Iris Murdoch

For Susan,

MERRY CHRISTMAS!

with much love,

Elaine

25th December 2004

Iris Murdoch

The Retrospective Fiction

Second Edition

Bran Nicol
University of Portsmouth

First published 1999
Second edition 2004 by
PALGRAVE MACMILLAN
Houndmills, Basingstoke, Hampshire RG21 6XS and
175 Fifth Avenue, New York, N.Y. 10010
Companies and representatives throughout the world

PALGRAVE MACMILLAN is the global academic imprint of the Palgrave
Macmillan division of St. Martin's Press, LLC and of Palgrave Macmillan Ltd.
Macmillan® is a registered trademark in the United States, United Kingdom
and other countries. Palgrave is a registered trademark in the European
Union and other countries.

ISBN 1–4039–1664–0 hardback
ISBN 1–4039–1665–9 paperback

This book is printed on paper suitable for recycling and made from fully
managed and sustained forest sources.

A catalogue record for this book is available from the British Library.

Library of Congress Cataloging-in-Publication Data
Nicol, Bran, 1969–
    Iris Murdoch: the retrospective fiction / Bran Nicol.—2nd ed.
        p.   cm.
    Includes bibliographical references (p.) and index.
    ISBN 1–4039–1664–0—ISBN 1–4039–1665–9 (pbk.)
    1. Murdoch, Iris—Criticism and interpretation.   2. Psychological fiction,
English—History and criticism.   3. Psychoanalysis and literature—
England.   4. Autobiographical memory in literature.   5. First-person
narrative.   I. Title.

    PR6063.U7Z745 2004
    823'.914—dc22
                                                                    2004046705

10   9   8   7   6   5   4   3   2   1
13   12   11   10   09   08   07   06   05   04

Printed and bound in Great Britain by
Antony Rowe Ltd, Chippenham and Eastbourne

For Ron and Norma Nicol

Human beings need fantasies. The novelist is potentially the greatest truth-teller of them all, *but he is also an expert fantasymonger.*

– Iris Murdoch, *Existentialists and Mystics*

Contents

List of Abbreviations

The following abbreviations of books and articles have been used in the text.

Novels by Iris Murdoch

B	*The Bell*, 1958 (London: Vintage, 1999)
BB	*The Book and the Brotherhood*, 1987 (Harmondsworth: Penguin, 1988)
BP	*The Black Prince*, 1973 (Harmondsworth: Penguin, 1975)
GA	*The Good Apprentice*, 1985 (Harmondsworth: Penguin, 1986)
GK	*The Green Knight*, 1993 (London: Chatto and Windus, 1993)
IG	*The Italian Girl*, 1964 (Harmondsworth: Penguin, 1967)
JD	*Jackson's Dilemma*, 1995 (London: Chatto and Windus, 1995)
NG	*The Nice and the Good*, 1968 (London: Triad/Panther, 1985)
PP	*The Philosopher's Pupil*, 1983 (Harmondsworth: Penguin, 1984)
SH	*A Severed Head*, 1961 (Harmondsworth: Penguin, 1984)
SPLM	*The Sacred and Profane Love Machine*, 1974 (Harmondsworth: Penguin, 1974)
SS	*The Sea, the Sea*, 1978 (Harmondsworth: Penguin, 1980)
TA	*The Time of the Angels*, 1966 (Harmondsworth: Penguin, 1987)
UN	*Under the Net*, 1954 (Harmondsworth: Penguin, 1988)
WC	*A Word Child*, 1975 (Harmondsworth: Penguin, 1989)

Non-fiction by Iris Murdoch

A	*Acastos: Two Platonic Dialogues*, 1986 (Harmondsworth: Penguin, 1987)
ad	'Against Dryness', in *The Novel Today* (1961), revised edition, ed. Malcolm Bradbury (London: Fontana, 1990)
em	'Existentialists and Mystics', *Existentialists and Mystics*, 1970 (Birmingham: Delos Press, 1993)
FS	*The Fire and the Sun: Why Plato Banished the Artists*, 1977 (Oxford: Oxford University Press, 1978)
S	*Sartre: Romantic Rationalist*, 1953 (Harmondsworth: Penguin, 1989)

sag   'The Sublime and the Good', in *Existentialists and Mystics: Writings on Philosophy and Literature*, ed. Peter Conradi (London: Chatto and Windus, 1997)

sbr   'The Sublime and the Beautiful Revisited', *Yale Review*, 49 (1959)

SG   *The Sovereignty of Good*, 1970 (London: Routledge, 1985)

MGM   *Metaphysics as a Guide to Morals* (London: Chatto and Windus, 1992)

Interviews

Interviews are identified by the name of the interviewer followed by the date, except in the case of the conferences at Caen and Amsterdam, where the place will be used.

Acknowledgements

Many people deserve thanks for their help and encouragement in the writing of both editions of this book. During my PhD at Lancaster University, Lee Horsley was an encouraging and patient supervisor, and I appreciate the advice of Tess Cosslett, Michael Wheeler and Richard Dutton. I wish to thank Patricia Waugh for her perceptive comments on some of the early material and for her support. Thanks are due to my former colleagues at University College Chichester: Jan Ainsley, Hugh Dunkerley, Alison MacLeod, Paul Norcross, Stephanie Norgate, Duncan Salkeld and Dave Swann.

For the second edition, I am grateful to Emily Rosser and Paula Kennedy of Palgrave Macmillan for their editorial support. I would like to thank Robert Hardy, David Herman, and Anne Rowe and the Iris Murdoch Society for invitations to write and speak about Iris Murdoch which helped deepen my interest in her work. Thanks, too, to Peter Conradi for his willingness to debate some of my ideas and share his own. Finally, my special thanks go to Karen Stevens, Joseph Furness and Jamie Nicol, who just about manage to keep me sane.

It goes without saying, however, that none of these people bear any responsibility for the faults which remain. Two editions, and I am still haunted by Arnold Baffin's comment in *The Black Prince*: 'Every book is the wreck of a perfect idea.'

I am grateful to Iris Murdoch, Random House UK Ltd and Penguin USA for granting me permission to quote from the works of Iris Murdoch. Some of the material in Chapters 3 and 6 and in Chapter 8 appeared in articles published in *The Journal of Narrative Technique* and *Modern Fiction Studies*. I wish to thank the editors for their permission to reprint.

Preface to the Second Edition

On 8 February 1999, while the first edition of this book was in the final stages of production, Iris Murdoch died from Alzheimer's disease after a much-publicized decline in health. Writing about the relation between retrospection and identity in the work of an author who had been so cruelly deprived of her own past was an awkward irony which was not lost on me as the book was completed. Yet while this parallel was of course entirely coincidental, the fact is that now, four years later, viewing Murdoch's fiction in terms of her life is almost unavoidable, given the number – and the revelatory nature – of a stream of new biographical works about her that have appeared in that time.

The new material in this second edition has, to a large extent, been inspired by the change in how we now perceive of Murdoch. It is not that I attempt to read her work 'biographically', in any crude sense, however – although a new postscript does consider the complex nature of the relation between Murdoch's life and writing. This book is concerned throughout with how her fiction works, and how it works on its readers, rather than with its genesis or potential autobiographical content. But the more we know about Murdoch as a person, the more it seems to me that her work is driven by contradictory impulses. This is not unusual, of course (why should we expect writers to be consistent?), nor is it a criticism, as I think the interplay of different ideas and desires behind her work accounts for much of its energy. But Murdoch was always a rather didactic writer, in so far as she made it clear in interviews and non-fiction what she stood for – and what she disapproved of – in both philosophy and literature. Now we know that there was 'another' Iris Murdoch throughout her life, a figure who contradicts much of the characteristics and values we associate with her previous public persona, we can explore more fully the other sides to her writing, where some of the central tenets of her thought turn out to be more complicated than she made them sound. The new Chapter 8 and the Postscript deal with two of these in particular: her insistence that philosophy and fiction should – and can – remain separate, and her conception of *authorship*, or the position an author should adopt in relation to her fiction.

The postscript also allows me to deal with a text which is discussed at only brief points in the first edition of this book, *The Sacred and Profane Love Machine*. Elsewhere I have taken the opportunity to explore two other novels largely absent from the original. Chapter 3 is devoted to *The Bell*, one of Murdoch's most retrospective novels, and one which exemplifies the central argument of this book about the 'retrospective dominant' of Murdoch's fiction. Chapter 8 includes an analysis of *The Philosopher's Pupil*, a novel which is something of a curiosity in Murdoch's work as it is the only one to combine her two favoured modes of narration, first- and third-person. Although its first-person dimension is radically different from her other six first-person 'retro- spective' novels, because the narrator represses the concern with his *own* past (this is why it was not considered in the first edition of this book), *The Philosopher's Pupil* is very much 'about' narration all the same. In a sense, then, my analysis of Murdoch's first-person fiction, which formed a major part of the first edition, can now be completed by examining this novel.

Adding readings of *The Philosopher's Pupil* and *The Sacred and Profane Love Machine* to this book highlights another, more implicit, argument that runs through the book. The novels to which I devote most attention throughout are, not uncoincidentally, Murdoch's most experimental, metafictional, works. I am interested in the moments in her fiction when she breaks away from her realist paradigm to create something more akin to postmodernism. Much of the energy of these more experimental fictions, I think (and will argue in Chapter 8), comes from the fact that they expose Murdoch's fictional technique and contradict many of the assumptions about literature and philosophy that underlie it. They work precisely because the author is attempting to remain faithful to her 'ethics' of fiction while also 'surrendering' to the logic of the writing itself.

My treatment of the more contradictory elements of her writing is underscored by an interest in what I think is one of the most overlooked aspects of her work, her literary theory. Though increasingly important in the fields of philosophy and theology, and still a presence in literary criticism, Murdoch's work has been neglected most of all perhaps by literary theorists. References to her thought are practically nowhere to be seen in contemporary literary-theoretical discourse. This is rather surprising, as her non-fiction develops a sustained theory of literary production. Murdoch's unwillingness to portray herself as a literary theorist due to her misgivings about the theoretical impulse in general is no doubt one reason for the neglect. Another is her perceived 'unfashionableness'. Contemporary literary theory is dominated (still) by insights from French thinkers like Barthes, Foucault, Derrida and Lacan, all of whom, in their different ways, articulate the problems with a kind of universalist or essentialist thinking about categories like the human being, reality and truth. Murdoch's discussions of literature exhibit some of the hallmarks of this way of thinking, especially its implication that 'good' literature is distinguishable from 'bad' literature, is of timeless importance no matter its socio-historical context, and exists to propagate 'human' values.

Nevertheless there are obvious areas of overlap between Murdoch's work and contemporary theory. She was always concerned with questions of otherness, difference and ethics, just as many literary theorists are now. In particular one of the things that fascinates me about Murdoch's work is its continual attempt to grapple with impossibility. Murdoch was determined to represent contingency in writing, when of course the very act of representation instantly transforms the contingent into something special and significant. Similarly she attempted to represent the accidental and even incorporate it in her fiction. Murdoch's philosophy and her ethics of fiction stress the value of respecting and representing otherness. But as a number of theorists – Blanchot, Baudrillard, Derrida – have said, otherness is impossible to represent because the very act of representation renders it the same.

To try to resolve such complex issues leads, not unsurprisingly, to contradictions, and I should add that my emphasis on these comes as much from the contradictory *responses* her presentation of these issues provokes in me. Murdoch's willingness to tackle such complex issues in her theory – and in her fiction (the backdrop of which is a concern with determining value in a post-religious world) – remains one of her most enduringly distinctive qualities amongst post-war English writers. Angela Carter, part of a different generation, but whose rich imagination and formidable mind suggests that she was in some ways a successor to Murdoch, once told of the occasion when her mother noticed her books on display alongside Murdoch's and said to her, 'I suppose you think that makes you an intellectual?' (Sage 1977: 40) This book, as much as it is a study of Murdoch's work, is intended as a tribute to her great intellect.

Preface to the First Edition

The aim of this book is to trace the preoccupation in Iris Murdoch's fiction with the way the past makes its mark upon us, haunting us and eluding our attempts to grasp it. Murdoch is one of the most important writers in post-war British fiction, partly because of the inventive ways in which she tackles the questions of our time, partly because she seems to stand outside the main currents of late twentieth-century thought. This is clear from her approach to retrospection. Interrogating the relationship between past and present has been a major concern in post-war fiction, one that has shown no sign of diminishing in postmodernity. Though she clearly shares some of the convictions which underlie this aspect of her contemporaries' work, what sets Murdoch apart from them is her comparative disinterest in history. Instead her fiction concerns itself with *personal* history. My focus is on the different ways in which the past is continually made present in her fiction: through guilt, nostalgia, the uncanny and the attempt to understand the past through rational investigation.

The book is an adaptation of a doctoral thesis on Murdoch's first-person novels, but its genesis came a few years earlier, when I first read *A Severed Head*. Like many readers new to Murdoch, I was drawn in by the cast of obsessive characters and the bizarre yet somehow entirely logical leaps of the plot. Most of all, though, I was struck by the narrator. His was a voice I had not come across before, direct, seemingly honest, but at the same time disingenuous in a way it was quite difficult to pin down. Turning to her other first-person novels I found similar protagonists, just as compulsive, deeply self-conscious almost to the point of paranoia – whose ancestors, I now realize, were the heroes in Dostoevsky or Nabokov. What made the plots particularly powerful, I thought (and still do), was the sense of being up close to these characters, looking over their shoulders as they stumbled, to use Murdoch's own words, 'from one awful blow to another' (Rose 1968). Later I realized something odd about my response to them, after I had become familiar with what had been written about Murdoch's fiction. These novels were commonly seen as ironic comedies, whereas I had not found them particularly funny – at least not on the first reading.

Now it may not be wise to admit to identifying with deluded over-sensitive anti-heroes or to missing the funny side of comic novels, but

I think what temporarily obscured their ironic effect was their retrospect-ive dimension. The strange power of these novels comes from the way they address the question of the past. This explains why I have chosen to devote a large part of this book to Murdoch's 'first-person retrospec-tive novels': *Under the Net*, *A Severed Head*, *The Italian Girl*, *The Black Prince*, *A Word Child* and *The Sea, the Sea*. Individually, most of these novels have been credited with being among the most challenging and successful in Murdoch's body of work. Yet their success has never been put down to the one major factor they have in common which her other fiction does not share: the first-person form. This is quite under-standable, for on one level there is nothing particularly unusual about them. They can be regarded simply as especially entertaining and thought-provoking versions of the fiction Murdoch has always set out to write, dealing with issues and presenting situations common to the Murdochian 'world'. But these novels are not just about the experiences undergone by their hero. They are about how he is affected by re-living these experiences, how he tries to make sense of them.

This book, then, does not pretend to be a comprehensive account of Murdoch's work. For one thing, there are plenty of other studies already in print which perform this function admirably: Elizabeth Dipple's *Work for the Spirit* (1984), Richard Todd's *Iris Murdoch* (1984), and Peter J. Conradi's excellent *Iris Murdoch: The Saint and the Artist* (1989). There has, it seems to me, been a relatively clear consensus of opinion among Murdoch's critics about what are the important issues in her work. Most studies, whether they deal in particular with one or two novels, or her fiction in general, stress the author's concern with what Peter Kemp has called 'the fight against fantasy', the need to overcome the temptation to 'aestheticize' our experience by attending properly to those contingent aspects of life which elude our attempts to make sense of them (Kemp 1969). This book is no different, though because of the critical consensus I have not felt the need to go over this ground again in any great depth. In one important sense, however, this study is very unlike some of the other works on Murdoch, which stress – like the author herself – the moral and critical value of difference over similarity. My overall intention is to concentrate on what Murdoch's novels have in common rather than what distinguishes them. One of my central aims is to emphasize the affinities, not the dissimilarities, between Murdoch's work and the late twentieth-century literary and philosophical context in which she writes.

In fact, as I argue in Chapter 1, her theoretical position is itself essentially retrospective, because it has developed by way of a productive engagement

with two previous literary traditions, classic realism and modernism.
A major concern of the next two chapters is to continue this process of
contextualization by situating Murdoch's retrospective fiction in the
tradition of the post-war novel. More specifically, both chapters set out
what I see as the 'double movement' of the past in Murdoch's fiction.
Kierkegaard said that life is lived forwards, but can only be understood
backwards. This logic illuminates the attempt of many of her characters
to somehow make sense of their past. But, as psychoanalysis reminds
us, life is also lived 'backwards', that is, we continually and involuntarily
return to moments of past trauma (or lost happiness), all the while
looking forwards to a point where we might be able to understand what
has gone before. Chapter 2 traces this double perspective in Murdoch's
fiction as a whole, placing particular emphasis on how her later work –
especially *The Good Apprentice, The Book and the Brotherhood* and *Jackson's
Dilemma* – dramatizes questions of guilt and redemption. This is further
explored in a detailed reading of *The Bell* in Chapter 3.

Chapter 4 turns to the first-person novels, and proposes that their
demonstration of the power of the past owes much to the author's use
of retrospective narrative form, a peculiar combination of *mimesis* and
diegesis which provides a fascinating counterpoint to her continued
interest in aesthetic patterning. This chapter clears the way for the three
following chapters, which offer detailed readings of the first-person
novels. In these I have chosen to discuss the novels in pairs to bring
out common concerns most clearly. Chapter 5 considers the attempt to
understand and represent the past in *Under the Net* and *The Black Prince*,
the only two novels in Murdoch's body of work where the protagonist
is a novelist. Chapter 6 explores uncanny recurrence in *A Severed Head*
and *A Word Child*, a phenomenon which motivates the characters and
also informs the narrative dynamics of each novel. Chapter 7 deals with
two works, *The Italian Girl* and *The Sea, the Sea*, which show the two
kinds of retrospective movement working against each other, in the form
of nostalgia and the uncanny. Chapters 4 to 7 also continue to examine
Murdoch's 'dialogue' with some of the principal schools of twentieth-
century thought: respectively, postmodernism and poststructuralism,
psychoanalysis and modernism. This is extended by Chapter 8, a reading
of the other novel which uses a first-person narrative voice (though it is
a very peculiar one), *The Philosopher's Pupil*, in the light of Murdoch's
engagement in her later philosophy with the work of Jacques Derrida.

Finally, I should add a note on my critical methodology. I have made
use of the insights of a number of different theoretical 'schools', especially
Bakhtin, narrative theory and psychoanalysis. One reason for this rather

maverick use of theory is because I have tried to let my arguments determine the theoretical approach rather than the other way around. But it also relates to my desire to consider Murdoch's relationship to recent theoretical trends. This is particularly illuminating, I think, in the case of psychoanalysis, the theory I draw upon most often. Besides some key similarities between Murdoch's thought and Freud's, which I shall explore at length in what follows, I am attracted by the parallels between Freud's (and, to some extent, Lacan's) conception of the psychic mechanism and the patterns which underlie Murdoch's presentation of character and her narrative technique. As the work of critics like Harold Bloom, Peter Brooks and Malcolm Bowie have shown, Freud is most illuminating when regarded less as a scientist or even a psychoanalyst than as a theorist who has much to say on the relationship between desire and the need to construct and believe in fictions – an estimation that could equally apply to Murdoch. This reading of Freud accounts for my debt to the work of Brooks, in particular.

1
Revisiting the Sublime and the Beautiful: Iris Murdoch's Realism

> We can no longer take language for granted as a medium of communication. Its transparency has gone. We are like people who for a long time looked out of a window without noticing the glass – and then one day began to notice this too. The beginnings of this new awareness lie far back... but it is only within the last century that it has taken the form of a blinding enlightenment or a devouring obsession.
>
> Iris Murdoch, *Sartre: Romantic Rationalist*

> I think in particular that it is in the aesthetic of the sublime that modern art (including literature) finds its impetus.
>
> Jean-François Lyotard, *The Postmodern Condition: A Report on Knowledge*

Iris Murdoch is an eccentric writer. Besides the oddity of her characters, their world and the plots they get wrapped up in (a strangeness that nevertheless taps into something in ourselves we all recognize) her fiction seems to position itself outside the central patterns of the post-war British novel. Her novels are difficult to place in any particular category (realism, comedy of manners, prose romance, metaphysical thriller, 'late modernism'), seeming to constitute one all by themselves. In her philosophy and literary theory, Murdoch consistently takes up an unfashionable position: she is a metaphysician in an age suspicious of metaphysics, a novelist who wishes to preserve the function of literary realism in a period marked by the 'crisis of representation'. While the generation of late twentieth-century writers to which she belongs is more self-conscious about their art and the ideas which inform it than any previous one,

1

Murdoch's status as a philosopher in her own right gives unusual emphases to her own self-awareness.

Naturally, then, the eccentricity of her position as thinker and writer is a line many studies of her work have chosen to pursue, concentrating on the ways in which she works against the flow of the contemporary novel. At the same time, however, to read her work is to grapple with some of the key moral and existential questions of our age – how to make sense of our situation in the absence of all-encompassing systems of thought, the role of language in constructing individual identity, the question of freedom from others and from the fundamental otherness at the heart of ourselves – and also to engage in dialogue with some of the foremost thinkers and writers of the twentieth century: James, Lawrence, Freud, Wittgenstein, Sartre, Derrida. This book concerns itself with an issue largely unexplored in Murdoch's work: its retrospective dimension. It is nevertheless a feature, as I will argue, which needs to be understood in the light of the fictional and intellectual traditions in which it is placed. In this chapter I want to set the scene for the more specific analysis which follows by considering the interface between Murdoch's work as a whole and key currents of twentieth-century thought.

My purpose is to consider how and where to 'place' Murdoch's fiction in relation to the most important strains in the twentieth-century novel: (classic) realist, modernist, postmodernist. To do so, of course, runs the risk of oversimplifying the complexities and discontinuities of the diverse range of fictional modes which interweave throughout the century. Considering any author in relation to broad generalized periods of literary history is something Murdoch herself would no doubt find redolent of the worst characteristics of 'theory', a profound distrust of which has been evident in her work ever since her first novel *Under the Net* insisted that 'All theorizing is flight' (*UN* 80). In her many discussions of literature over the years Murdoch has refrained from using periodizing terms like 'modernism' or 'postmodernism', preferring instead to regard each author or group of authors as a special case. Even when she does use a term conventionally associated with a literary period – romanticism, for example – it is not for its historicist value, but to denote an epistemo-logical or methodological strand apparent in literature as a whole. Her persuasive rhetoric in favour of particularity, like her eccentricity, explains why the broad contextualization of her work is not (until recently, perhaps) an avenue much Murdoch criticism has chosen to go down.

Yet the author herself – as befits someone sensitive to the arguments of philosophers like Heidegger or Wittgenstein – also insists on the impossibility of adopting any position 'outside' the object of study. While

I would not wish to misrepresent the uniqueness of any individual author, it is precisely because of Murdoch's seeming position 'outside the centre' that I think there is much to be gained by considering just where she conforms to and departs from contemporary fictional dominants.

Murdoch's conception of the novel, as it developed over four decades of theory and practice, depends on looking back to two previous versions. She positions herself against modernist notions of aesthetic autonomy and attempts to reproduce some of the characterological and formal achievements of the nineteenth-century novel and what she sees as Shakespeare's realism. Her status as one of the most prominent late twentieth-century advocates of a return to realism is a position she has largely manoeuvred herself into, consistently making clear her admiration for the achievements of great nineteenth-century authors like Tolstoy and George Eliot. The novel, she has repeatedly insisted, has a duty to portray the world as it is, and to strive to tell the truth about it, chiefly by portraying realistic characters not subordinate to the demands of plot or to the ideas which support it. Less commonly acknowledged is the fact that the flipside of this commitment is a sustained critique of certain aspects of modernist fiction. Modernism often functions in her thought as the antithesis of nineteenth-century realism, and the frequency and vigour with which she positions herself against it prove just as important to her work as her desire to return to realism. Rather than 'neo-realism', Murdoch's fiction could just as accurately be called 'anti-modernism'.

A pro-realism/anti-modernism dynamic is not by any means unusual in the work of a novelist beginning her career in the decade following the Second World War. The considerable feeling of societal rupture at the time was paralleled by a shift in the intellectual climate, which we could characterize as the movement to the condition of '*post-*'; the post-war world, as Malcolm Bradbury states, was also 'post-Holocaust, post-atomic, post-ideological, post-humanist, postpolitical, and indeed, some declared, post-Modern' (Appleyard 1990; Bergonzi 1993; Bradbury 1993: 268). Despite Bradbury's caution, this last term is certainly the most crucial in explaining the course taken by the post-war British novel. While a number of novelists (e.g. B. S. Johnson and Christine Brooke-Rose) were keen to pursue the experimental aspects of modernism still further, the majority were determined to place the novel firmly back on what they saw as its realist tracks. Authors turned their backs on modernism because it marked the pinnacle (or the end) of fictional innovation, but also because the modernist retreat into subjectivism and self-reflexivity rendered it unsuited to tackling the problems of the post-atomic era.

Given her commitment to realism, it is understandable that we find Murdoch first grouped alongside contemporaries like John Wain, Kingsley Amis and Angus Wilson – under different headings, like the 'Angry Young Men' or the 'New University Wits' (O'Connor 1963) – whose fiction centred on the dreary world inhabited by an anti-hero quite unlike the transcendent artist-protagonist of modernist works. Furthermore, her early novels, especially of the 1950s, bear the stamp of the changed post-war climate, where the need to make sense of the war and its social legacy found expression in a renewed faith in the political value of realism. The politically *engagé* Lefty Todd in *Under the Net* (1954), for example, seems like a token Brunet from Sartre's *The Age of Reason*; Mischa Fox in *The Flight from the Enchanter* (1956), for all his rootless mysticism, is a media mogul with great influence in the upper echelons of British politics. The labels are of little value now (the former especially inappropriate in the case of a female author who published her first novel at the age of 35, and was not particularly angry) but Murdoch clearly shares an affinity with the pro-realism/anti-modernism of such groups. On the whole, however, her fiction has always been largely uninterested in social analysis, politics or history; her characters, as Martin Amis once wrote, 'all inhabit a suspended and eroticised world, removed from the anxieties of health and money – and the half-made feelings on which most of us subsist' (Amis 1980). This is what made Murdoch's arguments for a return to realism distinct from those of many of her peers – and made them particularly valuable. Rather than call for renewed political commitment, her early writings insist that a new realism is necessary to supplant the weaknesses of recent literary (and philosophical) traditions.

Murdoch's 'aesthetic of the sublime': realism and the modernist inheritance

In her first book, *Sartre: Romantic Rationalist*, and two polemical essays she published at the tail-end of the 1950s and early 1960s, 'The Sublime and the Beautiful Revisited' (1959) and 'Against Dryness' (1961), Murdoch builds up an oppositional model of the development of the novel, one which, though she refrained from doing so as systematically in the following decades, she clearly still adhered to in principle throughout her career. On the one hand there is a *liberal* tradition, made up principally of Shakespeare and the nineteenth-century novelists (Austen, Scott, George Eliot, Tolstoy), and on the other a *romantic* tradition (she uses these terms in 'The Sublime and the Beautiful

Revisited') that stretches from the Romantic period as it is conventionally demarcated through Emily Brontë, Melville, Hawthorne and Dostoevsky, to modernist writers influenced by the Symbolists and their successors, contemporaries of Murdoch's like Sartre, Camus, L. H. Myers, the *nouveau romanciers*.

The title of the earlier essay suggests another way of describing this model. She uses Kant's famous distinction to argue that the romantic tradition she identifies typically values the creation of a 'beautiful' mythic pattern above the reflection of the sublime otherness of the world: romanticism 'is none other than Kant's theory of the beautiful, served up in a fresh form' (sbr 261). Its typical product is what Murdoch calls the 'crystalline' novel, a work in which each allusion and image fits in neatly to the structure of the underlying myth created by the author. The crystalline novel is a simplified version of the world, little more than the embodiment of a theory, a way to harness the enigmatic elements of life (the accidental forces in the world, the mystery of other people) by enveloping them in a theoretical structure. It is clear from her discussions of the crystalline novel – the most extensive example being her analysis of Sartre's *Nausea* in *Sartre: Romantic Rationalist* – that this is equivalent to the modernist ideal of aesthetic autonomy. She relates the ending of *Nausea*, where Roquentin decides to impose a self-contained aesthetic form on to his life, to the work of a number of other writers 'who have hoped for salvation through art'. These examples read like the beginnings of a list of key high-modernist novelists: 'Woolf, who attempts "to make of the moment something permanent" by finely embalming it; Joyce, who tries to turn life itself into literature and give it the cohesion of a myth; Proust who seeks by reminiscence to bind up and catch in the present the stuff of his own past' (*S* 46).

For 'romantic', for 'crystalline', for 'beautiful' in Murdoch's theory of the novel, then, we may profitably read *modernist*.[1] And for 'sublime' and 'liberal' we may (for now) substitute 'nineteenth-century realism'. Murdoch's diagnosis of the state of the contemporary novel is in fact reminiscent of that of Georg Lukács, the 'liberal Marxist' critic (as Murdoch calls him), who also worked with an opposition between modernism and realism. The finest realism, according to Lukács, is produced at key moments in history (Shakespeare, Tolstoy) when certain writers are able to comprehend the historical significance of their age and capture it in works which combine formal power (the use of symbolism, for example) with representative character. When history loses its sense of meaning, realism becomes diluted into *formalism* or *naturalism*, terms which have clear correspondences in Murdoch's 'crystalline' and 'journalistic' fiction (the other kind of fiction she identifies as dominant in the early 1960s).

The post-war fictional scene Murdoch surveys seems to be representative of just such a time, except that instead of the loss of historical depth bemoaned by Lukács she points to the bereftness in moral complexity. His influence can clearly be detected in her early writings, and like him, Murdoch responded to the weakness of modernism and the modernist inheritance by placing a similar emphasis on the combination of form and character.[2] Her model is the ability of great realists like Tolstoy and Shakespeare (whom she reads as a 'patron saint' of novelwriting) to combine in a 'wonderful magical way real character, I mean real independent people who stand up and who are remembered as individuals, and magical pattern' (Bradbury 1976). Or, as she puts it elsewhere, the novel should be *both* 'representational and autonomous [...] mimetic and formal' (Magee 1978).

What is particularly original about Murdoch's theory of the novel is her attempt to transform Kant's 'theory of the sublime [...] into a theory of art'. Usually defined by philosophers as 'an emotional experience resulting from the defeated yet invigorating attempt of reason to compass the boundlessness and formlessness of nature' (sbr 249), Murdoch finds the sublime 'pregnant with a concept of the tragic, and with a theory of the connection between literature and morality' (sbr 250). This is most visible in the novel, the form she regards as most linked to moral and spiritual experience, which can bring about

> the realization of a vast and varied reality outside ourselves which brings about a sense initially of terror, and when properly understood of exhilaration and spiritual power. But what brings this experience to us, in its most important form, is the sight, not of physical nature, but of our surroundings as consisting of other individual men. (sbr 269)

Though her career as a novelist was already well under way when 'The Sublime and the Beautiful Revisited' was published, it amounts to a powerful manifesto. What Murdoch aimed to do in her own fiction was to move away from the modernist aesthetic of the beautiful towards a true aesthetic of the sublime.

The most important part of this process is the return to a proper realist form of characterization. To counteract the diminished respect for personality in modern literature's aesthetic of the beautiful, Murdoch argues that the modern author must look back to the *tolerance* of the great nineteenth-century novelists: their capacity to display 'a real apprehension of persons other than the author of having a right to exist and to have a separate mode of being which is important and interesting to themselves' (sbr 257). The idea of tolerance reveals the extent to which Murdoch's way of regarding literature derives from her moral philosophy. Her brand of neo-Platonism insists that one can only approach Goodness by attending to the contingent and eliminating selfishness from the psyche. One must seek to emulate the benevolent condition of the mind in love, the ability of the lover to completely forget his or her own personality while trying to empathize with that of the beloved, to imagine what it is to *be* another person. The artist has a duty to portray the world as it is; his or her vision must not be distorted by the need for self-consolation. The creation of 'free' characters, desirable in order to restore faith in human difference, is achievable only through the *love* of an author for all aspects of the surrounding world. Characters must be more than just extensions of their creator's structure of thought, they must be portrayed as independent individuals. Like Keats, Murdoch especially admires Shakespeare's ability to suggest that his characters have individual importance independent of the requirements of the story, yet still fit in with its theme. She has referred to the process of authorial negation as 'merciful objectivity', a term which seems to correspond directly to Keats' 'negative capability' (Magee 1978).

At the heart of Murdoch's aesthetic of the sublime, then, is the Platonic ideal of *ascesis* (unselfing). 'Art is not an expression of personality, it is a question rather of the continual expelling of oneself from the matter in hand' (sbr 269). It is an ideal, incidentally, which explains her fondness for the myths of Apollo and Marsyas, and Orpheus, both of which relate to the process of artistic creation, and have at their heart the question of ascesis. Again, as much as this theory depends upon a positive analogy with realist authors like Tolstoy, it is also formulated in explicit opposition to modernism:

> A literary presence if it is too bossy, like Lawrence's, may be damaging; when for instance one favoured character may be the author's spokesman. Bad writing is almost always full of the fumes of personality [...]. I do not mind owning a personal style, but I do not want to be obviously present in my work. (Magee 1978)

While wishing to avoid the didacticism of a Lawrence, Murdoch does not seek to emulate the impersonality of early or late modernists like Flaubert, the *nouveau romanciers*, or Joyce. Murdoch is, I think, aware of the complaint levelled against such an ideal: that Flaubert's *Dieu invisible*, for example, too often seems like a 'bored God' watching impassively as passions are revealed and dramas unfold (Swinden 1973: 71). After all, she herself was similarly attacked. The obsession with 'the expunging of the self from the work of art' which A. S. Byatt saw in her early work led to her failure '*as a writer* [to] inhabit her action with the vigour with which she should' (Byatt 1965: 204). In her later work, she attempted to negotiate this opposition with care: impersonality should not mean non-existence, the author must be neutral but remain interested, and display a tolerant, impartial attitude to her characters.

As her thoughts on character suggest, Murdoch's appropriation of the sublime also depends upon a particular conception of literary form. A distinctive approach to form, the desire to create a beautiful autonomous object, is at the heart of the crystalline novel. The desire to console in this way, natural though it may be, can reduce 'our sense of reality as a rich receding background'. The novelist, according to Murdoch, has a duty to recomplicate our sense of reality by pitting the ideal of contingency against the crystalline conception of form. Creating individuals instead of types is one way to do this, for 'real people are destructive of myth' (ad 23). But Murdoch has tried in other ways to provide an alternative to 'beautiful' form. Most obvious is her deliberate refusal to create a coherent 'myth' in her novels. She uses mythic allusion to mystify rather than simplify. Although her novels typically contain a dazzling mass of symbolism drawn from diverse sources which makes the reader believe that a unified myth exists beneath the surface, any attempt to fit all the pieces into jigsaw-like order, each image accounted for, can only lead to frustration. The many references in each of her novels to other works of literature, to mythology and philosophy, are used on an *ad hoc* basis to enrich its overall flavour.

The Black Prince (1973) and *The Sea, the Sea* (1978) for example, meditate on *Hamlet* and *The Tempest* respectively, but it is impossible to match up the casts of novel and play; Murdoch has commented that she 'abhors' the idea of one of her novels being 'diagrammed by allusion' (Haffenden 1985). This is not always the case, however, in her fiction. She has conceded elsewhere that some of her own novels, like *A Severed Head* (1961) (and perhaps *A Fairly Honourable Defeat* (1970), which she has called 'a theological allegory') 'probably represent [. . .] a giving in to the myth' (Kermode 1963).[3] Yet even in these novels she tries to ensure, as Peter Conradi puts it, that 'myth belongs to the characters' (Conradi 1989: 81). It is most often her characters who draw comparisons between themselves and their situations and other sources. Once again, this can be seen as a response to the modernist practice of producing in a work an underlying myth which delimits the contingent world by making it representable and knowable.[4]

Another way Murdoch uses form to reflect contingency is by the use of plot to suggest the intrusion of accident into the lives of human beings. Her model for this comes again from what she regards as Shakespearean realism. Though it may seem excessively patterned, the Shakespearean plot is still open to the unexpected, as in the case of Cordelia's death in *King Lear*. The device Murdoch employs most obviously to this end is, similarly, the sudden unexpected deaths of characters in her novels. The most notorious example of this occurs in *The Sacred and Profane Love Machine* (1974) when Harriet, a bourgeois housewife, is suddenly gunned down in a random act of airport terrorism. More audacious still is when an accidental death is *repeated* in a novel. In *An Accidental Man* (1971), Austin Gibson Grey kills a six-year-old girl while driving drunkenly in his brother's car. His misery is partly reduced when the person who has been blackmailing him is himself reduced to a vegetative state as a result of another accident. At the end of the novel, the reader learns that another little girl, a minor character whose mischief has been commented on throughout, has died after falling from a scaffolding.

The device is made more central in the 1975 novel *A Word Child*, which begins with Hilary Burde trying to come to terms with his responsibility for the death of a friend's wife only to end with him partly to blame for the death of the same man's second wife. After reflecting on his part in the deaths of both women, Hilary hopes for a happy future with his sister Crystal, wryly quoting Lear's 'We two alone shall sing like birds in the cage' (*WC* 383). Richard Todd has argued that this reference alerts us to how *Lear*'s supreme image of what it means to suffer, Cordelia being carried dead in her broken father's arms, is matched in *A Word Child* by 'another kind of image, a pattern of experience' (Todd 1979: 57), the *repetition* of Hilary's role in both deaths. Rather than make a direct comparison between Lear and Hilary, the event reminds us 'that something is still to come after the "necessity" of the movement of the plot, some final contingent blow to the neatness of an artistic solution' (Todd 1979: 66). So the sense of pattern in *A Word Child* performs a similar function to the contingent horror of Cordelia's death; any redemption Hilary may gain through suffering after the death of Kitty is incomplete because such a tragedy may easily happen again. As in the case of *An Accidental Man* Murdoch's sublime plotting is a way of using form to suggest formlessness.

The paradox, however, is a problematic one for an author who consistently puts forward an ideology of literary openness, and as such has not been lost on Murdoch's critics. David Gordon suggests that Murdoch's view of aesthetic contingency is flawed because 'she seems to assume a literal correspondence between shapelessness in life and shapelessness in art' (Gordon 1995: 93). It is at the very point when the contingent is suggested in a novel, he continues, that form reveals itself. Bernard Bergonzi concludes something similar about the interchanging of sexual relationships in Murdoch's fiction, something which often vexes critics and readers. While recognizing that, for her, this is not a matter of 'authorial manipulation and pattern-making, but rather an insistence on contingency, a clear recognition of the fact that one never really knows what people might be up to', he remains unconvinced because 'what it implies is not so much contingency as a willed idea of contingency' (Bergonzi 1970: 48). Yet the contradictory nature of suggesting the contingent in a form which, by definition, always precludes the unplanned, means that a 'willed idea of contingency' is the best one can aim for. If Murdoch's sublime aesthetic is ultimately a defeat, it is at least a fairly honourable one.

Putting the real into realism: philosophy and fiction

Murdoch's use of form raises an important question about the relationship between her theory and practice of fiction. The accusation that her achievements are forced rather than natural has also been levelled at her characterization. Her characters are certainly unusual, but eccentricity is not quite the same as the contingent individuality she admires in realist character. As Frank Kermode has said, in Murdoch's novels there is a sense that 'contingency is conscripted' (Kermode 1971: 263). Her objectives are achieved by playing a manipulative game – brilliantly, but in which the devices which suggest the contingent (eccentric character, a mass of detail, accidental events) make us look the other way while she slyly lays down the myth which drives the work.

Hostile critics have seized upon this incommensurability between what Murdoch urges and what she does. She claims to be against rigid patterning and for 'free' individual character, the argument goes, but she takes an obvious delight in plotting and presents little more than variations on the same set of characterological archetypes. The outcome is that Murdoch's work is often more reminiscent of genres like the fantastic and the romance rather than realism. I have some sympathy with this conclusion (it does not need to be a criticism, of course, for resembling these genres does not in itself devalue her fiction) but I want to suggest that the gulf between Murdoch's theory and practice is not simply a matter of the author setting herself impossibly high standards which her gifts as a novelist simply cannot meet. Rather, the matter of returning to realism in the post-war period creates special problems which need to be solved in special ways.

It is now more or less accepted that the dominant mode in postwar fiction (at least in Britain) has been realism – a different form from nineteenth-century 'classic realism', and differing widely from author to author in terms of approaches and devices, but realism nonetheless (Alexander 1990; Gasiorek 1995). This recognition means questioning the once widely accepted realism/experiment dichotomy, as the actual practice of returning to realism has involved, in many cases, at least some degree of experimentation. Although the accurate reflection of social reality was considered a necessity in the aftermath of the war, realism was anything but straightforward in the new climate. For one thing, writers wondered how they were to go about representing contemporary experience which was often too horrific (e.g. the Holocaust) or so bizarre (e.g. American politics) that it was felt as 'a kind of embarrassment to one's own meagre imagination' (Roth 1961: 29). More importantly, the whole question of representation was at the top of the intellectual agenda. For if we had to pinpoint one issue at the heart of late twentieth-century literature, theory and philosophy, surely this would be it: the gulf between language and what it represents.

This is a question – as we can see from Murdoch's philosophical work – which stretches back to the philosophy of Plato and the fledgling literary theory of Aristotle, but it has been more directly resonant in the period of literature which can justifiably be called 'modern'. It has been suggested that the modern age really begins with Romanticism, a period marked by an erosion of faith in the referential capacity of words and which thus bears an obvious affinity with the cultural concerns of the twentieth century.[5] The beginning and ending of this century are distinguished, as Henry Sussman has said, by 'a firm sense, as firm as possible, of the linguistic constitution of reality, and the conceptual systems erected to qualify, modify, and contain it' (Sussman 1990: 130). But while representation was considered problematic at the modernist end of the century, I would contend that it is only in the postmodern age that it really enters a phase of crisis. After the Second World War powerful strands of anti-humanist thought from structuralism to poststructuralism and postmodernism were starting to make their influence felt. All of these bodies of thought are preoccupied by the gap between language and the real.

In the light of such epistemological changes, post-war writers were forced, as Andrejz Gasiorek says, to 'reconceptualize' or 'extend' realism 'in the wake of modernist and postmodernist critique' rather than simply return to any previous model (Gasiorek 1995: ii). This is just what we see Murdoch doing too, in fact for very similar reasons, and despite her repeated expressions of admiration for classic realist writers. Quite naturally for one who began writing at more or less the same time the term 'postmodernism' enters the theoretical vocabulary, the question of representation, in its complex late twentieth-century form, is central to Murdoch's approach to fiction. While this is not the impression we get from her writings on literature, her *philosophy* suggests otherwise. This book does not pretend to be a thorough analysis of her philosophy, but a consideration of her philosophical position casts some vital light on her particular reconceptualization of realism.[6]

Murdoch has often insisted that linking literature and philosophy is a troublesome business. Being labelled a philosophical novelist causes her discomfort because she regards the two disciplines as fundamentally opposed: where philosophy should aim at ultimate clarity and precision, art should teach by way of mystification. And she is always clear where her loyalties lie, should it come to the question of hierarchy between the two disciplines: 'For both the collective and the individual salvation of the human race, art is doubtless more important than philosophy, and literature most important of all' (*SG* 76). Nevertheless certain questions dominate her contribution to each discipline – the status of the individual, the consolations of aesthetic form, and so on – even though they are treated differently in each. 'One might start from the assertion that morality, goodness, is a form of realism', she has said. 'The chief enemy of excellence in morality (and also in art) is personal fantasy: the tissue of self-aggrandizing and consoling wishes and dreams which prevents one from seeing what is there outside one' (*SG* 59). Moreover, she herself invites the connection between her philosophy and fiction by giving a special role to art in her metaphysics, a practice which has tended to be limited to only a few philosophers, like Schopenhauer and, more recently, Derrida and Rorty.

What Murdoch has tried to do in her philosophy is neatly suggested by an illuminating comparison she makes in *Sartre*:

> What the psychoanalyst does for the particular consciousness of the individual the metaphysician does for the intellectual consciousness of the group he is addressing, and through them perhaps for the consciousness of an epoch. He presents a conceptual framework which is an aid to understanding. (*S* 137)

As the title of her latest work of philosophy puts it even more succinctly, Murdoch's philosophy aims to offer 'metaphysics as a guide to morals'. Broadly speaking, metaphysics, before Derrida's negative appropriation of the term, is a form of philosophy distinct from the analytical kind, one that concentrates on conceptualizing key philosophical 'first principles' (identity, time, knowing, etc.). Murdoch's approach is to focus on some of these metaphysical issues with the aim of providing an understanding of *ethical* first principles and an expanded notion of the human individual: 'I have views about human nature, about good and evil, about repentance, about spirituality, about religion, about what religion is for people without God, and so on' (Caen 1978). When she first emerged on to the intellectual scene in the late 1950s and early 1960s, and entered the debate about the novel, Murdoch set herself squarely against certain trends in contemporary philosophy – existentialism, linguistic philosophy, logical positivism – which provide, she argued, an impoverished picture of the individual. This is the result, she contends, of a misguided faith in transcendent rationalism based ultimately on the power of the human will (*SG* 1–45). In response she wants to counter the reductive understanding of the human subject which underlies such philosophy (and also capitalism, fascism and communism) and re-inject it with a moral function.

The philosophical scaffolding she relies on to reconstitute the individual is made up of concepts drawn from a number of influential predecessors, though it can never be reduced to them. One of the most important is Sartre. Like many in the 1950s Murdoch saw the value of existentialism as a tool for political and moral regeneration: 'Sartre's philosophy was an inspiration to many who felt that they must, and *could*, make out of all that misery and chaos a better world, for it had now been revealed that anything was possible' (*S* 9–10). This suggests why, although her study of his work is marked from the start by a keen apprehension of its weaknesses, Murdoch retained an enduring admiration for Sartre. His work, she suggests, stands as 'a last ditch attachment to the value of the individual' (*S* 137) – a phrase which applies equally, of course, to her own. Her philosophy, one might say, starts with the understanding that the human subject is, in Heideggerian terms, 'thrown' into an absurd world, surrounded by the contingent otherness of people and objects which resist our attempts to bestow meaning on them. Her fundamental empathy with this existentialist view of the world is revealed by the centrality throughout her work of Sartrean keywords like 'contingency' and 'opacity'.

From this shared point of origin, however, Sartre and Murdoch soon diverge. Confronted by the nauseating flux around them, Sartre and his heroes choose to embark on a process of systematic self-definition. Murdoch prefers a less sentimental response, one we can recognize from her literary appropriation of the sublime. Why, she asks, does Sartre 'find the contingent overabundance of the world nauseating rather than glorious?' (*S* 49). Like Simone Weil, another thinker who addresses the question of the subject's isolation and rootlessness,[7] Murdoch's alternative to existentialism involves turning to Plato. The human being should endeavour to strip away the layers of benighted self-mythologizing and approach the transcendent concepts of the Good and the True by a process of *ascesis*. While she approves of Sartre's 'liberal humanism', then, she is also aware of its negative side, the vivid picture he presents of 'the psychology of the lonely individual' (*S* 106). Sartre's is the logic of 'romantic rationalism' which ultimately demystifies the individual and the strangeness of the contingent world by following 'a deliberately unpractical ideal of rationality' (*S* 111). Freedom from the noumenal world is neither possible nor desirable, and building 'a general truth about ourselves which shall encompass us like a house' (*S* 113) is short-sighted and solipsistic.

Murdoch's Platonism is visible in her distrust of consolatory theorizing, but we can also detect the presence of another of her main philosophical influences, Ludwig Wittgenstein. The problem of theory is tackled head-on in her first novel, *Under the Net*. Its central image is drawn from Wittgenstein, who uses it to refer to the incapacity of language and theory fully to represent contingent reality, just as a net cannot fully contain whatever it is cast over. The influence of Wittgenstein – or at least the '*Tractatus* Wittgenstein' as she calls him in *Metaphysics as a Guide to Morals* – is pervasive in Murdoch's writing, though less directly than Plato. It is perhaps more visible in her fiction than her philosophy – almost literally visible, in fact, in the form of charismatic teacher-figures like Rozanov in *The Philosopher's Pupil* (1983) who lead ascetic lives, much of which are devoted to dissuading disciples from doing philosophy. His ghost also presides, more poignantly, over *A Word Child* in the figure of Mr Osmand, a schoolteacher who commits suicide and who is responsible for Hilary's passion for words. One of the key features of *A Word Child* – and one of its many parallels with *King Lear* – is its rhetoric about the difficulty of finding an appropriate discourse for suffering, and in this respect seems to be illuminated by the celebrated phrase which concludes the *Tractatus*, 'whereof we cannot speak, thereof we must remain silent'.

Her reading of Wittgenstein, perhaps the ultimate word child, can help us see that the significance of Plato for Murdoch extends beyond ethics.

Like Wittgenstein Plato was deeply concerned with the relationship between language and reality. For Plato, transcendent concepts exist *beyond* representation, in the realm of ideal forms, and are only properly accessible via *anamnesis* – extralinguistically, in other words. While words enable us to reproduce the shape of reality (its forms and ideas) they can just as easily lead us *away* from it. Language can produce its own forms, and therefore its own truth. Murdoch's work often centres on the difficult task of negotiating both kinds of language: one that is faithful to truth, one that is unfaithful. The question of language sheds some light on the 'Wittgensteinian neo-Platonist' label (Caen 1978) she has applied to her philosophy. But here we must again acknowledge the positive influence of Sartre. Many have recognized where the title of her first novel comes from, but it is less commonly acknowledged that the idea of the net is also explored by Sartre in *Nausea* (Danto 1991: 8). Roquentin is deeply troubled by the gulf between words and what they signify, and one of the main concerns of his creator was to come up with a more pragmatic method of reducing this gulf: 'if words are sick, it is up to us to cure them' (*S* 64).

This connection between these three major philosophical influences points to something curious about Murdoch's eccentric philosophy, how it often runs on similar lines to postmodernist and poststructuralist thought. To look back at it from a postmodern perspective, her philosophy amounts to a sustained critique of the Enlightenment project. She is keen throughout her philosophical writings to temper what she sees as a growing emphasis on the transcendent power of the rational mind and will by reminding us of the spiritual and irrational dimensions of human experience. This naturally involves questioning the possibility of adopting a position 'outside' the object of study: in *Metaphysics as a Guide to Morals* she refers approvingly to the Wittgensteinian concept of *sub specie aeternitae*, but she might just as well have turned to any number of poststructuralist or postmodernist philosophers who reject the idea of a 'view from nowhere'.

In exposing the fallacies of applying a theoretical framework to the world in order to understand it, Murdoch falls into step with the postmodern critique of metanarratives. In *The Sovereignty of Good*, for example, she rejects the 'prevailing myth' of Christian theology, explaining that 'there are probably many patterns and purposes within life, but there is no general and as it were externally guaranteed pattern or purpose of the kind for which philosophers and theologians used to search' (*SG* 78). Wittgenstein's conviction that the central questions of philosophy must be approached by recognizing they are actually questions about language meant that analytic philosophy became centred on language right at the point when the continental tradition was about to properly discover Saussure. Both traditions, in other words, were travelling on different tracks but towards a similar destination.

The affinity is something Murdoch recognizes, not least because she was following this route too, though as a result of being influenced by continental philosophy in the form of Sartre rather than structuralism. Speaking in 1978 about the title of *Under the Net*, she comments,

> It's interesting that the discussions which were in my head at that time, in the 1950s, are very much the discussions that we're hearing now about silence, about language moving toward silence, and the difficulty of relating concepts to anything which lies behind them, or under them. (Caen 1978)

Elsewhere in the same year she suggests that Wittgenstein was essentially a 'structuralist' and goes on to suggest why by using a familiar metaphor when considering the relationship between structuralism and literature: 'The writer must realize that he lives and moves within a "significance-world", and not think that he can pass through it or crawl under the net of signs' (Magee 1978). In her 1987 introduction to the reissue of *Sartre* she suggests that Derrida 'exposes philosophical fallacies which were earlier the target of Wittgenstein' (*S* 37). Wittgenstein and Murdoch use the image of a net where the postmodernists might prefer a map, but the sense is largely the same. As Terry Eagleton said in a review of *Metaphysics as a Guide to Morals*, the same qualities Murdoch admires in fiction and philosophy – contingency, anti-systematization – are valued by poststructuralism: 'if Murdoch is so keen to oppose it, it is because it represents her own vision of things pushed to an embarrassingly radical extreme' (Eagleton 1992).

Yet we must be cautious in pursuing the affinities between Murdoch and contemporary 'post' philosophy. Her Platonism (and her reading of Kant) stops her short of acknowledging that all order and meaning is always already an arbitrary construction. She affirms our need to maintain a belief in certain *a priori* truths, however difficult they are to establish. Some concepts, like the Good, endure despite the untenabilility of the Christian metanarrative. In the first of the Platonic dialogues Murdoch published as *Acastos* (1987), Mantias claims that 'really there's no such thing as "reality" or "nature", it's not just sitting there, we *make* it out of words – ideas – concepts'. Significantly, however, the stage directions have him 'floundering', in contrast to Socrates' confident response:

Of course words are not just names, the operation of language is very complicated, we use all sorts of conceptual tricks to relate to our surroundings, we often disagree about how to do it. It certainly does *not* follow from this, that there is no independent world such as common sense takes for granted. (*A* 35–6)

Given the status of Socrates in the play, and given Murdoch's similar pronouncements elsewhere, it is clear that he is speaking for his creator. Murdoch's rejection of prescriptive systems of belief does not lead her to Rorty's postmodern pragmatism but to an embracement of the irrational, the accidental and contingent. Furthermore, she turns structuralist and deconstructionist critique back on itself by suggesting that both viewpoints are fatally wounded by their tendency toward prescription and determinism. She regards it as paradoxical that the same French phenomenological tradition which led Sartre to attack predetermined structuration also produced deconstruction, the charms of which, she comments, 'are those of determinism, pleasing to the thinkers who exclude themselves from the fate of the codified' (*S* 37–8). When she turns her attention more explicitly to structuralism and poststructuralism (though she never uses this latter term) in *Metaphysics as a Guide to Morals*, it is clear that she regards them as late twentieth-century manifestations of the romantic rationalism which characterized the philosophy of the mid-century. Like the post-Kantian rationalism of Hampshire, like Sartrean existentialism, structuralism, deconstruction, postmodernism, she thinks, paradoxically attempt to place themselves outside the object of study (language, Western metaphysics, metanarratives, etc.) and in doing so invest too much faith in rationality. What she is less ready to acknowledge is the affinity between these forms of thought and her own. Murdoch's philosophy may be an eccentric amalgamation of strange bedfellows – Plato, Sartre, Wittgenstein – but in its concern with language it revolves around the issue which is firmly at the centre of late twentieth-century thought.

This interest, then, points to another of the key areas where Murdoch's philosophy and fiction coincide, though the connection is visible only fleetingly in her literary criticism. In a chapter in *Sartre* entitled 'The Sickness of Language' she offers, in a theoretical vocabulary which seems not unexpectedly outmoded now, a nonetheless typically dextrous view of what we have later come to call the crisis of representation as it affects philosophy and literature from Rimbaud and Mallarmé to *Finnegans Wake*. Her explicit purpose is to illuminate Sartre's view of how to harness language to his cause, but she implicitly puts forward her own case for the erosion of 'the traditional form of the novel' (*S* 74). Central to this is the increasing concern with language itself rather than what it refers to in the work of Joyce and Proust, the result, she implies, of 'a moral failure and crisis of value'.

There she stops, however, without going on to consider that the reasons for the modernist concern with language might have more to do with a loss of moral faith. Yet, clearly, the twentieth-century apprehension of language has important ramifications for the version of realism Murdoch wishes to install in place of modernism. The question of representation is at the heart of the poststructuralist critique (instigated by Barthes, and continued by the likes of Colin MacCabe and Catherine Belsey) of 'classic realism', those conventions adhered to by the same nineteenth-century writers looked up to by Murdoch in order to represent external reality faithfully. The nineteenth-century confidence about certain moral values (so the argument runs) is reflected firstly in the way the classic realist novel is organized, by setting up a hierarchy of voices and positions within its pages, with the author's reigning supreme at the top, and secondly in its conception of character, which is portrayed as essential and largely unchanging, individual yet *knowable*. Thus the classic realist novel persuades us that society is similarly dependent upon a tight, natural order. The problem with this ideology, however, is that it depends on a theory of language poststructuralism (and postmodernism) insist is false. Language does not represent the external world, but constitutes that world: to attempt to describe external reality is always already to interpret it.

Now, Murdoch's conviction that bad art ultimately tells a lie about reality depends upon there being an alternative, one she finds exemplified in great writers like George Eliot and Tolstoy. The logic comes ultimately from Plato, who says that language can *also* be used to mystify and falsify as well as telling the truth. Yet the poststructuralist approach to language insists that this is in fact *all* language can do: truth is never more than an effect of language, and even if it is 'out there' it eludes the grasp of signifying practices. Though devoid of explicitly post-Saussurian rhetoric, a similar recognition is never far from Murdoch's philosophy. The result is that a contradiction opens up in her work between the realist faith in referentiality and a counter-conviction about the fundamental inaccessibility of reality through language.

Liberal postmodernism/postmodern liberalism

Though at times it threatens to do so, this contradiction never quite engulfs Murdoch's fiction. Nevertheless, it does have important consequences for the pro-realist/anti-modernist basis of her sublime aesthetic. The question of the relationship between language and the real is often present in her fiction, as an issue which troubles her characters or underscores the situations they find themselves in. The central motif of *Under the Net*, that the more we theorize, the more we remove ourselves from the object of theory, reappears in a variety of ways in the novels which follow. Many of her protagonists, like Miles Greensleave in *Bruno's Dream* (1969) and Charles Arrowby in *The Sea, the Sea*, are troubled by the impossibility of producing a definitive prose description of an event or a person. In *The Black Prince*, part of Bradley Pearson's obsession with *Hamlet* is the play's awareness of 'the redemptive role of words in the lives of those without identity, that is human beings' (*BP* 199).

A variation of this is the powerful apprehension in Murdoch's work of our experience inside what Lacan calls the 'symbolic order' (also known as 'the big Other'), the network of contingent signifiers imposed from outside ourselves which makes up everyday reality. Both *A Severed Head* and *A Word Child*, for example, concern the various ways in which their protagonists' desire is reined in by the respectable veneer of civilized society. At one of the dinner-parties thrown by his socialite friends the Impiatts, Hilary Burde is forced to play by the rules of polite society despite his internal pain. 'How strange', he reflects, 'that behind a smiling chattering mask one may rehearse in the utmost detail pictures and conversations which constitute torture, that behind the mask one may weep, one may howl' (*WC* 97). Bearing in mind *A Word Child*'s concern with the inadequacy of language, and its meditation of *King Lear*, it is appropriate that these thoughts should include a specific allusion to the point in *Lear* where language breaks down. Put into psychoanalytical terms, the novel indicates Hilary's inability to symbolize a trauma at the heart of the real.

But the significance of the question of the real is not limited to its thematic exploration inside her fiction. It functions as a major contributing force behind its very shape. For support here we may turn to what may seem rather an unlikely source. Jean-François Lyotard's influential essay 'What is Postmodernism?' reminds us that the notion of the sublime is intimately bound up with the question of representation, in a way which calls to mind Murdoch's own appropriation of Kant's philosophy: 'But how to make visible that there is something which cannot be seen? Kant himself shows the way when he names "formlessness, the absence of form", as a possible index to the unpresentable' (Lyotard 1985: 78). Lyotard's thesis, that postmodern art, as a result of the peculiar cultural constitution of the era which produces it, is characterized by the effort to present the unpresentable, provides an alternative explanation for why Murdoch is forced to go to such elaborate lengths to approximate the seemingly effortless realism of her nineteenth-century forebears. The compatibility between the Murdochian and the postmodern sublime is testimony to how firmly she is situated in a late twentieth-century context.

Murdoch has, not unexpectedly, expressed her disapproval of post-modern fiction. In *Metaphysics as a Guide to Morals* she identifies 'a new sensibility in art, an attack on traditional art forms' which she calls 'structuralist' or 'deconstructionist' literature, a major characteristic of which is 'a search for hidden *a priori* determining forms, constituting an ultimate reality' (*MGM* 6). She criticizes the self-conscious quality of 'structuralist writers', 'poets [who] write about the nature of poetry, novelists about people writing novels' (*MGM* 4). The implication here is that the postmodern metafictional prerogative (though she refrains from calling the fiction she has in mind postmodern) is a symptom of the same kind of superrationalist, determinist logic which dominates modernism. By 'baring the device' and focusing on the telling as much as the tale, the metafictionist encourages the reader to take the book as a knowable structure of meaning in itself rather than one which is significant only in relation to the real world:

> The structuralist text may resemble a *koan* in having no solution, but being a play of meanings which stirs the client into meaningmaking activity for himself; whereas the traditional novel carries the ideal reader along, fascinated by the single authoritative 'reality' of its imagined world. A contrast between such proceedings has of course long existed unselfconsciously inside the huge realm of art. (*MGM* 90)

Though many theorists of postmodernism – both 'for' and 'against' – would find little to disagree with in this description, it makes clear that the source of Murdoch's critique of postmodern fiction is its rejection of the referential function. Novels which do this, however, are not typically postmodern. Critics who argue that postmodernism amounts to a break with modernism rather than a continuation of it hold that the most extreme experimental metafiction, which seeks to shatter the distinction between fiction and reality and is regarded by some as paradigmatic of postmodernism, is not in fact postmodern at all. Linda Hutcheon has argued that postmodern fiction 'proper' *retains* a referential function. A novel which does not, like the *nouveau roman*, is an example instead of 'late modernist radical metafiction', a form preoccupied with 'auto-representation...with its view that there is no presence, no external truth which verifies or unifies, that there is only self-reference' (Hutcheon 1988: 119). According to the logic of 'double-coding', which Hutcheon (and others) insists is typical of postmodernism, the distinction between realist and postmodern fiction is not a binary opposition: postmodern fiction is *both* realist *and* non-realist at the same time. Gasiorek suggests that such logic comes from realism itself, because of the 'doubleness' inherent in *mimesis*: 'Janus-faced, these texts look both outward to an external world that they attempt to depict in all its complexity and inward to the very processes by which such depiction is brought into being' (Gasiorek 1995: 14–15). In seeking to dissociate herself from postmodern fiction, then, Murdoch is rejecting the kind of metafiction which is really an overflow of radical modernism. In doing so, she aligns herself with a prominent current within *post*modernism, one that offers a critique of modernist autonomy and perseveres with the referential function of art, albeit problematically.

This conclusion is backed up by the fact that Murdoch's fiction itself, particularly since the 1970s, has often incorporated metafictional elements. This is most evident in the two novels, written ten years apart, which are her most formally innovative. In *The Black Prince* Bradley Pearson's narrative is embedded within a series of other narratives by an 'editor' and other members of the cast, a textual 'net' that serves seriously to call into question (as I shall explain more fully in Chapter 4) the origin and meaning of the fiction. The narrator of *The Philosopher's Pupil* is the enigmatic 'N' (for Nemo, or Narrator) who occupies the same hypodiegetic level as the other characters yet also appears to be blessed with all the omniscient powers of a nineteenth-century narrator at his most authoritative. His story concludes with a subtle reminder about its fictionality:

> The end of any tale is arbitrarily determined. As I now end this one, somebody may say: but how on earth do you know all these things about all these people? Well, where does one person end and another person begin? It is my role in life to listen to stories. I also had the assistance of a certain lady. (*PP* 558)

Normally, though, this certain lady's novels problematize the distinction between fiction and reality in a more subtle way. This is often achieved by a puckish form of self-reference, whereby a character who features in one novel crops up again in another. In *An Unofficial Rose* (1962) a bottle of wine is opened which bears the name Lynch-Gibbon, the wine-making hero of the previous novel *A Severed Head*. Septimus Leech, the boy-friend rejected by Julian for Bradley in *The Black Prince*, reappears in *The Sacred and Profane Love Machine* as one of psychoanalyst Blaise Gavender's patients.

Light self-reflexive touches like this seem to justify Murdoch's confidence that the metafictional aspects of her work (though she does not refer to them explicitly as such) do not jeopardize her aim of creating realistic fiction. At the conference in Amsterdam she comments that the reappearance of Septimus Leech is simply 'play', just 'a little game to amuse a small number of kindly readers' (Amsterdam 1988). The statement leads to a discussion of overtly metafictional authors like Fowles and Lodge, and it is clear that Murdoch wishes to distance herself from experimental currents within the contemporary novel. While in itself this disclaimer is unconvincing – playfulness is of course at the very heart of postmodernist fiction, and has been seen as its distinguishing characteristic (Alexander 1990: 3) – Murdoch is right in so far as metafictional elements of her fiction like self-reference serve ultimately to strengthen the mimetic illusion rather than expose the fictionality of both world and text. Or, to bear in mind the inclusive logic of post-modernism, it functions *both* as part of Murdoch's realist aesthetic of the sublime *and* also as an exposure of the flimsy foundations of realism. Septimus Leech's reappearance contributes to the reality-effect of the fiction, thrilling the reader familiar with her work into recognition of an extended world outside the compact focus of the novel. We can see this too in the kind of doubly charged comments which punctuate her novels, like 'if George was in a novel he would be a comic character' (*PP* 363), or 'people never fall in love suddenly like that except in novels' (*BP* 395). Comments such as these do subtly draw attention to the artificiality of the text in which they appear, but do not seriously threaten its sense of reality. Metafiction, as Hutcheon comments, is not necessarily 'revolutionary or progressive' (Hutcheon 1988: 188).

Nevertheless, the fact that certain aspects of her work tend more towards 'postmodern' realism than classic realism raises an important point about Murdoch's placing within the liberal tradition of the British novel. And it should be remembered that Murdoch, despite her strong criticisms of liberal philosophy in her early essays, essentially wishes to revitalize liberalism by returning it to its proper course (as followed by classic realism) rather than reject it outright. The 'great nineteenth-century novel', she says, is where 'one may see the liberal spirit at its best and richest disporting itself in literature, and not yet menaced by those elements of romanticism which later proved [...] so dangerous' (sbr 257).

Her criticism is more or less conventionally liberal humanist (intention-alist, nonhistoricist, resolutely anti-'theory' [*FS* 78]), her redefinition of the novel after modernism backed up by an appeal to what she sees as its essential liberal values: empiricism, individualism, particularity. Yet the metafictional dimension of her fiction illustrates that there is a doubleness to Murdoch's relationship to liberalism.

Nowhere is this more clear, it seems to me, than in her conception of subjectivity. While her notion of the subject is recognizably liberal as it is expressed in her non-fiction (essential, unique, etc.) the treatment of character in her novels at times stretches the notion of subjectivity into postmodernism. Character in the classic realist text is a fundamentally stable entity, a state of affairs which, it has been suggested, is the result of the ideological motivations behind the form: if the self is essential, then it can be known; if it can be known, it can be *placed* in a hierarchical social order.[8] Postmodern characterization responds to the perceived falseness and immorality of this approach by presenting character, to use a Bakhtinian term, as *unfinalized*, as a 'process' in which identity is constantly subject to change (Docherty 1991: 169). Murdoch's view of character, though not entirely free of suppressive ideological connota-tions, is more akin to this latter view than the former:

> Characters in novels partake of the funniness and absurdity and contingent incompleteness and lack of dignity of people in ordinary life. We read here both the positive being of individuals and also their lack of formal wholeness. We are, as real people, unfinished and full of blankness and jumble; only in our own illusioning fantasy are we complete. (*MGM* 97)

This view is transmuted into her fiction in the guise of characters who are preoccupied, we might say, with the *boundaries* of selfhood. This is especially striking in *The Sacred and Profane Love Machine* where Monty broods on the discrepancy between the familiar structure of one's face and the fluid personality which lies behind it, Emily complains of feeling 'hollow' and 'characterless', Harriet wonders about the 'form or structure or schema' (*SPLM* 16) of the human self, and so on. Marguerite Alexander has remarked on something similar in Murdoch's fiction, in that her characters, 'at each transitional point in their lives – most commonly, on falling in love – confer on their present state the distinction of finality'. Yet during each novel 'a number of "final" states may come and go'. The result is an intriguing mix of 'realist' and 'non-realist' character, 'a fruitful tension between, on the one hand, the autonomous character, suggested in the way that each character is delivered by the author to the reader in a highly "finished" form; and on the other, the individual as comprising fleeting moments of consciousness' (Alexander 1990: 182).

This approach to character indicates that Murdoch, in effect, is caught between two dominant traditions of the modern novel. Without being completely outside the 'neo-liberalist' and postmodernist traditions, she is at the centre of neither. She presents characters as 'unfinalized', yet does not go so far as to suggest that the self is entirely fragmented, or constructed wholly by language. Instead, she implies, an essence of selfhood may indeed exist, but it is impossible to find. This sets her apart from the neo-liberal realist tradition to which she clearly belongs in other ways, but which generally wants fictional character to be individual yet knowable.[9] Once again, though, it is worth noting that postmodernism and liberalism are not binarily opposed. To question liberal humanist concepts from a postmodern standpoint, Hutcheon reminds us, 'is not to deny them' (Hutcheon 1988: 57), a valid point even when it comes to the liberal notion of the subject, regarded so contemptuously by the poststructuralists. Decentring the subject is not the same as *denying* it (Hutcheon 1988: 158–9). The double logic of postmodernism applies in Murdoch's case: she is both liberal and postmodern. But while she is eccentric in this respect, an ambivalent position is common – if not the norm – in the late twentieth-century. Because of her historical location, her work is driven, as she herself has acknowledged, by 'sexual, mythological and psychological patterns, and not the great hub of society which a nineteenth-century writer relied on'.[10]

'A sort of post-Freudian Henry James':[11] Murdoch and the liberal soul

This comment suggests there is another dimension to Murdoch's under-standing of the personality, which complicates both the 'postmodern' and 'liberal' understandings of subjectivity. In her polemical pleas for a more adequate conception of the personality, Murdoch proposes that one area is especially neglected: 'for the Liberal world, philosophy is not in fact at present able to offer us any other complete and powerful picture of the soul' (ad 18). This is a particularly suggestive term, and its use in 'Against Dryness' opens up two of the major avenues in Murdoch's work. The first of these, the exploration into what we might call the spiritual side of subjectivity, is in line with the usual connotation of the word 'soul' (though it is not an area that figured largely in the cultural debate of the time, nor has it done so since) and is a question we shall return to in the following chapter. The second, however, seems more unexpected. Her attempt to regenerate the liberal conception of the soul chiefly involves recourse to the work of Freud.[12]

A consideration of the major intellectual influences on Murdoch's thought would not be complete without a consideration of her engagement with Freudian theory. Yet the connection is not immediately obvious from her discussions about her philosophical precursors. She was always keen to deny she was a 'Freudian'. This is chiefly the result of two major quarrels with psychoanalysis. First, its emphasis on introspection makes it prone to the same structure-building faults as 'romantic rationalist' philosophy and literature. This is morally wrong, in Murdoch's opinion, for good morality depends upon looking outside the self: 'the best cure for misery is to help someone else' (Haffenden 1985). Second, and this is the source of a more fundamental disagreement, Murdoch has serious misgivings about the therapeutic merits of Freud's foundation. Although analysis can be useful as 'a sort of first aid' where 'the analyst can fulfil a priestly role in making [people] feel there is hope' (Haffenden 1985), she finds the idea of the transference 'very alarming indeed ... this can disturb someone's life profoundly' (Caen 1978).

The dangerous power of the analyst leads to a line of charlatan psychoanalysts in her novels who abuse their 'priestly role'. Palmer Anderson in *A Severed Head*, the first and most memorable, uses his position as perceived possessor of a deep knowledge of human nature to justify his affair with Martin Lynch-Gibbon's wife, his patient, Antonia: 'Yes, perhaps it has a sort of inevitability [...]. This is ... something bigger than ourselves' (*SH* 28–9). After him there comes Francis Marloe, the discredited doctor in *The Black Prince*, who later publishes a psychoanalytic reading of Bradley's case, and Blaise Gavender, whose psychoanalytic training makes him the only character in the novel to display (smugly) a confident knowledge of his 'inner self'.

Despite these misgivings, however, Murdoch's conception of what drives us remains essentially Freudian.[13] Referring to her critique of Sartre, Robert Scholes has argued that Murdoch is a better novelist than Sartre, though not, as her proselytizing might lead us to expect, because she succeeds in presenting the irreducible difference of individuals, but because she portrays what unites us (Scholes 1974: 197). Although he describes this somewhat reductively as 'structuralist thinking', Scholes' point is nevertheless persuasive. Murdoch's reponse to the super-rationalist view of the personality embodied in Sartre's work is partly to take him on at his own game and urge that we *reason* ourselves into a position where we embrace the contingent rather than recoil from it. Yet her strategy also involves emphasizing the irrational forces at work within us which suggest a more complex relationship between self and external world than Sartre takes on board.

In particular, she regards Freud's picture of human nature as a realistic alternative to the fanciful existentialist notion of the free-choosing human self (and other versions of 'romantic rationalism', like Stuart Hampshire's notion of the 'ideally rational man'). She defines the condition of *angst*, not as Sartre does, as the tumultuous experience of pure freedom, but as 'a kind of fright which the conscious will feels when it apprehends the strength and direction of the personality which is not under its immediate control' (*SG* 38–9). Unlike existentialism, psychoanalysis takes account of the dark uncontrollable forces at work in the soul, the *mythology* of the psyche. It highlights the 'obscure system of energy out of which choices and visible acts of will emerge at intervals in ways which are often unclear' (*SG* 54). This energy is what Plato calls 'Eros', and is channelled in two main directions – towards self-gratification and self-delusion on the one hand ('low' Eros), and towards *ascesis* on the other ('high' Eros).

But Freud gives a particularly compelling account of 'low' Eros. What he does, in fact, can most easily be grasped by 'translating' the notion of Eros into more familiar psychoanalytic terminology: he presents us with a persuasive idea of the way *desire* drives the human being. More specifically, psychoanalysis shows how desire functions in a *mechanical* way, a comparison Murdoch consistently employs in her own discussions of the psyche. The metaphor is at the heart of *The Sacred and Profane Love Machine*, for example, which details Blaise's attempts to negotiate between both kinds of Eros, in the form of two very different women, his 'good' wife Harriet, and the earthy, sexy Emily McHugh. This is where the Murdochian and the Freudian vision of the subject coincide.

To summarize Murdoch's idea of the soul, we could do no better than use her own summary of Freud's:

> He sees the psyche as an egocentric system of quasi-mechanical energy, largely determined by its own individual history, whose natural attachments are sexual, ambiguous, and hard for the subject to understand or control. (*SG* 51)

Because this powerful force is easily mistaken, there is the risk that the subject comes to regard random events, like 'a series of accidents', as a kind of predestined pattern originating from *outside* the self. Not surprisingly, Murdoch regards such egocentricity as dangerous from a moral point of view, and her interest in this kind of behaviour is partly motivated by her insistence on the hazards of fantasy. It can ensure that in a person's unconscious 'a certain kind of drama shall be enacted and re-enacted'.[14] Murdoch believes people can become possessed by the idea of this internal drama, finding in it a 'mythological feeling of their destiny. They interpret a situation in some kind of doom-ridden way perhaps, and one can reasonably see this as a myth which has in some way got hold of them' (Bradbury 1976).

She has drawn attention to this mechanical energy as it manifests itself in fictional characters, like Raskolnikov (who is 'animated by a myth' [*MGM* 136]), or the Sartrean hero (sbr 254). (A similar view of the psyche, it should be noted, is also found in Lawrence, with whom a positive comparison is not as fanciful as it may seem.) But it serves well as a description of her own characters, in whom this personal myth is played out. Her characters feel deprived of choice, rigidly bound to a pattern, a kind of *machine infernale*, which once set in motion must be followed to its logical outcome. In a discussion about *A Fairly Honourable Defeat* (1970) Murdoch speaks of the 'notion of *arène* in which human beings can be seen as the puppets of their own emotions'. This is clearly exhibited, for example, in *A Severed Head* when Martin Lynch-Gibbon realizes his love for Honor Klein:

> Inevitable now Honor certainly seemed to be, vast across my way as the horizon itself or the spread wings of Satan; and although I could not as yet trace it out I could feel behind me like steel the pattern of which this and only this could have been the outcome. I had never felt so certain of any path upon which I had set my feet; and this in itself produced an exhilaration. (*SH* 124)

It is a state of mind which bears a strong resemblance to the Freudian concept of 'the omnipotence of thought', where one regards as an external magical force something which in fact originates in one's own mind (Freud 1987: 143–4).

Murdoch's interest in this aspect of human nature relates to her treatment of the question of myth in the novel. 'Modern literature', she has said, 'presents us with the triumph of neurosis, the triumph of myth as a solipsistic form' (sbr 265). This is an issue, of course, on which she is more than just an interested observer: she has admitted that when she attempts to populate a novel with independent-seeming characters she finds that 'the myth of the work has drawn all these people into a sort of spiral . . . which ultimately is the form of one's own mind' (Kermode 1963). The apprehension of being trapped within the imaginary is a clear point of similarity between Murdoch and psychoanalysis.

The comparison is also valid on a more general level. Peter Brooks has commented that 'according to psychoanalysis, man is a fiction-making animal, one defined by fantasies and fictions' (Brooks 1994: 108). This is a conclusion that could easily serve as an epigraph to Murdoch's own work. Murdoch is preoccupied throughout her writing with our need to construct fictions from our experiences, and then live in the fantasy world we create. Patrick Swinden, one of Murdoch's most perceptive critics, says of Murdoch's gallery of characters that

> They invent connections which impose a pattern and design on what is itself not patterned and designed. Then they go on to convince themselves and one another that these patterns, these designs, these *plots*, are inherent in the actions themselves. They convince themselves that they really exist. To do this they need to be inhabited. So the characters in Iris Murdoch's books find themselves living in an artificial world that has been imposed on them and constructed around them by their own inventive imaginations, by the need they feel to console themselves. (Swinden 1973: 235)

This seduction by the world of appearances can be explored within a Platonic framework. Yet what psychoanalysis has to say about the imaginary realm of human experience has an important resonance in the fictions produced by Murdoch's characters. In particular, psychoanalysis emphasizes how these are *retrospective* fictions, which testify to the hold the past has on us, and the hold we desire to have on the past. The aim of this book is to demonstrate that this dynamic informs one of the central currents in Murdoch's fiction.

2
The Insistence of the Past

> You've killed me and sent me to hell, and you must descend to the underworld to find me and make me live again. If you don't come for me, I'll become a demon and drag you down into the dark.
>
> *The Sacred and Profane Love Machine*

> I think memory works both ways [in narrative], in that the returns [...] are both returns to and returns of: moments when the past seems to come forward, as in the return of the repressed, or when memory takes us back into the past.
>
> Peter Brooks, *Psychoanalysis and Storytelling*

Making sense of the past is a common concern among post-war novelists, especially English ones. In *The Situation of the Novel*, published in 1970, Bernard Bergonzi argued that, as a result of the uncertainties brought about by recent history, contemporary fiction was poised somewhere 'between nostalgia and nightmare', alternatively or simultaneously imagining a brutal apocalyptic future and 'a vanished era', most often that of the 'Edwardian summer'.[1]

The desire to escape the future by returning to the past was not of course new to English culture, as any consideration of various reactionary or nostalgic strains in literary history from the Renaissance to modernism would testify (Renaissance pastoral, the 'Age of Sensibility', romanticism, Tennyson, Hardy, etc.). For a variety of political, social and historical reasons, looking back to a previous age is an integral part of the English psyche. Yet the tendency to look back does take on a new aspect and urgency in the fraught socio-cultural environment of the immediate post-war period in which Iris Murdoch first emerged.

After the trauma of the war, there was the conviction among writers and intellectuals that, as Bryan Appleyard puts it, 'some line of communication with the past had been severed' (Appleyard 1990: 3). The result was that it was all the more important to consider just what the past *meant* for those in the present. In a more recent analysis of the retrospective tradition in the post-war novel, David Leon Higdon delineates three distinct currents within the post-war novel devoted to doing just this. The first is made up of 'retrospective novelists in which the act of looking backwards transforms the individual who becomes subject and object', the second includes 'fiction imitating past fiction in a very self-conscious fashion', and the third is built around an interest 'in a new group of protagonists – biographers, bibliographers, historians, geologists, anthropologists and even paleontologists – whose lives are caught up with the past' (Higdon 1984: 9, 10, 11–12).

Higdon's survey is particularly useful, it seems to me, because it highlights the shared preoccupation with retrospection in modernism and postmodernism, and where the latter departs from the former. His first category conforms to what we might identify as the 'late modernist' strand in twentieth-century fiction, which continues to use the retrospective mode to facilitate *introspection* in the manner of modernists like Proust, Conrad and Ford Madox Ford. The modernist preoccupations with consciousness and time lend themselves to an inquiry into the relationship of the individual, or a group of individuals, to their past, and continues well into the post-war period, as we can conclude from one of its dominant forms, the *roman fleuve*: C. P. Snow's *Strangers and Brothers* (1940–78), Anthony Powell's *The Music of Time* (1951–75), Evelyn Waugh's *Sword of Honour* (1952–61), Lawrence Durrell's *The Alexandria Quartet* (1957–60). 'Late-modernist' retrospective inquiry does not preclude extreme nostalgia, as evidenced by Waugh's construction of a pervasive myth about the English aristocracy, but in its meditation on time and fictionality (as in Powell and Durrell) it approximates a more complex engagement with the question of the past.

This looks forward to what I see as a more characteristically postmodern kind of retrospection – which equates to Higdon's second and third categories – which is more self-reflexive about its status and methodology, and shot through with anxiety about the 'already-said'. One of the most common and representative forms of postmodern novel is what Linda Hutcheon terms 'historiographic', a kind of text which has appeared so often over the last thirty years or so that it indicates how deeply, almost obsessively, postmodernism is concerned with the past. The power of historiographic metafiction is rooted in the tension between two conflicting recognitions: that the need to understand the past is crucial, but is impossible to fulfil, for what we know of the past is always mediated and modified by forms of representation.[2] That this is a form which has proved particularly attractive to British authors, who have produced some of the most critically lauded examples of it (for instance, John Fowles' *The French Lieutenant's Woman*, Julian Barnes' *Flaubert's Parrot*, Graham Swift's *Waterland*) suggests that the form represents the perennial British preoccupation with the past dressed up in new (postmodern) clothes.

Murdoch's fiction offers a fascinating counterpoint to the 'retrospective dominant' in the post-war novel. Here her work again finds itself positioned both inside and outside the central currents of the post-war novel, in that it shares a prevailing interest of the period, but departs from the work of others in the way it actually explores the past.

Murdoch, to my mind, has been one of the most persistent and effective chroniclers of *loss* in late twentieth-century fiction. Her novels explore what we might call the 'natural' forms of loss we all inevitably experience – time, love, other people – and also a more unexpected, tragic kind of loss, which features in the large number of her novels which are concerned with guilt. Her theoretical counterpart in this sense is, naturally, psychoanalysis, for it too offers – as its later Lacanian formulation emphasizes – a suggestive, at times poetic, dynamic of loss. This is not to say that she draws directly on psychoanalysis to approach the question of the past. For one thing, as I have explained, her reservations about psychoanalysis prevent her embracing its precepts fully. More importantly, the question of the past is wrapped up in some of the other key concerns in her work: accident, spirituality, and the gulf between language and the real. But her retrospective fiction does share with psychoanalysis two clear convictions: the notion that the past will always find a way of making itself present (but never in precisely the way the subject wishes), and that the subject is compelled somehow to make sense of it – in psychoanalytic terminology, to bring it into signification. In this chapter I want to expand on this claim, but as a prelude to doing so wish to consider more precisely how Murdoch's work relates to the 'retrospective turn' in post-war narrative as I have outlined it.

Murdoch's dissimilarity to her contemporaries in the 1950s and early 1960s seems to extend to the dominant emotion in the group of post-war novels identified by Bergonzi. Nostalgia seems to belong to that part of the psyche bent on fastening on to illusory mythology and as such is an emotion Murdoch would have wished to resist. Nevertheless a powerful undercurrent of nostalgia is in fact evident in her work, though it is not as central nor is it directed towards the same ends as in some of her contemporaries.

As I have suggested, Murdoch's 'aesthetic of the sublime' is essentially retroactive, developed out of a dialogue with two earlier forms of fiction, classic realism and modernism. While this undoubtedly springs from deeply felt philosophical convictions, it is also partly motivated by a kind of nostalgia not too far removed from that of immediate peers like Powell and Waugh. Part of her 'project' to revitalize the twentieth-century realist novel involves the repeated assertion that the nineteenth-century novel is superior to the versions which supersede it. Yet the more we ponder the logic behind this, the more apparent it becomes that Murdoch values the technique of the nineteenth-century novel principally because of the more secure worldview which produced it. As the post-Marxist, 'cultural materialist' wing of theory dominant in British criticism since the 1980s has made clear, the question of literary value is endlessly relative. Murdoch's approbation of the classic realist novel is frequently supported by pronouncements which seem straightforward and commonsensical, but are in fact loaded with questionable terms.

She claims that 'the novel, the novel proper that is, is about people's treatment of each other, and so it is about human values' (*S* 138), without explaining why this should be the novel *proper*, or which values she has in mind. What the nineteenth century often seems to represent in Murdoch's work is a nostalgic zone, a home from which we in the twentieth century are sadly exiled. This becomes clear when she explains why it is impossible for twentieth-century writers to equal the achievement of the classic realists. In our age, writers are 'more timid', yet 'afraid of seeming unsophisticated or naïve':

> I think literature is about the struggle between good and evil, but this does not appear clearly in modern writing, where there is an atmosphere of moral diffidence and where the characters presented are usually mediocre. Many things cause literary change, and self-consciousness about language may be more of a symptom than a cause. The disappearance or weakening of organized religion is perhaps the most important thing that has happened to us in the last hundred years. The great nineteenthcentury novelists took religion for granted. Loss of social hierarchy and religious belief makes judgement more tentative, interest in psychoanalysis makes it in some ways more complex. (Magee 1978)

This is an accurate diagnosis, it seems to me, but not one which explains why the nineteenth-century novel is more *valuable* than what comes after it. Reading between the lines, this quotation stands as a lament for a time when a stable sense of morality and social order meant we could be less timid and more objective in our assertions, when we did not have to resort to irony to say what we meant, and were not so oppressively conscious of the role of language in constituting reality.

Though never actually set in the nineteenth century, Murdoch's fiction at times reflects a similar kind of nostalgia. Observations about contemporary moral diffidence, the dying-out of religion, the obfuscatory capacity of words, are repeatedly worked into her characters' conversations. For the most part, though, such nostalgia is felt implicitly rather than evoked directly (which is not the case with some of her post-war contemporaries). At its most basic, her preference for a previous age is conveyed as a subtle impatience with the present. There can scarcely be a novelist writing in the period from the 1950s to the 1990s who pays less attention to the massive acceleration of social and technological change which has occurred in the period: the electronic media, computers and aeroplanes are mostly absent from her fictional world, and cars and even the telephone are usually regarded with distaste. (This points, in fact, to a curious hint of nausea at the contingent which seeps into an otherwise exemplary tolerance for the messiness of life.)

On occasion, this unease with the present world creeps into her non-fiction, too. Terry Eagleton notes, tongue in cheek, that her critique of poststructuralism and postmodernism in *Metaphysics as a Guide to Morals* is bound up with a general hostility to modernity, 'which for Iris Murdoch includes television, computers, sociology and a good deal else' (Eagleton 1992). Generally, her novels do little to evoke the particular period in which they were written, though there are notable exceptions in her 'mid-period' novels, in the glimpses of youth culture in *The Black Prince* and *A Word Child*, for instance, or, more unlikely still, the appearance of UFOs in *The Nice and the Good* (1968) and *The Philosopher's Pupil*. For the most part, the high-bourgeois or aristocratic attitudes and lifestyles of her characters (particularly in her most recent novels, where some of them own houses in London as well as large halls with servants in the country) reinforce the impression that in its essential concern with human interrelations, Murdoch's fiction would lose little if set seventy or eighty years earlier.

Her fictional world, in fact, owes something to the nostalgia characteristic of the genre Northrop Frye calls 'prose romance', fiction which typically deals with esoteric coteries of people in an isolated, idealized setting, unlike the contemporaneous world though often analogous to it (Frye 1957: 305). The isolated community, as in *The Sea, the Sea* and *The Philosopher's Pupil*, is clearly a setting Murdoch is fond of, not to mention one her talents are particularly suited to portraying, and may plausibly owe something to her dislike of modernity.

Nostalgia: *The Book and the Brotherhood*

If we look in the right places, then, Murdoch's work can be seen to display a similar kind of reactionary nostalgia to that of her contemporaries in the post-war novel. The fact is, though, that the nostalgic attitude to the past occasionally on view in her theory and in her implicit dislike of the present is of a quite different order to the nostalgia which features in her novels.

This is clear from one of her most retrospective fictions, *The Book and the Brotherhood* (1987), which explores the collective and individual effects of the past on the members of a group of ageing Oxford friends. This 'brotherhood' long ago commissioned one David Crimond to write a book to promulgate the Marxist theories they once held dear. The problem is that the world and their views have changed – and so has Crimond, to the point at which, as one of Murdoch's demonic enchanter-figures, he now represents a threat to them which is many-sided. He challenges them intellectually by outwardly despising their new humanist convictions, and sexually and physically too: he seduces Duncan Cambus' wife and uses extreme violence to prevent him taking her back.

On a surface level, this absurd situation, of the group paying someone they no longer trust to write a book expounding ideals they no longer believe in, clearly points to a pressing need to come to terms intellectually with the past, and much of the novel's content is made up of discussions about the twentieth-century status of philosophy, religion and Marxism. Yet there is another, more emotional side to the novel's retrospective dimension, for, individually, the characters obscurely realize that something is missing from their lives. This aspect is prevented from descending into sentimentality by the superbly wistful, at times poetic, quality of Murdoch's prose – a style which, incidentally, marks an interesting contrast to the ironic narration of the novel's predecessor, *The Good Apprentice*. The sense of loss ranges from the vaguely nostalgic, as when Rose looks out at the tower of an Oxford college and is reminded 'of something, some kind of theatre, some time, perhaps many times, when she had seen illumined buildings at night and heard superhuman voices' (*BB* 14), to a more concrete and sustained sense of longing.

Both Rose and Gerard Hernshaw (the chief protagonist, though as in many Murdoch novels, many of the cast figure prominently) still suffer from the death of Sinclair, Rose's brother and Gerard's one real love. Sinclair figures as the 'absent centre' of the book, indicating that loss works on a technical level too. Murdoch has referred to an intriguing experiment she has used while writing a novel in order to make the peripheral characters as real and important as the principal ones: she creates a central figure, and then removes him (Bradbury 1976).[3]

At the beginning of the novel, however, Gerard is faced with a new and unexpected loss which serves as the point of convergence for all the others: his father dies. Though their relationship has been happy overall, there remains one unresolved area of contention between them. As a boy Gerard owned and adored a parrot called Grey, whose significance was more than simply as a companion: 'The parrot was a world in which the child was graciously allowed to live, he was a vehicle which connected Gerard with the whole sentient creation, he was an avatar, an incarnation of love' (*BB* 58). For no apparent reason, but perhaps bound up with jealousy or worry at the child's misdirected love, his father gave away the parrot when Gerard was at boarding school. Gerard is now filled with remorse at not having confronted his father with this grievance before he died. Grey's role as a nostalgic signifier, denoting some indefinable, inaccessible happiness, is increased with his father's death. The parrot is now associated with the two great losses in Gerard's life, Sinclair and now his father, a symbol which is made even more poignant by Gerard's realization that Grey may actually have survived both.

One of the most moving scenes in the novel, and in Murdoch's work as a whole, is when, walking home one winter, Gerard comes across a parrot in the window of a pet shop in the Gloucester Road. As in *Nuns and Soldiers* (1980), another novel concerned with the effects of the past, there is an echo of the device Joyce uses in 'The Dead' to underscore Gabriel Conroy's meditation on the passing of time (Scanlan 1992): 'The snow fell slowly like a visible silence as if it were part of the ritual making a private place wherein Gerard and the bird were alone together' (*BB* 216). Watching the parrot, separated from it by the glass and half-consciously acting out his childhood movements of opening the cage and stroking the parrot, Gerard's thoughts turn to his father, whom he saw on his deathbed similarly wrinkled and clawed: 'Did the dead know how much we loved them, *did* they know, for they know nothing now?' (*BB* 217).

The Book and the Brotherhood is a novel which deals thoughtfully with nostalgia, but is not itself nostalgic like the work of many of Murdoch's contemporaries. The poignant desire to return to the past does not characterize the *overall vision* of the novel in quite the way it does in, say, Powell and Durrell. Murdoch is too attached to her ethic of authorial withdrawal to allow the novel to be an expression of her own nostalgia (though the novel may be read in this way). Nostalgia here belongs firmly to the characters, not the author. And this, to my mind, points to the key difference between Murdoch's approach to the past and that of other post-war writers.

Where her contemporaries are primarily concerned with a *collective* version of the past – albeit one often visualized in terms of how it is experienced by one individual – Murdoch's interest is in a localized, personal past, the implications of which extend little further than the effect of a particular past experience on a particular character. This has much to do with the hierarchy she seeks to preserve of character over form, derived from her instinct against using the novel as a way of dramatizing a set of extra-fictional ideas. But it is also the consequence of the diminished status of *history* in her work.

Her novels, it has often been pointed out, come across as palpably disinterested in history, politics and the ways in which wide-ranging social forces motivate or constrain the individual. They prefer to shift between a focus on the timeless rather than the diachronic aspects of experience (love, the good, the mechanical mythology of the psyche, etc.), and, conversely, a portrayal of what is so particular about human experience that it is irreducible to any universal theory. Although in their discussions the characters in *The Book and the Brotherhood* are concerned with a shared experience of the past, this is far removed from the kind of sustained self-conscious inquiry into the past which characterizes historiographic metafiction.

This is not the same as saying that Murdoch's fiction is entirely ignorant of history, however. For one thing, her awareness of the consequences of being 'post-Freudian' necessarily implies a sensitivity to the changing historical backdrop behind the epistemology of the subject. In *The Sacred and Profane Love Machine*, which implicitly contrasts nineteenth- and late twentieth-century notions of character, Monty claims to be suspicious of Blaise's faith in the 'dreary old historical self' (*SPLM* 123). More explicitly, a number of specific historical referents do recur in Murdoch's fiction. The title of her 1965 novel *The Red and the Green* echoes Stendhal's *Le Rouge et le Noir* and it similarly blends together fictional character with a specific historical location, in this case Easter 1916 in Ireland. Though this is her only outright departure into historical fiction, in many other books the cold hand of recent history touches the lives of individual characters. The troubled political past of Poland, for example, is embodied in the strange Luciewicz twins, part of the cast of refugees in *The Flight from the Enchanter*, and also in a much later novel, *Nuns and Soldiers*, where 'The Count' envisages his present situation as a small-scale repetition of the history of his motherland. Several characters are haunted by their experience – or non-experience – of war: in *An Accidental Man* Ludwig Leferrier has fled the United States after draft-dodging Vietnam, and *The Nice and the Good* and *A Fairly Honourable Defeat* feature in Willy Kost and the evil Julius King two opposing moral responses to surviving the Nazi concentration camp.

But these examples serve to emphasize that 'real' history in Murdoch's fiction figures mostly as part of a particular character's emotional baggage. As Margaret Scanlan argues, there is no sense that her characters feel something might be gained from an analysis of their own historical situation: 'Enmeshed in the permanent crisis of a largely uncommunicable personal past, they "do not even know they do not know" a shared world of public history' (Scanlan 1992: 186).

Public history may be visible in Murdoch's fiction, then, but it is subsumed by the question of the *personal* past, which looms much larger. Making sense of the past takes place on an individual level in her novels. Late-modernist and postmodern retrospective fiction, on the other hand, ultimately attach some collective importance to their interrogation of the past. The former, by suggesting (often through nostalgic elegy) that the past contains important values which are worth preserving or resurrecting, serves to draw conclusions about cause and effect, how we got *here* from *there*. The past may well be a foreign country, as *The Go-Between* famously has it, but, as the novel itself affirms, it is still possible to visit and learn some of the language. By doing the opposite, by turning upside-down the accepted understanding of the relationship between cause and effect, historiographic metafiction lays bare the very workings of retrospective inquiry and concludes that any act of reconstruction must involve subjective processes of construction. The writer-hero of Julian Barnes' *Flaubert's Parrot* learns that 'hypothesis is spun directly from the temperament of the biographer' (Barnes 1984: 40).

In Murdoch, where the sense of a shared past is minimal, and the overall ideology of the book less transparent, such conclusions are not so easy to come by. Yet, in an important sense, her retrospective fiction does resemble the more overtly postmodern variety in that it insists on the double logic of the past: it is fundamentally inaccessible yet nevertheless unavoidably significant. A comparison between *The Book and the Brotherhood* and *Flaubert's Parrot* can make the comparison clear.

Just as a parrot is used in Barnes to symbolize the always already absent historical referent, Grey is more than simply a lost companion to Gerard Hernshaw, but stands for the lost world of his childhood, his relationship with his father, and, implicitly, with his first love Sinclair. The coincidental choice of the same image by two very different authors emphasizes that the personal past functions in Murdoch much like the public past in historiographic metafiction. Standing outside the pet shop Gerard Hernshaw resists the temptation to buy the parrot and take it home, recognizing that recovering the past in the form of a 'dream parrot' (*BB* 218) is impossible. Nevertheless the compulsion remains almost irresistible because of his need to squeeze out as much significance as possible from the key events of his life.

This impulse figures centrally in other novels where Murdoch focuses on old age. In *The Sea, the Sea* (a novel I shall say more about in following chapters) retired theatre director Charles Arrowby retreats to a lonely cottage beside the sea to write his memoirs, a project which chiefly involves trawling through his childhood memories. The 1969 novel *Bruno's Dream* is built upon Bruno Greensleave's deathbed reflections on his past. He has invested a great deal of time in building up a huge stamp collection, an obsession which symbolizes the need to piece together the events of his life. By the end of the novel, however, the collection has been swept away by the flooding Thames.

Jackson's Dilemma: making sense of the past

Characters like Bruno do their best to ensure the past is continually present, though they struggle to make final sense of it. Other characters find that the past returns in spite of their efforts to escape it, and this makes the need to determine its significance all the more pressing. Murdoch's 1995 novel, *Jackson's Dilemma*, contains examples of both kinds of character. Although shorter than any of her novels since the 1970s, and although its compressed form is at times more reminiscent of a fable than its sprawling realist predecessors, it nevertheless provides a good example of the extent to which her compulsive characters and plots are motivated by the past.

Edward Lannion has never forgiven himself – nor been forgiven by his father – for failing to save his brother from drowning in a childhood accident. Marian Berran is suffering terrible guilt after jilting Edward the day before she was due to marry him – the key event on which the plot turns. Benet Barnell is wistfully and vaguely nostalgic, missing his dead Uncle Tim, lingering at the Peter Pan statue in Kensington Gardens. For

Tuan, a Jew, the public guilt of the Holocaust has taken on personal significance, and has prevented him from seeking happiness or entering into any relationship with man or woman. 'It is about the past', he reflects, '– oh, the past, how soon it can vanish and be forgotten. Even the hugest and most hideous things may fade – yet such things also must never be forgotten' (*JD* 165–6).

The problem of coming to terms with the past explains the title of the novel. As a result of being surrounded by people so troubled by the past Jackson becomes aware that 'he carried a weight, a burden placed upon him by *them*' (*JD* 122). He is one of Murdoch's most successful characters, remaining enigmatic and sympathetic, displaying elements of many of her familiar types without conforming neatly to any: the unattractive yet good man (like Tallis Browne in *A Fairly Honourable Defeat*), the remorseless evil man (Julius King, Tallis's adversary) the pathetic servant-figure (Francis Marloe in *The Black Prince*), the charismatic manipulator like Mischa Fox (*The Flight from the Enchanter*). In the course of the book he is compared to numerous artistic or mythic forebears: Christ, Othello, Macbeth, the Fisher King and Caliban. In one sense, these references in the novel illustrate the working of Murdoch's 'anti-modernist' use of mythic allusion, in that none of them seem to apply absolutely. But the connection with *The Tempest* – as is often the case in Murdoch's fiction – goes further. Like this play the atmosphere of the book is subtly magical; the plot begins expectantly only for a quiet to descend over it as the characters seem to achieve contentment sooner than we thought. With about a third of the book to go, seasoned readers of Murdoch anticipate a shock, but the surprise in this case is that there is none. This is because Jackson has been playing the role of Prospero, presiding over the cast, registering their movements and knowing everything about them – yet not exploiting this power like Murdoch's other Prosperos, like Mischa Fox or Charles Arrowby. He has worked to ensure that there are no shocks and no unhappiness, engineering the situation so that it resembles the conclusion of one of Shakespeare's comedies, the cast neatly paired off in three weddings, Jackson himself agreeing to settle down with Benet to ensure he is happy too. The energy he has expended in doing so leaves him exhausted, much as James' similarly selfless rescue of Charles in *The Sea, the Sea* exhausts him.

For most of the novel Jackson's inner world remains enigmatic and we are unsure whether he is working for someone, or for some darker purpose. But at the end we recognize that Jackson's dilemma is a moral one. Specifically it relates to his decision about whether he should return the confused Marian to Cantor, the man she loves, or 'turn her in' to an over-protective network of friends and family. On a wider level, though, Jackson's dilemma is how to help those around him deal effectively with their pasts. By directing them into situations where their guilt can be assuaged he allows them practical solutions which point to a way out of their own deluded self-mythologizing (Benet's indulgence in matchmaking fantasies, Owen's demonic fantasies of power, Edward's self-destructive ones).

The importance of the past in *Jackson's Dilemma* is reinforced by an apparent eccentricity in its organization. Though the chapters are set out in conventional numerical order, one of them (the third) is given the subtitle, 'The Past'. Rather than marking a new departure in Murdoch's fiction, this simply makes more explicit the device upon which a great number of her stories in fact rest: a significant event occurs in the past with which the characters must somehow come to terms. In some, like *Under the Net* and *The Bell* (1958), this event takes place in the past of the hypodiegetic world, that is, outside the time frame of the plot. Jake Donahue has published a transcript of his conversations with Hugo Belfounder without asking his permission, and Michael Meade has been forced into a shameful departure from his schoolteaching job because of his homosexual love for a pupil. Other plots begin with the pivotal event. *The Nice and the Good* (1968), for example, along with *The Black Prince* and *The Green Knight* (1993), one of Murdoch's periodic reworkings of the conventions of the detective novel, begins with the discovery of a body. *The Good Apprentice* (1985) opens with another death, an accidental one in this case, simultaneously horrific and hilarious: Mark Wilsden, high on the LSD fed him by his friend Edward Baltram, leaps out of a window in the mistaken belief that he can fly.

In some of her books, the metaphorical presence of the past is given a more material expression. *The Sacred and Profane Love Machine* and the more recent *The Green Knight* both begin with a similar dreamlike tableau, where a strange person is seen standing at the bottom of a garden at night. In the former, this turns out to be Luca, the child borne by Blaise Gavender's mistress, and whose appearance signals the interpenetration of the two worlds he has until now successfully managed to keep apart. The latter, more strangely still, marks the return of Peter Mir, the man who intervened in Lucas Graffe's attempt to murder his brother Clement and was killed himself. These openings figure as a kind of primal scene, constantly returned to in the minds of those it affects: 'The story, so frequently run through, enacted, polished, probed and interrogated in Clement's mind...' (*GK* 80). Clement's situation exemplifies those of Murdoch's other past-obsessed characters, who are determined to make sense of what has happened to them. As one of them, Paula Biranne in *The Nice and the Good*, insists, 'one must do something about the past. It doesn't just cease to be. It goes on existing and affecting the present, and in new and different ways, as if in some other dimension it too were growing' (*NG* 122).

These last instances are suggestive of the Buddhist notion of *karma*, the belief that we inevitably pay for our past actions, an idea which is clearly attractive to Murdoch as part of her continued interest in theology (Conradi 1989: 81, 233). Seeing the child in the Gavenders' garden, for example, Monty Small imagines it is the ghost of his dead wife. He is haunted by more than just bereavement: in one of the most cleverly worked revelations in Murdoch's fiction, we come to realize that partly because of his wife's extreme pain from cancer, but also because of her relentless goading, Monty performed an impulsive 'mercy' killing.

But a more pertinent comparison than *karma* for the symbolic returns in Murdoch's fiction is psychoanalysis, the fundamental law of which is that past trauma will always find a way of returning. These symbolic returns illustrate that the past functions in Murdoch's work as *insistence*, the term Lacan uses for the 'compulsion to repeat', the mechanism Freud discovered at work in the human subject, and which, Peter Brooks has suggested, is also a fundamental pattern in narrative (Brooks 1992). One way or another, the past cannot be ignored; it insists on being taken into account, on being interpreted, and signified.

The repetition-compulsion operates according to a distinctive logic. While we must move beyond the past, we are also compelled to return to it. These two distinctive movements, Brooks observes, are central to the working of memory itself: returns *to* and returns *of*, the deliberate interrogation of what has gone before, and the return of the repressed or the inescapable (Brooks 1994: 119; see also Brooks 1992: 90–142). Both movements are at work in Murdoch's retrospective fiction. For every character like Gerard Hernshaw and Bruno Greensleave (and later, as we shall see, many of the heroes of Murdoch's first-person fiction) whose desire is to return to the past, or at least to understand what it means, there are others, like Monty Small or Edward Lannion, who find themselves unable to escape it.

Redemption, spiritual and secular: *A Word Child* and *The Good Apprentice*

The second process is most clearly at work in those novels which explore the nature of guilt. As the examples I have given so far confirm, the sheer number of guilt-ridden characters in the pages of Murdoch's novels is quite striking. This, in itself, is not unprecedented in the twentieth-century English novel, a prominent tradition of which is made up of Catholic novelists like Waugh, Graham Greene, Muriel Spark and David Lodge. But what is unusual is that the work of a Protestant British author – a 'puritan' as she has described herself (Caen 1978) – should return so frequently, almost obsessively, to the question of guilt.

It is an interest which was there from the start, and one which, as her 1980s and 1990s novels demonstrate, did not diminish. An explanation for this is not too difficult to advance, however, as guilt brings into play two of Murdoch's most consistent concerns: the disruptive intrusion into our lives of contingent or accidental forces, and the question of the status of spirituality in the late twentieth century. But these questions are themselves bound up with Murdoch's concern with retrospection, as is apparent in the two novels which pursue the question of guilt and the possibility of redemption most relentlessly, *A Word Child* and *The Good Apprentice*.

At the centre of each is an example of the Murdochian 'accidental man', the course of his life changed forever by a tragic mistake. Hilary Burde has killed his lover during a furious row while driving, Edward Baltram is partly to blame for Mark's death. Each man has tried different ways of coming to terms with the past – Hilary rigorously structures his life, Edward seeks refuge in a mysterious retreat called Seegard – but neither is able to forget the past, or to redeem himself. Edward receives hate letters from Mark's grieving mother, urging him to '*Think* what you have done. I want you to think of it at every moment, at every second. I would like to stuff it down your throat like a black ball and choke you' (*GA* 9). Not that these are necessary. He cannot rid himself of the conviction that 'One momentary act of folly had destroyed all his *time*' (*GA* 10). At the end of *A Word Child* Hilary sits in St Stephen's, the church where T. S. Eliot was a warden, and thinks of the lines from 'Burnt Norton': 'If all time is eternally present all time is unredeemable' (*WC* 384).

The main problem for both men is that they seek redemption in a world where God does not exist. Hilary comments bitterly on the 'marvellous myth' that is the Christian notion of redemptive suffering, 'this denial of causation and death, this changing of death into a fairytale of constructive suffering' (*WC* 291), while Harry Cuno speaks for many of the characters in *The Good Apprentice* when he says that 'the fact about human nature is that things are indelible, religion is a lie because it pretends you can start again' (*GA* 441). These comments offer a neat picture of the moral world that all of Murdoch's characters inhabit. Carel Fisher, the most demonic version of a number of agnostic priests in Murdoch's work (along with Father Bernard in *The Philosopher's Pupil* and Cato Forbes in *Henry and Cato*) describes theology as no more than an 'act of concealment': 'One must be good for nothing, without sense of reward, in the world of Jehovah and Leviathan, and that is why goodness is impossible for us human beings' (*TA* 173–4). Though Christianity is described repeatedly in her fiction as magic or myth, Murdoch does not go along with Fisher's nihilistic assumption that goodness is therefore impossible.

The problem of how to establish a moral framework in the absence of one provided for us by Christianity is at the heart of Murdoch's moral philosophy. In *The Sovereignty of Good*, her most impressively concise work of philosophy, she argues that we need to replace God with the idea of Good, retaining the moral guidance which a divine being offers but avoiding personification of an abstract concept. We should instead envisage the values God represents as metaphysical concepts which can offer 'a guide to morals', and turn for guidance to empirical examples of the good at work – especially love, which involves a clear respect for the alterity of another, and is visible in its 'highest' form in the greatest art (*SG* 74–5).

Murdoch's conviction about the invalidity of God does not mean that religion has no place in her philosophy, despite her often-acknowledged atheism and her belief that the status of religion is much diminished in our culture. Her most recent fiction makes it clear that some aspects of its moral framework are important to hold on to. *Jackson's Dilemma* contains a background discussion about religion and mysticism, conducted chiefly through Tuan, who is writing a book on the subject, and Mildred, who wants to be a priest. Speaking no doubt for the author herself,[4] Mildred values the 'deep mystical understanding, which had once belonged to Christianity, [but] had been therein eroded by the great sciences and the hubris of the new Christian world which had kept their Christ and their God as stiff literal persons who cannot now be credited' (*JD* 186). There is an echo here of Murdoch's earlier objections to traditions in modern thought like existentialism and analytic philosophy which fail to pay sufficient attention to the irrational and the contingent. But at the same time, the danger is that the mythological elements of the theory lead the subject away from the real ascetic aims: 'This was religion, the giving away of oneself, the realization of how small, like to a grain of dust, one was in the vast misery of the world – and yet how vast the power of goodness, of love like a great cloud, lifting one up out of the meanness, the deadliness, of the miserable ego' (*JD* 207). Similarly, in *The Green Knight*, Father Damien warns Bernard about picturing God as a soldier: 'This sort of "dramatization" of what is holy is, in your case, a form of egoism' (*GK* 113).

In other words, Murdoch is opposed to the idea of religion as a metanarrative, but values its endorsement of *ascesis*. Christ himself, removed from the specific framework of the Bible, remains an important model for Murdoch's ascetic ideal. He is never far from Murdoch's recent fiction. Jackson is compared to Christ, his loss of energy after ensuring those around him are more at ease with the past reminiscent of Christ's suffering to enable others to live again. The myth is treated more obviously in *The Green Knight*, where Peter Mir is mysteriously 'resurrected' and comes to confront Lucas Graffe with his past actions. As Clement Graffe realizes, 'Peter saved his life and gave his life for me' (*GK* 430). Murdoch's Platonic reworking of Christian beliefs accounts for the increasing interest in her fiction, from the 1970s onward, in the form of characters like James in *The Sea, the Sea* and Uncle Tim in *Jackson's Dilemma*, with Eastern forms of religion, those which offer a picture of valuable moral concepts like unselfing shorn of the illusory, 'magical' elements of Western religion.

Murdoch's dissatisfaction with the notion of redemptive suffering is linked to her convictions about the falsely consolatory nature of artistic form, the motivation behind the development of her own sublime aesthetic. Previously, I referred to the link Richard Todd makes between *A Word Child*'s 'sublime' use of form and the obscure reference to *King Lear* in 'Against Dryness'. Murdoch's discussion of this play in *Metaphysics as a Guide to Morals* proves that his instinct is right. She argues that *Lear* largely manages to avoid consolation by refusing to conform to the (Aristotelian) 'tragic ideal'. Rather than experiencing *catharsis* after watching it, 'we go away uneasy, chilled by a cold wind from another region' (*MGM* 121). Murdoch describes how the 'bird i' th' cage' speech – quoted by Hilary as he begins to glimpse his own redemption – 'must often have been the cry of defeated people who suddenly saw a holy vision of peace inside pain, of forgiving and being forgiven, of redemptive suffering' (*MGM* 119).

These observations point to Murdoch's wider purpose in her reading of *Lear*, her connection between the 'tragic ideal' and the Christian doctrine of redemptive suffering. The play's 'absolute cancellation' of this idea, she says, embodies 'Shakespeare's (true) tragic understanding that religion, especially and essentially, must not be consolation (magic)' (*MGM* 119–20). There is no reason for Cordelia's death (it is unnecessary for the dynamics of the plot) and thus it exposes Lear's blissful prison dream, his vision of consolation, as an illusion. *King Lear* is therefore a true tragedy because it has become 'some sort of contra-diction, destroying itself as art while maintaining itself as art' (*MGM* 123). This phrase could serve as a neat exposition of her aesthetic of the sublime, for which Shakespeare and *Lear* in particular are the supreme models.

Reading *Lear* in terms of the Christian notion of redemptive suffering is not particularly original, of course, but Murdoch does go on to propose a more radical analysis of the play which sheds further light on her approach to redemption. Although *Lear* repudiates the 'tragic ideal' by denying the audience a consolatory *catharsis*, although Lear's death is by no means heroic and remains disturbing because it comes before the evil forces at large in the play are defeated, still, she suggests, it risks an element of consolation:

> As it is, one might go further and ask would it not be an even better tragedy if Lear were left alive at the end, if we were left with his sense of consciousness, bearing this terrible knowledge, continuing to be. (We are not to be consoled by the idea that he is mad, he is not mad, he knows and sees it all.) (*MGM* 120)

It is precisely this dimension that *A Word Child* and *The Good Apprentice* add to their heroes' suffering. At the end of the novel Hilary and Kitty, his second lover, are swept into the Thames. Hilary, though, does not drown. He gets another chance – or, more likely given Murdoch's suggested improvement on *Lear*, stays alive with his tormented con-sciousness. To die would be a consolation, because it would prevent the chance of the tragedy being repeated. Similarly, in *The Good Apprentice*, Edward considers suicide, but his author will not allow him the comfort of committing it. Thomas McCaskerville, one of the more sympathetically presented psychiatrists in her work, informs him that 'Your endless talk of dying is a substitute for the real needful death, the death of your illusions. Your "death" is a pretend death, simply the false notion that somehow, without effort, all your troubles could vanish' (*GA* 71).

Blocking her characters' passages to death is surely the most severe example – puritanical, we might say – of Murdoch's anti-consolation ethic. It underlines the fact that all the obvious paths to redemption are cut off for Hilary and Edward. Christian mythology is too much like a fairytale for them to believe in, and neither is allowed to aestheticize his predicament in the way that Miles Greensleave in *Bruno's Dream* responds to the accidental death of his first wife by composing a poem. The world of each novel may be uncanny and obsessional but it is quite unlike the magical world of *Jackson's Dilemma*: there is no Jackson figure to achieve their redemption for them. These novels emphasize, in other words, that Murdoch complicates the whole notion of redemption, demanding that we understand it in contexts other than purely the religious or aesthetic. But this complication is also a clarification, as is clear if we consider the different senses of the word itself. To redeem is to exchange, or to recover or restore – to gain something anew, or to regain something we previously possessed. Redemption, in other words, is really about making sense of the past. How can we *exchange* the past for something significant, that will make sense of what happened and allow us to progress?

This question returns us to psychoanalysis, what we might see as the secular version of redemption. For there is of course a similarity between the role of a psychoanalyst in 'redeeming' the patient's past, and that of the priest – something Freud himself acknowledged.[5] It is a connection from which Murdoch draws a certain amount of comic capital in *The Green Knight* when she makes her 'Christ-figure' Peter Mir pretend he is a psychoanalyst. The aim of the psychoanalytic process is to find a way of making the past fully present, of releasing into full consciousness the trauma which has previously been locked in the unconscious. Central to this process is the Freudian distinction between 'remembering' and 'repeating' (Freud 1924, 1986). In a successful analysis, the analysand is required to bring a repressed experience fully into his or her consciousness and understand it, rather than simply continuing to replay it (by, for example, transferring identical feelings from the original cause to the analyst). The buried experience is thus transformed into a language which will make sense of it; by being re-enacted properly, time is effectively redeemed.

This is not to say that Murdoch's characters need therapy, however, any more than they need a priest. What is important is that they are able to 'remember' their past by confronting it properly, without getting stuck in the loop of their own mechanical self-mythology or any other aestheticizing process. This lesson is what lies behind one of the most memorable Gothic 'set-pieces' in Murdoch's fiction. In *The Good Apprentice* one of the main impulses behind Edward's journey to Seegard is to seek out his real father, Jesse. (He is partly driven by mysterious Oedipal feelings which demonstrate that he is motivated by more than just the tangible events of the recent past.) Once reunited, however, Edward begins to realize that Seegard is far from the pastoral haven it first seemed to be.

Having lapsed into a feverish state, troubled by vivid nightmares, imagining the fruit-juice he has been drinking has been laced with some potent substance, Edward takes a walk by the river and is sure he sees his father's face staring up at him under the water. He is engulfed by guilt and paranoia:

> Edward thought, my God, it's an *hallucination*. It's like something I saw in a dream that night when I was drugged. *They* have done it to me. [...] Will I go on being like this, am I *breaking up*? And he thought, no, *they* aren't poisoning me. It's my own doing. It's that awful drug I used to take, it'll never go away, never. What a horrible vision. I'm coming to pieces. *This* is what I've come to, this is where I'm being *driven*. And I thought I was recovering, I was getting off. But of course the punishment is automatic. (*GA* 307)

That this is a symbolic death for Edward is reinforced by the title of the novel's final section, which follows it, 'Life after Death'. Like Orpheus, he has to descend into the underworld of his unconscious and confront both his feelings for his father and about himself before he can begin to recover. The reference to the drug which was instrumental in Mark's death indicates, too, that rather than any 'magic' solution to his problem, he must truly revisit his past in order to approach redemption.

Something similar occurs in Murdoch's other retrospective fictions. In *A Severed Head*, for example, the metaphorical underworld into which Martin Lynch-Gibbon must descend in order to fetch back his unfaithful wife is symbolized by a fight with the 'infernal' Honor Klein which takes place in a cellar described as a vision of hell, complete with 'sulphurous odour' (*SH* 109). Similarly, as Hilary Burde sinks into the mud on the riverbank in the dramatic climax to *A Word Child*, he feels as if 'fiends' were clutching on to his arms and legs and pulling them down into the river, 'that cold hell' (*WC* 376–7). This kind of Orphic descent into one's own past and one's own mind – a journey which is also analogous to the psychoanalytic process – explains the way some of Murdoch's guilt-ridden characters must seek redemption.

The past speaks insistently to two kinds of past-obsessed characters in Murdoch's fiction: those who wish to recover it, like Gerard Hernshaw, and those who cannot help *re*-covering it, like Martin Lynch-Gibbon and Hilary Burde. It is no coincidence that *A Severed Head* and *A Word Child* are first-person novels, for there is something about the way Murdoch has harnessed the claustrophobic potential of this form, where everything is presented to us through the consciousness of one character, which makes the return of the past seem particularly insistent. But the first-person form is also particularly suited to the desire to return *to* the past, something which quasi-autobiographical novels like *The Black Prince* and *The Sea, the Sea* demonstrate effectively. In other words, the double movement I have identified as running through Murdoch's fiction is at its most visible and powerful in those novels which conform to the definition of the first-person retrospective novel, one in which the narrator tells a story about his own past: *Under the Net, A Severed Head, The Italian Girl, The Black Prince, A Word Child* and *The Sea, the Sea*.

As these works show, the past is naturally – inevitably – made to seem more significant when the protagonist of a novel is also its narrator. The key to each is not just the story the narrator tells, but his very experience of using a narrative to look back on his past. To return to a familiar Murdochian metaphor, his narrative figures as a *net* cast over the real of the past, a way of imposing form on top of raw material, an attempt to symbolize what is unsymbolizable. Before considering Murdoch's first-person novels, however, it is worth turning to *The Bell*, a novel which explores both the values and dangers of constructing a narrative about one's past in a way which also underlines the argument I have put forward in this chapter.

3
Narrative as Redemption: *The Bell*

The Bell is one of Murdoch's most important and popular achievements. Less melodramatic and less willing to deploy the devices of the romance than many of her others (even though it trades in familiar scenarios and character-types) its sense of restraint renders it more like a 'traditional' version of realism than much of her early work. The novel also shows how naturally a preoccupation with the past functions as the motor in Murdoch's fiction, driving the other themes she is perhaps more consciously keen to deal with, such as religion, subjectivity, and the nature of love.

What is especially powerful about *The Bell* is the way that the insistence of the past acts upon the reader, who is made subtly to feel the power of the past through the symbolic texture of the fiction, rather than being confronted with it directly through dialogue or stream of consciousness. My intention in this chapter is to expand on this point, showing the extent to which *The Bell* can be thought of as a 'retrospective' fiction, in the terms I outlined in the previous chapter. But the way this particular novel links retrospectivity with the idea of *narrative* – a way of making sense of the past – also looks forward to the following chapters, which are concerned with this connection as it figures in Murdoch's first-person 'retrospective' fiction, where it becomes integral to their form.

The Bell is the first of Murdoch's novels to make use of the audacious grand flourish of plotting which characterizes *An Accidental Man* and *A Word Child*, where a shocking event that happened in the past comes to happen again, as if predetermined. Before the time of the story Michael Meade has faced ruin in his career after falling for one of his male pupils. He has begun a new career as a leader of an Anglican lay community in Imber Court in Oxfordshire, the family home he inherited, which shares its grounds with an ancient Abbey. But having apparently freed himself from the scandal of his past, exactly the same thing occurs. His attempt to make sense of this experience, to come to terms with it so that he can open the way to a happier future, is central to the story.

Michael only gradually emerges as the main character, however. *The Bell* is really the story of three people, their significance suggested by the fact that the story as a whole is told only from their perspectives. Dora Greenfield, a former art student, arrives at Imber to try and resume her volatile relationship with her estranged husband Paul, a medieval historian who is working on a set of ancient documents in the Abbey. Toby Gashe has just left school and is spending the summer with the community as a prelude to going to university. Dora and Toby arrive at the same time, and figure as the innocent outsiders who must become accustomed to the ritualized pattern of life at Imber. When they arrive the community is looking forward to two symbolic events: a new bell is to be hung in the Abbey to replace the old one which was lost mysteriously hundreds of years before, and one of the community, Catherine Fawley, is formally to enter the Abbey to become a nun.

In the first part of the story we see both newcomers becoming acquainted with the history and lifestyle of Imber. Toby is more comfortable than the non-religious Dora, who feels out of place and twice tries to 'escape'. By contrast Toby quickly gets to know his new home, roaming through the grounds of Imber and the Abbey, and swimming in the lake. On one swim he comes across what he will later realize is the huge lost bell stuck in the mud at the bottom of the lake. Early on we are also introduced to the internal politics of the community as the two leaders, Michael Meade and former missionary and army man James Tayper Pace, debate the day-to-day business. James is in practice if not in name the 'governor' of Imber, its 'superego', imposing and preserving order. Michael leaves decisions to him, and decisions are something he apparently finds simple to make.

While we are introduced to the main characters and shown the apparently harmonious day-to-day existence of the community, two ominous notes are sounded. First, we realize that living in a lodge away from the main building of the court, is Nick Fawley, Catherine's brother, and the agent of Michael's downfall when he was a schoolboy. He is now a cynical damaged alcoholic. Second, Paul relates to Dora a story about the legend of the lost bell he has discovered during his research. It is said that some time in the fourteenth century one of the nuns had a lover who, climbing over the high wall of the Abbey to visit her, fell and broke his neck. When the nun involved failed to come forward the Bishop placed a curse on the Abbey, whereupon, so the ancient manuscript claims, 'the great bell "flew like a bird out of the tower and fell into the lake"' (*B* 42). Soon after the nun ran out of the Abbey and drowned herself in the lake. As Paul says, 'there is a story about the bell ringing sometimes in the bottom of the lake, and how if you hear it it portends a death' (*B* 43).

The crisis that these portents herald occurs when Michael suddenly, on impulse, kisses Toby after a day spent together, and is plunged into an agony of desire and remorse. As befits a novel so directly concerned with religion, this is the most obvious of a number of 'falls'. It is Michael's second fall from grace, while Nick himself figures as a kind of fallen angel, once innocent and beautiful, now exiled into a contemptuous alcoholic hell. The event also brutally effects young Toby's passage from the innocent world of sheltered childhood to the ambivalent world of adult sexual desire. The kiss is a transgression against the order of the community, and once it has occurred it seems to usher forth a more general breakdown in the prevailing law. As Toby reflects, 'suddenly it seemed that since everything was so muddled, anything was permitted' (*B* 176). Before long he has impulsively climbed the wall separating the Abbey from the Court, clumsily attempted to seduce Dora, and hatched with her a ridiculous plan to replace the new bell with the rediscovered original by hijacking the ceremony and unveiling it.

'Outside inwards'/'inside outwards'

Setting the story in a religious community enables Murdoch to address, in detail but in an uncontrived way, the question of how to determine spiritual meaning in an increasingly atheistic world – a question, as we have seen, which could sum up the philosophical backdrop for her fiction as whole. What is notable about its treatment in *The Bell*, though, is that the specificity of the novel's geographical and historical location gives the philosophical interest an added sociological precision. Where *A Word Child* and *The Good Apprentice* present us with characters involved in a *private* drama intensified by their atheist convictions, here we have a group of people at a particular point in history actively and collectively involved in trying to come to terms with the modern erosion of spiritual value.

In her 1970 essay 'Existentialists and Mystics', Murdoch writes of the large number of people in the late twentieth century who are growing up outside Christianity and have thus lost access to the ready 'protective symbolism' of religion, 'the instinctive philosophical background of the ordinary person' (em 12–13). Her ideal (although she never expressed it as directly as this) was that a replacement be erected for this ready-made metaphysical scaffolding, so as to ensure, as the title of her sprawling last work of philosophy puts it, that metaphysics could be a guide to morality. Elsewhere she improvised an idea of 'metaphysical utilitarianism', a 'less optimistic, more desperate' version than Bentham's and Mill's. Where these philosophers had argued that people were entitled to tangible, practical things like food and shelter, Murdoch wondered why these basic requirements could not be extended to things like 'freedom, democracy, truth and love'. This is persuasive in principle, but it seems to me typical of Murdoch as a thinker that she never attempted to set out precisely *how* this kind of 'metaphysical utilitarianism' might actually be imposed, beyond a kind of Arnoldian gesture towards embracing the value of art and its 'implicit moral philosophy [. . .] unobtrusively supported by religious belief' (em 16–18). Her analytical brilliance meant that Murdoch could clearly isolate one of the most pressing voids in modern life. Filling the gap, however, was a different matter altogether. If people were no longer being enticed into church through the attractive imagery of Christianity, surely philosophy and art, the preserve of only a minority, were hardly likely to fare any better.

But it is interesting to consider *The Bell* in this context, for it presents us with a society who are attempting to address the problem practically rather than philosophically. The original conception of the community, Michael recalls early in the book, came after the Abbess spoke to him of the need for a '"buffer state" [. . .], between the Abbey and the world, a reflection, a benevolent and useful parasite, an intermediary form of life' (B 81). Her idea comes from her conviction that the modern world is full of people 'who can live neither in the world nor out of it'. They suffer from a kind of sickness, yearning for the value that God can bestow on their lives, but lacking the strength or character to give up their everyday existence. The Abbess does not criticize such people for being weak. Rather their predicament is an inevitable response to the realities of a modern society dominated by the work ethic. Only professions like teaching or nursing offer a modicum of spiritual value; most others, while demanding commitment, fall short. Life at Imber, then, is not directed towards 'seek[ing] the highest regardless of the realities of our spiritual life' but rather 'seek[ing] that place, that task, those people, which will make our spiritual life most constantly grow and flourish' (B 81). It is a quest, says the Abbess, which requires a particular kind of 'divine cunning', the kind suggested by Christ in Matthew 10:16: 'As wise as serpents, as harmless as doves' (B 81).

Imber might therefore be regarded as a fictional realization of what, as Conradi notes (Conradi 1989: 115), Murdoch refers to in her essay 'A House of Theory' (1958) as 'the vision of an ideal community in which work would once again be creative and meaningful and human brotherhood be restored'.[1] But rather than see Imber as a didactic illustration of the author's views on how religion might be made to work in a godless world, it is better to regard it as a microcosmic portrait of late twentieth-century society. Positioned between the ascetic world of the Abbey and the numinous 'real' world Imber is not quite a version of purgatory (though it has been pointed out that its circular geography recalls Dante[2]) but it is certainly poised between two extremes: the spiritual world of the Abbey and the secular outside world. Although it deals with an enclosed community, the preserve of the prose romance, *The Bell* is one of Murdoch's more historically specific fictions: the outside world is suggested by pubs and car journeys and, most clearly perhaps, in the sudden appearance in the sky above Imber of a formation of aircraft – a reminder of the proximity of this real world.[3] Michael Meade, who readily acknowledges that he suffers from the sickness the Abbess refers to, is thus a kind of representative Everyman of this in-between state, someone who once harboured ambitions towards the priesthood, but ended up being a schoolteacher instead. James Tayper Pace is another 'half-contemplative', as the Abbess terms them (*B* 81), who had begun to train as a missionary but instead ended up running settlements and boys' clubs in London.

The novel has a dialogical balance typical of Murdoch's writing. This is most clear from the way that the sociological/philosophical subtext is conveyed, via two sermons, given in turn by James and then Michael. Each opens with the line 'The chief requirement of the good life' (*B* 131–200), each considers the question of innocence, and each uses the image of a bell to reinforce what they have to say. For James, goodness is a matter of adhering to rules – an approach to ethics which resembles the Kantian 'categorical imperative', where we are allowed to do what we have to do because we *must* do it, it is our duty. For him, adhering to the law of God means preoccupying ourselves not with 'what delights us or what disgusts us, morally speaking, but what is enjoined and what is forbidden'. Truth, for example, 'is not glorious, it is just enjoined', nor is sodomy 'disgusting, it is just forbidden' (*B* 132). This means renouncing any sense of personality, working 'from outside inwards'. Simply obeying the laws of God unquestioningly means that innocence can be preserved and the reward will be knowledge.

Michael's view, though he does not present it as such in his sermon the next week – nor even realize it fully until he begins to speak – is the precise opposite. Goodness, he argues, is the result of knowing oneself, acting from 'inside outwards' (*B* 204). What he values is 'exploring one's personality and estimating the consequences rather than austerely following the rules' (*B* 205). We cannot simply do what we are told if what we are told runs counter to what we perceive spiritual reality to be. This is how he interprets the Abbess's quotation of Christ, 'as wise as serpents, as harmless as doves'. In the Bible it refers to Jesus's advice to the disciples about how to proceed in dangerous circumstances: they must be sufficiently aware of evil not to be drawn into its clutches, but equally must remain innocent enough not to prejudge people according to the standards of evil. In Michael's conception of the good life it translates as 'exploring and hallowing every corner of our being, to bring into existence that one and perfect individual which God in creating us entrusted to our care' (*B* 204–5). Another reference point here, quoted directly from and disapprovingly by James, is Milton's *Areopagitica* speech of 1644.[4] Michael endorses Milton's viewpoint that knowledge of good requires a knowledge of evil: they are inseparable and can only be distinguished if we know them both.

'We never discuss our past lives here': the rational and the uncanny

The positioning of these two sermons, and their self-conscious echoes of each other, reminds us of the repetitive ritualistic nature of life at Imber but also suggests a rational dialogue, an exchange of views. Interestingly, a similar strategy of repetition operates at a deeper, more symbolic textual level, and this serves to puncture the sense of rationality conveyed by James's and Michael's speeches. Just as the two sermons echo each other, at times word for word, so there are two parallel episodes, in Chapters 6 and 18, which are almost identically worded in the first 6 lines of each. In both Michael is awakened from his sleep 'by a strange hollow booming sound which seemed to come from the direction of the lake' (*B* 78–223). The first turns out to be another example of a 'sinister and uncanny' (*B* 78) recurring dream Michael has, as he watches the nuns drag a corpse out of the lake and wonders whose it might be. On the second occasion this dream appears to have been predictive as Michael is really wakened by the sounding of the old bell after Toby and Dora have pulled it out of the water.

This portentous quality is central to the side of the novel which pertains more to the suspense and drama of gothic romance than classic realism. It is clear that the 'geography' of the novel – isolated ancient buildings surrounding a deep lake – plays on gothic conventions. These are suggested in the many points in the novel when one of the three central characters looks out at the lake, especially Dora. Early on, for example, she looks out at the moonlit lake and 'with a shock of alarm, she saw that there was a dark figure standing quite near on the edge of the water, very still' (B 43–4). Later she feels 'There was something incredible about the proximity of that dark hole and that silence' (B 69). This gothic quality is something that Murdoch was to make more central in a sequence of novels which followed The Bell: A Severed Head, The Unicorn (1963) and The Time of the Angels (1966).

As in much Gothic fiction, we are in the realm here of the Freudian 'uncanny', the phenomenon where something familiar becomes troublingly unfamiliar (or vice versa) when it occurs in an unexpected context. The effect is disturbing because it puts us in contact with the mechanism of the unconscious. The mechanical nature of the unconscious means that the uncanny often operates via repetition, when, for example, we experience a coincidence, déja vû, or we see a double. Freud's exploration of the concept comes in an engagement with a work of fiction, E. T. A. Hoffman's strange story 'The Sandman' (Freud 1990), and the concept of the uncanny has close affinities with literature, since literary texts trade in precisely the same kind of things (repetition, doubling, symbolism). The literary theorist Tzvetan Todorov terms 'uncanny' one of the predominant forms of the literary fantastic: unlike its counterpart the 'marvellous' (where unrealistic events are to be taken by the reader as 'really happening' in the world of the fiction), the uncanny is where unrealistic events are ultimately the products of a character's perception, informed by his or her unconscious fantasy. As I shall argue in later chapters, the strange and coincidental events that frequently appear in Murdoch's fiction are usually to be seen in this light: the strangeness of the world is the result of it being perceived that way through the heightened, often deluded, senses of her characters.

In The Bell the uncanny is not simply there to create a Gothic atmosphere. Instead it serves as a counterpoint to the passionate rational dialogue between James and Michael which is conducted across its pages. It is important here to acknowledge the extent to which the community at Imber is preoccupied by the past. In the most obvious sense, like all communities and institutions, Imber sustains itself by continually invoking tradition. This is shown most directly by the puritanical Mrs Mark's directions to Dora, telling her of the rituals that must be observed at Imber ('we don't normally allow any sort of personal decoration in the rooms' [B 61]) and informing her of its historical features, its architecture, how the stables were once ravaged by fire. Imber's history is also backed up more formally by the updates Paul Greenfield gives his wife about his research. But the deliberate practice of looking back is accompanied by a counter-movement by which the past continually makes itself felt in the character's minds involuntarily or problematically.

Central to this is the symbol of the bell. Murdoch's plot contains numerous echoes of the myth recounted by Paul to Dora: when, for example, Toby climbs the high wall of the Abbey, like the nun's lover, or when Catherine, the faithless, lovesick nun, runs into the lake to drown herself. Once told, the premonitory quality of the story resounds throughout the novel, instantly creating suspense. Knowing the sound of the old bell means death, the reader expects a death to occur. This anticipation increases once Dora and Toby have rescued the bell and accidentally caused it to ring – as a result of their own illicit flirtation. The question, of course, as so often in Murdoch, is: *whose* death will it be? The chief red-herring here is Catherine, a nun who has been secretly in love with Michael for years (we learn at the end), and who confesses at one point, 'I often dream about drowning' (*B* 138). Her Ophelia-like destiny is almost fulfilled when she attempts to drown herself in the lake, only to be rescued by Dora at the last moment. In fact the victim is Nick, disillusioned and perhaps jealous at Michael's passion for Toby. His suicide recasts Michael's kiss as a smaller-scale version of the illicit affair of the legend but with equally serious consequences.

We can see here how insistent the past is in Murdoch: the past will not remain past, the curse will come true. More precisely, the story of the bell shows the 'double movement' I discussed in the previous chapter clearly at work in her fiction. The old bell is the marker of an original time of trauma to which the characters look back, or by which they are obscurely haunted. At the same time, it heralds, portentously, an event in the future. It is a reminder of a story of inappropriate love which leads to tragedy, and as such cannot be forgotten until a similar story is played out again. Mrs Mark warns Dora that 'we never discuss our past lives here' (*B* 63). The implication is that entering the community involves tacitly agreeing to renounce one's individual past in favour of a collective, historical past. The myth of the bell, however, insists that one's personal past cannot be simply repressed in this way. The story that unfolds turns on the fact that Michael and Nick are in fact unable to bury their own past.

We can see, then, that just as the plot of the novel revolves around repetition (the repetition of Michael's desire for a young man which has disastrous consequences) so the symbolic and philosophical texture of this novel works according to the logic of repetition too. The repeated sermon episodes signify the repetitive rhythms of a community sustained by a rational, traditional ideology in which the personal past is renounced for a collective past. But these are paralleled by the disorienting effect of Michael's repeated wakening to the booming of a distant bell, the first a dream that seems like reality, the second reality that seems like a dream. These replayed episodes remind us of the irrational, insistent power of the past – another symbol for which is the lake itself, the dark dangerous hole at the centre of the community. This uncanny undercurrent also invites us to see the rituals of the community in another light: more than simply signifying routine, they convey a sense of circularity and *inevitability*.

Narrative acts

What makes this sense of an ending particularly effective is the fact that we become actively implicated in its logic ourselves as we read the novel rather than simply passively 'watching' the characters grappling with it. Nick's suicide effectively asks the reader to choose between the 'rational' and the 'irrational' positions in the text: because the legend promises a death and a death occurs, does this mean that the old curse is *true*? Does superstition win out over rationalism? More importantly than deciding on an answer, the point is that the very ambiguity is central to what the novel is 'about', as it mirrors exactly the dilemma which the central characters face in relation to their own past. What can they learn from it? Are sequences of events to be regarded purely as coincidental and unrelated, or are they a kind of narrative from which the characters should learn?

We are confronted in other words with the philosophical conundrum which is never far from Murdoch's writing. Life is a random chaotic flux but we are predisposed to regard it as patterned. To what extent should literature seek to reflect this by remaining as formless as possible? Or should the novel glory in pattern and its own artifice? Literary devices such as repetition and symbolism (employed in *The Bell* in relation to the old bell or the lake) seduce us to interpret, to make links between different aspects of the text. This process is integral to what we might call the 'narrative act' – the process by which author puts together a patchwork of events and signifiers and the reader organizes these into a meaningful sequence. Like most fictions this general law applies to *The Bell*. But its subtle use of repetition makes the law operate particularly powerfully.

As we see time and again in Murdoch (and as we have already briefly considered in the case of Martin Lynch-Gibbon in *A Severed Head*) it is easier when placed in a troubling situation to succumb to a 'mythological feeling of [-] destiny', as Murdoch herself put it (Bradbury 1976): that is, to interpret events in terms of a narrative imposed by some external force and to act subsequently in a way which conforms to its apparent logic. This is a very real danger to Michael, even though he is far less of a fantasist than Martin Lynch-Gibbon. The problem, as is made clear early on, is Michael's tendency to interpret his life in religious terms. In the Abbess's 'foundational' speech, where she suggests how the establishment of Imber can help assuage the prevailing modern spiritual 'sickness', Michael instantly recognizes himself in her words, hearing in them precisely the kind of summons he has always been expecting: 'It was an aspect of Michael's belief in God, and one which although he knew it to be dangerous he could never altogether reject, that he expected the emergence in his life of patterns and signs. He had always felt himself to be a man with a definite destiny, a man waiting for a call' (*B* 82).

The dangers are apparent in the way he has chosen to interpret his original 'fall', his relationship with Nick. When initially considering whether to try to become a priest, he is worried that his homosexuality is likely to fatally compromise his religious ambitions. He resolves the dilemma by deciding that 'in some curious way the emotion which fed both arose deeply from the same source' (*B* 100). This enables him to give up sexual desire and redirect its energy into his religion. But in the midst of the crisis caused by his relationship with Nick, he begins to look at this from the opposite perspective. Rather than his religious impulses being tarnished by his sexual desire, surely his sexuality could be *purified* by its proximity to noble spiritual impulses? 'Vaguely Michael had visions of himself as the boy's spiritual guardian, his passion slowly transformed into a lofty and more selfless attachment' (*B* 105). On one level, of course, a serious debate is being conducted here about the Platonic theory of low and high Eros – or to put it in Freudian terms, sublimation. But on another level (and the choice of word 'vaguely' is the clue) it suggests the dangers of using a mythical or theoretical framework to make sense of experience. There is something here reminiscent of *Death in Venice*, in which an older man also justifies his pursuit of a younger one by invoking Platonic philosophy.

The appeal to religious narratives is Michael's favoured way of coping with traumatic events. As he prepares to put the scandal surrounding Nick behind him and start a new career at Imber, Michael reflects that 'the catastrophe which destroyed his first attempt [to become a priest] had been designed to humble him' (*B* 108). And when Nick unexpectedly reappears in Michael's life at Imber he is sure that 'Nick had been brought back to him, surely by no accident' (*B* 114). It is therefore a natural response during the events of the second crisis, his desire for Toby and Nick's subsequent death, to interpret both occurrences as somehow predetermined. One of his immediate responses to Nick's suicide is to think that by killing himself Nick must have hit upon a more elaborate form of revenge than simply crudely seducing Toby: 'Instead, Nick had forced Toby to play exactly the part which Nick himself had played thirteen years earlier' (*B* 295). The reader knows this is unlikely, having been party to the rather awkward, distanced relationship that Nick and Toby have in fact had.

It is important to note at this point that in fact the neat balance of the two opposed sermons in *The Bell* is significantly offset by the existence of a third 'sermon', which is what a drunken Nick calls a bitter and ironic statement, far removed from the calm rhetoric of James's and Michael's speeches, which he delivers to Toby shortly before his suicide. He begins by presenting Imber as a world where innocence has been lost, something which certainly applies to Toby's recent experience there. He then suggests that there is something masochistic about religion, as sinning enables the sinner to gain the exquisite *jouissance* of repentance and confession. Although Nick is, as Toby protests, 'raving', his point seems to be that Michael's apology to Toby and the anguished monologue of repentance he is running through in his mind (which we can vouch for, having just read it) provides him with a masochistic kind of pleasure. As a counterpoint to the two previous sermons, Nick suggests that besides renouncing the personality and adhering to the law of God, or interpreting the law of God according to a detailed knowledge of the limits of one's personality, there is a third position: the spiritual masquerade which pretends to look at the self unflinchingly but in doing so only submits to another form of self-deception, one that substitutes forbidden pleasure for something sanctioned by the church.

Ultimately, however, the novel suggests that, although Michael flirts with this kind of response to the tragedy, he is able to recognize his mistakes without wrapping them up in a self-aggrandizing narrative. Nick, he eventually realizes, 'needed love, and he [Michael] ought to have given him what he had to offer, without fears about its imperfection' (*B* 307). He is able to understand that '[t]he pattern which he had seen in his life had existed only in his own romantic imagination. At the human level there was no pattern' (*B* 308). As a result, he sees signs of overcoming the numbness which has afflicted him since Nick's death: 'Very slowly a sense of his own personality returned to him' (*B* 309).

Having apparently found a way of achieving self-knowledge without succumbing to the dangers of narrative to facilitate the inquest, Michael ends the novel returning to school-teaching – a more healthy kind of repetition. This outcome amounts to a certain vindication of the truth of his sermon rather than James's (or Nick's). Reflecting on how he was unable to apologize to Toby for his actions in a way which closed the matter properly while also protecting the boy from a sense of guilt, Michael concludes that 'a person of great faith could with impunity have acted boldly: it was only that Michael was not that person. What he had failed to do was accurately to estimate his own resources, his own spiritual level' (*B* 201). A greater self-knowledge, in other words, has indeed led Michael to an understanding of goodness.

It is clear here that the value of self-knowledge extends to his sexuality, even though this is not directly acknowledged by Michael. The central repetition in *The Bell* is not quite the result of an accident, as it is in *An Accidental Man* or *A Word Child*. Instead it is a fairly likely consequence of Michael's sexuality. Social attitudes towards homosexuality – perhaps even ones that predominate in religious ideology – are as responsible for his humiliation and Nick's death as the carelessness of his actions. References to this wider social prejudice occur in the novel, in Michael's ironic reference to his sexuality as 'what the world calls perverted' (*B* 99) and by James's homophobic reference to Nick as a 'pansy' (*B* 116).

At one level, then, *The Bell* considers the dangers of *narrative* – the way that random or simple causal occurrences can be regarded as a grandiose sequence of meaningful events by which the perceiver can inflate his or her sense of self-importance. What makes it particularly effective is that reading the novel inevitably puts the readers in a similar position, as we are invited to weave together into a coherent narrative a sequence of events and a network of symbols. The potentially dangerous reservoir of symbols and narrative tropes provided by religion and drawn on by Michael, is paralleled ironically by the novel's own attitude to symbolism. Like the rest of Murdoch's fiction, *The Bell* contains a wealth of imagery and intertextual allusion which tempts us to construct a grand explanatory metanarrative which will make sense of the entire text. We might note, as an example, the references contained in the text to angels. Besides Nick's casting as 'fallen angel', there is the fact that the original bell was named after the angel Gabriel, known for the Annunciation (Luke 1: 26–38), and is inscribed with the words '*Vox ego sum Amoris. Gabriel vocor*' ('I am the voice of Love. I am called Gabriel'), while Michael also has the name of an archangel, Michael the 'Prince' of angels, the defender of heaven who is called upon to rescue our souls at the hour of death. Both names have an ironic air, given what happens in the novel: the old bell 'speaks' of love, but it is a warning about inappropriate or excessive love, and Michael leads others to potential salvation at Imber only to find himself almost damned.

The fact that the readers the of novel engage in a similar process to the characters of linking together apparently unrelated elements of the world of the novel, reminds us of the complexity of constructing narrative. Constructing narrative, *The Bell* suggests, is a potentially harmful activity yet also a potentially valuable one – perhaps even valuable precisely because of its dangers. Ultimately Michael gains a valuable degree of self-knowledge, which seems to underline his potential for goodness in his renewed appreciation for others, because of his capacity to reflect objectively on his own story. The value of this achievement is underlined by the fact that this is precisely what the two other central characters achieve too.

It is most straightforward in the case of Toby. It is clear that he is damaged by Michael's advances, the narrator telling us that 'Toby had received, though not yet digested, one of the earliest lessons of adult life: that one is never secure' (*B* 160). Immature for his age, Toby has had a rude awakening. Yet by stressing his inexperience (e.g. *B* 161) in descriptions of him, the narrator shows that this apparently traumatic event is really just an integral part of gaining maturity. Toby slips out of the novel after being advised to leave Imber by an over-cautious James and is not mentioned again until he sends Michael a letter, once he has begun life at Oxford. Michael is relieved to discern from it that Toby has apparently suffered neither from guilt nor anxiety, nor is he especially curious about Imber: 'He was in a new and wonderful world, and already Imber had become a story' (*B* 305). Toby's experiences at Imber have clearly been shaped into a narrative about his development, a narrative which has performed the crucial function of making sense of a traumatic episode in the past. The implication is that, as in Michael's case, this has also involved coming to terms with his sexuality. Toby's ambivalent feelings towards both Michael and Dora seem at points in the story to exceed the standard confusions of adolescent sexuality and point to a more permanent bisexuality.

While Dora has seemed throughout to be a freer character than most of the inhabitants of Imber, not least because of her own comfort with her sexuality, she has suffered from a pronounced inability to feel in control of her life. She is stuck in a cycle of dependence on her husband

Paul, unable to live happily with or without him: 'the persecution of his presence was to be preferred to the persecution of his absence' (*B* 7). Rather than being grateful to her for returning, Paul uses her return to renew his intimidation of her, claiming that her indecision has 'diminished [her] permanently in my eyes'. 'How', she reflects, 'could he assess her like this because of something which had happened in the past? The past was never real for Dora' (*B* 41). The unreality of the past is Dora's strength and her weakness. Not respecting the value of the past puts her at odds with the rest of the community at Imber. This at once enables her to be freer than they are and means that she suffers from anxiety at her inability to conform to the codes of behaviour that operate there.

The novel ends, however, with Dora having separated finally from Paul and on the point of leaving Imber to stay with a friend. She has managed to free herself from her dependence on her husband, and also from the imposed norms of the community at Imber. Not surprisingly the bell and its symbolic connotations have played a major part in this transformation. The crucial scene occurs as Dora, in a typical agony of indecision over whether to proceed with her plan to switch the old bell for the new, stands alone with the old bell she and Toby have rescued and concealed in a barn. Suddenly she recalls James's image of the bell in his sermon as 'the truth-telling voice that must not be silenced' and decides to ring it continuously. This has the effect of bringing the existence of the bell into the open in the most direct way. But it also heralds a newfound openness about what she wants to do – and also about her relation to her past. The last line of the novel is seemingly a throwaway: 'Tonight she would be telling the whole story to Sally' (*B* 316). But it suggests that the story of the past is now hers, and it tells the 'truth' about her experience at Imber and with Paul.

Michael Levenson has argued that one of the outcomes of *The Bell* is that Dora has 'gained' a past which enables her to have a future. She has secured this partly 'by living through a time of difficulty; but partly, and more subtly, she comes to assume a more profound relation to time' (Levenson 2001: 576). Her increased sense of embodiment in the world is suggested by her newfound ability to swim in and to row across the lake. Water, as so often in Murdoch, comes to represent the flux of real life, and Dora is able to navigate it. Levenson argues that the 'act of memory' which the last line of the novel 'anticipates' relates to Murdoch's philosophical conviction about the value of narrative in making sense of moral experience: 'parables and stories', she argues in an early essay 'Vision and Choice in Morality',[5] can function as 'moral guides' to an

incomprehensible world. As with Michael and Toby, Dora has woven
her experiences at Imber into a valuable tale.

Just as it highlights the dangers of storytelling, then, *The Bell* also
indicates its value in making sense of the past. Narrative is, of course,
usually about the past, about a sequence of events which have already
happened. But it tells a different kind of truth about these events than
philosophy can, a more mysterious truth, one that reflects the incomprehensible, contingent nature of the world, without making it seem
knowable. Where imposed narrative conventions – such as the religious
ones so central to *The Bell*, or psychoanalytic or historiographic ones –
carry with them the danger of falsifying the reality of events by offering
a consoling myth to the storyteller, a personal story, composed with
sufficient detachment, can tell a kind of truth.

What *The Bell* implies is what (as we shall see) Murdoch's first-person
novels assert more dramatically: narrative needs to be made personal,
written from the 'inside outwards' rather than being either the opposite
or – worse – written from a position where the inside is *mistaken* for the
outside, as Michael is tempted to do for much of the novel. *The Bell*
affirms that the most valuable source for redemption in a world where
faith in God has diminished is one's own story.

4
Author and Hero: Murdoch's First-Person Retrospective Novels

> Perhaps we would do best to speak of the *anticipation of retrospection* as our chief tool in making sense of narrative, the master trope of its strange logic.
>
> Peter Brooks, *Reading for the Plot*

In her 1978 interview with Bryan Magee, Murdoch addresses the question of why twentieth-century novelists are unable to emulate the achievements of their nineteenth-century predecessors:

> An author's relation to his characters reveals a great deal about his moral attitude, and this technical difference between us and the nineteenth-century writers is a moral change but one which is hard to analyse. In general our writing is more ironical and less confident. We are more timid, afraid of seeming unsophisticated or naïve. The story is more narrowly connected with the consciousness of the author who narrates through the consciousness of a character or characters. There is usually no direct judging or description by the author speaking as an external authoritative intelligence. To write like a nineteenth-century novelist in this respect now seems like a literary device and is sometimes used as one. (Magee 1978)

Murdoch's insights here are valuable, not least because they offer an interesting counterpoint to some of the theories of classic realism advanced by the likes of MacCabe and Belsey, Barthes, and, especially, Mikhail Bakhtin. What is interesting is that she should regard the key to understanding the difference between the nineteenth- and twentieth-century novel as the question of narrative voice.

This is not a surprising interest for an author so concerned with form, of course. Nor does it represent an obvious threat to her aim to re-inject the late twentieth-century novel with the virtues of classic realism: some critics – both outright admirers and those who are less persuaded about her achievements – have seen Murdoch's third-person narrative voice as the modern equivalent of that of the nineteenth-century author. 'Her triumph', Peter Conradi says, 'has been to reconstitute the direct address (in all its ambiguity) of traditional fiction, and it is clear that many of her readers feel as "spoken to" as did Dickens' audience' (Conradi 1989: 261). Harold Bloom compares, unfavourably, Murdoch's 'authorial interpolations' to those of George Eliot because her 'narrative voice lacks George Eliot's authority, being too qualified and fussy when a rugged simplicity is required. She is no less acute a moral analyst than Eliot, but she does not persuade us that her judgements are a necessary part of the story she has made for us' (Bloom 1986: 3–5).

Yet, to my mind, despite her admiration for the nineteenth-century novel, Murdoch's own third-person fiction actually employs the narrative voice she regards as characteristic of the twentieth century – one which speaks 'through the consciousness of a character or characters', without direct judgement from 'an external authoritative intelligence'. Close analysis of her work demonstrates that she does not intend her voice to resemble George Eliot's – that is, didactic, indistinguishable from the 'implied author' and keen to interrupt the flow of the story to pass moral judgement. True, the fiction of the 1980s sees her third-person voice becoming more demonstrative, more omniscient (Todd 1984: 93) but, on the whole, her work prefers the kind of narration narrative theorists have termed 'external focalization' or 'psychonarration', the rules of which are neatly summarized by Roland Barthes: 'the narrator must limit his narrative to what the characters can observe or know, everything proceeding as if each of the characters in turn were the sender of the narrative'.[1]

In this sense, of course, a far more accurate precursor for Murdoch's narrative voice would be Henry James. He is an author for whom she has often expressed her admiration. James is similarly concerned with how to combine the faithful representation of reality with a tight organic pattern, and like Murdoch, is an author who maintains a firm commitment to the tradition of moral realism, but whose historical placing means that he cannot help but take on board contemporary ideas about consciousness and psychology. This, incidentally, reminds us that, despite her implicit quarrel with modernism, some of Murdoch's paradigms for shifting the novel beyond the restrictions imposed on it by the modernist legacy come from a prominent part of the modernist movement itself.[2]

Another principal exemplar is surely Dostoevsky, at least in the way that Bakhtin understands his work:

> Nothing which is in the least essential is ever left outside the realm of the consciousness of Dostoevsky's leading characters [. . .]; they are confronted dialogically with every essential element that enters into the world of his novels. [. . .] Dostoevsky never retains for himself an essential *superiority of information*, but only that indispensable minimum of pragmatic, purely informative omniscience which is necessary for the development of the plot. (Bakhtin 1973: 60)

Murdoch's role is by no means identical, for she looks on her characters from above, from an external extradiegetic position, where Dostoevsky is always 'amongst his characters', in dialogue with them. In terms of impartiality and fairness to her characters, however – or 'merciful object-ivity', as she would prefer – she is a natural successor. There is, moreover, a genuine comparison to be drawn between Murdoch and Bakhtin, even allowing for the ease with which Bakhtin has been appropriated by different forms of theory. The value she places on authorial tolerance and her commitment to Jamesian 'centre of consciousness' narration is similar to Bakhtin's conception of the 'polyphonic' author, one who does not impose a single vision upon the reader but presents characters' points of view without attempting to show where they stand in relation to his or her own. Murdoch's 'crystalline' novel, the antithesis of her own fictional ideal, is one which corresponds to Bakhtin's idea of the 'monologic' text, where the various points of view contained within are suppressed in order to conform to the author's desired unity of ideological effect. The similarity seems all the more persuasive when we compare the more wide-ranging philosophy which lies behind each literary paradigm (while again bearing in mind the fundamental difference between Murdoch's liberal background and Bakhtin's formalist-Marxist roots). Bakhtin regards the attempt to make dominant one's own point of view futile because of the dialogic nature of language: all discourse, no matter how forcefully or persuasively articulated, can be challenged by other voices, even in its very expression. Murdoch's philosophy, one might say, runs on a parallel, more explicitly ethical track. She stresses the need to *respect* these other points of view and thereby recognize the individuality of the other person, to acknowledge the contingent aspects of life and accept what we cannot control.

It is important not to overplay the connection between the two, however. The key term in Bakhtin's theory is carnival – and it has no real counterpart in Murdoch's. For Bakhtin, the spirit of carnival is the end to which the polyphony of a work of art naturally moves and indeed *should* be directed. Though it is present in Murdoch, as Barbara Stevens Heusel has shown (1995), chiefly through the critical power of laughter (consider the parodic and self-parodic elements of *The Black Prince*, for example) there is no real social, collective impulse behind it. Nor, for that matter, is there anything resembling the Bakhtinian grotesque body to be found in her work. Nevertheless, her novels are still governed by what Elizabeth Dipple has called a 'dialogic impulse' (Dipple 1988: 187). Typically, that is, they are built on a series of interweaving voices, or points of view, which counter or balance one another. Her characters often seem constructed – as Bakhtin says of Dostoevsky's – around a particular idea, which enters into dialogue with the others. (Both novelists have been accused of continually reproducing the same characters who all speak the same language, but what is more important in a Bakhtinian sense is the fact that an equilibrium is maintained among these voices.)

It is not surprising, in this respect, that Murdoch was so interested in the Platonic dialogue form. It plays a small but vital role in her first novel, and is used to express the philosophy of *Acastos*. A polyphonic balance is also implied by her fondness for titles which emphasize opposition (*The Nice and the Good, The Sacred and Profane Love Machine, The Book and the Brotherhood*). The dialogic dimension was in fact part of her fiction from the outset. The members of the cast of *Under the Net*, A. S. Byatt has suggested, 'are used in the story almost as a dream allegory would use them'. Hugo, for example, represents the 'nostalgia for the particular', Lefty the 'subjection of everything to political experience' (Byatt 1965: 190). The characterization of *Under the Net* functions as an almost systematic representation of each way of looking at a particular situation. Though by doing so it almost compromises Murdoch's aim to avoid creating 'characters who "represent" particular ideologies' (*S* 139), she has learned in later novels, I think, to avoid the kind of mechanical polyphony of *Under the Net* while remaining true to the dialogic principle.

Dramatizing narrators

The ethical motivations behind her approach to narration and her commitment to a form of polyphony give some indication as to why Murdoch prefers writing in the third person to the first. Acknowledging this at Caen in 1978 she explains that choosing which type of narration to employ makes her 'anxious', 'for I know that things will turn out quite differently if it's written in the first person'. To decide on first-person form is to confront a particular 'danger': 'it's harder then to create other characters who can stand up to the narrator, because they're being seen through his eyes'.

The first-person form, in other words, represents a real threat to the sense of polyphony which is so important to Murdoch. And in an important sense her first-person novels do seem at odds with her approach to fiction. In her view, the modern author's preference for introspection results in a fondness for 'the symbolic individual who *is* the literary work itself' (sbr 266) instead of portraying a number of different characters. In showing the world from the deeply subjective viewpoint of one character, then, her first-person novels might seem uncomfortably like the introspective modern fiction she has criticized. It is this apparent contradiction which perhaps accounts for the disinclination among critics to treat the first-person novels in isolation.[3] Until quite recently those writing on Murdoch have been keen to ensure that discussion of her work takes place on the ground she herself has set out. A work like *The Bell*, which has no specific hero but a number of characters presented impartially, is more obviously an attempt to remain faithful to her realist ideal than, say, *A Word Child*.

At the same time, however, there are obvious advantages to writing in the same form of fiction one critiques. Portraying a solitary consciousness enables Murdoch to underscore her complaint against 'romantic rationalist' currents within modern thought through a subtle form of deconstruction. The hero of her first-person novels resembles the hero at the centre of these systems of thought, one who covers up his fears and prejudices behind a misplaced faith in the power of the will. I am not suggesting that Murdoch deliberately sets out to portray in fiction what she discusses in her non-fiction: the notion of dressing up an idea in the form of a character would deeply offend her principles of characterization. She recognizes that her heroes are psychologically more complex than the men she finds at the centre of Hampshire or Sartre. Nor is it the case that this character is denied the authorial tolerance on which she places so much emphasis elsewhere – on the contrary, she has admitted that she feels 'very close' to him.[4] But I think her first-person novels can be read as a fascinating game – or dialogue – between author and character, one which enables her to expose the questionable attitudes of her heroes by a subtle process of distanciation without threatening her aesthetic principles.

Critics agree that the characterological balance of Murdoch's fiction is founded upon a central opposition between the saint and the artist (Conradi 1989; Dipple 1984; Todd 1979). As she puts it herself, her work revolves around 'the struggle between the wouldbe artist and the would-be saint; the man who's silent and the man who speaks; the man who's unconsciously good and the man who's consciously, aesthetically, creating his life' (Bradbury 1976). The artist-figures range from sensitive, neurotic questors (like Ludens in *Message to the Planet* [1989], or Benet in *Jackson's Dilemma*) to dangerous enchanters (Mischa Fox in *The Flight from the Enchanter*, David Crimond in *The Book and the Brotherhood*) and – just as in life, as Murdoch would argue – they outnumber the saints and get all the best tunes.

Her first-person retrospective novels show us this Murdochian Every-man especially close-up, because more of the narrative is given over to him than any other. Each of her narrators is highly intelligent, an unsuccessful artist or artist-*manqué*, extremely self-conscious, capable of exuding winning charm, a master of language. They suggest another comparison with Dostoevsky, for there is something in them of his tormented heroes, imprisoned by the relentless energy of their own consciousness, endlessly interpreting their own actions.[5] But another link would be with the men in Freud's writings, intelligent people from privileged backgrounds who struggle to reconcile the world of their mind with the world outside.

It would of course be absurd to try to psychoanalyse Murdoch's characters, marking them down as *clinically* neurotic or even psychotic. Yet they clearly exhibit symptoms of both fundamental forms of pathology: their dogged pursuit of the truth, for example, is reminiscent of an obsessional neurotic like 'The Rat Man', and their obsessive determination to read the world around them occasionally tips over into a kind of paranoia. The paranoiac, as Freud realized through his dealings with Schreber (another highly sensitive first-person narrator) projects his internal catastrophe outward, and begins a 'process of reconstruction' to build it up again in his own image (Freud 1984a,b). Each of Murdoch's narrator-heroes attempts to divide his life into separate compartments which he guards jealousy from becoming interwoven. Jake Donahue, for example, divides London into two distinctive areas, the 'necessary' and the 'contingent', and tries to remain in the former. Bradley Pearson fears that friends from different parts of his life should become acquainted behind his back.

Just because the paranoiac is sensitive and vulnerable, however, does not mean it is easy to sympathize with him. Besides their obvious charm, Murdoch's first-person heroes are also, to varying degrees, misogynistic, bullying, ruthlessly selfish. Power is as often the motivation behind their need to compartmentalize their lives as fear, as Hilary Burde's brutal organization of his and everyone else's lives shows. The victims of their régime are most frequently women – unpredictable, fickle creatures who must be kept under control. In its crudest form, this containment is achieved by imprisoning them – metaphorically in *A Word Child* (where Hilary intimidates his sister into staying at home and receiving only the visitors he authorizes), physically in *The Sea, the Sea* (Charles Arrowby locks his beloved in a bedroom to prevent her escape). But it is also manifested in the more subtle form of misogynistic generalization. Bradley Pearson regards his ex-wife Christian as an example of a 'predatory woman', and his sister Priscilla and friend Rachel as belonging to a category of women he calls 'pear-shaped ladies' (middle-aged, over-affectionate, distressed at growing less physically attractive) – both types he can rely upon to act in the same way at all times.

All this contributes to the neat dialectic of form and content in Murdoch's first-person retrospective novel, for both the mind of its narrator and his narrative are characterized by limited perspective. In another way, though, narrative form succeeds in exposing the narrator's false assumptions. It is here, I think, that Murdoch's instinctive dialogism finds its most novel and effective expression. In a later reading of *Under the Net* Byatt describes the outcome of the novel by remarking that Jake 'tries an internal monologue, but discovers that the world is full of other people whose views he has misinterpreted but *can learn*. [. . .] No single view of the world, no one vision, is shown to be adequate' (Byatt 1976: 19). The pattern is repeated in most of the other first-person retrospective novels, where the heteroglossia of the fictional world provides numerous counter-perspectives which chip away at the hero's monologic vision. (An exception would be *The Italian Girl* where all of the characters seem caught up in the same delusion, apart from Maggie, who does not carry sufficient rhetorical weight to effectively counter this collective ideology.)

The key to the process is the hero's acute self-consciousness, revealed most clearly by his keen apprehension of being observed. *A Word Child*, for example, is a novel replete with images of looking, and opens with Hilary Burde and his lodger in the claustrophobic setting of a lift, regarding each other in a mirror made large 'to intensify mutual inspection' (*WC* 1). Hilary is painfully aware of himself as a spectacle, often imagining how he appears to his friends or office-mates: 'I also very much wanted to turn to look at Lady Kitty whose gaze I could feel burning my right cheek [...] Gunnar kept on looking at me with the intent yet somehow sightless, somehow horrified, glare' (*WC* 218). Self-consciousness, for Bakhtin, is the 'artistic dominant' in the construction of the polyphonic hero, and it is this which 'breaks down the monologic unity of the work (without, of course, violating artistic unity of a new and nonmonologic type)' (Bakhtin 1996: 93). Dostoevsky incorporates within his hero's 'field of vision' all those elements which have gone into creating him, such as where he stands in relation to other characters' points of view, how 'sociologically typical' he is, even what he looks like to others. Where 'the self-consciousness of a character was usually seen merely as an element of his reality, as merely one of the features of his integrated image, here, on the contrary, all of the reality becomes an element of the character's self-consciousness'.

This requires one condition for it to work, however: the novel must preserve the distance between author and hero so that it remains a work of art instead of becoming 'a personal document' (Bakhtin 1996: 92–3). And this is something Murdoch's fictional ethic of 'merciful objectivity' is designed to do. By giving over a whole novel to a character whose point of view she does not share, she effectively manages to have it both ways: she can subtly advance her own ideology all the while staying true to her own polyphonic ideal. What she does, in other words, is allow her hero to undo his own point of view. Although he monopolizes the text he is forced to acknowledge the counter-words of others. One character in particular tends to assume this dialogic role: Hugo in *Under the Net*, Honor in *A Severed Head*, Arnold in *The Black Prince*, Tommy in *A Word Child*, James in *The Sea, the Sea*. Bakhtin states that 'Dostoevsky always introduces two heroes in such a way that each is intimately connected with the interior voice of the other' (Bakhtin 1973: 215) and, though it would be wrong to suggest that every character in Murdoch's first-person novels is treated, Dostoevsky-fashion, as if s/he were another hero, this is largely true of the pairing between the narrator and this character.

This is particularly noticeable in *The Sea, the Sea*, where two voices enter into a consistent and powerful dialogue with Charles. The first of these is Ben, the brusque husband of the women he has captured in an insane misrecognition of love. When Ben tells him, 'Things change and people have their own worlds and their own places', Charles' reaction is telling: 'I listened to his rigmarole almost without any surprise, almost as if it were a cassette which I myself had invented' (*SS* 151). More powerful still as an opposing voice is Charles' cousin James. He resembles the *alter ego* figure Bakhtin noticed in Dostoevsky's novels, a physical embodiment of the other half of a dialogue which resides in the hero's consciousness: 'When I was young I could never decide whether James was real and I was unreal, or vice versa. Somehow it was clear that we could not both be real; one of us must inhabit the real world, the other one the world of shadows' (*SS* 57). In each case Charles is so familiar with a viewpoint diametrically opposed to his own because it is the externalization of an alternative position which is already suppressed within his own consciousness. *The Sea, the Sea*, like *Under the Net*, and *The Black Prince* (as we shall see) are novels which portray the hero's gradual progression to a certain degree of enlightenment. Central to this process is the gradual acknowledgement of this internal dialogue. Early in *Under the Net* Jake confesses that 'the substance of my life is a private conversation with myself which to turn into a dialogue would be equivalent to self-destruction' (*UN* 31). The novel is the story of his own rejection of his previous self, largely as a result of turning his private conversation with himself into a dialogue.

Murdoch's first-person retrospective fiction, then, is characterized by the kind of double-voicing typical of what Bakhtin calls 'internal polemic', the influence of which is 'extremely great in autobiographies and in *Ich-Ehrzählung* forms of the confessional type' (Bakhtin 1996: 107–8). Another way of putting this is to say that in these works Murdoch displays a remarkable facility with the ironic mode. Characters who betray themselves unintentionally – as when Charles complains about Ben, 'That's what mad people do, see everything as evidence for what they want to believe' (*SS* 223) – is a typical feature of 'structural irony', another device especially suited to first-person narrative. A recognition of this is in fact what lies behind Deborah Johnson's excellent feminist reading of Murdoch's first-person novels. She argues that Murdoch, a female author masquerading as male narrator, is able to deconstruct masculine pretensions by 'attacking from within' and ironically exposing their misogynistic assumptions.

Murdoch's use of the ironic mode indicates that her first-person novels bear an interesting relation to the tradition of the first-person novel. It is a form with a history as long as the novel itself, being favoured by many of the early practitioners of the novel proper when it emerged in the eighteenth century (Davis 1983) and being instrumental in some of the great novels of the next century (e.g. *Wuthering Heights* and *Great Expectations*) despite the growing preference for the external omniscient narrator as historical novels gave way to classic realism proper. With the advent of the twentieth century, the first-person form again becomes dominant. One of the key modernist narrative situations is where a central character looks back on his past (and it is usually *his* past), recovering it in words, analysing its significance. Examples include, most famously, Proust's *A la Recherche du Temps Perdu*, but also Thomas Mann's *Doktor Faustus*, Joyce's *A Portrait of the Artist as a Young Man*, Ford Madox Ford's *The Good Soldier*. Its use by modernist writers demonstrates how closely linked the first-person retrospective form is to a particular version of the *Bildungsroman*, the artist-novel, where the narrator's inquiry into the past involves tracing out the genesis of his vocation as artist (Beebe 1964; Fletcher and Bradbury 1976). The use of retrospection to facilitate introspection does not die with high modernism, however, but continues as a major genre throughout the century, particularly in the English novel. The late-modernist retrospective tradition I sketched out in the previous chapter is especially suited to the first-person form (e.g. Christopher Isherwood's *Goodbye to Berlin*, Evelyn Waugh's *Brideshead Revisited*, L. P. Hartley's *The Go-Between*, Lawrence Durrell's *The Alexandria Quartet*). And as many examples of historiographic metafiction show (*Flaubert's Parrot*, *Waterland*, etc.), the form is also ideally equipped to convey the postmodernist rhetoric about the validity of 'little' narratives as opposed to grand universalizing master-narratives.

The twentieth-century tradition of the first-person novel sheds light on the deconstructive use to which Murdoch puts the form. What is noticeable about the modernist and late-modernist first-person retrospective novel is that its use of irony is limited. This is not to say, of course, that narrative ambiguity is absent from modernism – on the contrary, as James' unreliable narrators, Conrad's framing devices, or Joyce's discursive pyrotechnics show, this is one of its defining characteristics, and one which is certainly apparent in the first-person retrospective narrative of the time (see, for example, Gide's *Les Faux-Monnayeurs*). Yet in telling of the 'sentimental education' of their narrators, a passage from ignorance to enlightenment, these novels give the impression, on the whole, that the author *endorses* this progression. The author shares the narrator's desire to inquire into the past and also supports his conclusions. One of the simplest ways this existential coincidence is advertised is by Proust's narrator taking his author's own first name.

Murdoch's first-person novels, by contrast, draw on this form ironically. She subverts and problematizes the journey towards enlightenment which her heroes undergo – or at least think they undergo. This is most evident in *The Black Prince*, in Bradley Pearson's grandiloquent discussions about art and its capacity for enlightenment, but all of her narrators conceive of themselves as something akin to the modernist artist-hero, believing they have been led by a mixture of experience and the aestheticization of this experience to Truth. But Murdoch's way of gradually undercutting their conclusions problematizes this outcome.

There is also a valid connection to be made here with another genre particularly suited to first-person narration, the prose romance. Besides her interest in isolated communities, which I mentioned previously, other structural and thematic features of prose romance feature heavily in Murdoch's fiction: the enjoyment in patterning and storytelling apparently for its own sake (despite her efforts to check this habit), or the way her characters often resemble the 'stylized figures which expand into psychological archetypes' of prose romance. Even her focus on wealthy, upperclass groups of people may be seen as typical of the fascination with privilege in the romance (Frye 1957: 304–5).

Such similarities can explain why Murdoch's work is often judged according to standards of classic realism and found wanting – what she writes, for all her realist aspirations, owes a great deal to the romance. She herself is happy to be described in this way, so long as one draws a distinction between romance and *romanticism*.[6] She has said that she considers the spirit of Shakespeare's late romances in particular to be a valuable model for her kind of fiction, and her novels allude most frequently to two of the greatest romances of all, *The Tempest* and *Peter Pan*. Yet the romance is primarily a subjective form, born typically of the author's desire to recover a lost world. Its prominent modern examples (e.g. Stoker's *Dracula*, Alain-Fournier's *Le Grand Meaulnes*, Fowles' *The Magus*) display a similar existential empathy between author and hero to that of the modernist retrospective artist-novel. (It is worth noting in this respect that both genres seem to be about a particularly 'male' quest.) Murdoch's fiction, however, eschews authorial wish-fulfilment, and the result is that the prose romance is another predominantly 'sincere' first-person genre which Murdoch draws on ironically in her own first-person novels.

At the beginning of *The Sea, the Sea*, for example, Charles has decided, like Prospero, to 'abjure magic' (*SS* 2) by retiring from his life in the theatre and living a reclusive life. What this signals, though, is less a renunciation of power than a desire to play Prospero in another way. This is clear from the way he casually assigns people around him parts from *The Tempest*: Lizzie, for example, who sings 'Full Fathom Five' at one point, is Ariel (a part she played on the stage), and Gilbert, who chops wood for him, is Ferdinand.

Yet, true to Murdoch's 'anti-modernist' approach to the question of underlying myth, the sense of authorial collusion characteristic of the romance is absent. The network of allusion works from one viewpoint only, the narrator's; as Conradi says, 'In the sense that the remote enclosure is always the setting for romance, it might be said that the bad man in Murdoch's work carries the box-like world of romance around in his head' (Conradi 1989: 81). Charles' attempt to match up the people in his life to the archetypal figures of the romance, proves a failure. Ben, whom he casts in the role of Caliban (Cali*ben*; 'let him think anything his foul imagination can beget' [*SS* 275]) proves himself incapable of acting as basely as Charles expects him to, while it is James, not Charles, who brings the less tyrannical side of Prospero, his wisdom and magic, into the world of the novel. 'The maddening fact was', Charles reflects, 'that I now had all the pieces for a solution, but would I be allowed to fit them together?' (*SS* 260). By subtly dismantling the foundational myth beneath him, Murdoch frustrates his efforts to force the contingent elements of his life into a self-gratifying version of *The Tempest*.

Writing in retrospect

In a sense, then, Murdoch reinvests the first-person retrospective novel with some of the irony it displays before the advent of romanticism (e.g. in the works of Defoe or Sterne). Her first-person novels effect as seamless a synthesis of form and content as her fiction could hope to achieve – though not quite in the way we would expect from the dialectic of form and content set forth in her aesthetic of the sublime. They are motivated by a subtle interaction between author and hero which manages to remain true to her ethic of fiction. But this does not wholly account for the compelling effect of her first-person fiction. At work in these novels is a very different kind of engagement between author and hero, one which brings into play a more complex notion of subjectivity produced as a result of the protagonist's relationship with his past. We have already touched on this, in considering how these heroes are forced to grapple dialogically with the existence of two different perspectives within their own consciousness. But this too is a particular consequence of the first-person form itself – as we can see if we consider this kind of narrative in more detail, this time concentrating on a synchronic rather than a diachronic approach.

To begin with, let us return to the question of how the dramatized narrator dominates his narrative. Although we can still detect the presence of the implied author at the extradiegetic level 'above' the narrator – something made clear by Murdoch's ironic undercutting of his word – the first-person novel nevertheless gives a peculiarly powerful impression that the narrator is solely responsible for the book we read. As narrative theory suggests, this is more than just a matter of rhetoric. Käte Hamburger, in her influential *The Logic of Literature* (1957), argues that the first-person novel is uniquely equipped to convey the impression of reality. The language it uses (e.g. the narrator's avoidance of verbs of inner action in the description of another character) ensures that it inhabits the realm of the *feigned*, that which masquerades as something it is not, rather than the *fictive*, which does not attempt to hide its artificiality. Unlike the third-person novel, it 'posits itself as non-fiction, i.e. as a historical document', to the extent that in some novels 'it cannot be determined with certainty whether we are dealing with a genuine autobiography or with a novel' (Hamburger 1973: 312, 314–15). Bertil Romberg supports Hamburger's conclusion by arguing that the impression of verisimilitude is principally the result of the 'epic situation'. Just as 'all epics can ultimately be related to a situation where a narrator presents a story orally to a listening public' (Romberg 1962: 33) so, Romberg believes, the reality effect of a first-person novel is enhanced (or collapsed) by the author's incorporation of the epic situation into the novel: the narrator may reveal that he or she is speaking or writing the account, or may appear among the characters. Whereas the epic situation is not a part of the third-person novel because it is *outside* the fiction, in the first-person novel it belongs to it.

The work of critics like Hamburger and Romberg can explain why the autodiegetic narrator maintains a degree of autonomy not matched in other forms. While the reader is constantly aware that this surrogate author is a fictional creation, he also possesses an independence quite unlike even the most realistically drawn character in a third-person text, because every word of the narrative originates only from him. He is individualized by no other narrator (except where there is another in the same text, like the editor Loxias in *The Black Prince*) and there are no direct interventions in his text by a heterodiegetic narrator representing the views of the implied author. Our mental construction of this persona is not limited to what he 'writes' on the page; rather, we must look into the silences around his words for a sense of this fictional author existing in a world surrounding his text and actually constructing his narrative, just as we do with a 'real' author.

Steven Kellman's work on what he calls the 'self-begetting novel' (although it does not draw explicitly on narrative theory) can further explain the semantic significance of this sense of autonomy, in a way that can help explain how it relates to Murdoch's fiction. The self-begetting novel displays a distinctive circular movement in both structure and theme: it 'projects the illusion of art creating itself [. . .] it is an account, usually first person, of the development of a character to the point at which he is able to take up his pen and compose the novel we have just been reading' (Kellman 1976: 1245). As its central concern is the story of its own composition, it thereby projects the illusion of narratorial independence I have described: its protagonist is not only the subject of the story but also the producer of the entire novel in which he features, making the real author appear somewhat redundant.

Kellman includes *Under the Net* as part of his study of this kind of fiction. It is a novel which possesses many of the trademarks of the self-begetting novel proper, including the physical begetting motif itself, a cast of artists, much intertextual reflection on art and numerous connections with what Kellman proves is the guiding force behind the sub-genre, the French literary tradition. Jake is a typical self-begetting hero, a rootless solitary intellectual, looking for a direction in life which his novel will ultimately provide. Kellman suggests that *Under the Net* effectively re-writes Sartre's *Nausea*, itself a prominent member of the self-begetting tradition. The sense of magic inspired in Jake as he listens to Anna's song towards the end of the novel – an epiphany which, many critics have recognized, echoes the significance of the Negress's song at the end of Sartre's novel – leads him to realize 'the potential power of art' (Kellman 1980: 91). It is a recognition which is neatly made to serve Murdoch's philosophy, for the lesson Jake learns, and which leads to his decision to write a novel, means that he will not shy away from 'the *stuff* of human life' (S 146) in the way Roquentin (and Sartre) does. Having previously abhorred contingency, preferring 'everything in my life to have sufficient reason', he is now able to accept the mysterious mixed breed of Mrs Tinckham's newly-born kittens as 'just one of the wonders of the world' (*UN* 253).

Under the Net is the only one of Murdoch's first-person novels to conform fully to Kellman's requirements for the self-begetting novel. Her other hero-narrators, as we shall see, do not always *consciously* decide to write a fiction and thereby beget a self, and many of the typical themes and imagery identified by Kellman are absent. Yet, for the reasons I have given above, each of her novels is as self-sufficient as legitimate examples of Kellman's sub-genre. The story in each, that is, looks forward to the point at which the narrator will look back: it demonstrates clearly Brooks' assertion that '*the anticipation of retrospection* [is] our chief tool in making sense of narrative' (Brooks 1992: 22–3).

Another way of describing this effect is to refer to Gérard Genette's division of narrative fiction into three parts: *story* (the causal, chronological series of events), *text* (the aesthetic reworking of these events in plot form) and *narration* (the actual production of the text) (Genette 1980). In the first-person retrospective novel, Genette's second and third categories of narrative (text and narration) are effectively part of the first. The story includes an event which is not always explicitly featured within, but which we know must occur, namely the narrator's actual *narration*, or composition, of the novel – what Romberg refers to as the 'epic situation'. In other words, the reader deduces that the chronological sequence of events which makes up the story must always end with a final event: 'Narrator Constructs Narrative'. This stage exerts an influence over the story as we read it which is almost uncanny: it is present yet absent, something vital to the plot yet not exactly part of it. It is this which is largely responsible, I would argue, for the 'emotional charge' Murdoch appreciates in first-person narrative (Caen 1978). In the typical third-person novel, the description of the past life of a hero is unlikely to carry the emotional significance which results from this hero describing his *own* past.[7]

The role of the dramatized narrator as fictional author, or at least supreme organizer of the material in his text, has a number of important implications. For one thing, it returns us to the question of Murdoch's relationship to postmodernist fiction, because the first-person form lends itself quite naturally to an exploration of the nature of fictionality. Her novels are aligned to the prominent tradition of twentieth-century fiction which Malcolm Bradbury and John Fletcher term the 'introverted novel', where the method of narration becomes 'a good deal more than simply a convenient narrative device, as it might well have been in less sophisticated narrative structures of earlier date: it is in fact the very essence of the novel' (Fletcher and Bradbury 1976: 398). While Murdoch's fiction as a whole, as I suggested in the first chapter, is consistently yet not *radically* metafictional, her first-person novels *are* formally self-conscious in a way which her others are not. The peculiarity of the first-person form means that the narrator inhabits two different narrative levels; in Genette's terms he is not just autodiegetic but extradiegetic: 'author-narrators…are at the same level as their public – that is, you and me' (Genette 1980: 229). The narrator exists as a man composing a novel in both a fictional world and the 'real' world. His book is simultaneously an artefact in both worlds, and serves as a bridge between the two. The result, although the reality effect is still never seriously threatened, is that there arises a confusion between fiction and reality in the manner of more overtly self-conscious postmodernist fictions. If the fictional author straddles two different levels of reality, this must raise in the reader's mind questions of a specifically ontological nature. The form of the first-person novel – the narrator's dual status of existing in a fictional world but narrating to real people – ensures that the narrator emerges from the fictional world while the reader is brought in. The question 'which level of reality do the narrators belong to?' corresponds to the question 'which level of reality do *we* belong to?' If the narrator inhabits both our world and his own, do we inhabit a fictional world too? Both *The Black Prince* and *The Sea, the Sea* would have us think so, addressing the reader as if s/he is familiar, from coverage in the 'real' media, with Bradley Pearson's notorious trial and Charles Arrowby's status as a well-known public figure.

What we might call this natural metafictional dimension of the first-person novel is something Murdoch capitalizes on, particularly in *Under the Net, The Black Prince* and *The Sea, the Sea*, where each narrator is a writer. Jake Donahue and Bradley Pearson are disaffected novelists, one who spends his time translating the works of others, the other whose bitterness at his lack of success causes him to adhere to a puritanical aesthetic of silence, while Charles Arrowby is writing a kind of autobiographical account which he chooses to call a 'novelistic memoir'. This is significant because although Murdoch's books are replete with artists and writers – professional or aspiring painters, poets and philosophers, and also numerous amateur writers completing a scholarly work, and craftsmen concerned with the aesthetics of their vocation – there are comparatively few novelists.[8] Garth Gibson Grey in *An Accidental Man*, or the thriller-writer Emma Sands in *An Unofficial Rose* have minor roles which do not enable Murdoch to exploit the narcissistic attitude towards their work which makes the narrators of the first-person 'artist-novels' so interesting.

The opportunity to present a self-conscious commentary on her craft is most obvious in *The Black Prince*, but is there also in *The Sea, the Sea*, a work which Marguerite Alexander says should be placed alongside those novels in British fiction which are 'finally more about themselves than about aspects of the real world that are being mediated through them' (Alexander 1990: 168). It is also there in *Under the Net*, Murdoch's debut novel (and the first to be narrated in the first person). As we have seen, it is a self-begetting novel, and this means that it ends in a similar (though less mystifying) way to *The Black Prince*, pointing the reader partly back into the work of art instead of simply to the world outside.[9] Like *The Black Prince*, it features an ironical discussion about the nature of art (centring on the extract from Jake's philosophical work which is cleverly planted in the novel) which deals with the problems of representation, whether art can allow one to crawl 'under the net' and access the truth beyond words and theory. *The Sea, the Sea* offers a different version of this search, as Charles Arrowby looks for the truth of his own past. In all three novels, the question of truth is bound up with the actual process of writing. Although Murdoch criticizes 'deconstructive' literature for trying to convince us that 'language, not world, transcends us, we are "made" by language, and are not the free independent ordinary individuals we imagined we were' (*MGM* 151), the first-person novels posit a not dissimilar argument.

As its title suggests, *Under the Net* asks whether it is possible to slip beneath the structure of language, a question returned to implicitly throughout *The Black Prince*, where Bradley is impressed by Shakespeare's awareness in *Hamlet* of 'the redemptive role of words in the lives of those without identity, that is human beings' (*BP* 199). Like the characters in *The Sacred and Profane Love Machine*, the narrators long to grasp the 'essence' of their personality (each confesses to lacking a sense of his own identity) all the while fearing there is nothing really there. 'Being is acting', Bradley continues; 'We are tissues and tissues of different personae and yet we are nothing at all' (*BP* 200).

This statement is verified by the instances of role-playing in Murdoch's first-person fiction. *Under the Net* features a mimetheatre where Jake's friends appear on the stage in masks, a situation which neatly prefigures the hero's consistent inability, as the plot continues, to penetrate beneath their surface behaviour to their real desires. *The Sea, the Sea*, as befits a story told by a stage director, is also full of theatrical imagery. Bradley Pearson at one point admits to his 'excitement at playing a new role' (*BP* 185). He also explains what the other artist-narrators come to realize, that the most effective mask one can do is language. When writing of Arnold he feels 'as if I were building a barrier against him composed of words, hiding myself behind a mound of words' (*BP* 82).

Charles Arrowby applies this metaphor to his whole narrative: 'This chattering diary is a façade, the literary equivalent of the everyday smiling face which hides the inward ravages of jealousy, remorse, fear and the consciousness of irretrievable moral failure' (*SS* 483). Role-playing does not feature only in the three most metafictional first-person novels. As one would expect in the work of a writer who consistently stresses the importance – and often the impossibility – of grasping hold of reality, many of Murdoch's novels could fruitfully be read as demonstrations of the theatricality of everyday life. We should note, however, that this tends to be regarded less positively in her fiction than in that of other twentieth-century novelists, as Alan Kennedy has suggested in

The Protean Self (1974), his study linking the profusion of 'metaphors of drama' in modern fiction to contemporary sociological 'role theory'. He sees Murdoch as something of an exception to his rule that major modern novelists use dramatic action to indicate how the self can relate positively to the public world (role-playing preserves free will while still allowing the subject to engage with society) because in all her novels, except the *Hamlet*-obsessed *The Black Prince*, 'drama' figures as a negative term.

One sense of this is provided by *A Word Child*, a novel in which the idea of pantomime is a recurrent motif, and where role-playing is repeatedly presented as a source of anguish. Hilary Burde admits on one occasion that 'I could not slip out of my role, however agonizing it was to play this role to this audience' (*WC* 226). His adoption of roles is accompanied by an unnerving sensation that not only is he powerless to choose which role the external environment thrusts upon him, but also that the mask he is bound to wear simply covers an emptiness, a vanished sense of identity. Arranging his life into 'days', where he knows in advance what he will be doing, offers him 'identity, a sort of ecto-skeleton' (*WC* 28).

But the negative connotations of role-playing also involve something less sympathetic, for the ability to perform in a certain environment is part of the domineering nature of Murdoch's narrators. Deborah Johnson remarks on Martin's ability to address an exclusively male audience of imagined readers by 'playing to the gallery' in *A Severed Head* (Johnson 1987: 26). Murdoch responds to this, however, by a further use of roleplaying metaphor. When his world begins to collapse, Martin feels 'flayed. Or more exactly as if the bright figured globe of my existence, which had been so warmly symmetrical to the face of my soul, were twisted harshly off, leaving my naked face against a cold window and darkness' (*SH* 33). The image is a favourite of Murdoch's. Her reading of the Marsyas myth, she has explained, is to do with the death of the self (Hartill 1989). The emphasis on masks and role-playing, then, also relates to the way she forces her heroes through the process of *ascesis*.

The way she harnesses the suggestive potential of the status of the first-person narrator as fictional author explains why critics who have included Murdoch in discussions of less extreme varieties of metafiction have almost invariably supported their case with reference to her first-person novels.[10] It is also this supplementary dimension of the narrative (one which indeed works according to the Derridean logic of the supplement, as the epic situation casts its shadow over all the events leading up to it) which complicates the relationship between author and hero, because the narrator is both surrogate producer of the narrative and its protagonist. This means that in considering the deconstructive aspect of Murdoch's first-person fiction we must take into account the narrator's own potential for deconstruction. The real author, in other words, may well 'attack from within' in her first-person novels, but it is just as plausible that it is the narrator, in his 'creative' role, who deconstructs the section of his narrative which relates to his pre-enlightened persona. In other words, rather than regarding certain aspects of *Under the Net* as its author's covert critique of her protagonist's misogynistic assumptions, could it not equally be Jake himself who wishes to expose the counterfeitness of a previous incarnation of himself of which he is now slightly ashamed?

Determining how and when Murdoch undercuts the perspectives of her heroes is therefore a much more complex process than it may appear. But instead of representing a threat to the polyphonic process Murdoch depends on to subtly reinforce her ethical outlook, this ambiguity makes it more truly polyphonic – more adherent, that is, to the spirit of her artistic ethic of tolerance. If the dialogical game was clearly won by the author, then the novel would tend more towards the monologic than the dialogic.

Recovering the past: two kinds of retrospective novel

The peculiar rhetorical status of the first-person narrator, then, complicates the intriguing dialogical relationship between author and hero in Murdoch's fiction. But the real significance of his role as surrogate author – at least as far as our consideration of Murdoch's retrospective fiction is concerned – is that it underlines the degree to which the first-person retrospective novel is about *time*.

The first-person retrospective novel works, as narrative theory explains, on two main temporal levels: the time of the present, when the story is narrated, and the time of the past, in which the events told of actually occur.[11] This means that the narrator is in effect split into two different manifestations of the same self, one who *narrates* and one who *experiences* (or *focalizes*). We might describe this distinction either in a structuralist sense (the former operates at the level of 'text', the latter at the level of 'story') or in Aristotelian terms (mimesis and diegesis). It means, as Hamburger remarks, that the narrator is not just a subject of the discourse (like most characters in third-person fiction); by recalling his past, he *objectifies* himself. It is not surprising that the first-person form should prove so suitable for introspection, for the narrator is obliged to consider himself as he was, and, by implication, how he *is* at the time of narration. We must recognize, however, that the difference between these two temporal positions varies according to the novel in question. The narrator may still identify more or less completely with his earlier self when he comes to write about the past, or he may wish to dissociate himself from it.

Dorrit Cohn has characterized this distinction systematically, imagining the various degrees of identification as a scale, using the terms 'consonance' and 'dissonance' to describe each of the poles (Cohn 1978: 143–72). Complete consonance is rare, she insists, though, for narrators more commonly misunderstand themselves and mix consonance with dissonance. More often than not, first-person texts conclude with a dissonant relationship between past and present self. This is most clearly the result of the 'sentimental education' of the modernist artist-hero, who seems wiser at the end because of changes in his outlook caused by the events he recounts.

Murdoch's six first-person retrospective novels can be divided into two groups according to Cohn's model. The distance between the narrating self and the experiencing self is not as apparent in *A Severed Head, The Italian Girl* and *A Word Child* as it is in *Under the Net, The Black Prince* and *The Sea, the Sea*. The former trio is more consonant, the latter more dissonant. This basic formal characteristic underlies, we might say, many of the differences between these two kinds of novel. The narrative theorist Franz Stanzel has suggested that the existential connection between the narrator as object and the narrator as subject is a significant pointer to his 'motivation to narrate'. This, he says,

> is directly connected with his practical experiences, with the joys and sorrows he has experienced, with his moods and needs. The act of narration can thus take on something compulsive, fateful, inevitable, as in the case of the first-person narrator of *The Catcher in the Rye*. The motivation to narrate can also originate, however, in the need for an organizing overview, in a search for meaning on the part of the matured, self-possessed 'I' who has outgrown the mistakes and confusions of his former life. (Stanzel 1984: 93)

Both the alternatives Stanzel offers accurately account for the motivation to narrate which lies behind each kind of novel in Murdoch's first-person canon. We can make one further distinction, however: each protagonist's desire to narrate is governed by the nature of his relationship with his past. And this is determined by the two ways in which past is made present in Murdoch's work: deliberate recovery or involuntary re-covering.

I mentioned before the relevance of the psychoanalytic distinction between 'remembering', the process by which the subject manages to make the past truly past, and 'repeating', where the subject remains in the grip of the past, compelled to replay the same traumas. By the time they come to write their narrative, the dissonant narrators in Murdoch's fiction (in *Under the Net*, *The Black Prince* and *The Sea, the Sea*) have managed to 'remember' the past. They come to understand, in other words, the deluded nature of their experiencing self (the lesson, of course, the author has subtly been guiding them to all along). The consonant narrators, on the other hand (in *A Severed Head*, *The Italian Girl* and *A Word Child*) simply 'repeat' the experience, maintaining the same prejudices and locked into the same obsessional logic which characterize their former selves. (Both patterns will become clearer in the studies of these novels which follow.)

The particular way the past is made present in each group of novels is underscored stylistically in another way. In his seminal work of narrative theory, *The Rhetoric of Fiction*, Wayne Booth differentiates between 'self-conscious narrators', 'aware of themselves as writers' and 'narrators or observers who rarely if ever discuss their writing chores, [...] or who seem unaware that they are writing, thinking, speaking, or "reflecting" a literary work' (Booth 1961: 155). Booth's categories are equivalent to those of recollection and repetition. Those narrators who have remembered acknowledge directly that they are writing and are open about the need to tell their story. Those who have simply repeated, on the other hand, dramatize the epic situation only implicitly and infrequently, as if consciously unaware of why they have decided to narrate – it is in fact as if they are *compelled* to do so.

It is no surprise in this light that the most obviously metafictional of Murdoch's first-person novels should be those where the narrator 'remembers' his past: in each case, as I have suggested, he is a writer, and accompanies his narrative with extended reflections on his art. In contrast, those still bound by the repetition-compulsion tell their story with as little interruption as possible. We are provided with so little information about the writing process that we cannot simply examine their attitudes to the act of composition, as we can in the case of the more self-conscious narrators: their thoughts about their story as they tell it are never made clear, the epic situation is only implied throughout.

At the end of *A Severed Head* and *The Italian Girl* and – less so – *A Word Child* it seems that the narrator has undergone something like the progression from illusion to enlightenment, from consonance to dissonance, that figures in *The Black Prince* or *The Sea, the Sea*. Yet where the latter texts do suggest that some kind of wisdom has been reached as a result of the experience undergone and the act of writing about it, the narrators of the former remain, to paraphrase their author, benighted creatures trapped in a reality they deform by fantasy (ad 22). They long to be 'in the truth' (as Edmund Narraway of *The Italian Girl* puts it), and might even believe they have arrived there by the ends of their novels, but in fact remain possessed by the insistent power of the past working within them – the repetitive mechanism at work in the psyche, 'a myth which has in some way got hold of them' (Bradbury 1976). As well as models drawn from narrative theory, the Orpheus myth is again particularly apt in symbolizing the different relationship to the past in each text. The 'repeating' narrators are compelled to revisit the dark realm of the unconscious, only to be caught looking back and be forced to remain there while telling the story. But Orpheus also figures as an archetypal figure of the artist. So unhappy is he at losing Eurydice that he turns to his lyre to assuage his pain. This aspect of the myth is commonly seen to nourish the idea that art emerges out of unhappiness and loss. In *The Black Prince* Loxias says of Bradley Pearson, 'Every artist is an unhappy lover. And unhappy lovers want to tell their story' (*BP* 10).

While both types draw on the tradition of the confessional novel, in other words, only one involves anything resembling a genuine 're-birth'. The difference can simply be illustrated by comparing *The Sea, the Sea* and *A Word Child*, both of which revolve around a 'primal scene' of lost love which causes both heroes to mistake the powerful pattern released from deep within themselves for an external determining force. Where Charles ends up with neither his love nor a substitute, and is forced to realize the immorality of attempting to impose form upon contingent events, Hilary Burde's first tragic love affair comes to be repeated almost exactly, with only a suggestion that he has come to any recognition of the instrumental role played by accident in his story. Though this re-birth takes place in a particularly Murdochian context – the need to confront the contingent – it is clear that, in one sense, the self-consciously artistic novels draw on the modernist artist-novel in a way which is not simply ironic. All three, that is, are concerned with the transfigurative power of art. Even *The Black Prince* and *The Sea, the Sea* (albeit not as clearly as *Under the Net*) resemble the self-begetting novel – more of a modernist than a postmodernist form – in that the change undergone by each author is only fully apparent at the end of the book. In effect, it invites us to read the novel again in the light of this knowledge. Bradley Pearson is most forthcoming about the narrative technique this involves, deciding to 'inhabit my past self and, for the ordinary purposes of story-telling, speak only with the apprehensions of that time' despite being conscious that it is 'a time in many ways so different from the present' (*BP* 11).

The novels, to varying degrees, advertise their dissonance in a similar way to the modernist artist-novel. In *The Black Prince*, for instance, during Rachel's clumsy attempts to begin an affair with Bradley, he lies on the bed beside her feeling as if he is 'outside, seeing myself as in a picture' (*BP* 158). The sensation resembles a feature common to the novels Maurice Beebe examines in *Ivory Towers and Sacred Founts*, his study of the tradition of the artist-novel in modern literature, which he terms the 'divided self'. The artist-figure is struck by his own split identity, and wonders how he can simultaneously suffer the agonies of the real world while remaining detached enough to observe this suffering objectively. This is another respect in which the plot of the first-person novel is paralleled by its form, for each half of the divided self corresponds to the experiencing and narrating selves of the first-person narrator.

Like the modernist hero, then, these protagonists attempt to reunite their past and present selves through a fictional meditation on their own past. But, as we shall see, this is either a failure, or is not accomplished in quite the way they envisage. For Murdoch understands the past differently from the modernists. Brian McHale regards modernist retrospective fiction as clearly exemplifying the modernist 'epistemological dominant': 'The past is known, fully accessible; it is just a matter of telling (or indeed *re*-telling) it' (McHale 1992: 148). This approach to the past, as I have suggested, is one which is difficult to reconcile with Murdoch's retrospective fiction. It presupposes a faith in our power ultimately to control the past which is too rationalist – too 'romantically rationalist', in fact. The first-person novels which are marked most powerfully by the inescapable insistence of the past (*A Severed Head* and *A Word Child*) demonstrate this emphatically, as we shall see in due course: the past is capable of controlling us. I want to turn first, though, to two novels – *Under the Net* and *The Black Prince* – which show that the epistemological quest in Murdoch's fiction is less straightforward, more analogous to the postmodern understanding of the past. That the past *happened* is not in question; the problem is, how do we gain access to it?

5
Reading Past Truth: *Under the Net* and *The Black Prince*

> The final judgement rests with common and moral sense: one cannot, however frenetically one tries, pluck out the heart of that mystery.
>
> Iris Murdoch, *Sartre: Romantic Rationalist*

'The key to the artist's mind', says Bradley Pearson, the writer-hero of *The Black Prince*, is what he is afraid of (*BP* 82).[1] Asking this question is one of Murdoch's own strategies in her criticism, and among a number of contenders for Bradley's own greatest fear is the fear of contingency she detects in Sartre. But another is surely identified by Rachel towards the end of *The Black Prince* when she tells Bradley that all along he has been 'somehow in the dark, not understanding anything, under all sorts of misapprehensions' (*BP* 361). On several occasions he attempts to determine the 'truth' behind an episode with a zeal that seems disproportionate to its importance. At the beginning of the novel he is so frustrated by his inability to penetrate the 'mystery' behind Rachel and Arnold's violent marital row, so curious, 'that I almost turned back to snoop around the house and find out what had happened' (*BP* 53). This is soon followed by another mystery, when he implores Rachel to recount in exact detail the events after her clumsy efforts to seduce him, insisting: 'Please try. Truth does matter. What exactly happened yesterday after Arnold arrived back and we were – Please describe the events in detail. I want a description beginning "I ran down the stairs"' (*BP* 177).

Truth matters to Bradley, to an extraordinary degree. The state of mind he displays in these episodes resembles the way of thinking Freud called *epistemophilia*, the delusion that innocuous situations and coincidences are mysteries which must be unravelled. The epistemophiliac, as Freud said of the Rat Man, is 'prey to an obsession for understanding', determined 'to understand the precise meaning of every syllable [...] addressed to him, as though he might otherwise be missing some priceless treasure' (Freud 1984a: 70). This kind of behaviour is of course in keeping with the paranoid nature of Murdoch's characters I referred to earlier. Bradley Pearson is one of the most extreme cases. He is often troubled by a vague sense that something bad is about to happen to him. He regards music as a disturbing language he cannot quite understand but which is somehow about him (*BP* 257). And like many paranoiacs, the manifestation of his condition is combined with a dim awareness that he might be mistaken: 'One perceives a subterranean current, one feels the grip of destiny, striking coincidences occur and the world is full of signs: such things are not necessarily senseless of symptoms of incipient paranoia' (*BP* 144). This way of perceiving the world ranges from the mildly paranoid insistence in the early part of the novel that truth matters to the fully blown paranoia he displays later on, when convinced Julian's banal letter to him contains a coded subtext.

Although it borders on the pathological,[2] Bradley's extreme curiosity does not make him unusual among Murdoch's characters. It is a quality which many of the other writers in her fiction display (Emma Sands, Monty Small and Arnold Baffin).[3] All the first-person novels feature 'a poor, rather gullible, confused man stumbling on from one awful blow to another' (Rose 1968), a process which makes him long to be 'in the truth'. Extreme curiosity, on a lesser scale, is the motivation behind an activity in which a great number of Murdoch's characters are engaged: the quest for knowledge. This takes many different forms, like the academic acquisition of facts (Bruno Greensleave's study of spiders, for example) or the professional or personal investigation (Radeechy's inquest into the suicide of a former colleague in *The Nice and the Good*, or Edward Baltram's search for his father in *The Good Apprentice*). The predominance of the quest for knowledge is symptomatic of what I see as the overall epistemological basis of Murdoch's fiction. In other words the world-view of her characters demands that they ask the kinds of cognitive questions Brian McHale sees as typical of modernist fiction, 'How can I interpret this world of which I am a part? And what am I in it?' (McHale 1992: 33). The importance of these questions is linked to a related activity, common among other characters: the attempt to provide final and authoritative descriptions of an experience, a sensation, or of each other. Needless to say, this attempt is almost always defeated, but it does not stop them from trying. Leaving aside for the moment the question of how Murdoch's fiction relates to the 'shift of dominant' from modernism to postmodernism which McHale has explored, I think we can conclude that the will to interpret and describe is one of the characterological dominants of Murdoch's fiction. As Franco Moretti says, 'interpretation and description are not antithetical, but in fact "two directions" [...] in which the cognitive process can tend' (Moretti 1983: 134). And these two directions are at the heart of *Under the Net* and *The Black Prince*, two of the most sustained examples of the epistemological quest in Murdoch's fiction.

'Some things can't be unravelled ...': reading *Under the Net*

There is a close similarity between the expectant anxiety of epistemophilia and the state of the reader's mind while reading fiction, an activity governed by what Barthes termed 'the passion for meaning'.[4] Barthes points out that the single events in a narrative really mean nothing in themselves, but point towards something else, a conclusion which will render them significant (Barthes 1977: 123–4). The reader knows this of course, though it is not usually made explicit in the text. The effect of observing the epistemophilic narrator in Murdoch's first-person novels, who reads the world around him as if it were a complicated text, full of clues and promising a coherent ending, is to remind the reader that reading the novel involves adopting a similar mindset. Encouraging readers' curiosity by alternately rewarding and frustrating it is something fiction has always done, of course, especially through complex plotting like Murdoch's which continually activates the hermeneutic code. Furthermore, according to Tzvetan Todorov, the reader of fiction is assisted in constructing its imaginary world by a similar process being represented in the work itself, by the characters building up a picture of their environment and the other people who surround them: 'thus, reading becomes (inevitably) one of the themes of the book' (Todorov 1980: 78). This kind of self-consciousness is something which is clearly on display in many postmodernist texts. Linda Hutcheon has explored what she calls the 'metafictional paradox' whereby readers are simultaneously distanced from the text by being reminded that the hypodiegetic world is artificial and made to acknowledge their active role as co-producers of meaning. One of her examples is *A Word Child* where the philologist Hilary Burde's reflections on language serve as 'an almost allegorical commentary on the act of reading' (Hutcheon 1984: 102).

At times in Murdoch's fiction, more subtly than in more radical postmodernist fiction perhaps, we are invited to reflect on our active role at the same time as playing it. The reader becomes aware that s/he is being invited to interpret what is going on in the hypodiegetic world in the same way as the characters who 'exist' there. For one thing, this is the result of her rejection of the modernist 'underlying myth' in her work, which works by seducing the reader into believing something similar lies under the surface of her own fiction, only for this belief finally to be frustrated. A more obvious way this occurs is on the numerous occasions throughout her novels where the activity of interpretation is foregrounded in the way Todorov suggests. When characters make observations about the 'drama' they are involved in, the 'machine' which traps them, the 'pattern' they see in events, they are offering, on another level, a covert commentary on the novel which contains them – they are, in effect, reading the story as it unfolds around them. Bradley Pearson's friends continually give concise, confident summaries of his appearance and character: 'You're such a funny fellow, Bradley. You're so unphysical. And you're as shy as a schoolboy' (*BP* 117). In *A Word Child* similar résumés are often given in front of Hilary, but as if he were absent.

In each of the first-person novels the duty of reading the narrator's character seems to belong to one character in particular. Francis Marloe in *The Black Prince* is furnished with the same touches as previous characters like Honor Klein in *A Severed Head*. He tends to arrive silently and unnoticed, or to be found looking in from outside a window. Francis dogs Bradley throughout the story, offering support and explanations of events and people (which support and explanations Bradley always rejects) almost as if he is following Bradley's story with as avid an interest as the reader. In *The Sea, the Sea* Charles comments that his cousin James has never been 'much of an actor in my life' (*SS* 57). The implication, borne out by his understanding of Charles' behaviour, is that he has instead been observing Charles from afar. James first enters the novel as discreetly as Francis Marloe, catching Charles unaware. The suggestion is that these reader-figures are invisibly present throughout, capable of entering the text at any time, witnessing all. This is not to say that the protagonist functions simply as the object of the voyeuristic gaze. According to Freud, the epistemophilic instinct is one of two component sexual instincts which take root in the 'anal-sadistic' stage of childhood. The second is the scopophilic instinct, or the concern with looking. A similar pairing between the desire to know and the desire to look is manifested in the first-person narrators, where voyeuristic urges often service their epistemophilia. In *The Sea, the Sea* Charles conceals himself outside the window of his beloved and her husband in the hope of determining what is really going on in their relationship. As he describes the scene, he speaks of his inability to interpret a marriage (a failure which, we have seen, Bradley is conscious of too) in appropriately voyeuristic terms: 'Whoever illicitly draws back that curtain may well be stricken, and in some way that he can least foresee, by an avenging deity' (*SS* 194). Later he watches them through binoculars.

The first-person novels, then, cause the reader to reflect on his or her interpretive role by establishing a claustrophobic, almost paranoid, atmosphere in which the act of reading is constantly suggested: all the time the narrator is voraciously reading what goes on around him, someone else is reading him. But where the activity of reader-figures like Marloe and James parallels, as Todorov says, the process of construction engaged in by the real reader of Murdoch's novels, the narrator's epistemophilia exemplifies the process of reading as *mis*-construction. His narcissism stops him seeing himself as he is or the situation around him as it is, a lack of self-knowledge which makes Charles Arrowby's comment to Hartley especially comic, 'that's what mad people do, see everything as evidence for what they want to believe' (*SS* 223). Hilary Burde is so enveloped in self-concern that he is fatally unable to recognize the seriousness of Clifford's situation, mistakenly believing his continual threats of suicide are empty. Martin Lynch-Gibbon is unaware that his wife is having affairs with, first, her analyst, and then his brother. Edmund Narraway spends almost the whole of *The Italian Girl* blind to the fact that Flora and Isabel are in genuine misery; that he is unable to see past the superficial is emphasized by the novel's many suggestions of façade, like Isabel's 'pinned-on' hair (*IG* 101). As these last two examples suggest, however, the narrator's inability to read certain people or situations is not entirely the result of his egocentrism, for the reader is often no clearer. The emphasis on misconstruction, by reminding us just how difficult it is to interpret what goes on around us, relates to the Murdochian insistence on the need for careful attention.

Once we recognize the ubiquity of this focus on reading and misreading in Murdoch's work it is interesting to look back to her first novel and see just how central it is there. An exploration of the problematic business of interpretation is as much at the heart of *Under the Net* as it is in *The Black Prince*, though it is foregrounded less directly. The parallels between these two novels, the two which deal most profoundly and directly with the relationship between writing and artistic truth in the Murdoch canon, has been acknowledged, as has their value in understanding a novelist so concerned with the state of the contemporary novel.[5] But in both, the treatment of writing is intimately bound up with a deep concern with reading. This dual concern actually means that the concern with interpretation which recurs throughout Murdoch's fiction becomes in these texts more literal – it relates to the process of reading *fiction* as much as to reading a situation or other people.

Noting the affinities between the two novels, A. S. Byatt has pointed out that both are narrated by artists obsessed with 'the tension between the attempt to tell, or see, the truth' (Byatt 1976: 35). In the case of *Under the Net* this obsession explains Jake's infatuation with Hugo Belfounder. Jake has always been in pursuit of grand philosophical truth and upon meeting Hugo, a man who expounds and lives by a philosophy which distrusts generalization in favour of the particular, he thinks he has found it. He publishes a book, *The Silencer*, which ironically not only theorizes Hugo's anti-theory but attempts to give voice to his ethic of silence. The complex plot of *Under the Net* revolves around Jake's subsequent efforts to find Hugo and explain the reasons for this betrayal. He goes about this task with such energy, however, that it appears Hugo himself has come to represent the kind of truth Jake is longing for. At the end of the novel Jake realizes that he has been guilty of constructing a myth around Hugo: he is not Truth – he is a far more humble and bewildered creature than Jake remembers. This realization ushers in the more concrete, more valuable truths that are necessary for Jake's enlightenment, which Byatt categorizes as 'social, moral and aesthetic' (Byatt 1965: 193). In other words Jake has had to find a way to reconcile his bohemian ideals with the demands of the real world around him, while also learning to respect the otherness of people he has previously taken for granted and exploited. Along the way he discovers, almost by accident, the aesthetic truth which has eluded him. The prizewinning success of Jean-Pierre Breteuil, the novelist whose works Jake has somewhat scornfully translated, jolts him into realizing that the creation of original art, free from purely economic concerns, is still a worthy goal in a cynical world. The novel ends, in the way Steven Kellman has suggested, with Jake looking set to undergo an artistic regeneration.

In fact, to return to the question of how Murdoch's first-person novels relate to the modernist artist-novel, the role which art plays in *Under the Net* is greater than any of the others, even *The Black Prince*. The hero's transformation comes about not because he experiences overwhelming love for another person, as is usual in Murdoch's novels, but because he realizes he can write a novel. In other words, the key event in the plot is not Jake's relationship with Anna, but his 'treacherous' publication of *The Silencer*. It is important therefore not to underestimate the power of art in *Under the Net*. Nor should it be misunderstood, something I think Kellman does at times: Jake does not come to a sudden recognition of the power of art but regains a previously held faith in it. This faith is absent at the beginning of the novel. Where once Jake had 'ideals' and felt he could write anything he wanted, he now believes (like many in the early 1950s) that 'the present age was not one in which it was possible to write a novel' (*UN* 19). His earlier idealism has been replaced by the cynical view that one can live comfortably if one 'is prepared to write anything which the market asks for' (*UN* 21). As this comment implies, his refusal to produce original work owes much to his disgust with the political situation of the time (the eponymous hero of the one original piece he admits to having written, an epic poem, 'symbolized big business'). Yet his renewed conviction about the worthiness of art eventually comes not from any Sartrean belief in the need for political engagement (he refuses the socialist Lefty Todd's offer to write for the Party), but because he comes to believe one has a duty after all to write in the name of Truth. For all his empathy with Hugo's philosophy of silence, he rejects this at the end in favour of words. The rejuvenation of his artistic impulse thus partly explains the novel's epigram from Dryden: ''Tis well an old Age is out/And time to begin a New'.

As this brief summary indicates, *Under the Net* portrays a search for truth which embodies the key principles of the moral philosophy its author was developing at the time while also conforming to the 1950s' preference for social realism. But in the light of the concern with reading I have been focusing on so far, I think it is worth describing Jake's search for truth in another way. He is constantly in pursuit of an altogether more mundane kind of truth, but one which is hugely important to the epistemophiliac: knowledge of what is going on around him. The hero spends most of *Under the Net* being propelled from one inexplicable event to another, with 'a fever of curiosity [...] raging in my blood' (*UN* 163). The narration displays an early mastery of the typical devices of the romance that were to become characteristic of Murdoch's fiction – unexpected arrivals and disappearances, dramatic escapes, mysterious notes found in improbable places, and so on – and Jake reacts to them all with increasing anxiety: 'What did it mean? Oh, why had I not come earlier! What was this offer? Perhaps Hugo...' (*UN* 112). His paranoid need to understand is not completely unjustified, however, as part of the plot of *Under the Net* concerns a conspiracy where some of his friends try to use one of his translations for a film script without his knowledge. But most of Jake's epistemophilic energy is centred on what he thinks is a tangled love-plot being played out around him, even though the situation is quite straightforward. Jake is unable to understand who is in love with whom because he has failed to read the other characters with enough care despite all the clues in front of his eyes. His overall situation is reminiscent of the scene in the mime theatre, where he is confronted by a number of characters wearing masks, inviting him to guess who is behind them. With its sense of the action being frozen, and the emphasis on the dim half-light suggesting one of Murdoch's preferred metaphors, the Platonic cave, this scene distils the book's whole concern with interpretation into one fractal image.

Jake's misreading of the love-plot comes hard on the heels of his underestimation of Breteuil's ability as a writer. 'I had classed Jean Pierre once and for all. That he should secretly have been improving his style, ennobling his thought, purifying his emotions: all this was really too bad. [...] It wrenched me like the changing of a fundamental category' (*UN* 171). This revision later becomes a literal rereading, as Jake picks up Breteuil's book. It prefigures the metaphorical outcome of the novel: what has changed in Jake at the end is that he has learned to read more accurately. Part of the lesson involves taking heed of Hugo's advice: 'Some situations can't be unravelled... they just have to be dropped. The trouble with you, Jake, is that you want to understand everything sympathetically. It can't be done. One must just blunder on. Truth lies in blundering on' (*UN* 228). Reflecting on how Anna 'existed now as a separate being and not as part of myself' Jake wonders,

> When does one ever know a human being? Perhaps only after one has renounced the possibility of knowledge and renounced the desire for it and ceased to feel even the need for it. But then what one achieves is no longer knowledge, it is simply a kind of co-existence; and this, too, is one of the guises of love. (*UN* 238)

As well as his moral regeneration Jake has learned something about his own epistemophilia. In Byatt's words, this passage reflects the fact that 'understanding, in Murdoch's thought, is a good ideal, but one impossible of complete achievement' (Byatt 1965: 36). Jake's renunciation of the passion for knowledge is not final, for soon after this admission comes his most outrageous attempt yet to gain knowledge, when he blows up a safe in order to find documents which expose the conspiracy going on behind his back. Yet the ending of the novel suggests the lesson is likely to endure. He returns to his place of refuge, the mysterious Mrs Tinckham's shop in Soho, and when asked if he can explain the biological marvel of why each of her litter of kittens should look so different refuses to speculate: 'I don't know why it is... It's just one of the wonders of the world' (*UN* 253). *Under the Net*'s last sentence shows that the truth-seeker has finally conquered his epistemophilia.

The framing of Bradley Pearson: *The Black Prince*

Under the Net is about a search for truth, but there are in fact two parts to it. In order to arrive at what we might call the *metaphysical* truth – Byatt's 'social, moral and aesthetic' categories – Jake has to understand what is happening around him, he has to learn *circumstantial* truth. In a clear sense his failure to 'read' his situation and other people conforms to the ethical pattern typical of Murdoch's fiction. What I have stated in textual terms could easily be translated into Murdoch's characteristic philosophical vocabulary: Jake's misreading is of course a failure to attend properly. But, as I have suggested, observing this causes us to reflect on our own efforts to make sense of the text. In *Under the Net* this is accomplished largely at an implicit level. Its direct descendent, however, the more overtly metafictional *The Black Prince*, makes the reader even more aware of his or her interpretive role by approaching the question of textual reading more directly. The basic motivation for the story is the same – a writer searches for two kinds of truth, metaphysical and circumstantial – but this is overlaid with a more self-conscious framework built up partly by its narrator's constant theorizing about fiction, and partly by the complex paratextual form of the novel. Bradley finds that conveying both kinds of truth in his narrative is more problematic than it seems. Like many postmodernist novels, *The Black Prince* reminds us that representing the truth – especially the truth of the past – is a troublesome business.

At the beginning Bradley makes it clear that he thinks he is already in possession of both kinds of truth. He sets out his motives for writing: 'I have endeavoured in what follows to be wisely artful and artfully wise, and to tell truth as I understand it, not only concerning the superficial and "exciting" aspects of this drama, but also concerning what lies deeper' (*BP* 11). His first priority, in other words, is to tell the true story of the murder of Arnold Baffin, his friend and fellow novelist, in order to exculpate himself. While doing so, he intends to reveal the deeper philosophical truths which he believes this story contains. This dual purpose is reflected in the structure of his narrative, which alternates the telling of his story with a series of meditations on life and the nature of artistic truth. But as soon as he sets about his task, in the longest section of the narrative, '*The Black Prince*: A Celebration of Love', he realizes it is one thing to know the truth, quite another to express it. He opens by saying, 'It might be most dramatically effective to begin the tale at the moment when Arnold Baffin rang me up and said, "Bradley, could you come round here please, I think that I have just killed my wife."' He is right of course, but then he remembers that dramatic effect is not his main concern – it is more urgent that he sets out clearly what really happened. As soon as he has decided on one beginning, then, he realizes that perhaps another might be more accurate: 'A deeper pattern however suggests Francis Marloe as the first speaker [...] who, some half an hour before Arnold's momentous telephone call, initiates the action' (*BP* 21).

What he has been forced to recognize here is the fact that setting out clearly what happened is not as simple as it might seem, for the very act of expression changes the past. This conclusion is of course similar to the rhetoric of historiographic metafiction, which explores in a different way the same question as *The Black Prince*, how to write past truth. The issue is also in fact at the heart of *Under the Net*, and explains its eponymous metaphor, derived of course from Wittgenstein, but which (as I suggested in Chapter 1) could be restated in the light of current theoretical insights as referring to a condition of textuality, the sense of being inextricably enveloped in the fabric of language. Hugo explains to Jake that the description of anything in the past – a feeling, a state of mind, a conversation – is 'falsified from the start. [...] The language just won't let you present it as it really was' (*UN* 59). Both *Under the Net* and *The Black Prince*, then, underline the interdependence of Moretti's two directions of the cognitive process: description always already involves interpretation.

Given that stating the truth is complicated by the net of textuality, it follows that using a whole novel to express the truth is only likely to magnify the problem. Bradley is aware of this. In his first address to Loxias, a long soliloquy in which the thematic terrain of the novel is mapped out, he outlines his conviction that art is 'the only available method for the telling of certain truths', while admitting that because art is complex and truth simple, there is a danger of allowing 'the marvels of the instrument itself [to] interfere with the task to which it is dedicated'. Yet to try to avoid this problem by stating the truth as simply as possible is doomed to failure because the personality of the author inevitably colours what he describes. Or, as Bradley puts it, how can a person be described 'justly' when even a statement like 'I am tall' is true only in a certain context? If art is to tell the truth it is therefore essential to choose an apt form. And his preferred form is one which emphasizes the fictionality of a work in order to present what is true, a process which offers 'a diagnosis' by a sort of momentary artificiality. Since his book is both about art and a work of art itself, Bradley hopes it 'may perhaps be permitted, now and then, to cast a look upon itself'.

This method may mean that form gets in the way of content: 'Yet what can one do but try to lodge one's vision somehow inside this layered stuff of ironic sensibility, which, if I were a fictitious character, would be that much deeper and denser?' (*BP* 80–1).

In this remark we can of course sense the mischievous presence of the author herself, for to find the 'truth' of *The Black Prince* the reader must lodge his or her vision inside the more complex ironic layers of Iris Murdoch's novel. Although what he actually says is somewhat cryptic, tackling the question of form head on in the way Bradley does reminds the reader of his or her role in producing the meaning of the novel. By this stage, in any case, we have already been given signs that truth is unlikely to be told straightforwardly in this book, for in order to get to Bradley's main narrative we have had to get through two prefaces. The result of such narrative framing is that the artificial status of the novel (and by extension all fiction) is foregrounded right from the start. Bradley's admission that he has chosen a convoluted metafictional form also works as an implicit invitation to the reader to discover the truth by a process of careful interpretation. In this respect *The Black Prince* seems equivalent to what Murdoch calls – rather derogatorily, we recall – the 'structuralist text', where 'a play of meanings [. . .] stirs the client into meaning-making activity for himself' (*MGM* 90).

Urged to interpret with care, one of the things the reader is likely to be most suspicious of is the very notion of truth itself. Bradley insists that 'truth is simple'. However, if the insights of poststructuralism and postmodernism have taught us anything, it is that truth is far from simple to determine. The concept of one truth, as all-governing *logos* or transcendental signified or metanarrative, is now regarded with suspicion. It is more sensible to talk of truths plural, for the validity of each truth depends upon who is speaking and from which vantage point. As the philosopher Richard Rorty has argued, distinguishing between truths is actually a matter of choosing between persuasive vocabularies. Rorty insists our duty is to choose between attractive descriptions of the world while recognizing simultaneously that they cannot claim absolute veracity (Rorty 1989). There is a parallel to be drawn, I think, between the 'liberal utopia' Rorty imagines can follow from this understanding, and Bakhtin's conception of the novel. To recap briefly, Bakhtin shows, in a way which resembles later poststructuralist analyses of fiction, how the novel comprises a number of different truths which co-exist within its pages. It is by definition a polyphonic genre despite the efforts of monologically inclined authors to limit and stabilize these truths by ordering them into a hierarchy which places the authorially endorsed word at the top.

Those texts which are happiest to let various truths stand freely, even when they are in conflict (a category which includes a large percentage of postmodernist novels) represent microcosmic versions of Rorty's utopia, which would be achieved, one might say, by the dialogic interaction between different descriptions of the world. As I previously suggested, Murdoch's fiction is fundamentally dialogical. This is especially true of *The Black Prince* even though much of it is dressed up as a didactic monologue. My view is that the dialogism of *The Black Prince* produces an effect which can comfortably be aligned with postmodern theory and practice, but which departs from the course typically plotted by historiographic metafiction. This novel stands as the finest example of the 'polyphonic irony' which functions (as I suggested in Chapter 3) in Murdoch's first-person fiction. For this reason alone it would be worth examining in detail – but more significant for the present purpose is the way *The Black Prince* uses the dialogic interpenetration of different truths to highlight subtly but effectively the problems of describing and interpreting the past.

Peter Conradi has aptly suggested that '*The Black Prince* partly resembles a *Death in Venice* written by Dostoevsky's Underground Man' (Conradi 1989: 184). We can say of Bradley, as Bakhtin does of the Underground Man, that

> [he] thinks most about what others think or might think of him and strives to keep one step ahead of every other consciousness, everyone else's thoughts about him, every other point of view toward him. At all essential points in his confession he strives to anticipate possible definitions and assessments of him by others, to guess the sense and tone of those assessments, and to carefully formulate the potential words of others, interrupting his own speech with the imagined remarks of others. (Bakhtin 1973: 42)

These other points of view are, in other words, layers of 'ironic sensibility' inside which the truth-seeker, by virtue of his awareness of them, may 'lodge his vision'. From the very beginning of his narrative, Bradley shows he is aware of these alternative viewpoints by attempting to justify his actions and disarm potential criticism at all times. Frequently this criticism takes the form of an explicit dialogue with an imaginary reader:

> I will not pause to answer the cynic, possibly the same one whom we heard from just now, who will say: 'And how long does your Romantic foreverness last, pray?' or rather, I will simply reply: 'True love is eternal.

It is also rare; and no doubt you, Sir, were never lucky enough to experience it!' (*BP* 210)

But what he says is influenced more often by the anticipated response of specific characters in the novel whose word functions according to Bakhtin's logic of the internal polemic. Like Raskolnikov or the Underground Man, Bradley does not treat other people as individuals or actors in his drama, but living embodiments of a counter-philosophy to which he must address himself. He continually engages in dialogue with, for example, Francis Marloe, who becomes a self-styled psychotherapist specializing in Bradley's 'case'. He is aware of Marloe's Freudian reading of his character – that he is a repressed homosexual who loves his mother and detests his father – and this leads him to expect a hostile response on occasions when he describes himself: 'My mother filled me with exasperation and shame but I loved her. (Be quiet Francis Marloe)' (*BP* 15).

Likewise he is continually forced to consider the word of others when discussing art. Where Bradley believes art is something sacred, only to be indulged in sparingly by those who seek the realm of the divine, Arnold does the best he can as often as he can, as befits the 'professional writer' (*BP* 50). Many of Bradley's ruminations upon the practice of writing are therefore influenced by the need to answer Arnold, even before his rival has been mentioned in the novel.[6] Two other voices, Julian's and Loxias's, also feature in the ongoing dialogue about art, even though the ideological position each adopts is closely related to Bradley's. Julian holds a rough-edged, juvenile version of Bradley's grandiose aesthetic, while Loxias embodies the divine artistic ideal to which he aspires. Yet despite this common ground, the dialogue he maintains with each of them is instructive, for he alters his word according to his anticipation of his addressee's response. To Julian, he presents a simplified version of his view of art, as befits the wise artist speaking to the inexperienced beginner, and during the periodic contemplations of life and art which are addressed to Loxias, he adopts a philosophical tone which suggests an ability to generalize confidently about human behaviour.

The effect of the co-existence of various discourses is to emphasize the fact that truth is a more fluid, more unstable entity than Bradley wishes to make it. He intends his novel to function like the classic realist text, as a 'hierarchy of discourses' which places the reliable, unchallenged 'metalanguage' of the author outside them, pointing out where the other discourses stand in relation to 'truth' (MacCabe 1974). His voice is to function as this authorial metalanguage, but in fact his word is challenged and subverted by those of others. The dialogical principle ensures that any point of view is not only measured against alternative discourses, but is partially formed by these discourses. To read each of Bradley's affirmations of a particular 'truth' – about love, life, and art – is to realize an alternative ideological position exists, one in fact which his own word observes 'half-consciously'. So while he may choose to conduct a reasoned debate about his own and Arnold's conflicting ideas of artistic truth, his expositions about art are also unavoidably modified by the crude psychoanalytical theory of art expounded by Francis Marloe, whose voice he cannot silence. This is the inevitable result of trying to assert authoritatively one's idea of truth in a polyphonic form.

What is especially interesting about *The Black Prince* is how Murdoch has used the structure of the novel to emphasize this point. Like the other first-person novels, the illusion is maintained that Bradley is the sole author of his novel. Yet there are in fact six other texts which go alongside Bradley's narrative (which includes his own prologue and postscript) to make up the complete book: Loxias' two sections which open and close the novel, and the four postscripts written by main characters. This paratextuality is the most radical formal experiment ever employed by Murdoch. The postscripts each continue the same point of view its writer has adopted throughout the novel, and with which Bradley has unwillingly entered into dialogue. This consistency of character leads Conradi to argue that the effect of these appendices is limited because they 'service our sense of the plot more than they destabilize our grasp of it' (Conradi 1989: 187). Murdoch herself, characteristically keen to downplay the experimental aspects of her fiction, has declared that the postscripts are simply playful.[7] Yet when taken as a whole, I think the postscripts have the effect of deconstructing almost every 'truth' Bradley presents, more powerfully than the other voices which act implicitly on his word, even though each writer merely restates their previous ideological position.

As Douglas Brooks-Davies has remarked, the postscripts set free the voices Bradley's monologue has attempted to silence (Brooks-Davies 1989: 179). Like him, each of the authors is, in Susan Lanser's terms, a 'public narrator', one who addresses an extrafictional reader. Each postscript is itself a self-contained literary document, a first-person retrospective narrative with as strong a reality-effect as Bradley's. It is in keeping with the logic of this novel about novels, which constantly affirms the power of the word, that when something is written it possesses a greater persuasive force, and this is true of the postscripts.[8] (It is true even though, as Murdoch claims at the conference in Amsterdam, the postscripts are far shorter than Bradley's narrative: 'it would be an entirely different kind of novel if one divided the space up equally between the different versions' [Amsterdam 1988]). Yet the main source of the disruptive power of the postscripts is that they are part of the metafictional method so central to the novel. Like Bradley's commentary, which accompanies his story, the postscripts allow Murdoch to draw attention to the artificiality of the story. They force us to recognize how our emotions have been manipulated by the narrator's rhetoric. They underline the dialogical point that the deep 'truths' Bradley tells are constructed subjectively and are true from one viewpoint only. Furthermore, they question the veracity of the very events from which he derives these truths.

They confirm at a formal level what is implied at the level of story, something often overlooked in discussions of the novel, that *The Black Prince* is a murder-mystery – or, more accurately, an *anti*murder-mystery. The distinctive way a story of the detective genre progresses, by continually posing and solving enigmas (the process Barthes calls the hermeneutic code) is frequently paralleled in Murdoch's novel. Bradley's epistemophilia suggests he is obsessed with establishing the true course of events long before the murder of Arnold makes it necessary to write 'a truthful account of what has been so universally falsified and misrepresented' (*BP* 14). *The Black Prince* can be read on one level 'simply' as a thriller, the story of the murder of Arnold Baffin. But the novel refuses to conform to the pattern of the traditional murder-mystery, because it is impossible to know for sure who did in fact do it. Even though he appears innocent (Rachel seems to cleverly 'frame' him for Arnold's murder) he still had the means, motive and opportunity to commit the crime. Furthermore, the postscripts, despite being of dubious credibility themselves, as each writer has a motive to harm Bradley, cast serious doubt on his status as a reliable truth-teller.

There is no help either from the one person who seems able to clarify what actually happened. By ensuring that he has the last word, Loxias sets himself up as the revealer of final truth: 'I had intended to write a long analysis of my own, rather like a detective's final summing up, pointing out discrepancies, making inferences, drawing conclusions.' His divine nature seems to make him uniquely capable of providing such a conclusion, but he decides instead to omit the dénouement: 'Partly because Bradley is dead. [...] And partly because, rereading Bradley's story, I feel that it speaks for itself' (*BP* 413). This conclusion is ironic, for the novel continually casts doubt on the hermeneutical process. The reader cannot finally be certain what really happened in the murder of Arnold Baffin and is thus placed in a similar position to the epistemo-philic Bradley Pearson, longing for the truth but unable to satisfy his sense of an ending. Although the outcome of Bradley's trial may be symbolically just – Marsyas is flayed after his duel with Apollo – in the 'real' world justice is not done, for it seems that the wrong person is convicted. Such injustice is of course anathematical to the conventional detective story.[9]

Brian McHale has called the detective story 'the epistemological genre par excellence' (McHale 1987: 9), for it is all about using ratiocination to uncover the truth. The refusal of *The Black Prince* to conform to the pattern of this genre underlines the point made continually by its pol-yphony: the representation of truth is always a matter of interpretation. Ending with a 'trial', the novel represents a variation on the common Murdochian theme of redemption, frequently explored by evoking a *karmic* need to pay for past deeds; as Mir says in *The Green Knight* 'the idea of retribution is everywhere fundamental to justice. [...] An eye for an eye and a tooth for a tooth serves as an image for both restitution and revenge' (*GK* 126). As he writes his novel, Bradley shows a continual awareness of being judged by authorities higher even than the British legal machine. He often considers how human beings appear to the angels which look down on them. This sense of judgement by divine agents is partly explained by the fact that his confession is oriented towards Loxias. But he assigns judicial roles to others: when Arnold surprises him at the seaside he asks to be allowed to 'defend myself' (*BP* 338). He believes Julian will one day 'be the just judge who under-stands and forgives' (*BP* 285). And she notices his preoccupation with justice, wondering why he wants to 'justify everything' (*BP* 320).

Judgement is also, of course, a question of interpretation. Or to put it differently: if truth is 'an effect of successful rhetorical performance', as postmodernism insists, 'how can one talk of justice when one cannot talk of truth?' (Waugh 1992: 150). When he faces a real jury, Bradley's fate depends upon the interpretation of a 'story', an activity the novel constantly reminds us is fraught with difficulty. This is made clear during the trial, when Bradley's various actions are claimed by different 'lobbies' to support their case. His reaction to Priscilla's death, for example, is seen as proof of insanity by some, and of callous premeditation by others. This state of affairs is reminiscent of the case of the nineteenth-century murderer Pierre Rivière, which so interested Foucault. The structure of *The Black Prince* also resembles Foucault's book on the case, in which Rivière's memoir is framed by a collection of modern-day and nineteenth-century texts, and the effect is similar: it suggests that truth floats somewhere between different discourses, never coming to rest (Foucault 1978). Bradley's real trial only begins after his conviction for murder. The material disputed by prosecution and defence, his story, is judged in its literary form by a jury made up of the four characters who write the postscripts. Bradley is in effect re-tried, with his account used as an extra piece of evidence to be debated. In such a self-referential novel, it is fitting that the real trial should be textual.

Loxias' postscript, which closes the novel and exposes the flaws in the arguments of the others, invites the reader to contribute to the regression of deconstructive readings by interpreting the text for himself. He advises that 'The reader will recognize the voice of truth when he hears it' (*BP* 412), that 'the work of art laughs last'. His conviction that 'art tells the only truth that ultimately matters' (*BP* 416) suggests that the facts of Bradley's case are irrelevant, the lesson which his novel tells is more important, and it is up to the reader to decipher it. His rhetoric in my view figures as the supreme piece of irony in a supremely ironic novel. The interpretative situation of *The Black Prince* is reminiscent of another framed narrative, Marlow's tale in *Heart of Darkness*, which, according to Peter Brooks, conveys the fact that meaning is 'dialogic', located somewhere in the relationship between teller and listener, but impossible to pinpoint (Brooks 1992: 260–1). The reader of *The Black Prince* is placed in a similar position to Marlow's listeners, invited (by Loxias) to sum up, to complete the message contained in the narrative, but incapable of doing so because of the indeterminacy of the text.

It is possible to maintain that the experience Bradley undergoes – and writing about it – does lead him to a kind of truth. Losing his one true love and being wrongly convicted of murder has taken him through pain to the knowledge required to create genuine art. Guided through his ordeal by the two gods, Apollo (disguised as Loxias) and the Black Prince, Eros, he learns that true love – a dark fusion of 'sex and true moral vision' (Conradi 1989: 204), 'low' and 'high' Eros – requires the loss of self. Bradley does achieve *ascesis*, but when competing with the divine the stakes are high and he must pay for his transition, as Marsyas did, with his life.[10] This reading is certainly plausible, but does not in my view account for the deconstructive effect of the postscripts. This might be Bradley's truth, but it is not Marloe's or Julian's, for example (both of whom also manage to publish work as a result of their very different experience of the same story).

Nor is it the reader's. For the reader, as Byatt has said, *The Black Prince* 'offers an endless series of receding, unattainable, focused images of truth, but nothing believable, nothing habitable' (Byatt 1979: 36). Even after repeated readings, there is a sense that it is impossible finally to prise the truth of the novel away from its grasp. This is not to say the experience of reading the novel is frustrating; rather it is a thrilling, moving narrative which does manage to leave the reader feeling that s/he has learned something profound, even if what this is precisely is unclear. The reason for this can be explained, I think, if we exchange the word 'knowledge' for the word 'truth'. The novel continually promises knowledge and urges its reader to look carefully for it, but frustrates these expectations: neither metaphysical nor circumstantial knowledge is forthcoming.

It might seem surprising that in interviews Murdoch has supported the conclusion that Loxias' rhetoric directs us towards: that, with careful attention, one can tell where Bradley should be believed. At the conference in Amsterdam she insists that she intends 'mystification to be something of a further intensification of the story: not a contradiction of it, but a kind of shadow hiding the story which people could see if they could unveil it' (Amsterdam 1988).[11] This statement suggests, in other words, that her view of the outcome of the novel's metafictional layering coincides with Bradley's. This is not as unlikely as it may seem, for despite the repeated warning in her criticism of the dangers of being seduced by fictional form we should remember that her aesthetic of the sublime – as *A Word Child* demonstrates – does not preclude the use of complex form to tell simple truth. In the case of *The Black Prince*, however, the fact remains that as well as the brilliant opacity of much of the prose, Murdoch's use of form is largely responsible for the opacity of knowledge in this novel. Its emphasis on fictionality underlines the fact that any truth is always already subjectively constructed. Loxias' rhetoric at the end of the novel, to the effect that Bradley's novel 'speaks for itself', suggests that the reader is to arrive at the deeper 'truth' of the novel by employing the logical hermeneutical method of literary interpretation (and detective work) – to construct a coherent *fabula* from the *sjuzet* which will enable him or her to deduce from it a moral. But if the dialogic language and form have cast doubt on Bradley's representation of truth – factual and philosophical – how can we realistically draw accurate conclusions about its meaning? Bradley's comment at the end of his narrative is crucial: 'Art is a vain and hollow show, a toy of gross illusion, unless it points beyond itself and moves ever whither it points' (*BP* 392). This has been plausibly interpreted as a statement of Murdoch's belief in the referential nature of (realist) fiction. Conradi argues that the self-reflexive elements of the novel 'are not simply self-regarding but point to the charmless and dangerous world that lies, undomesticated, outside' (Conradi 1989: 209). Yet our difficulty in sorting through 'the layers of ironic sensibility' to construct a final version of events means that in one important sense the novel does indeed point only towards itself: the one truth we can reliably draw from it is the truth it has expressed all along: all truth is fictional.

Another aspect shared by *The Black Prince* and *Under the Net*, then, besides its obvious interest in the transformative capacity of art and love, is the concern with misreading. Bradley's search for truth is even more marked by epistemophilia than Jake's. But where the reader of *Under the Net* was for the most part able to determine where Jake was guilty of misreading, the seductive yet opaque rhetoric of narrator and editor, and the dialogic nature of the text, mean that in *The Black Prince* the reader becomes as much of an epistemophiliac as the narrator. In *The Pleasure of the Text*, Barthes improvises a psychoanalytic 'typology of the pleasures of reading' which makes the link clear. A paranoid reader, he says, 'would consume or produce complicated texts, stories developed like arguments, constructions posited like games, like secret constraints' (Barthes 1976: 63). The reader of *The Black Prince*, urged by Bradley, Loxias, and implicitly by Murdoch herself to pin down the truth of the novel, becomes just this kind of reader.

Despite her apparent faith in the ultimate decipherability of *The Black Prince*, this state of affairs is entirely compatible with the 'antimodernist' position of Murdoch's fiction. One of the key elements in the movement from modernism to postmodernism, according to the Lacanian theorist Slavoj Žižek, is the change in 'the very status of interpretation'. The typical high modernist work (*Ulysses*, *The Waste Land*) demands that we recuperate its fragmented, superficially incomprehensible elements through interpretation. It is effectively unfinished until a commentary is provided by the reader (or discovered within the text) (Žižek 1992: 1). The strong emphasis this places on interpretation results in what Žižek has elsewhere termed an 'interpretive delirium' (Žižek 1990: 109). Paranoid reading, in other words, is more than just one of several types of textual pleasure, as Barthes describes it, but the necessary way to approach modernist literature. In fact, according to another diachronic comparison between modernism and postmodernism, Brian McHale's, the influence of modernism has been such that paranoid reading, 'the mind-set of *tout se tient*', has become institutionalized as the literary critical orthodoxy (McHale 1992: 81–2). Because of this, McHale contends, the response of some postmodern novels like Pynchon's *Gravity's Rainbow* and Eco's *Foucault's Pendulum* has been to deliberately encourage the reader's (modernist) paranoia in order to frustrate it. My view is that *The Black Prince* achieves a similar resistance to the practice of modernist reading.

To test this it is worth considering that the novel's emphasis on misreading involves highlighting the shortcomings of literary criticism – an irony not lost on Murdoch's critics. Bradley's charge that Arnold Baffin is too prolific and adorns his work with too much unnecessary intellectual baggage is an ironic reproduction of similar complaints made by reviewers about Murdoch's own fiction. His critique of Arnold's work is in fact bad criticism, driven by a desire to justify his own artistic viewpoint, and make excuses for his own meagre output. His reading of *Hamlet*, which is at the thematic heart of the novel (and, as Dipple says, the only occasion where criticism successfully illuminates a work of art [Dipple 1984]) crucially involves dismissing the classic Freudian reading of the play as accurate but too narrow to explain adequately such a complex work of art. The psychoanalytical interpretation is paralleled by the reductive Freudian reading of Bradley's narrative given by Marloe. And the postscripts of course betray a similar tendency to over-simplify, serving to gratify the egoism of the critic rather than focus objectively on the work in hand.

Patricia Waugh argues in *Practising Postmodernism/Reading Modernism*, *à propos* the term 'postmodernism', that before coming in the last two decades to refer to the way the cultural logic of late capitalism has finally collapsed our faith in the Enlightenment project, it first became used in literary critical circles in the sixties and seventies to describe an emerging 'art of the surface' which reacted against the 'surface-depth' model of interpretation so central to the modernist aesthetic. Although *The Black Prince*, published in 1973, does not present a world of the surface as radically as some of its contemporaries, its continual casting of doubt on the interpretive process makes it conform to this earlier definition of the postmodernist text. This is in keeping with the fact that Murdoch's liberalism is compatible with the liberal postmodernism of the likes of Rorty. But Murdoch's literary theory, on the other hand, as we have seen, is quite resistant to the openness of postmodernism. *The Black Prince*, it seems to me, highlights this uncomfortable mixture.

I have spoken mainly of modernism and postmodernism in this chapter, saying little about Murdoch's preferred mode, realism. What is clear is that though this novel aims to tell a broadly 'realistic' story with convincing 'rounded' characters, naturalistic description, a sense of real time, and other staples of classic realism, it also firmly rejects the basic ideological structure of this convention. As I suggested above, the polyphony and polysemy of *The Black Prince* subtly but effectively work against the monologism of the classic realist text. The novel's layers of irony force us to recognize that asserting objective truth in a narrative is impossible; even if concrete truth does exist somewhere within the pages of *The Black Prince*, it is inaccessible to the reader. In deconstructing the classic realist method this novel thus figures as a moment of *aporia* in Murdoch's work, for by implication the reliability of her other novels is subtly questioned. For an author who has so often and so strongly affirmed a commitment to realism, this outcome is radical and unsettling. As such it suggests another explanation of her comments at Amsterdam: in defending the truth-telling capacity of her novel, she continues to discuss a postmodernist text in a realist discourse. Although a few of the novels which come after *The Black Prince* (*A Word Child*, *The Sea, the Sea*, *The Philosopher's Pupil*) again use a certain amount of formal experimentation to remind us of the constructed nature of past truth, Murdoch never really builds on the destabilizing achievement of *The Black Prince*, feeling perhaps that the referential chasm that novel opened up was just too dangerous for a committed realist fully to explore.

6

The Writing Cure: *A Severed Head* and *A Word Child*

> Love obviously in its genesis belongs with sex, but it's able to transcend sex – I don't mean in any sense of moving away from the carnal expressions of sex but simply that sex is a very great mystifier, it's a very great dark force. It makes us do all kinds of things we don't understand and very often don't want to do. The kind of opening out of love as a world where we really can see other people and are not simply dominated by our own slavish impulses and obsessions, this is something which I would want very much to explore and which I think is very difficult. All these demons and so on are connected with the obsessional side of one's life, which in a sense has got to be overcome.
>
> Rose, *London Magazine*

A Severed Head and *A Word Child* belong in the category of her fiction Murdoch has referred to as 'closed-up, rather obsessional novels' (Rose 1968).[1] Other novels in this group would include works from the earlier part of her career like *The Italian Girl*, *The Unicorn* and *The Time of the Angels*, where an entire community of characters seems to be living out a collective fantasy, and the solipsism of the cast is paralleled by the melodrama of the plot and the claustrophobia of the setting. The obsessional novels often draw on the Gothic tradition (in *The Unicorn* a governess goes to stay in a foreboding castle) and, in their compulsive patterning, are close to Murdoch's conception of the crystalline novel. They underline just how difficult it is to achieve the 'opened out' form of love Murdoch speaks of in the above epigraph.

The dilemma is intrinsically connected to her specialized conception of Eros, the fusion of spirituality and sex which she derives from Plato and Freud. In her obsessional novels the Platonic ideal of *ascesis* is conspicuous only in isolated glimpses; for the most part, the characters remain locked into a way of behaving that resembles Freud's baser version of the soul. *A Severed Head* and *A Word Child* are typical of the 'Murdochian Gothic' in their brooding wintry settings, enclosed locations, and cast of characters small enough for each to be a play. But I think there is something deeper and more complex about the portrayal of the obsessional side of life in these works than most of the other 'closed-up' novels. For one thing, because each is narrated in the first person, we are given a particularly powerful insight into how the obsessional mind works. Both novels, as I have already indicated, are more than any other illuminated by the Orpheus myth. The experiences both of their heroes undergo involve a descent into the particular kind of underworld Murdoch excels at portraying: the destructive mechanism of the unconscious.

Both novels offer an especially 'psychoanalytic' version of Murdoch's interest in the gulf between the contingent elements of reality and those networks (language, theory, art) with which we try to gather them up. In general terms, they are concerned with the overturning of imposed rational order by the irrational force of desire. Time and again in each text – to put this in Lacanian terms – the real intrudes into the symbolic in the form of unsymbolizable trauma or the libidinal energy of desire. At its most obvious, as I suggested earlier, this is achieved by contrasting the veneer of social convention with the powerful emotions this normally manages to keep reined in. *A Severed Head*, for example, is on one level a very English 'drawing-room' comedy, where the hero remains resolutely 'stiff-upper-lipped' in the face of outrageous partner-swapping and taboo-breaking. Desire also erupts – or threatens to erupt – in the form of the aggressive impulses of two naturally violent protagonists (Martin Lynch-Gibbon is an ex-boxer and punches two people, while Hilary Burde, though he tends to direct his anger inward, still ensures those he subjugates can 'smell' his violence [*WC* 35]). But in each novel naked desire erupts to much more devastating effect. The kernel of the story in *A Word Child* is the car crash in which Anne Jopling dies, an event which, like all tragic accidents, defeats Hilary's attempts to determine exactly what it means. He is unsure how to behave after this event, unsure what he now *signifies*: 'I imagined that I would carry the placard *Murderer* around my neck for ever. [...] I had a problem about responsibility for the past which became a problem of identity' (*WC* 127). At the heart of the traumatic event, furthermore, is desire. As much as being in love with Anne, Hilary 'was dreadfully in love with the sort of black certain metaphysical love that cuts deeper than anything and thus seems its own absolute justification. [...] I think this is true of the one and only Eros' (*WC* 125).

What we might call the psychoanalytic understanding of Eros (as opposed to the Platonic) performs a similar function in *A Severed Head*, where desire also emerges as a force which cannot easily be incorporated into the symbolic. This kind of desire is most clearly embodied by one of the characters, Honor Klein, who stands for the power of the id, in a world where the imposed rationality of the ego is dominant. Before she has even entered the action, Georgie remarks that 'there is something primitive about her' (*SH* 7), a comparison Martin later recalls before noting that she resembles 'something black and untouchable', and which is emphasized by her anthropological research, the study of 'primitive savages' (*SH* 64). He slowly comes to recognize that she brings out his own dark side: what he finds 'repellent' in her – her 'animal-like' (*SH* 55) quality – he also finds unconsciously attractive. He likes the fact that their 'conversations were refreshingly lacking in formality', removed from the repressions of social convention. As the only person who has spoken for violence all along, it is not surprising that she should be the person Martin hits first.

Psychoanalysis is relevant in exploring these novels not simply by chance, however. As I have suggested, certain aspects of Murdoch's thought, notably her conception of human nature, run along similar lines to Freud. But in the case of *A Severed Head* Freudian allusions are placed there deliberately to establish a specific context to help the reader interpret the events in the novel. The novel comes from a period, the early 1960s, when Murdoch seems to me to be at her most 'Freudian'. A. S. Byatt has said that *A Severed Head* wears its Freudianism 'sceptically' (Byatt 1991: 33). But although it does show psychoanalysis to be a dangerous tool in the hands of a miscreant like Palmer Anderson, the fact is that this novel is far less agnostic about psychoanalysis than a later work like *The Black Prince*, which, as we have seen, incorporates a psychoanalytical reading but is careful to expose this as reductive. In *A Severed Head* the invitation to interpret psychoanalytically functions less ironically; it is not limited to the predilections of one character but carries the endorsement, as it were, of the author. This is most easily demonstrable by considering the knowing way in which it sets up a psychoanalytic framework. The twin themes of the castration-complex and mother-fixation (which I shall say more about in due course) are made central in the novel by a layering of suggestive references. For example, Martin has an Oedipal dream in which he is about to penetrate with a phallic sword a conflated image of his mother, Honor and his sister when the restraining figure of his father arrives. The psychoanalytic connection is also explicitly foregrounded by comments made by the characters. Martin's brother Alexander, a sculptor who specializes in heads, explains this obsession by directing him to 'Freud on Medusa. The head can represent the female genitals, feared not desired' (*SH* 44).

This is a neatly suggestive comment, though frequently, as when Martin tells Honor that his mother-fixation dictated his choice of wife (*SH* 114), such examples conform more to the Jamesian notion of telling rather than showing, and remind us that at the time of *A Severed Head* Murdoch is still struggling between her instinct for didactic patterning and her desire for a looser, more character-centred version of form. This is not the case in *A Word Child*, which comes from a period where Murdoch is at the height of her powers.[2] Yet there is more to explain this novel's dearth of psychoanalytic references, explicit or implicit, than simply the question of an author becoming more skilful in her craft. I spoke earlier of Murdoch's ambivalent attitude towards Freud and would guess that by the time she wrote this novel she had distanced her own thought from Freud's, with the result that the psychoanalytic aspects of her fiction had become distilled into an altogether more ironic treatment. (This too will be significant later in the chapter.) Nevertheless although it seems clear that reference to Freud has been avoided just as studiously in *A Word Child* as it is carefully built into *A Severed Head*, the effect of this novel also depends upon a strongly psychoanalytic framework. As well as a general concern with the relationship between real and symbolic, both novels explore an obsessive concern with the past in a way which resembles the psychoanalytic approach to *repetition*.

Repetition, as the title of one of the most significant of Lacan's series of seminars indicates, is one of the 'fundamental concepts of psychoanalysis' (Lacan 1986: 17–66). I have already made the link between Murdoch's use of repetition and its importance in psychoanalysis, but here it is worth dwelling further on the notion of the 'compulsion to repeat'. Our tendency to repeat the most traumatic events in our lives, and even paradoxically take pleasure in them led Freud, in one of his most controversial theses, to postulate the existence of the death drive, a force that works in opposition to the pleasure principle, and demonstrates the need of the human organism to *return* to a state of inactivity (Freud 1986: 229). Thus, Freud could claim that the aim of all life was death. The compulsion to repeat springs from deeper within the soul than the pleasure principle: it seems 'more primitive, more elementary, more instinctual than the pleasure principle which it overrides' (Freud 1986: 232). At this point we are reminded once again of the affinity between the

Freudian and Murdochian understanding of the soul, a link embodied in Palmer Anderson, the charlatan psychoanalyst in *A Severed Head*, who could almost be speaking for his author when he remarks

> The psyche is a strange thing [...] and it has its own mysterious methods of restoring a balance. It automatically seeks its advantage, its consolation. It is almost entirely a matter of mechanics, and mechanical models are the best to understand it with. (*SH* 31)

It is the repetitive patterning of this machine working within them which strikes Murdoch's characters when they become possessed by their own myth. There is something powerful and other-worldly about this: as Neil Hertz reminds us, the 'demonic' nature of the repetition-compulsion is created 'not by being reminded of whatever it is that is repeated' but by 'being reminded of the repetition compulsion' itself (Hertz 1985: 101). In the protagonists of *A Severed Head* and *A Word Child* the experience of falling in love induces this distinctive inertia. In each case there is the sense that this love is waiting to happen, a sensation which should of course alert each hero to the fact that it owes more to the projection of internal wishes than external chance. Instead, ironically they feel that this epiphanic realization promises escape from their normal selfish state of being, when in fact it is just an intensification of it. Or, in Murdoch's own phrase, 'an unexamined sense of the strength of the machine is combined with the illusion of jumping out of it' (*SG* 42). Reflecting on his loss of Antonia, Martin imagines he requires, as salvation, 'some colossal and powerful love such as I had never known before' (*SH* 54). Similarly, after Gunnar's reappearance Hilary describes himself as a 'waiting machine' (*WC* 189). Both heroes are struck, after recognizing their love, by how *true* this state of mind feels, how, in Martin's words, it has 'utterly to do with me' (*SH* 126): 'I was chosen, and relentlessly, not choosing. Yet this very image brought home the insanity of my position. I was chosen, but by whom or what?' (*SH* 124). Such feelings are not surprising, for both men have been 'chosen' by the power of their own psyches. This experience of love, as so often in Murdoch, is based on enchantment and self-dramatization rather than selfless attention. It takes place at the level of what Lacan calls the imaginary: each man identifies with an image *he* has invested with libidinal energy, but which he mistakes for its essence. As Murdoch observes in *The Fire and the Sun*, we have a tendency, when in love, to 'de-realize the other, devour and absorb him, subject him to the mechanism of our own fantasy' (*FS* 36).

While repetitive patterning, then, is a dominant feature in Murdoch's fiction as a whole, both in terms of plot (especially in the retrospective novels) and character, it is particularly important to *A Severed Head* and *A Word Child*. It provides us with a powerful insight into the peculiar hold the past has on Murdoch's characters; the two heroes, for different reasons, find it impossible both to escape the past and to understand it. The compulsion to repeat is most clearly the driving force behind *A Word Child*, where the entire plot revolves around the unfolding of a terrible repetition-compulsion. Many years after being responsible for the death of his Oxford friend Gunnar Jopling's wife, Hilary Burde then falls dangerously in love with his second wife and eventually becomes partly responsible for her death too. But repetition of a more disguised but no less resonant kind also features strongly in *A Severed Head*, and it is to this novel I want to turn first.

The textual uncanny: *A Severed Head*

Whatever our response to *A Severed Head* – amusement, infuriation, pleasure – it is likely to come from its use of repetition. Antonia's announcement at the beginning of the novel that she is leaving Martin for Palmer sets in motion a bizarre catalogue of couplings among the cast of characters, where, as has frequently been acknowledged, almost every permutation is tried out. The way this works testifies to the importance of repetition in interpreting any narrative: what initially seems contingent is in fact revealed to be part of a pattern which we can then understand. In the case of *A Severed Head* the recurrence of what is at first shocking causes us to revise our early opinion of the novel as, say, an exercise in realism and to regard its significance as more allegorical – as a social satire, perhaps, or a 'Freudian comedy'. Yet it is beneath the plot, at a more symbolic level, that repetition functions most powerfully in *A Severed Head*. It is informed throughout by a particular manifestation of the compulsion to repeat, the uncanny: the phenomenon whereby a familiar but repressed fear resurfaces in an unfamiliar way – when, in the words of Jean Laplanche and J.-B. Pontalis, 'qualities, feelings, wishes, objects, which the subject refuses to recognize or rejects in himself are expelled from the self and located in another person or the environment' (Laplanche and Pontalis 1981: 66).

The concept is relevant to Murdoch's work as a whole. Her use of fantasy could be categorized as uncanny in the sense in which Tzvetan Todorov uses the term, to describe fantastic elements which most probably originate from the preoccupations of a particular character's mind (Todorov 1973).

We might consider as examples the appearances of the sea monster in *The Sea, the Sea* (another novel in which repetition is a major theme) which represents Charles Arrowby's jealousy, or the scene in *The Good Apprentice* where Edward Baltram appears to come upon his missing father floating underwater in a stream. Yet *A Severed Head* contains such a concentration of uncanny episodes and images that it seems certain it is designed to explore the uncanny directly.[3] This results in a number of explicit pointers – the kind of heavy-handed references I noted earlier, as on the occasion when Martin comments that Honor's sudden appearance 'had something of the uncanny' (*SH* 72). But the uncanny is woven into the fabric of the text in more subtly suggestive ways too. The title itself is included by Freud in a list of things which 'have something peculiarly uncanny about them': 'dismembered limbs, a severed head, a hand cut off by the wrist [. . .], feet which dance by themselves' (Freud 1990: 347).[4] What these examples have in common is precisely what unnerves and thrills those characters in Murdoch's novels about the mechanics of their psyche – the quality of 'independent activity in action' (Freud 1990: 366) which comes from something the subject knows well, being expressed in an unfamiliar way.

The novel continually evokes the image of the severed head – playfully, but in ways which are faithful to Freud's definition. Alexander has produced a version of Antonia's head which ominously suggests to Martin how she would appear to another man in love with her. Georgie, feeling rejected by Martin, sends him a box full of her hair, which she has cut off in despair before taking an overdose. As he opens the package and sees the hair, Martin – and the reader – is shocked, believing her severed head lies underneath. But the uses of the eponymous image increase with the arrival of Honor Klein, the novel's most uncanny character. Soon after she appears on the scene she leans out of Martin's car window in the fog, her body jolting beside him 'like a headless sack'. He is disconcerted by her ghostly habit of following him with her eyes but not moving her head. She makes one of the most significant gestures in a novel of stylized theatrical flourishes, when she offers a dazzling demonstration of her expertise with a large ornamental Samurai sword which hangs on the wall (*SH* 96–8).[5] As she performs, Martin reflects on the weapon's use in Japan for decapitation, and instinctively crosses his legs in order to feel less uncomfortable.

The fear of castration is of key importance in *A Severed Head*, and not only because this is what the severed head ultimately signifies in Freudian theory. In her discussion of the novel in *Degrees of Freedom* A. S. Byatt reflects that Martin has a 'quite complex character', but which is obscured by the crystalline nature of the novel. '[I]f we look too closely', she says, 'we may even see that the study of Martin's *character* would lead us to require to explore a quite different situation from the one we are given to contemplate as the logical conclusion of the "enslavement" and "liberation" themes' (Byatt 1965: 201). A close look at Martin's character reveals that he is driven by an intense desire to control his world and the people around him. In this respect, *A Severed Head* tells of how this power is systematically stripped away from him. When we first encounter him, professionally and privately Martin enjoys a role as lord over all he surveys. Before long, though, his wife has revealed that she has been having an affair with her psychoanalyst (Palmer), he finds out she also had a long-standing relationship with his brother, and realizes, moreover, that his sister has known about this all along. Slowly but surely he is made to realize that he is merely on the periphery of a larger world outside his own ego. His metaphorical impotence soon becomes physical, and he realizes that even his business can function without him. Martin is forced, like Freud's ego, to accept that he is no longer master in his own house. But the decline does not end there. The disruption of order in his personal affairs is only the first of the two central crises which make up Martin's story. So far he has managed to maintain a certain civilized dignity while his comfortable life has been dismantled all around him. But this is about to change too, because his *internal* world soon becomes violently upset as he falls in love with Palmer's sister Honor Klein.

If we confine ourselves to the character of its hero, then, *A Severed Head* tells a story of disempowerment. It is interesting that the eponymous image offers a kind of short-hand version of this reading of the text. After Antonia's departure, Martin's position as head of his 'kingdom' is first of all usurped. Then his head's role as ruler of the body – the dominance of the rational mind over the emotions – is undermined when he falls for Honor Klein. But this comparison has to do with more than just rhetoric. In Freudian terms the severed head primarily denotes castration and this is again knowingly conveyed by the metaphorical texture of the novel. Our discomfort at manifestations of the uncanny – specifically the 'bodily' uncanny, those parts which remain animate despite being separated from the whole – originates, Freud suggests, in the fear of castration and the fantasy of 'inter-uterine existence' (Freud 1990: 366–7). He points to the fear aroused in the male by the myth of Medusa (mentioned twice in *A Severed Head*), which 'occurs when a boy, who has hitherto been unwilling to believe the threat of castration, catches sight of the female genitals, probably those of an adult, surrounded by hair, and essentially those of his mother' (Freud 1974: 273). We find the uncanny unnerving because it is suggestive of an inability to control our environment; by provoking the fear of physical castration, it represents metaphorical *impotence*.

It is in this light, then, that we can consider those numerous instances of the uncanny in *A Severed Head* which suggest metaphorical decapitation. One of the most important is Honor's designation of herself as 'a severed head such as primitive tribes and old alchemists used to use. [...] And who knows but that long acquaintance with a severed head might not lead to strange knowledge' (*SH* 182). As severed head, as Medusa, her significance to Martin is the 'phallic mother' whose sexuality is the source of fear and not desire: sex with her prompts connections with being swallowed up and emasculated, rather than gratification (Freud 1973: 53). The 'strange knowledge' she speaks of refers to incestuous desire – strange knowledge that is repeatedly suggested in other ways in the novel, in Alexander's comment about Freud on Medusa, for example, Martin's remark that 'a sculpted head alone seems to represent an unfair advantage, an illicit and incomplete relationship' (*SH* 44), or his dream featuring a sword, a severed head, and Palmer and Honor entwined.

Martin's fascination with incest goes hand in hand with another form of repetition-compulsion, his mother-fixation, which leads him throughout the novel to transfer maternal characteristics on to various others. He notes, for example, how Alexander resembles his mother: it is he who 'plays her role' and is thus 'the real head of the family' (*SH* 39). The piece Alexander is currently working on, in fact, and which reminds Martin of 'something sad and frightening', turns out to be a replica of the head of the family herself. 'I recalled her clearly', he says, 'with a sad shudder of memory, and with that particular painful thrilling guilty sense of being both stifled and protected with which a return to my old home always afflicted me' (*SH* 162). The association with a symbolic return to the womb is particularly rich here because of the explicit link with homecoming, a central idea in Freud's theory of the uncanny, the *unheimlich*.[6] Martin is well aware that his attitude towards his mother has dictated his choice of wife (Antonia is an older woman who has sometimes been mistaken for his mother and is given to calling him 'my child') but does not fully register that the powerful psychic myth of mother-fixation is also what attracts him about Honor in her role as Medusa. As phallic mother, she represents what Lacan calls 'the Thing', the forbidden object of incestuous desire. This symbolic role is emphasized when the *literally* incestuous affair she has with Palmer is revealed. Surprising them in bed, Martin reacts just like the child spoken of by

Freud who stumbles upon his parents having sex: 'How naïvely had I imagined that Honor must be free; I had even, it now occurred to me, imagined that she must be virgin: that I would be her conqueror and her awakener' (*SH* 131). It is quite natural that he should fall so extremely for this person. But as a replica of his mother, there is more of a threatening edge to her than there could ever be with Antonia. The closer he gets to her the closer he gets to his forbidden desire: he loves her but at any moment she may devour him. A key factor in the subject's integration in the symbolic order is the setting in place of the incest taboo, in the form of the Oedipus complex. In transgressing this rule – in affirming, as Lévi-Strauss famously put it, that incest is 'bad grammar' – Honor again figures as the eruption of the real in the symbolic.

Although uncanny repetition (in the form of the castration complex and incestuous desire) functions mainly at a shadowy half-conscious level in Martin, at times he is more consciously aware of the recurrence of certain events. At one point, for example, he experiences 'a sudden repetition' of a feeling that Palmer and Antonia want him 'out of the way' (*SH* 160). He notices 'something vaguely reminiscent' when Antonia pours the rest of her wine into his glass when about to tell of her affair with Alexander (*SH* 186), because it is the same gesture she makes before revealing her love for Palmer (*SH* 22). But more significant are the occasions when Martin frequently replays in his mind crucial 'setpiece' scenes involving Honor. For instance, her demonstration with the Samurai sword recurs in his thoughts on several occasions (e.g. *SH* 100).

Another of these dramatic episodes, his struggle with Honor in the cellar, is particularly rich in *narrative* connotation, and is illuminating as a result. What it suggests I think is that the instances of the uncanny in *A Severed Head* are paralleled by the way the novel works *as* narrative. Repetition is central to both psychoanalysis and fiction for similar reasons: both are essentially about constructing narrative accounts of past events. It seems natural, then, that the psychoanalytical understanding of the motivations behind repetition in the psyche can teach us something about repetition in narrative.

This logic lies behind the psychoanalytic slant Peter Brooks has brought to narrative theory. He suggests that the patterns of repetition in certain 'texts of compulsive recurrence' resemble the involuntary return of a particular trauma in the psyche (Brooks 1992: 99).[7] Other critics have shown how Freud's work on the uncanny can illuminate the act of writing itself, how, in the words of Elizabeth Wright, the uncanny is writing which 'reveals or conceals unconscious intention' (Wright 1984: 137). A particularly inventive version of this is offered in Marjorie

Garber's *Shakespeare's Ghostwriters*, where she describes the psychoanalytic patient's involuntary repetition of what has been repressed from his or her past as 'restaging or replaying' (Garber 1987: 14). Her intention is to explain the function of the ghosts in Shakespeare's plays by linking theatre with the return of the repressed, but her comparison applies equally well to first-person retrospective narrative, by its very nature of course a repetition of the past. In *A Severed Head* Martin *replays* a crucial period of his past by writing about it. He does so, as I remarked before, without referring extensively to the act of narration, nor commenting once on his motives for narrating. He is simply compelled to narrate.

This is particularly clear in the evocative cellar-scene. Many scenes in the novel are memorable, but here Martin's powerful rhetoric is compounded by the urgency of his tone. He speaks directly to the reader – unusual in this book – imploring him or her to believe that what he tells is true: 'What happened next may seem a little improbable, but the reader must just believe me that it did occur.' His use, twice, of the phrase 'in retrospect' (*SH* 111, 121–2) suggests that he has replayed the scene many times since the original and has built up an interpretation of it. It ensures that the reader constructs the event in his or her imagination from a different angle. Our viewpoint is elevated to a position where we do not just experience the situation as Martin originally did, through his eyes, but witness him in the process of recollecting the scene. To use a cinematic analogy, we do not view the episode as if we held the camera recording the action, but through the lens of a secondary camera recording the scene *as it is being interpreted*. Only when this happens in *A Severed Head* does the form of narration resemble the more 'dissonant' first-person novels, like *Under the Net* and *The Black Prince*, where the narrating self is foregrounded. Then we are aware that Martin is no longer just acting in the scene but observing it as well.

The phrase 'in retrospect' is used again two chapters later as he replays the scene once more:

> But I recalled the scene itself even with a certain satisfaction: satisfaction mingled with some more obscure and disturbing emotions. I kept returning with wonderment to the thought that I had now *touched* her: 'touched' was putting it mildly, given what had happened. But it seemed, perhaps for that very reason, almost implausible in retrospect; and although I could picture her face screwed up with pain and fury, although I could see her black oily hair rolling in the dust and hear her gasp as I twisted her arm further, I could not altogether recall any sense of the contact of my flesh with hers. (*SH* 121–2)

His concentration on a certain aspect – here the importance of physical contact, the breaking of a taboo – prompts a comparison with the novelist's (or film director's) capacity to foreground a particular part of his or her material and underline it as especially important. From this point on, this kind of retrospective reflection – what Genette calls 'repeating analepses', or 'the narrative's allusions to its own past' (Genette 1980: 54) – is increasingly conspicuous. Martin uses the phrase 'in retrospect' on three further occasions as he recalls crucial scenes: Honor and Palmer in bed (*SH* 138), his attack on Palmer (*SH* 164) and his car journey with Honor after collecting her from the station (*SH* 179). He is curious about a similar reflective urge in Antonia: 'Now the taboo had been broken Antonia could talk of nothing but Palmer, endlessly remaking her relationship with him retrospectively' (*SH* 169).

Early in the novel Martin remembers a rash hint he once made to Georgie that they may one day marry, and comments: 'These remarks had had no sequel, but they remained between us as a text which must some day be revised, ratified or at least explained' (*SH* 20). The literary analogy is particularly appropriate in a novel where repetition *in* the story (at the level of events) is paralleled by repetition *of* story (the text itself functions as replay). This overall pattern is prefigured in miniature when, immediately after the cellar-scene, Martin replays it again but this time actually in the form of literature. He composes three draft letters to Honor into which he puts 'more intellectual effort...than I had expended since I wrote *Sir Eyre Coote and the Campaign of Wandewash*' (*SH* 117). These contain various interpretations of his own character – he calls them 'implausible hypotheses about the state of my psyche' (*SH* 115) – which indicate the kind of self-consciousness normally noticeable only by its absence from his narration. (It is in these letters that Martin addresses directly the question of his mother-fixation.) The mention of his book is notable, too, for his passion for history reflects a desire to recapture the past – as, incidentally, do the professions of Palmer the psychoanalyst and his sister the anthropologist.

Where this kind of self-consciousness would herald enlightenment in the case of the dissonant narrator, here the pattern of the past is too powerful to be destroyed. Instead of respecting the contingent, Martin turns to an artistic process which promises to allow him to control the contingent factors which have left him impotent. He has already expressed his envy for the '*technique* for discovering more about what is real' (*SH* 43) which sculpting gives Alexander. He once dominated his immediate environment; writing a novel about his past will enable him to regain this power. In contrast to Palmer, who has informed him on his departure that he feels no need to provide a 'commentary' on what has taken place, Martin *does* require a commentary, as *A Severed Head* proves. There are some things which he cannot understand. When he falls in love with Honor, Martin realizes that 'although I could not yet trace it out I could feel like steel the pattern of which this and only this could have been the outcome' (*SH* 124). His need to 'trace out' the pattern, and by doing so control it, is what leads him to write the novel. He may not 'yet' be able to do so, but he will try when he writes. This urge is, incidentally, one way to account for the importance of mythology in *A Severed Head*. Mythology becomes a symbol in itself to inform the reader that Martin is tracing out, replaying, his own kind of psychic myth. He takes to reading mythology, and also *The Golden Bough*, in order to satisfy his need for information on incest.[8] But there is perhaps another reason for his research. He is discovering associations between his own story and Greek mythology which will allow him to present his own myth more persuasively. For this reason there are a bewildering number of allusions to Greek mythology in *A Severed Head*.[9]

Martin's narrative comes into existence because he is compelled to repeat experiences which have left a profound impression upon him. This compulsion verifies Palmer's view that the psyche 'automatically seeks ... consolation' (*SH* 31). In other words, balance is restored by the compulsion to repeat: if a vital focus of psychic energy – an object of desire, for example – is absent, it will be 'recreated' by the process of transference. But more pertinently, repetition also promises to transform impotence into power. As Freud realized upon fathoming the famous '*fort/da*' game, where he witnessed his grandson overcoming the pain of his mother's departure by making a passive experience active, the act of repetition can enable the subject to achieve a kind of mastery over an unpleasant situation, the need for which originates in the psyche's desire to 'follow its own path to death' (Freud 1986: 247). Brooks sees this insight as a 'suggestive comment on the grammar of plot, where repetition, taking us back again over the same ground, could have to do with the choice of ends' (Brooks 1992: 98). Martin's need to write about the past can be regarded in this light; his narrative allows him to re-enact unpleasurable experiences and gain some degree of control over them. Lacan's reading of the '*fort/da*' game characteristically emphasizes its linguistic nature: the game foregrounds the question of signification, as the child moves from 'the lived experience of the Real' to focus first on an object (the cotton-reel he plays with) and then on language (the words 'fort' and 'da') (Lemaire 1977: 52). His narrative functions in a similar way, providing a way of signifying what initially escapes signification.

Martin's replaying of the past in narrative is a form of repetition less involuntary and unnerving than the uncanny, but repeating in order to master remains more instinctive than full recollection. Nevertheless, although the replaying of the past owes more to compulsion than choice, he is still *conscious* of a desire to write. We can be sure of this, despite the absence of references to the epic situation or direct reflections on the writing process, for we have been given clues from the outset that Martin is capable of writing an autobiographical narrative. Displaying a comic sense of self-aggrandizement typical of Murdoch's first-person narrators, he likens himself to 'a cross between the philosopher Hume and the actor Garrick'. He relishes the reputation of 'having become morose, something of a recluse, something indeed of a philosopher and cynic, one who expects little and watches the world go by'. In other words, he describes himself as a familiar kind of artist-figure. Of course, having composed the narrative in which these words appear, he is safe in the knowledge that he *is* something of an artist. Despite the domestic upheaval depicted in the story, one cherished item of furniture has remained present, as if waiting in the wings for its grand entrance. The Carlton House writing-table accompanies Martin as he moves from house to flat and back again, heralding the literary mission to come. Towards the beginning of the novel he informs the reader that 'The story which follows will reveal, whether I will or no, what sort of person I am' (*SH* 15). Despite his reluctance to probe deeply into his own character, his narrative proves him right.

Narrative exchange: *A Word Child*

Hilary Burde has much in common with Martin Lynch-Gibbon. Though he is much less charming, this is the result of careful affectation on his part – he has decided that his process of self-punishment must involve making himself as repugnant as possible. He is as obsessed with order as his predecessor is with power, organizing his life into a rigid routine. His unpleasantness does not prevent him from being cared for by people around him, though, and like Martin, he rules over the women in his life – his sister Crystal, his lover Tommy – with an iron hand. He allows his sister's lover Arthur to visit her every Thursday, until he himself 'removes' him, while Tommy is allowed to visit Crystal once a month, 'disappearing at my nod about ten past seven' (*WC* 57). Like the previous novel, the story of *A Word Child* on one level details the gradual breakdown of this ordered existence. Where Martin's wife leaves him, the catalyst for Hilary's decline is the return of the man whose wife he killed,

Gunnar Jopling, to become head of Hilary's department. Not long after the other characters who have for so long been under his coercive spell rebel against him: Tommy visits him at work despite being forbidden ever to do so, Arthur and Crystal get engaged. Even at work, where the mundane pointlessness of civil-service routine provides a comic counterpoint to the dedication to order in his personal life, he finds one day his workmates have moved his desk. His self-control collapses completely – like Martin's – when he falls dangerously in love with Lady Kitty, Gunnar's new wife. The novel ends when the sense of awful momentum built up in the plot delivers what it promises, as Hilary becomes partly responsible for her death.

In a more obvious way than *A Severed Head*, then, *A Word Child* shares with psychoanalysis the understanding that past trauma has an uncanny capacity to return. But a significant difference between the two novels is that where Martin tells his story in order to master the events which have left him powerless, when his novel begins, Hilary is already going through a process of repetition as mastery. He has chosen his strict daily régime precisely to prevent his past repeating itself. He has deliberately chosen not to pursue a potentially successful academic career in favour of the humdrum routine of the civil servant. Yet this response to the past is, in its own way, as much the product of fantasy as his belief that he has fallen in love with Kitty. (That there is something not quite right about her as love-object is suggested by her trademark perfume, which is remarked on wherever she goes.) Rather than see Anne's death as a terrible accident with which he must somehow cope, he views it as a judgement on himself. As Conradi perceptively points out, Hilary's 'crime', 'was not that he exonerated himself but rather that he puritanically made himself, like Lucifer, totally responsible' (Conradi 1989: 81). His determination to believe that his condition is unalterable leads to a tendency to over-dramatize it, suggested by his conviction, expressed in different ways, that 'Powers which I had offended were gathering to destroy me' (*WC* 89). Such behaviour is, again, in line with the Freudian notion of repetition-compulsion. His state of mind resembles the 'omnipotence of thought', which Freud regards as a manifestation of the uncanny, the feeling common to children and neurotics that what they wish or think will alter the course of real events (Freud 1990: 362).

The prominence of the repetition-compulsion in *A Word Child* means that detailed analysis of any Freudian subtext in the novel is superfluous. Suffice to say that the larger operation of the repetition-compulsion is paralleled in many more subtle ways throughout. Hilary has a 'mechanical and regular' Saturday row with the porter (*WC* 48) and his arguments with Tommy have a 'characteristic hopeless mechanical structure' (*WC* 43). One of his pastimes is riding aimlessly round the Circle line on the London Underground. There are also suggestions of the uncanny in the way in which the lives of Gunnar and Hilary are entwined. In an early encounter with Gunnar, Hilary says his name 'like someone calling to a ghost or speaking idly yet eloquently to the dead' (*WC* 204). It is clear that Gunnar is in a sense Hilary's double: he has been as obsessed with Hilary as Hilary is with him, harbouring fantasies of revenge.

Although *A Word Child* clearly invites a psychoanalytic reading, however, we must bear in mind that unlike *A Severed Head*, this owes little to any deliberate incorporation of psychoanalytical ideas by the author. Its audacious plot, as I argued previously, exemplifies the Murdochian aesthetic of the sublime, whereby pattern is used simultaneously, and paradoxically, to convey the sense of accident.[10] Of more conscious interest to Murdoch at this stage of her career is how we understand redemption in the absence of an appropriate religious metanarrative. All the while Hilary is superstitiously guarding against somehow reproducing his past, he is also able to analyse his situation in more level-headed terms:

> Did I repent? That question troubled me as the years went by. Can something half crushed and bleeding repent? Can that fearfully complex theological concept stoop down into the real horrors of human nature? Can it, without God, do so? I doubt it. Can sheer suffering redeem? It did not redeem me, it just weakened me further. (*WC* 126)

Appropriate here, too, is Conradi's view that Murdoch's fondness for repeating plots owes as much to the Buddhist concept of *karma* as to Freud: 'we pay for all we do, say and think, but not necessarily at once' (Conradi 1989: 81). Hilary's concern with payment is obsessive. He explains his delinquent childhood as the result of being born illegitimately: 'I hated the universe. I wanted to cause it pain in return for the pain it caused me' (*WC* 202).[11] Appropriately his job in the civil service is to deal 'with pay, not with the metaphysics of pay, but with its mechanics' (*WC* 6).

But while the treatment of the question of return in *A Word Child* demands to be seen in spiritual as well as Freudian terms, the theological treatment of redemption in the novel is also given a psychoanalytical twist. Hilary's dilemma is neatly summed up in his remark, made while agonizing over the possibility of redemption, that he 'would have been willing to pay, only I had nothing to pay with and there was no one to receive the payment' (*WC* 127). This reminds us of how central the idea of *exchange* is to the question of redemption. What can be redeemed, offered up in exchange, that can adequately make up for what happened in the past? And it is precisely this kind of exchange that psychoanalysis is particularly eloquent about. Central to the psychoanalytic process is the transference, a special kind of situation where the past is reproduced, but on a particular 'stage' constructed between analysand and analyst and which paves the way for repetition to become full recollection. In Lacanian terms (Lacan has much to say, of course, on the question of exchange in psychic life) transference allows past desire to be made present, and *re*-signified to ensure it remains past. Transference is all about presentation and representation of 'story', in other words. This has led Brooks to develop a transferential model to illuminate the dynamics of narrative. Like analysis, he suggests, narrative properly comes into being as a result of the interaction between teller and listener (reader); a story of the past is offered, which is incoherent and full of gaps and which must be interpreted by the listener and thereby made complete. In emphasizing the dialogic nature of the narrative process, Brooks envisages narrative as a process of *exchange*, a transaction, as he describes it, between teller and listener. It is a model he thinks applies to all narrative, though the transactive process itself is dramatized in particular texts.[12] *A Word Child*, I propose, is one such text.

For more than anything else, perhaps, *A Word Child* is a story about telling stories. At the heart of the plot is Lady Kitty's attempt to arrange a meeting between her husband and Hilary, which is really an attempt to engineer a effective narrative transaction: a psychoanalyst, she says, 'might not help him, but you might help him, and only you' (*WC* 170). Each man must tell his version of the story of Anne's death to the one narratee who can make it worthwhile, the other. No substitute will suffice, as is clear when we consider Hilary's efforts ever since the original tragedy to find someone to play the role of narratee. Soon after the accident he confesses everything to Crystal, but realizes later that this has done nothing but cause her misery too. Later he confides in Arthur ('because I had to tell somebody, I had to let the monstrous thing out of the sealed sphere which composed my consciousness and Crystal's' [*WC* 111]) but this attempt also fails. These efforts to narrate prove unsatisfactory because the wrong person is in the place of narratee, and because the story Hilary tells is incomplete: he keeps from Crystal the fact that Anne was pregnant when she died, and in telling Arthur, he 'omitted certain things, though nothing of importance, and I doubtless told it in a way which was sympathetic to myself' (*WC* 111). Part of Lady Kitty's attraction for him, by contrast, is that she knows everything. At one stage she seems likely to occupy the position of 'subject supposed to know' (Lacan's phrase for the position the analyst must come to occupy during the transference). 'I dare to say these things to you', he tells her, 'because of the extraordinary opportunity which you have, it seems knowingly, given me' (*WC* 221). This does not work either, however, partly because the telling takes place on a non-transferential stage (he writes to her), but also because he is by then involved in a different, more dangerous kind of transference: he is in love with Lady Kitty.

The importance of Hilary's need to tell his story is emphasized by the needs of other characters to tell theirs. He often wonders, for example, about the tale behind his friend Clifford's signet ring, a story which, it is likely, has something to do with his suicide towards the end of the novel. There is also ironic reference to the telling of secrets. Hilary begins to think that 'there were tales which Biscuit [the Joplings' servant] could tell' (*WC* 342) about her employers. Laura Impiatt, in typically melodramatic style, falsely 'reveals' to her husband that Hilary is in love with her while confessing herself to having a crush on his lodger, Christopher – to cover up an actual affair with the latter. This emphasis on storytelling has more than a thematic significance: it is essential to the dynamics of the plot. The ground on which *A Word Child* is fought, one might say, is stories. The dramatic highpoint of the novel is the scene in which Hilary tells a sceptical Crystal about his love for Lady Kitty. In response his sister reveals her own secret, about an encounter with Gunnar soon after Anne's death in which she lost her virginity, and in doing so breaks the 'tacit pact' which she and Hilary had formed, 'never to inquire, never to "go over" what had happened' (*WC* 249). The meaning of Crystal's story is crucial for the workings of the novel. Up until now, Hilary's misguided determination to preserve an ideal of 'goodness' in an otherwise persecutory world has led him always to take a perverse pride in Crystal's virginity. Her story means Gunnar and Hilary are in fact 'even': Gunnar has 'taken' Crystal from him as surely as he had taken Anne. It also appears to be a factor in Clifford's death, as he has derived perhaps even more comfort than Hilary from the fact of her virginity. His anger is directed towards the story itself as much as its contents. He shouts at Hilary, 'And – and – you shouldn't have told me!' (*WC* 359). But most importantly, telling her secret proves that Hilary's pact with Crystal is more damaging than protective: it is necessary for those traumatized by past events to talk about them.

Of the two proper meetings Hilary and Gunnar do eventually have, the first is entirely ineffective. Faced with Gunnar's extreme coldness, Hilary is reduced, as is his way, to making sarcastic remarks which conceal his real feelings. It dawns on him 'with a terrible final sense of despair, that really Gunnar did not want me to talk at all' (*WC* 265). The problem, in other words, is that this is not a true narrative *exchange*. Their second meeting, however, is more dialogic. Hilary is honest about the accident and his feelings for Anne, Gunnar is genuinely interested in him, and they are able to touch on the key moral questions about contingency and forgiveness which their situation raises. The result is significant:

> 'What a perfectly – extraordinary – negotiation –' Gunnar laughed. It was more like weeping. The big mouth opened and shut convulsively, a little saliva dribbled over the lip, the blue eyes closed as if in anguish. (*WC* 327)

A suitable narrative transaction seems to be on the point of being effected. But the story does not end there. Any therapeutic benefit Hilary might draw from this conversation is compromised by his love for Kitty. He is still, in other words, immersed in his fantasy world, a fact which is about to ensure the compulsion to repeat is played out. That this is still to come is suggested by Kitty's sudden appearance at the end of the transactive scene. Hilary notes that 'her dark hair was particularly Dionysian and glowing' – the only occasion in which her role resembles that of Honor Klein. Her appearance frightens and annoys him: 'There was something dangerously frivolous in this manifestation, in her evident wish to see these men together' (*WC* 328). The ominous tone is justified when a botched rendezvous between them soon after ends with her being drowned in the Thames, Hilary unable to save her.

A significant result of this second catastrophe is that Hilary's frustration at being unable to tell his story is increased. He notes that his involvement has gone unremarked: 'once again I had dropped out of the story as if I had never existed' (*WC* 377). While this might seem to be a source of relief because he avoids greater punishment, it is also a source of anguish for Hilary, for it limits his opportunities to tell his tale. Furthermore, his two longstanding confidants are unavailable. Clifford, who has functioned throughout as someone he can confess to (he is the only person besides Crystal who had known about Anne's death, until Hilary tells Arthur too), is dead. He decides not to tell Crystal this time to avoid burdening her with the pain. He feels that 'there was no one now to whom I could speak at all of the things which were hourly and minutely devouring my heart' (*WC* 379).

Yet there is of course one way he can tell of these things. Reflecting on the deaths of Kitty and Clifford as he sits in St Stephen's church, his thoughts turn to its erstwhile warden, T. S. Eliot. He too has 'vanished from the catalogue of being. But I could feel a lively gratitude for words, even for words whose sense I could scarcely understand' (*WC* 384). Hilary has earlier confessed that he has little concern for literature, and reads it only for the beauty of its linguistic structure. Here he is beginning to formulate an appreciation of its signifying potential. This developing awareness reminds us, I think, that Hilary is, after all, writing about his experience, a task which enables him at last to tell his story in full. Once we register this, we can look back at the novel retrospectively and consider that the relief brought by writing an account of the past is evident at certain junctures throughout – not least when he reaches the point where he must describe his affair with Anne:

> I will now tell the story which is at the centre of this story, and which it was necessary to delay until the moment when, in this story, I told it. I will tell it now, as far as it can be told by me, truthfully and as it was, and not as I told it that Friday night to Arthur. (*WC* 111)

The repetition here is clumsy but emphatic. Hilary's words remind us that his novel is born of the same impulse to tell of past trauma which sustains the 'talking cure' itself, with the reader placed in the position of analyst.

'Ambiguously ever after'

As much as it is about origins, psychoanalysis is concerned with endings. Its central aim, to evoke Brooks' emphasis on the link between psychic and narrative dynamics, is to provide an ending for the plot rather than to let it recur continually. When it comes to the ending of *A Severed Head* and *A Word Child*, both remain ambiguous. Whether each narrator is still compelled to repeat his past or has 'worked it through' is a moot point. As recent narrative theory stresses, retrospectivity is of key importance in making sense of narrative; to quote from Brooks again, 'only the end can finally determine meaning, close the sentence as a signifying totality' (Brooks 1992: 22).[13] If we apply this logic specifically to the first-person retrospective text, it follows that knowledge of the narrator's epic situation is required if we are to make full sense of the novel. And such knowledge, we recall, is lacking in *A Severed Head* and *A Word Child* (and also *The Italian Girl*) where the narrator does not acknowledge that he has written or is telling the account we read.[14] In effect, these novels are incomplete because we are unsure how exactly they end; it remains unclear just how the narrator has been affected by the experience he narrates.[15]

A Severed Head seems to end on a clear note of hope, with Martin on the point of beginning a new life with the object of his desire. Ostensibly, he has changed for the better. He is keen to impress upon us the fact that he is now worthy of Honor: 'An intoxicating sense possessed me that at last we were treating on equal terms' (*SH* 204). But, appropriately enough for a text so concerned with symbolic appearance, there is something patently false about this ending. This could be the result of Murdoch's failure to breathe life into Honor as anything other than a demonic icon. Yet there is something about the very fact that Martin ends the novel as Honor's partner that suggests his transformation is an illusion. He has chosen her not through any respect for her individuality – he does not *see* her as a separate person – but because he remains under the spell of his psychic machine. Or, to put it in more baldly Freudian terms: in choosing merely the latest in a line of mother-substitutes Martin does not conquer his castration-complex but remains driven by his mother-fixation. The unsatisfactory flavour of this conclusion is reinforced, it seems to me, in a significant feature of the last scene when Martin and Honor are reunited and plan a future together. Attention is repeatedly drawn to Honor's *gaze* (no less than eight references are made in the space of three pages [*SH* 202–5]). This, of course, recalls the Sartrean use of the Medusa myth to suggest how we become imprisoned in another person's definition of us.[16] In this light, the outcome to the novel casts serious doubt on Martin's freedom and future well-being. Murdoch underlines the uncertainty when, in the interview with Rose, she agrees that the pairing-up of characters at the end of the 'obsessional novels' is 'an *effect* of compulsion': 'In *A Severed Head* there's no resolution. Martin is just lucky – or is he lucky? – in his relationship to one of his enslavers' (Rose 1968).

A Word Child also ends, to use David Lodge's description of the post-modern fondness for open closures, 'ambiguously ever after' (Lodge 1986). In this case, we are not sure that the pairing-up will even occur, as it is unclear whether Hilary and Tommy will get married. Hilary does seem to have learned a typically Murdochian lesson about apprehending the reality of other people: he allows Crystal to be married and recognizes that he has neglected Clifford, a friend who had been in need of his help all along. He comes to understand that accident played an important part in both deaths, and that the real source of his guilt is, paradoxically, his determination to punish himself completely for what he did by living a mediocre life. Against these indications that Hilary might now be ready to change, however, must be set the fact that throughout the novel he inhabits his previous self with so very few – almost no – proleptic glimpses into a transformed later self. There is little evidence, in other words, that he wishes to distance himself from his earlier behaviour. Seldom does he let fall the ironic, cynical mask of his prose. On several occasions – for example, when he realizes that he has hurt Arthur by cruelly mocking Crystal in his presence – he expresses regret at acting in a particular way, but his regret seems to have been felt at the time of the story and not after.

Nor is there any guarantee that marriage will amount to salvation. The conventional signifiers of joy which operate in the closing scenes (Christmas-time, a wedding, the prospect of a baby) are offset by Hilary's obvious discomfort, and also by the fact that the novel contains such a strong internal critique of the Christian concept of salvation. As in the case of *A Severed Head*, Murdoch has explicitly stated that an open ending was her intention. At Caen, in one of her few published reflections upon the novel (and her only discussion of the first-person form), she admits at first that she regrets not making 'Hilary's telling of the story itself into part of the story' before concluding that the resulting ambiguity is actually quite appropriate:

> I felt myself that the end was meant to be unresolved: whether Hilary would find any sort of salvation, either by himself or with Tommy, or whether he would fall back into some hopeless kind of repetition of what had happened, so that the next twenty years of his life might resemble the twenty years which are described in the book. (Caen 1978)

That both novels effectively end on a suspended chord is in keeping with the spirit of narrative transference – not to mention in keeping with the psychoanalytic session. It is left to the reader to interpret, to choose between the possibilities, or to consider new ones. Like *The Black Prince*, both texts bear out Brooks' conviction of 'the dialogic relation of narrative production and interpretation' (Brooks 1994: 50), ensuring that the full significance of the narrator's experiences – whether he is able to recollect or simply go on repeating – rests somewhere in a dialogic interzone between text and reader.

7

The Ambivalence of Coming Home: *The Italian Girl* and *The Sea, the Sea*

> To identify oneself absolutely with oneself, to identify one's 'I' with the 'I' that I tell is as impossible as to lift oneself up by one's hair.
>
> Mikhail Bakhtin, *Mikhail Bakhtin: The Dialogical Principle*

The Italian Girl and *The Sea, the Sea* have less obviously in common than the other pairs of novels we have considered. They are worlds apart in terms of critical appraisal: one is almost universally agreed to be Murdoch's weakest novel, the other stands as the Booker Prize-winning peak of her 'great decade', the seventies. *The Italian Girl* more closely resembles the obsessional 'closed-up' books *A Severed Head* and *A Word Child*. It is an uncanny Gothic tale narrated in an anachronistic voice which more often seems like a pastiche of Poe than anything convincing in its own right. All of its characters seem caught up in a collective delusion. As Isabel remarks, 'We are all prisoners here. We are like people in an engraving' (*IG* 41). *The Sea, the Sea*, on the other hand, is closer to *Under the Net* and *The Black Prince*. It is a novel written by an 'artist' self-consciously engaged in a quest into the past to find truth, both circumstantial and metaphysical. Charles Arrowby, its hero, displays an epistemophilia which is at times more pronounced than that of his predecessors as he tries desperately to make sense of events going on around him and to unravel the 'terrible mystery' of why his first love left him. Yet for all their dissimilarity, I think there is something in both novels that is largely absent in the others, and which is central to Murdoch's work as a whole: the sense of nostalgia.

Nostalgia features elsewhere in Murdoch's fiction, as I have argued. It is movingly present in the 'dream parrot' episodes in *The Book and the Brotherhood*, works as a motivating force behind her concern with spiritual vacancy or the state of the novel, and also appears in her work in a more reactionary way, as an implicit uneasiness about the modern world. The term 'nostalgia' tends perhaps to be used most often in a derogatory sense, to suggest an overburdened attachment to the past. This accounts for its presence in critiques of a dominant mode of postmodernism, what Fredric Jameson calls 'the pastiche of the stereotypical past' (Jameson 1991: 21).

Yet we should not, I think, underestimate the positive value of nostalgia as a literary mood. It is, after all, at the centre of one of the greatest and most influential achievements of the century, Proust's fictional exploration of 'involuntary memory'. While not entirely synonymous with the Proustian concept, nostalgia is also brought on typically by accident, when something occurs which causes the mind to jump backwards to a significant time or place. As a particular form of melancholy triggered specifically by the feeling of being absent from home (a sense suggested by its Greek roots: *nóstos*, return home; *álgos*, pain) nostalgia is a profound emotional and creative force.[1] It is thus a kind of flipside to the uncanny: where one involves an unwilling return to a forgotten home, the other is the desire to return to an inaccessible home. The uncanny is where the familiar resurfaces in an unfamiliar way, nostalgia is where unfamiliarity activates the desire to bring about the familiar. In exploring both kinds of homecoming, *The Italian Girl* and *The Sea, the Sea* foreground the two distinctive ways in which past is made present in Murdoch's fiction, especially her first-person novels: the return to the past, and the return *of* the past. As in *A Severed Head* and *A Word Child*, the past re-emerges as uncanny recurrence; as in *The Black Prince* and *Under the Net*, both novels are to some extent driven by the deliberately backward-looking energy of the epistemological quest.

A strange memory: *The Italian Girl*

The Italian Girl begins with Edmund Narraway's return home after the death of his mother. Coming back to his childhood home involves a psychological return to his childhood, and the anguish and excitement he felt then, particularly as a result of the suffocating love of his mother. It is a situation which recalls Freud's description of the uncanny as a kind of homecoming, a familiar yet unfamiliar experience. Soon after his arrival Edmund enters the room where his mother's corpse lies, and cannot dispel an eerie feeling that she may not be dead after all. Her long hair seems 'vital still, as if the terrible news had not yet come to it. It seemed even to move a little at my entrance, perhaps in a slight draught from the door' (*IG* 27). As Edmund looks upon the 'live, still burnished hair' (*IG* 20) he reflects that she 'had got inside me, into the depths of my being, there was no abyss and no darkness where she was not' (*IG* 19). This sense of the uncanny is accompanied, as it is in *A Severed Head*, by numerous instances of replay. There has been a constant stream of Italian housekeepers for as long as Edmund can remember, so that 'they were indeed all, in our minds, so merged and generalized that it seemed as if there had always ever been only one Italian girl' (*IG* 22). Edmund's eventual decision to begin a new life with the latest version, a calm, wise, older woman called Maggie, resembles Martin Lynch-Gibbon's final inability to escape the compulsion to repeat by ending up with Honor Klein. As one of the chapter headings – 'Edmund Runs to Mother' – emphasizes rather heavy-handedly, this outcome means Edmund too has decided on nothing other than a mother-substitute.

Deborah Johnson has described *The Italian Girl* as 'a poetic curiosity, a "severed head"' (Johnson 1987: 35), and indeed it does at times seem to be little more than a replay of its predecessor. Themes central to and fully developed in *A Severed Head* are reanimated unconvincingly in *The Italian Girl*. There are, for example, echoes of the Medusa legend (Isabel's 'shorn-off' hair and Maggie's 'severed' ponytail [*IG* 154]), which serve no function other than to recall – uncannily – the previous novel. It stands as something of a 'problem-novel' within Murdoch's fiction, in that there is a question about when it was written. Elizabeth Dipple has suggested, plausibly I think, that it is a resurrection of an early novella. This would certainly explain why Murdoch, who by 1964 had already published some very assured fiction (*Under the Net, The Bell, A Severed Head*) should suddenly fall so far below par. *The Italian Girl* fails to blend convincingly the issues which dominate her philosophy (like the role of the contingent and the desire to be good) with the plot and characterization. Frequently she leaves it to the utterances of the characters and the narrator to provide an insight into the myth behind the story and the personalities of the people within. The result is that the dialogue – usually one of her strengths even in less successful novels – buckles under the weight of this responsibility. One curious result of the novel's defectiveness is that there is a crucial ambiguity about how much Murdoch intends and how much she does not, a factor which must affect any interpretation of the novel. Johnson has remarked that 'it is never clear how far the author is in collusion with [Edmund]. He lacks the rhetorical presence of Iris Murdoch's other dramatised narrators and has no clear relationship (of complicity or otherwise) with his readers' (Johnson 1987: 30–1).

Yet his rhetorical absence is also peculiarly appropriate for someone so unsure of his identity and seen by all around him as withdrawn. We might put his strange quality of detachment down to the 'rapacious violence' (*IG* 17) of his mother's devouring attentions. In common with many Murdoch characters (Charles Arrowby, for example) Edmund notes with distaste 'female' symbols such as open mouths (*IG* 79), and regards married people as 'obscene animals' (*IG* 107). His prudishness is the source of comedy later on, as Murdoch makes him seek comfort in Maggie's kitchen while a huge pair of Otto's underpants dry above his head. But there is another explanation for his inability to inhabit himself properly. Edmund's detachment is suggestive of melancholia, the condition brought on, in clinical terms, by a need to mourn the separation from the mother, and which is characterized, as Julia Kristeva says, by those 'states of withdrawal in which the subject takes refuge to the point of inaction'. And the particular form of melancholy Edmund exhibits is nostalgia. Kristeva makes clear the affinity between the two conditions:

> Riveted to the past, regressing to the paradise or inferno of an unsurpassable experience, melancholy persons manifest a strange memory: everything has gone by, they seem to say, but I am faithful to those bygone days, I am nailed down to them, no revolution is possible, there is no future. (Kristeva 1989: 60)

Edmund is 'riveted to the past', longing to remove himself altogether from the adult world.

One of the fascinating things about *The Italian Girl* is that its very flawed quality allows themes worked elsewhere more skilfully, more subtly into the texture of Murdoch's fiction, to emerge in a more naked form. Something similar is observable, to a lesser extent, in *Under the Net*, an extraordinarily accomplished first novel (particularly in comparison with *The Italian Girl*) but which contains an odd moment near the end where Jake's voice slides from its characteristic jaunty picaresque register to something more lofty and gnomic:

> So we live; a spirit that broods and hovers over the continual death of time, the lost meaning, the unrecaptured moment, the unremembered face, until the final chop that ends all our moments and plunges the spirit back into the void from which it came. (*UN* 244)

Jake at this point has just recognized his potential as a writer of high literature, but this passage seems to represent more than simply a desire to try out his new vocation. We can detect the trace of some other voice in his words (Bryan Appleyard thinks these lines display 'a rhetoric which would have been unthinkable in tone and manner to many of her contemporaries' [Appleyard 1990: 160]) and it is a profoundly nostalgic one, aware of the elegiac power of prose. Murdoch's facility with the elegiac mode is what emerges strongly in *The Italian Girl*, in the form of Edmund's longing to return to the absent world of his childhood, a desire which is in turn revisited in greater depth in *The Sea, the Sea*. It is also a desire which is hardly felt in *A Severed Head*, and advances this strange novel's case to be read as more than simply an offcut from its predecessor.

Edmund's anguish at having left childhood behind is conveyed less lyrically or directly than in *The Sea, the Sea*. Instead, appropriately enough for a novel bearing the stamp of Murdoch's 'Freudian period', it is suggested by a form of transference. Edmund conflates the idea of himself as a child with that of his niece, Flora (whose name appropriately suggests the blossoming of youth), whom he persistently refers to as 'child' even though she is old enough to be pregnant. Richard Todd has suggested that Edmund 'seems obscurely to desire' her (Todd 1984: 58) and while there is truth in this, far stronger is the suggestion that his desire is for a return to the state of childhood which Flora represents. When he first enters his old bedroom in the dead of night upon arriving home, he is shocked by the ghostly 'hallucination' of a girl (Flora) upon his bed. His move to retreat immediately 'and close the door in a shock of guilty terror' may indeed spring from sexual attraction, but his next sentence implies that his motives are more complex: 'This was a magic of exclusion which was too strong for me. A moment later, like an evil spirit put to flight, I was stumbling away down the stairs' (*IG* 20). Both Edmund and the sleeping girl are, appropriately, compared to ghosts: he, the ghost of the adult the child will become, she the ghost of the child he once was. Their mutual connection is strengthened when Flora reveals that she is pregnant and turns to Edmund for help. Besides his disgust at sex, Edmund is shocked by her revelation because it tarnishes the sense of childhood innocence he associates with her: 'I felt as much horror and instinctive disgust at her pregnancy as if she had told me that she had some loathsome disease. *Mingled with this* was a moral nausea at her plight and at its suggested remedy' (*IG* 65–6, my italics). Before long he finds himself following her towards the overgrown part of the garden, furthest from the house. He realizes that 'the place had me now under some sweet compulsion, and I followed' (*IG* 60–1). Flora leads him to the cascade and he wonders if it perhaps 'really did live in the past'. The cascade 'had been my place. Now it belonged to Flora' (*IG* 62).

Flora's significance for Edmund involves the juxtaposition of time and space: he invests psychic energy in a particular object because it stands in for a particular time. It is, in fact, a dynamic inherent in nostalgia itself, which refers to being emotionally bound to a period in life more desired than the present *and/or* to a particular absent place. Such interconnectedness is characteristic of melancholia in general: Kristeva mentions Kant's view that 'nostalgic persons did not desire the place of their youth but their youth itself; their desire is a search for the *time* and not for the *thing* to be recovered' (Kristeva 1989: 60).

Yet though nostalgia may really be about time, space remains a crucial element in the equation, as it offers a means of precisely locating a particular time. This is shown clearly in nostalgic literature, where one place in particular comes to symbolize a certain time – as a kind of chronotope, the spatiotemporal location important to Bakhtin's theory of the novel.[2] In *The Italian Girl* this location is the garden. 'For us children', Edmund says, 'it had formed a vast region of romance. I sighed. I could not remember being happy in childhood, but now it was as if the woods remembered it for me' (*IG* 35). The choice of words is suggestive, for the garden performs the same function as the device commonly found in the prose romance which John Fowles calls 'the domaine', an expanse of natural landscape which represents escape from the mundane world and where creative potential is realized.

Such a space figures often in Murdoch's fiction, in the form of the mystical pastoral clearings in *The Good Apprentice* and *The Message to the Planet*, or the secluded garden in *The Sacred and Profane Love Machine* where Monty, like an Elder spying on a whole troupe of Susannahs, watches seven nymph-like schoolgirls dancing. In *A Word Child* the park represents for Hilary Burde a 'great divide between myself and a happier land' (*WC* 5) – somewhere he later associates explicitly with childhood (*WC* 117, 234, 339). The park is actually Kensington Gardens, a Neverland (where the statue of Peter Pan stands) in which Hilary seeks respite from the claustrophobic spirals of his life.

Yet the garden in *The Italian Girl* represents something more than the oppositional space of the romance. It figures as the zone around which Edmund's conflicting desires about the past are circumscribed. This role is suggested above all by the recurrence several times in the novel of a particular scene where Edmund pursues a woman through the garden. On the first occasion he follows Flora to the cascade and is struck by a sense of freedom. Like a child he begins to run for no reason, but 'with a sort of excitement' (*IG* 61). This excitement is transformed into the more adult sensation of sexual arousal when the scene is replayed in the suggestively titled chapter 'The Magic Brothel'. This time, in 'a frenzy of anxiety' he chases Elsa, a young woman who makes him feel deeply ambivalent, repulsed and attracted at the same time. The chasing scene is repeated for a third time towards the end of the novel, with Flora again the object of Edmund's confused desire. Now he pauses to consider his motives: 'Was I pursuing or was I fleeing?' (*IG* 171). Is he following the representation of himself as a child back into childhood? Or is it simply because there is something about the house that he must escape? (It is 'not [...] the first time that I had run out of the house in sheer horror of what I had seen within' [*IG* 171].) Whichever, he recognizes that his impulse is 'to capture her and to retrieve some innocence for us both, to find in her again the child that I had known' (*IG* 172). This phrase is deliberately and finally ambiguous. Is Edmund searching in Flora for the child she was – or the child he himself once was?

What is clear is that these scenes represent the crux of the dilemma depicted in *The Italian Girl*. Its hero attempts to run away from the forward movement of the past while simultaneously trying to reach back into his own history and find something to hold onto. The chasing sequences symbolize the ambivalence of Edmund's relationship with his past. On the one hand he wishes to recover a time of innocence, yet one which allows excursions into the dangerous, thrilling world of adult sexuality. On the other, he recognizes all too keenly that the past is also full of things he fears and must escape.

A demon-ridden pilgrimage: *The Sea, the Sea*

A similar search – both literal and symbolic – features in *The Sea, the Sea*, only this time it is taken much further. Charles Arrowby's dogged pursuit of Hartley, the woman he loved and lost in his youth, is, as in Edmund's case, the result of more than simply the rekindling of dormant love. He is not attracted to Hartley physically or for her mind; he wants her because she is an embodiment of a lost world of innocence. In her presence he feels 'so helplessly, vulnerably close to my childhood' (*SS* 327). So seduced is he by his desire to repossess the past that he is patently unable to recognize – nor does it matter – that the Hartley he has carried around in his imagination is quite unlike the rather dull, happily married elderly woman she is now. Where Edmund's motives are ambivalent and his behaviour passive, Charles is aggressively demonstrative. Once he has failed to cajole Hartley into dropping everything and leaving her husband for him, he imprisons her (in an episode reminiscent of Proust) in a locked room in his house.

Such behaviour makes a mockery of his original intention to retire to a lonely house by the sea to renounce the illusory world of the theatre and 'learn to be good' (*SS* 4). In her book on Plato Murdoch remarks that the 'subject of every good play and novel' is 'the pilgrimage from appearance to reality' (*FS* 14). His treatment of Hartley demonstrates that Charles has a long way to go before he can pass fully from the state of *eikasia* to enlightenment. Yet as much as it is about a pilgrimage, *The Sea, the Sea* is also about a symbolic homecoming. His new home represents something different from the nomadic, dislocated life of the actor, who has to contend with the excitement of beginning a new play and 'the homeless feeling when it ends' (*SS* 36). His attitude towards his new life is suggested by the evocative German word *sehnsuchen*: the longing to return to a place one has never been. But there is also the suggestion that its significance comes from a place which he does know well, but has had to leave behind. Describing his house, he notes that 'the yellow light of the "blinded" room somehow and sadly recalls my childhood, perhaps the atmosphere of my grandfather's house in Lincolnshire' (*SS* 14).

Yet the move marks another kind of symbolic homecoming. From his arrival the loneliness and oddness of the house make him uncomfortable. He notes nervously some of its inexplicable features, like the mysterious 'inner room', and his uneasy sensation that the sea is on the point of engulfing the house by way of a 'hidden channel' (*SS* 14) underneath. The house is where some of the most disturbing episodes in the novel take place: some that are eventually explained, like the shattered vase, some that are not, like the appearance of a face in the window at the top of the inner room at a height where only someone hanging from the ceiling could appear. Its evocation of the uncanny contributes to the peculiar depth and power of *The Sea, the Sea*. The novel explores the darker side of the human personality in a way that touches on something genuinely unpleasant, making even Murdoch's other masterly portraits of an obsessional mind – *The Black Prince, A Word Child* – pale in comparison.

Unlike these novels, where we can trace the repetitive mechanism working within the hero more or less back to its cause, the impression in *The Sea, the Sea* is that Charles is driven by something so deeply rooted in his psyche that it is impossible to know exactly what it is. In this way, it is closer to the Lacanian notion of the real than anything else we explored in the previous chapter, for what Charles has repressed is truly unsignifiable. Things can only stand in metaphorically for the trauma. And what stands in for it primarily – thus functioning as a kind of '*objet petit a*', the excessive character of which obstructs the process of symbolization – is the huge green-eyed sea monster which Charles sees rising from the waves at the beginning of the novel. He is *'excessively frightened'* (*SS* 20) by this image and struggles to explain it. Perhaps it was a giant eel appearing to be further away than it was? Perhaps an optical illusion in which a worm he had just been looking at became superimposed into something else? He settles on the conclusion that it is a throwback to a bad LSD trip several years before, not because it resembles what he saw visually, but because of the way it terrifies him:

> It was something morally, spiritually horrible, as if one's stinking inside had emerged and become the universe: a surging emanation of dark half-formed spiritual evil, something never ever to be escaped from. (*SS* 21)

The episode is a quintessentially Murdochian one, where a rational mode of understanding is confounded by something which eludes its grasp. As a device it indicates her particular ability to create a suggestive image which remains beautifully opaque. Yet where the severed head or the bell can be given a more or less final 'signified' – indeed the novels go some way to providing one for us – this is not the case in *The Sea, the Sea*. The sea monster can plausibly be explained as many things: a symbol of jealousy, an emotion central to the book, or (as I suggested above) a displaced expression of the fear of female sexuality. But what makes this image so effective is that it has the power to absorb all of these interpretations and still seem to represent something more. We are left in the same position as Charles, trying to signify the traumatic kernel at the heart of the real. The climax of the plot comes as Charles is pushed headlong (by a jealous Perry) into Minn's Cauldron, a dangerous whirlpool, only to be miraculously saved by his cousin James. When the amnesia induced by this traumatic experience clears, Charles remembers something horrifying about the fall: 'The monstrous sea serpent had actually been in the cauldron with me' (*SS* 466). The realization that the creature is somehow about *him* is instrumental in Charles' journey from appearance to reality. His experiences in the novel force him to descend into the underworld of his own unconscious and confront whatever compels him before emerging into the light.

The claustrophobic heart of darkness in *The Sea, the Sea* is what sets it apart from the other 'artist-novels', *Under the Net* and *The Black Prince*, which it otherwise closely resembles. As in her other quasi-autobiographical novels, a large part of the disturbing effect comes from Murdoch's mastery of first-person retrospective form. We find ourselves colluding with its hero's warped view of the world and having to draw back and restore some perspective. At the same time, however, Charles is more than simply an obsessive crypto-paranoiac. We empathize with him because of his nostalgia. While it does not excuse his despicable behaviour to others, his attitude to the past can at least explain it. He claims, for example, that Hartley's teenage son Titus, whom he uses to lure her to him, is the son he has always wanted. Yet this is belied by his unwillingness to assume the mundane responsibilities of fatherhood. It is more likely that with his own particular 'family romance', and his desire to enter the theatre, Titus resembles Charles' youthful self. As Titus 'plays boyishly with himself' by the sea Charles watches him 'with a piercing mixture of affection and envy' (*SS* 258). Towards the end Charles tells his cousin that, 'the past is in some ways the most real thing of all, and loyalty to it is the most important thing of all' (*SS* 354).

Coming to terms with his need to recover the past is crucial in Charles' pilgrimage, and to this end the allusive framework of the novel is significant. There is a wealth of references to specific works of literature in *The Sea, the Sea*: Valéry's 'Le Cimetière Marin', from which the title is taken, *The Tempest*, *The Divine Comedy*, J. M. Barrie's *The Admirable Crichton*. But there is one novel which stands out as its key intertext: *A la Recherche du temps perdu*. In broad terms, there is much the two novels share: both are studies of obsessive, jealous love, central to which is the hero's spiritual journey away from the world of illusion. John Bayley's comment that for Proust, 'A can never love B but only his idea of B, and *vice versa*, with confusing and depressing results', could apply equally to *The Sea, the Sea* (Bayley 1960: 161). This is backed up by a number of allusions, both explicit (James speaks of Proust) and more subtle: there is a homosexual called Gilbert[e], and Charles' mention of 'the kiss withheld, the candle taken' (*SS* 79) when remembering his childhood recalls '*le drame du coucher*'. Yet the significance of Proust in this novel is more than simply to offer *ad hoc* symbolic support.

At Caen in 1978, just after completing the book, Murdoch claimed that 'the French novelist who is closest to me is Proust'. The comparison is not as obvious as those with other predecessors like James or even Lawrence. It is not something she has chosen to develop, apart from comments that reveal her sympathy with Proust's handling of issues explored in her own work, like 'good and evil'.[3] But from the general thrust of her pronouncements on literature we can speculate about what she finds so valuable in Proust. It seems especially likely that she admires the strong realist dimension of *A la Recherche*, a substantial achievement often unfairly overlooked by critics more interested in the treatment of involuntary memory: the presentation of a vast panorama of the *haute bourgeoisie*, among which there are many artists, diplomats and intellectuals, as in Murdoch's own work. It is possible to read Proust, in other words, as a writer following on from the classic realists rather than a modernist concerned with exploring the psychic experience of time. The crystalline side of his work, by contrast, the use of fiction to expound a theory which had preoccupied him in his earlier non-fiction, is likely to be less palatable to Murdoch. Yet it is just this aspect of the novel, the attempt to recapture time in art, which proves most resonant in *The Sea, the Sea*.

Proust's protagonist overcomes his deep regret at the absence of the past by realizing that it is in fact eternally available within the unconscious, and can be brought about either accidentally (via involuntary memory) or deliberately (through the connective power of art). As Murdoch herself describes it, Marcel discovers that there are moments 'set free from the order of time, an experience of time in a pure state, an enjoyment of the essence of things'.[4] Her definition of involuntary memory, the 'particular way in which reality is suddenly apprehended in the midst of illusion', reminds us of another connection with Proust, for to portray this is one of the major aims in her own fiction. It is illustrated most effectively at the point in *The Black Prince* when Bradley Pearson, wandering around Covent Garden at the height of his anguished love for Julian, becomes aware of a 'unique but unidentified smell, carrying awful associations'. Soon after he realizes the bitter irony of what it is: '"Strawberries!" The smell of youthful illusion and transient joy' (*BP* 266).

Marcel's experience in *A la Recherche* – or more accurately, his experience of composing it (it is the archetypal self-begetting novel) – leads him to enlightenment, as Murdoch explains:

> This intense perception-memory which the narrator realizes he has often experienced before without understanding or profit, prompts the reflections upon illusion and reality, general and particular, the unreality of the self, the nature of art, which enable the narrator to begin writing the book.

With this knowledge on board he 'can now set about recovering his life in the light of truth'. It is this backwards-moving dimension of *A la Recherche*, where introspection meets retrospection, which is most illuminating in comparison with *The Sea, the Sea*. Like Marcel, Charles believes in reminiscence as the source of truth, and in his narrative sifts through the experiences of what he calls his 'far past' – memories of his friends and acquaintances in the theatre, his parents and his Aunt

Estelle and cousin James – to find the one period where he thinks truth is located, the time he spent long ago with his childhood sweetheart Hartley. This experience resembles those events in Marcel's past which, Louis Dudek comments, are 'like diamonds in the dark internal caverns of the pysche [...] intuitions of permanence beyond time and change' (Dudek 1976: 43). Charles also uses the cave metaphor (one of Murdoch's favourites of course) to explain his state of mind. Its dark cavernous chambers are illuminated by the memory of Hartley, 'the great light towards which I have been half consciously wending my way'. The process of writing about this memory is central to discovering if this light is the artificial glow of illusion or 'the light that reveals the truth' (*SS* 79).

There are generally agreed to be two different ways in which 'lost time' is confronted in Proust. On the one hand, to use Paul Ricoeur's terminology, there is 'visitation' (involuntary memory) and, on the other, 'search' (the deliberate quest into the past) (Ricoeur 1984: 357). *The Sea, the Sea* is more concerned with the latter kind, the artistic project dedicated to reactivating the past and discovering its truth. The first-person retrospective form is particularly relevant here. The purpose of *A la Recherche du temps perdu* is not just to understand the past, as we might argue that most past-obsessed postmodernist novels (historiographic metafictions) do, but actually to *grasp* it. (This, incidentally, is what makes the English translation of the title, *Remembrance of Things Past*, particularly weak, as 'remembrance' lacks the sense of active endeavour suggested by the French *rechercher*.) And it is this kind of activity which attracts Charles from the start. He begins his narrative because he feels the 'need to write something that is both personal and reflective'. He has 'very little sense of identity' and this, he implies, must be put right; it is 'time to think about myself at last' (*SS* 3). Naturally this is a process which involves considering the far past, though this initially takes him by surprise: 'Do I really want to describe my childhood?', he asks (*SS* 27). Unlike theatrical writing, which is ephemeral and reflects 'the profound truth that we are extended beings who yet can only exist in the present' (*SS* 36), prose autobiography offers something more: 'This is for permanence, something which cannot help hoping to endure' (*SS* 2). As he writes he quickly comes to appreciate this form's strange capacity to enable shadowy areas of the past to be brought to light. 'Since I wrote [about Hartley]', he says, 'so many more pictures of her, stored up in the dense darkness of my mind, have become available' (*SS* 87). Charles soon recognizes, in other words, the aesthetic logic so central to Proust: the first-person retrospective narrative is the perfect vehicle for a return to the past.

At this point it is worth noting a significant difference between *The Sea, the Sea* and Murdoch's other first-person novels. A substantial part of it – the entire opening section – is in the present tense. Because of this, we know Charles begins writing *before* the events which come to form the plot have occurred. The book is not born as a consequence of the events it describes, as is the case with the other narrators (Edmund included), but has been conceived earlier, along with his original intention to retire to his seaside home. Once we recognize that Charles sets out to write his journal specifically to recapture the past, we can read the events which make up the plot of the novel in another way. The reflective first section of his journal is not, as it first seems, rudely hijacked by the hectic events of the present, but is something which serves as a *prelude* to these events. This section, 'Prehistory', ends with Charles claiming to be haunted by the past (a fact which has been suggested all along by his former lover Rosina occupying his house and pretending to be a poltergeist) and wondering, 'Can a woman's ghost, after so many years, open the doors of the heart?' (*SS* 89). Soon after this, as if conjured up by the narrative itself (a kind of 'omnipotence of writing' perhaps) the real Hartley appears in his life. His attempt to capture her is a way of doing literally what he first intended to accomplish metaphorically by writing his novel. In Charles' story, form appears to motivate content more exactly than the Russian Formalists would have considered possible.

A preoccupation with form is not, of course, unusual in Murdoch's work. Charles resembles many of her artist-figures by using form to counteract his fear of the contingent in various ways. He is struck by the *senselessness* of the rocks outside his house and takes to ordering them obsessively on his lawn. Yet the concern with form in *The Sea, the Sea* is more than just a matter of its author reworking old tricks. Considering it as part of her interest in the danger of form as a source of consolation fails to explain why the question of *narrative* form should be foregrounded to a degree unsurpassed anywhere else in her fiction, with the exception of *The Black Prince*. From the start Charles reflects continually on the particular shape his work is taking, trying it out in various generic categories: is it a diary? a memoir? a chronicle? Especially noticeable is how often his meditations on narrative form refer to the specific act of joining together past and present. This is a fantasy Charles indulges in more than once in the novel. Looking over old photographs of Hartley as a child, for example, he tries 'to build connections between the young face and the old, the old face and the new' (*SS* 156). It is she who can connect his past and present selves, making him 'whole as I had never been since she left me' (*SS* 186). He is also dimly aware of how his narrative does this too, announcing his intention early on to 'bring the story gradually up to date and as it were float my present upon my past' (*SS* 3). But it is only much later that he realizes its full potential, in an insight which also allows him to settle on what to call his narrative: a novel. A novel, he reasons, enables him to combine the need to tell his story with his liking for philosophical reflection, 'to inhabit the far past or depict the scarcely formulated present'. 'The past and the present are after all so close, so almost one, as if time were an artificial teasing out of a material which longs to join, to interpenetrate, and to become heavy and very small like some of those heavenly bodies scientists tell us of' (*SS* 153). The more he writes, and the more he is confronted by the past in the present, the more he recognizes that the first-person retrospective form, with its dual temporal structure, promises to join together his experiencing and narrating selves, his past and present.

The attention paid to Charles' narrative project in *The Sea, the Sea* at once highlights the novel's strongest similarity to Proust and its most significant departure from *The Italian Girl*. While Edmund is visited by the past as a form of involuntary memory, the corresponding introspective *search* is conspicuous by its absence. Levkin recognizes that a lack of self-knowledge is at the heart of Edmund's problems: 'You are a buffoon just like your brother, but you don't even know it! He at least, he knows that he is a perfectly ludicrous animal' (*IG* 130). While Edmund realizes this too, and admits to being perplexed by the mystery of his own character, the awareness never develops into real introspection. He never makes the link between writing about himself and the desire to achieve a greater degree of self-understanding. The detachment that is the dominant feature of his character is reflected in his style of writing, which often gives the impression that he is viewing himself from the outside. He describes his shadow following him, something which would be more likely to strike an outside observer. He speaks of himself as if he were describing another character: 'In acute distress I turned to the window' (*IG* 43), 'In a sort of fright I looked at my watch' (*IG* 52), 'I slunk from the room' (*IG* 88). The position as outside observer is one he is keen to claim ('After all I was the one that watched') and would seem to prefigure the typical role of the retrospective narrator, the 'second self' who watches himself during the story. Yet Edmund remains a consonant narrator, hardly ever analysing his previous actions objectively in prose. He almost never speaks in the present tense apart from his repetition of the phrase (though it is not an insignificant one) 'I can recall'. Unlike *The Sea, the Sea*, this is retrospection without real introspection – Proust, one might say, without Proust.

It would be a mistake, though, to push the comparison between *A la Recherche* and *The Sea, the Sea* too far. Charles is never allowed fully to inhabit his past self to the extent that Marcel is. This is not just a matter of the different lengths of the two novels, but a question of the ideology which holds each text together. Proust builds his text upon a particular conception of time which depends on the existence of a pure form of psychic time removed from the linear order of 'clock' time. Past and present, according to this idea, are able to co-exist: firstly in the unconscious, but also, and most enduringly of all, within the pages of a book. The treatment of time in *The Sea, the Sea* is altogether different. Charles gradually comes to realize that the connective power of narrative form is illusory. For one thing, the very activity of writing teaches him the lesson that he must always already be separated from even his most recent past; all narrative, as Gérard Genette says, is essentially retrospective. The phenomenon is especially visible in the 'Prehistory' section of the book, which employs the form of narration, common to journal or epistolary novels, which Genette calls 'interpolated' (because it occurs 'between the moments of the action'): 'Here the narrator is at one and the same time still the hero and already someone else: the events of the day are already in the past, and the "point of view" may have been modified since then' (Genette 1980: 217–18).[5]

Deborah Johnson has remarked on the way Charles, in his diary, is 'divided from his luminous present by the very act of writing about it' (Johnson 1987: 47).[6] In one line he celebrates the idyllic experience of looking out to sea only to record in the next the disappointing absence of seals. This ironic process extends beyond the level of the sentence to his narrative as a whole. The process of narration ensures that his narrating self unavoidably becomes divorced from his experiencing self, and he is forced implicitly to question some of his previous actions or opinions: 'I felt for her a desire which was marvellously indistinguishable from pure love' (*SS* 279). This formal inevitability is instrumental in Charles' sentimental education. Eventually he reaches the point where he can acknowledge that 'I had deluded myself throughout by the idea of reviving a secret love which did not exist at all. [...] How much, I see as I look back, I read into it all, reading into my own dream text and not looking at the reality' (*SS* 499). This admission signals that the pilgrimage from appearance to reality is more or less complete. It is in fact a process which we could alternatively describe as a movement from narratorial consonance to dissonance. Central to his enlightenment is the realization that he cannot fully inhabit his past self, despite the power of narrative form. James has already hinted at this, asking him, about the past:

'What is the truth anyway, that truth? [...] Can you determine exactly what you felt or thought or did? We have to pretend in law courts that such things can be done, but that is just a matter of convenience' (*SS* 175). Only much later, after James' death, does Charles begin to realize the significance of what James says, that retrospective writing can bring only a limited degree of self-knowledge:

> Time, like the sea, unties all knots. Judgements on people are never final, they emerge from summings up which at once suggest the need of a reconsideration. Human arrangements are nothing but loose ends and hazy reckoning, whatever art may otherwise pretend in order to console us. (*SS* 477)

Charles ends the novel aware of the journey he has undertaken, looking into the future not the past: 'Upon the demon-ridden pilgrimage of human life, what next I wonder?' (*SS* 502). His narrative indicates that this pilgrimage is far from straightforward, but involves going forward, back and also within.

Murdoch's ambivalence

A la Recherche du temps perdu, another story about obsessively living a lie, portrays a similar pilgrimage. Murdoch suggests that Proust's novel depicts a journey from the illusion of life to the reality of art:

> Redemption or salvation is the discovery of oneself as an artist. Then, when one writes, one seeks scrupulously, and with closest attention, for the truth; whereas, out in life, one destroys oneself for illusions, *on se tue pour des mensonges*. The narrator here recalls how he had never really believed in Albertine's love, but was ready to destroy his health, his work, his whole life for what he really knew to be a lie.

Yet this comment indicates a crucial difference between Proust's novel and her own. For Charles Arrowby, both realms, 'out in life' *and* in art, in so far as each is a vehicle for his attempt to recapture the past, are *equally* illusory. The subtle rhetoric at the end of *The Sea, the Sea* points outward to an enlightened way of life, different to the previous one. Rather than retreating into an aesthetic world, Charles must learn to relate differently to his past. We can see this in the section titles, which – if we follow the logic of the 'feigned reality statement' – he must have added after completing the novel. The most immediate past, the story about re-encountering Hartley, is consigned to 'History'. Life must go on, despite and because of what has happened in the past: 'what next I wonder'. It is a lesson firmly at odds with the affirmation at the end of *A la Recherche* (at least in the way Murdoch reads it) that art figures as a form of redemption.

> In an important sense, the narrator's life cannot be recovered, and those, including himself, whom he harmed by an imperfect way of living, remain irrevocably harmed; how much harmed the story ruthlessly reveals, the story which also exhibits true goodness and true love, as well as the *mensonges* for which the narrator was ready to destroy himself.

As in Murdoch's other studies of redemption, like *The Good Apprentice* and *A Word Child*, the point is that the past cannot be redeemed for something new. At the end of his pilgrimage Charles recognizes that he must live in the present, a conclusion that involves acknowledging the alterity of the world and its surrounding inhabitants. Much as she admires it, the Proustian vision of pure time is not, in Murdoch's view, 'a general guide or pointer to a good or spiritual way of life, it is about the artist, not about the saint'.

The distinction between artist and saint, a variation on other dualisms which run through her theory, like open and closed, sublime and beautiful, reminds us that Murdoch's theory works according to an oppositional logic. Ultimately such paired terms tend to be versions of a central opposition between modernism and anti-modernism. Murdoch's reading of Proust is essentially her critique of modernism and the modernist inheritance restaged. While she clearly loves Proust for his mastery of the art they both share (an achievement which earns him one of Murdoch's most important accolades for a writer, 'a great moralist') and while her discussion of *A la Recherche* makes clear her view that Proust has hit upon a fundamentally accurate analysis of how the conscious mind works, still she has reservations about the approach to time embodied in his work. She describes the 'revelation' in Proust as 'an aesthetic one, whereby the dead serial moments of ordinary life, with its obsessions and illusions, are contrasted with a vision which sees them as of value as the material of art'. A typically modernist revelation, in other words. And Murdoch objects to the modernist approach to time, its faith in the transcendent power of the epiphanic moment. 'Put it this way', she says, 'why do we have to wait for accidental inspirational experiences which may, if we are lucky, make us artists? Should we not attempt to turn most of our time from dead (inattentive, obsessed, etc.) time into live time?'

The Sea, the Sea is notable in that it articulates Murdoch's critique of modernism chiefly in formal terms. In its quest for past time, *A la Recherche du temps perdu* is an archetypal example of one of the classic high-modernist fictional forms, the artist-novel, where the narrator-hero attempts to recover past experiences and make sense of them. As such, it is true to what McHale sees as the epistemological bias of modernism. Its narrator may discover 'aspects of his past experience that he did not know, or did not know that he knew' (McHale 1992: 148) but the point is that these are always *available* to him. Just how far McHale's model can stretch is questionable (it struggles to explain a novel like *Heart of Darkness*, for example, which is epistemologically dominated in that Marlow's narrative is the vehicle for the attempt to know the truth, but ends indeterminately) but it certainly applies to *A la Recherche*. After a long period of frustration about the past's elusiveness, Marcel's previous experience gradually opens out for him as something fully accessible. This is not what we find in Murdoch. *Under the Net* and *The Black Prince*, I have already suggested, rework the modernist artist-novel ironically. Where modernist first-person retrospective narrative is typified by the sense of proximity between author and narrator, in these novels, Murdoch subtly problematizes her hero's point of view. *The Sea, the Sea* develops the general anti-modernism of these earlier fictions by taking a specific modernist text as a model and underlining the fact that the epistemological quest is not only futile, but also undesirable.

What makes this particularly effective is the nostalgic energy directed towards this quest. We understand why it must be unsuccessful because we are made to share – at least to some extent – in Charles' intense desire for the past. But this underlines an ambivalence at the heart of the novel. While Charles' illusory world is exposed for what it is by the subtle contrapositioning of his author, there remains something genuine about the sense of loss in this novel that amounts to more than simply an exposure of a particular false mindset. Murdoch, it seems to me, finds herself drawn to and partly seduced by the Proustian quest, but aware at the same time of the ethical flaws in such an activity. There is an ambivalence about Murdoch's reading of the modernist inquiry into the past, and the self, as there is about her relation to other aspects of modernism. She has more in common with the modernists than she might imagine. Her particular form of nostalgia, as revealed subtly in her criticism and fiction, is closer to 'the pain of a properly modernist nostalgia with a past beyond all but aesthetic retrieval' (Jameson 1991: 19) than the empty stylized nostalgia of postmodernism. Against this similarity must be set her deep-seated conviction that inquiry into the self must be rejected, or at least regulated, in favour of looking outside it. She is drawn to looking backward, but wary of looking inward; in favour of retrospection, but suspicious of introspection. This is why she has outlined her preference for third-person fiction, and criticized the introspective modernist tradition. She is clearly fascinated by this form, but is aware of its ethical shortcomings. *The Sea, the Sea* draws much of this power, I think, from this tension.

It also highlights a related tension in Murdoch's work: the connection between the desire to recapture the past and the desire to impose form. When Charles confronts James over knowing a mutual friend long before Charles introduced them, he exclaims: 'You've made all your words into lies, you've devalued your speech and – in a moment you've spoilt the past – and there's nothing to rely on any more' (*SS* 410).[7] Peter Brooks has traced from modernism to postmodernism the modern 'nostalgia for plot', our desire to seek final meaning despite the fact that we have 'become too sophisticated as readers of plot quite to believe in its orderings' (Brooks 1992: 314). Murdoch continually keeps in check a similar desire to create pattern, for it runs counter to her ethical requirements for good fiction. This is a lesson Charles learns too, for in one sense his attempt to bring about the past by effecting a conjunction between his past and present incarnations is a failure.

Yet we must also recognize that, up to a point, he *does* manage to secure his past within the pages of his novel. When we take into account the completed novel as a whole – written of course by Murdoch, but masquerading as Charles' – we can see that his metaphorical capture of Hartley is a partial success. He imagines telling her one day about the other great love of his life, Clement, and reflects 'How important it seems to continue one's life by explaining oneself to people, by justifying oneself, by memorializing one's loves' (*SS* 244). Hartley herself is 'memorialized', captured within his novel. Because he is successful in this aim it follows that his attempt at wrapping up the diverse elements of the world is not wholly in vain either. Peter Conradi has pointed out that the sea is the ultimate example of formlessness (Conradi 1989: 249). In the novel James observes that the sea itself is 'sublime'. But in a way Charles does manage to build form around it: the sea is metaphorically contained in his novel, as its title indicates. In moulding reality into form he is altogether more successful than has previously been understood. Dipple is right to point out that the book's 'meandering refusal of closure' (Dipple 1984: 85) comically highlights the problems of ending a work of fiction, but there is nevertheless a circular unity about it: Charles begins by writing a meditative diary in a strange house and ends that way too. Although its form is undoubtedly ragged, he does manage to create a self-contained art-object with the quality of 'permanence' he envisages.

The Sea, the Sea, then, both a retrospective fiction and *about* a retrospective fiction, highlights the inevitable ambivalence in our relationship to the past. More than this, though, it encapsulates the profound ambivalence of Iris Murdoch. She is an author who prescribes classic realism more or less unproblematically in her theory, yet questions it implicitly in her fiction. She is hostile towards poststructuralist and postmodernist currents in fiction and theory while pursuing similar lines of inquiry in her own work. She concentrates on the failings of psychoanalysis while a similar logic – evidenced by the relationship between real and symbolic, the effects of compulsion, the law that what is not said is more revealing than what is – operates in her own work. She attacks modernism from many quarters, all the while adhering to similar principles, like authorial impersonality and the transcendent value of good art. An ambivalence lies behind her technique in writing novels too. She is clearly attracted to, and excels at, plotting and patterning, yet has repeatedly affirmed an ideal which is the exact opposite. This leads to what I have called the aesthetic of the sublime, which contradictorily attempts to suggest accident by way of rigid pattern. Murdoch is in fact, for all her authorial withdrawal from her fiction, and because as a rule she has said very little by way of exposition of any one of her novels, an author who tends towards the didactic: we are very clear what she stands for, what her intentions are. As with Charles Arrowby's narrative, though, the fiction she produces often strays from her intentions – and is all the more intriguing for doing so.

8
Philosophy's Dangerous Pupil:
Metaphysics as a Guide to Morals, Derrida and *The Philosopher's Pupil*

> The anguish of the philosopher comes about because philosophy touches impossibility [. . .]. It's impossible for the human mind to dominate the things which haunt it.
>
> Haffenden, *Novelists in Interview*

I ended the previous chapter by highlighting areas where Murdoch's theory does not correspond to her fiction. To summarize, we might say that the source of the contradictions in her work is the clash of two powerful and perhaps irreconcilable impulses: the desire to totalize and the desire to reflect what is irreducible and particular. This is hardly surprising given that this theme is constantly played out in various ways within her characters and plots – for example, in the 'artist–saint' dichotomy which runs through her fiction. In this chapter I want to consider further the contradictory nature of Murdoch's thought and writing by turning to a novel which bears a curious relationship to her first-person retrospective fiction, and indeed to the rest of her work, *The Philosopher's Pupil*.

The Philosopher's Pupil depicts a community in the grip of a kind of collective hysteria brought on by the presence in their town of the famous philosopher John Robert Rozanov. It is tempting to regard this as a fictional version of the situation Murdoch witnessed with regard to both Sartre and Derrida, of the 'philosopher being hailed as a prophet' (*S* 10). It also demonstrates how one of the major functions of the 'enchanter figure' in Murdoch's fiction is, like Lacan's 'big Other', to *hystericize* everyone else. That is, Rozanov's presence causes the other characters to try to ascertain his desire and become its object, looking for some sense of self-definition in the 'truth' of their relation to him. It is thus, like *The Italian Girl* or *The Message to the Planet*, another example

150

of Murdoch's unique take on the story of the emperor with no clothes, a study of how a tyrannical man 'reigns' over other people because they permit him to do so. They perceive him through the frame of their own fantasies rather than recognizing what he actually is. This is made especially clear in *The Philosopher's Pupil* as Rozanov is portrayed as particularly unattractive, the grotesqueness of his physical features frequently described in detail. Nor, despite all his undoubted egoism, is he interested in cutting a 'brilliant' persona in public, preferring to be left in peace. Yet the people of the town still become obsessed with him, especially the self-styled demonic figure George McCaffrey, a man who was once his pupil (hence the novel's title), and the disillusioned priest Father Bernard Jacoby who seeks him out for conversations that might help him clarify his relation to God.

The plot is extremely convoluted, even by Murdoch's standards: an exuberant carnival of dramatic 'set-pieces', sudden love affairs and unexpected violent events. As a result Murdoch's critics have seldom been sure quite how to deal with the novel, a position summed up by Peter Conradi's ambivalent comment that '[p]erhaps there is just too much in this book; or perhaps – as with late work by, say, Titian or Verdi – this is simply a new kind of art' (Conradi 1989: 269).

So is *The Philosopher's Pupil* the 'standard' Murdoch novel done to excess, or a completely new departure? My view is that it is both. Like the first-person retrospective novels, which present us with the familiar Murdochian world but through the distorted lens of the dramatized narrator, *The Philosopher's Pupil* resembles her other work, but employs an unusual mode of narration. On one level it conforms to Murdoch's favoured third-person form of narration, designed to approximate the classic realist achievement of presenting many diverse characters from both 'inside' and 'outside' their consciousness. In this respect the novel eschews the limited perspective of the first-person novels. But even third-person novels have a narrator, of course, though it is usually a hidden, omniscient and objective figure, existing on a higher diegetic level than the characters, and *The Philosopher's Pupil* reminds us of this fact by dramatizing its omniscient narrator. We know who he is – a shadowy figure named 'N' – and know that he lives among the characters he tells us about and has been present during the events he describes in his story, even intervening at crucial moments (e.g. to offer shelter to George's wife as she tries to escape him). While most of the time he remains unobtrusively in the background (we can easily forget that it is not Murdoch's standard third-person narrator telling the story) the fact that he has made himself known and still claims objectivity means that we cannot help questioning his pretensions to omniscience and detachment: can we trust him? Most puzzlingly – and this is where N differs most from his counterparts in the first-person retrospective novels we have explored over the last few chapters – his motivation for telling the story, what he *gains* from doing so, remains impenetrable.

In the context of Murdoch's narrative technique *The Philosopher's Pupil* is therefore a paradox, a combination of the two literary forms she favoured, first-person retrospective novel and omniscient Jamesian 'loose baggy monster'. N combines the categories of first- and third-person narrator so that he both coincides with and departs from Murdoch's preferred narrative voice. We could describe *The Philosopher's Pupil* by paraphrasing the Russian Formalist critic Victor Shklovsky's famous comment about Sterne's *Tristram Shandy*: it is at once the most typical and untypical novel in the Murdoch canon.[1] Shklovsky's point is that *Tristram Shandy* is unusual in literature because of the extreme degree to which it foregrounds the sheer artificiality of presenting a fictional world, something which normally remains hidden in fiction. Yet because artifice is, by definition, a property of all novels, it is in fact quite typical. This accounts for the subversive effect of the principal conceit of *The Philosopher's Pupil*: the novel does something similar to Murdoch's third-person fiction, subtly defamiliarizing the mechanics of her fictional universe.

N introduces himself as 'a discreet and self-effacing narrator [...] an observer, a student of human nature, a moralist, a man [who will allow himself] the discreet luxury of moralizing' (*PP* 23). He proceeds to give an obsessively detailed description of Ennistone and its inhabitants – even down to the exact look of the brass taps and crockery (*PP* 29). This is a familiar exercise in what Shklovsky called 'baring the device', especially common in postmodernist fiction, and it calls into question the convention of the realist narrator, reminding us that any story is the product of subjective strategies of selection, interpretation and representation. The implication is that nothing in the story – even the name of the town where it is set, which he calls 'N's Town' or 'Ennistone' (*PP* 23) – has escaped the narrator's process of aesthetic shaping. Coming after the first part of the prelude, in which we are plunged into an almost self-parodically Murdochian piece of drama (George driving the car into the canal), the implication is that this device does not just lay bare the conventions of traditional realism, but *Murdoch's* realism in particular. Indeed it would not be pushing things too far to regard N's portrait of Ennistone as a careful analogy of how Murdoch goes about constructing her fictional universe. N's town is really 'M's town', the narrator's detailed description of the elaborate machinery that allows the Baths to operate signifies the symbolic and conceptual apparatus at work in the typical Murdoch novel.

The twin devices of N and the exposure of the internal workings of Ennistone cast subversive new light on Murdoch's other fiction. Consider, for example, her first depiction of the workings of an enclosed community, in *The Bell*. In the light of *The Philosopher's Pupil* we can see now that while it is not overtly metafictional, nor is it entirely free of self-reflexivity. As Imber is described in the early stages of the novel it is as if we are observing not just the workings of a fictional community but the way that this fictional community is itself constructed as a necessary backdrop for dramatic events to unfold. To consider its elaborate scene-setting in this way is to see *The Bell* – one of Murdoch's most realist fictions, certainly in comparison to a novel like *The Philosopher's Pupil* – as much less realistic after all. Imber Court becomes defamiliarized as a device which enables Murdoch to explore the philosophical concerns which interest her (the nature of religion, the value of introspection) by setting up a microcosm of the modern 'God-hunted' world.

This example accounts for the shadow that *The Philosopher's Pupil* can cast over the rest of Murdoch's fiction, if we choose to see it that way. It is one of Murdoch's most self-deconstructive texts, in its own way more radical than the more flamboyantly experimental *The Black Prince*. In particular it threatens to expose Murdoch as a writer who uses her fiction to explore *ideas* rather than other people – a description of course which is incompatible with her ethics of fiction. Literary realism, though it may seem otherwise, is really the product of great artifice, the equal in fact of any experimental or 'postmodern' form of literature. Its energies are devoted to making the presentation of its fictional world seem natural and effortless, the narrator functioning as simply a mediator rather than what s/he actually is, a *creator* of the fictional world (directed of course by the hidden figure of the author). Realist fiction is thus founded upon an implicit ideology or *philosophy* – not something as conscious or clearly thought-out as, say, a romantic or postmodernist aesthetic manifesto, but a philosophy nonetheless. The implications of this fact for Murdoch's fiction is that it complicates the relationship between the 'philosophical' and the 'literary' in her work. In what follows I want to concentrate primarily on how this relationship is played out in her last work of philosophy *Metaphysics as a Guide to Morals*, before returning to *The Philosopher's Pupil*, where the peculiar form of narration means that it is explored in a different way.

Philosophy and literature: Murdoch and Derrida

Murdoch was always clear about how she felt her philosophical writing and her fiction related. She maintained that while her novels did contain philosophical discussions they were certainly not 'philosophical novels', nor did she set out deliberately to dramatize in fiction the philosophical questions which interested her. Speaking in 1976 she explained that in her fiction 'there's just a sort of atmosphere and, as it were, tension and direction which is sometimes given by a philosophical interest, but not anything very explicit' (Bradbury 1976). In 1985 she claimed even more forcefully that she felt no 'tension' as a result of the demands placed on her by philosophy and art other than that brought by the fact that 'both pursuits take up time' (Haffenden 1985). Her opinion seems to be justified by the work itself, which manages to preserve a remarkably stable outward distinction between her two writing identities. Philosophy, in other words, is often present within Murdoch's fiction but only in an 'atmospheric' sense, contributing to the discussions and disagreements between characters, while her non-fiction (with the exception of interviews and conference papers) is largely devoid of references to her status as a practising novelist, even in the early essays concerned with the state of the contemporary novel like 'The Sublime and the Beautiful Revisited' or 'Against Dryness'.

Nevertheless, that Murdoch should use the word *tension* in both of these remarks is interesting, for tension is precisely what we might expect to be produced in the practically unique case of a writer who continued to produce both philosophy and fiction side by side throughout her long career. She conceived of her two disciplines as not just different but quite *opposite* in crucial respects. While the fundamental aim of both was to convey 'truth', philosophy should try to clarify while literature must mystify. Literature was about play, magic, entertainment, arousing emotions, whereas philosophy had a duty to strive towards an 'unambiguous plainness and hardness [. . .] an austere unselfish candid style. A philosopher must try to explain exactly what he means and avoid rhetoric and idle decoration' (Magee 1978: 264–7). Each discipline is governed, in other words, by a opposite impulse or *desire*. In psychoanalytic theory, the co-existence of mutually exclusive desires is likely to lead to anxiety, even neurosis. How valid is Murdoch's insistence that her two main interests created only a small, productive amount of tension? And what would be the textual equivalent of neurosis in her writing?

The answer might be found in two of the rare moments in her work when the boundary between her double writing identity is temporarily broken down. One occurs, not unexpectedly, in *The Philosopher's Pupil*, where we learn that Rozanov had once published a 'seminal work' called *Nostalgia for the Particular* (*PP* 83), which also happens to be the title of one of his author's own early philosophical essays. Self-reference, we recall, is one of the 'postmodern' indulgences Murdoch sparingly allows herself in her fiction – sparingly because, as this example shows, the practice subtly serves to snag the fabric of Murdoch's realism by exposing the fictionality of her work even as it strengthens its sense of verisimilitude by suggesting an extended fictional universe beyond the confines of the text. Here, though, it prefigures N's curious admission at the end of the novel, 'I also had the assistance of a certain lady' (*PP* 558), a statement which points implicitly to Murdoch as despotic creator of the fictional world. The title of Rozanov's book strengthens this implicit sense of confession and, most importantly, seems to suggest that the philosophy discussed within, and even the eponymous relationship between philosophical master and pupil is informed by Murdoch's own philosophical career.

Even more striking is a moment in *Metaphysics as a Guide to Morals* when the boundary is crossed in the other direction. While glossing Derrida's idea (as she understands it) that there is 'only a network of meanings (the infinitely great net of language itself) under which there is nothing', Murdoch remarks parenthetically 'See a philosophical discussion of these matters in my first novel, *Under the Net*' (*MGM* 187). The comment is clearly intended to strengthen the point she is making about priority in philosophy, how Wittgenstein and Heidegger got there before Derrida. Yet, stylistically, this is actually a highly unusual move in Murdoch's philosophy. Because of her conviction that 'philosophical writing is not self-expression, it involves a disciplined removal of the personal voice' (Magee 1978: 165), she seldom writes in the first person in her non-fiction – and acknowledges her 'other' career far less often. But one of the immediate implications of this remark is to contradict Murdoch's assertion that her novels are not directly related to her philosophical concerns, even though it refers to *Under the Net*, the only novel Murdoch has been happy to call a philosopher's novel 'in a very simple sense' because 'it plays with a philosophical idea' (Kermode 1963: 122). It also seems especially appropriate that the traversing of the boundary should come in a reading of Derrida, of all philosophers.

Until now this book has treated Murdoch's philosophy and literary theory as *supplementary* to her fiction – that is, as a body of writings which can be used to clarify certain aspects of her fiction or to provide support for readings of particular novels if so desired, but consideration of which is not essential to understanding her art. Yet the notion of supplementarity is one which Derrida has taught us to approach with caution – especially when it comes to the question of the relation between philosophy and literature. His famous reading of Rousseau in *Of Grammatology* interrogates Rousseau's persistent use of the word 'supplement', highlighting its strange doubleness: a term referring to something which might be added optionally to an already complete entity but that also implies a lack in this entity as a result. Derrida shows that this contradictory element at the heart of Rousseau's writing is in fact typical of the conceptual logic of philosophical (or 'logocentric' or metaphysical) thought in general, which operates by setting up a central opposition, in which one term is privileged over another subordinate term. But in fact, as the intricate process of deconstructive reading demonstrates, his secondary term points to a structure which determines the very shape of the prioritized concept, and, moreover, *limits* it by threatening to contaminate or collapse it. It is precisely this 'dangerous' quality of the supplement (Rousseau's description) that explains why it needed to be suppressed in the first place. This analysis of the term 'supplement' suggests how Derrida goes about undoing the various key binaries which structure Rousseau's thought: culture/nature, melody/harmony, speech/writing. What is particularly significant in the case of Rousseau, is that his 'literary' writing, the *Confessions*, powerfully performs the contradictions between speech and writing which his philosophy attempts to suppress. This exemplifies the fact that the dangerous supplement is particularly associated with *literary* writing, a kind of writing which philosophy has to position as its other in order to police and keep at bay.[2]

Iris Murdoch clearly conforms to Derrida's understanding of the 'logocentric' thinker, not least because the single most characteristic feature of her philosophical rhetoric is its preference for oppositions: the sublime and the beautiful, the crystalline and the journalistic, existentialism and mysticism, low and high Eros, the necessary and the contingent, fantasy and imagination, appearance and reality. And to consider her work in a Derridean light can help us see that one of the most pervasive oppositions in her work is the one between literature and philosophy, the latter functioning as a kind of problematic supplement.

What happens when a definitively metaphysical thinker like Murdoch comes up against the great exposer of the problems of metaphysical thinking? Derrida is perhaps the key presence in *Metaphysics as a Guide to Morals*. The book contains more references to him than to Freud and even Sartre, a signal that he plays a similar role in Murdoch's late thinking to that of Sartre in her early period. In a sense his work might be seen as the catalyst for the entire book, for Murdoch is clearly troubled by what she regards as Derrida's mission to move philosophy into an entirely new way of thinking, one which takes for granted the death of metaphysics more provocatively than Nietzsche and Heidegger. As a result she sets about building up an extensive critique of his work. Her strategy is to attack his work on two main fronts: (1) its inherent flaws and contradictions, (2) its style.

Her main tactic is one that she has used to good effect before (and which might be described, ironically, as a deconstructive move), that is, demonstrating that work which likes to think of itself as non- or anti-metaphysical is actually founded upon a central metaphysic. This was central to her reading of Sartre, which showed how reliant his work was on the metaphysical notion of freedom operating within it. Here Murdoch argues that Derrida is a metaphysician in so far as the idea of *archi-écriture* or *différance*, to which his work constantly appeals, is an overarching transcendent concept similar to the Saussurian notion of *langue* in that it exists 'behind' Derrida's readings rendering them meaningful. And for all the general accuracy of his understanding of language, because it depends upon a metaphysical structure (the idea of language as a system) it 'obliterates a necessary recognition of the contingent' (*MGM* 194). Derrida's conviction about undecideability means that necessary 'ordinary-life truth-seeking' (*MGM* 195), which depends upon everyday, old-fashioned but *workable* distinctions between what is true and false, is obscured. Like her engagements with other philosophers in *Metaphysics* Murdoch is effectively reading Derrida through Plato: 'The fundamental value which is lost, obscured, made not to be, by structuralist [*sic*] theory, is truth, language as truthful, where "truthful" means faithful to, engaging intelligently and responsibly with, a reality which is beyond us' (*MGM* 214).

Murdoch's second major objection to Derrida's work emerges more implicitly in *Metaphysics as a Guide to Morals*, but it appears to worry her even more. In the chapter devoted to Derrida she comments that his thinking is not like other philosophy in terms of style, as it lacks 'the kind of careful lucid explanatory talk and use of relevant examples which good philosophy, however systematic, includes and consists of' (*MGM* 197). She finishes the chapter with a passionate appeal for a rearguard action to be fought in order to put the Western tradition back on track and resurrect its '*method* of imaginative truth-seeking and lucid clarification' (*MGM* 210–11). The note of passion is significant because this section does not mark the end of her consideration of Derrida in the book even though she goes on to address other issues and the work of other philosophers. She keeps coming back to him as if she cannot escape him, the discussion becoming more and more rhetorical until eventually she is moved to break with her philosophical voice and speak directly – once again breaking free from her dispassionate stylistic constraints. She says that she first read *Writing and Difference* in the original on publication in 1967 'and was impressed and disturbed by it', going on to read other books up until more the recent Derrida of *Glas* and *Psyche: The Invention of the Other*. She pays compliment to him as 'a remarkable thinker, a great scholar, a brilliant maverick polymath, a *pharmakeus*', who is capable of creating brilliant works like *Glas*, concluding that 'one should not ignore (as some of his critics do) these unique literary marvels'. But she has a rhetorical question, which she immediately answers herself (lest we misinterpret her rhetoric perhaps):

> So what is wrong, what is there to worry about, should we not enjoy and profit from his versatile writings, his scholarship, his gorgeous prose, his large literary achievement? [...] What is disturbing and dangerous is the presentation of his thought as philosophy or as some sort of final metaphysic, and its elevation into a comprehensive literary creed and model of prose style and criticism, constituting an entirely (as it were compulsory) new way of writing and thinking. (291)

Derrida is brilliant but dangerous, in other words, because he brings an element of the *literary* into philosophy, where it has no place. This is a quite accurate assessment, of course, though it is more than a little surprising coming from a philosopher who also happens to be an accomplished writer of literature herself. For one might reasonably imagine that properly bringing the literary into philosophy is just what a thinker like Murdoch, who continually emphasizes the value of literature in taking account of the contingent in the world, might seek to do in her own work.

This contradictory element is not too surprising, however, for the dual strategy of Murdoch's critique – attacking Derrida's content and style – actually leads to a central contradiction in her response to his work. On the one hand her portrayal of Derrida as a metaphysician carries with it the implication that we should not take seriously his pretensions to bringing about the end of philosophy. On the other hand, she simultaneously seems to regard his 'literary' style as posing a very real threat to philosophy as we know it. At this point we must acknowledge that where there is much that is valid in Murdoch's reading of Derrida – like the idea that *archi-écriture* is essentially a metaphysical concept[3] – it contains some serious misrepresentations of Derrida's thought. It is misleading to suggest that deconstructive reading practices are motivated by the *'quest* for the hidden-deep . . . meaning of the *text'* (*MGM* 189), for this description is more applicable to a psychoanalytic methodology: the very idea of 'deep truth' is something Derrida constantly questions. It is also a mistake to view Derrida's notion of the endless deferral of meaning as a version of relativism, for certain values – like the respect for otherness and difference – are carefully preserved in his work. Above all, her view of Derrida's dependence on an overarching metaphysical system of language may be a valid critique of *structuralism* but is entirely misrepresentative of Derrida. It clearly overlooks the fact that Derrida begins his career – for example, in *Writing and Difference*, the book Murdoch read in 1967 – with some far-reaching critiques of structuralism. Derrida takes great care to avoid imposing a system on his readings, avoiding where possible the use of the same 'blanket' terminology when analysing different texts in favour of terms chosen precisely because they are integral to the work he is considering (this is why he uses the word 'supplement' in his reading of Rousseau).

Murdoch's misreading here brings us to the most unsatisfactory aspect of her discussion of Derrida, the consistent characterization of Derrida as the originator and leading proponent of *structuralism*. The error is compounded by the fact that Murdoch's definition of structuralism seems at times staggeringly wide of the mark: what we know as structuralism does not encompass poststructuralism, deconstruction, modernism and postmodernism as she claims it does (*MGM* 5, 185). No doubt there is, to some degree, a polemical impulse behind Murdoch's gesture. It could plausibly be argued that although Derrida is not a structuralist it is possible to observe the 'influence and effects' of structuralism through his work and that of others who pursue the logic of structuralism as far as it will go (*MGM* 185). And we *can* see poststructuralism, deconstruction, modernism, postmodernism, to varying degrees, as the product of a general 'Saussurian' worldview – namely the conviction that language constitutes the world rather than refers to it. Nevertheless what we are faced with here is a failure or unwillingness on Murdoch's part to read another philosopher on his own terms. And this in fact exemplifies a tendency in her thought as a whole.

While Murdoch's rhetoric in her non-fiction is unfailingly about the necessity of preserving a sense of real, contingent experience away from the totalizing impulses of theoretical systems, it actually *performs* something quite different. She criticizes Derrida and structuralism for their adherence to a system which falsifies the true nature of contingency and particularity in the world. In order to make this point, however, she disregards the particularity of the work of the different intellectual movements she mentions. Her apparent desire to reduce to a set of common characteristics a vast and diverse array of radically different writers and thinkers associated with the four terms she groups together (poststructuralism, deconstruction, modernism and postmodernism) is surprising in one who so often insists on the difference between individual people and texts: does Murdoch really believe that (to make a random list of names conventionally associated with these movements) Lévi-Strauss, Derrida, Lacan, Deleuze, Joyce, Proust, Picasso, Pynchon, Baudrillard, Don DeLillo and Toni Morrison are more similar than different?

This preference for the general is exhibited, often more visibly, elsewhere in her non-fiction. The insistence on the value of 'irreducible dissimilarity' (sag 216) tends to involve reducing philosophy or literature to a set of similar groups or sub-groups. A characteristic feature of her non-fiction from early polemical essays like 'The Sublime and the Beautiful Revisited' onwards is the attempt to persuade us that various dominant twentieth-century intellectual approaches are guilty of presenting a reductive account of otherness and the individual. For all the undoubted accuracy of this claim, in practice this means divesting a range of distinct philosophical and literary movements and their members of their particularity and historical context, flattening the history of ideas into one great horizontal line of equivalence: Romanticism=existentialism= Hegelianism=formalism=Derrida=structuralism=poststructuralism, modernism, postmodernism and so on.

This strategy is most readily apparent, in fact, in her literary theory, a form of writing which, from a Derridean perspective, is firmly rooted in the 'philosophical' rather than the 'literary'. Central to Murdoch's view of literary criticism is that it should not be 'theoretical': 'any so-called critical "system" has in the end to be evaluated by the final best instrument, the calm open judging mind of the intelligent experienced critic, unmisted as far as possible by theory' (*FS* 78). Literary critics must speak 'as *individuals* and not as scientists' and resist the temptation to apply 'non-evaluative structures and codes' to the work they discuss (*MGM* 189). Yet with the exception of her book on Sartre and the excellent readings of *King Lear* and Proust in *Metaphysics as a Guide to Morals*, nowhere in Murdoch's writings on literature do we find extensive analyses of specific literary texts. On its own terms, there is a failure in Murdoch's criticism to respect the irreducible dissimilarity of individual texts.

Murdoch's reading of Derrida, then, illuminates a central contradiction within her thought: despite all the appearance to the contrary, she is in fact a rigorously systematic thinker. Her philosophy and literary theory set up a pervasive opposition between 'absurd irreducible uniqueness' (*S* 246) on the one hand and totalizing intellectual systems or aesthetic patterns which eliminate the difference between things on the other. This hierarchy serves another fundamental pair of oppositions: literature is, by implication, prioritized over philosophy. To put this another way, although to all intents and purposes the 'literary' takes priority over the 'philosophical' in Murdoch in so far as it deals with the contingent, in practice, the nature of her philosophical writing destabilizes the opposition. As befits a metaphysician, Murdoch makes the typical philosophical move which Derrida has repeatedly exposed and challenged in metaphysics: she defines literature as the realm of contradiction and irreducibility, of chaos and muddle. But this move, he demonstrates, is precisely the means by which philosophy creates its own other, placing the literary outside the boundaries of philosophy and thereby implying that philosophy is *not* all about contradiction and unchecked rhetorical play.

Murdoch's insistence that philosophy is distinguished from literature chiefly as a result of style would seem to endorse this view. But in fact what functions as the supplement in her thought – philosophy – not only is equal in importance to literature, but also, as deconstruction stipulates, actually gives the prioritized term (literature) its very definition, for the whole idea of irreducibility and contingency is a fundamental property of her philosophical system. What is contingency if not a philosophical category? Indeed the implicit equation of 'the contingent' or 'the particular' with 'truth' that we find in Murdoch is problematic for this reason. The contingent can only be regarded as truth – can only be represented at all, perhaps – from *within* a particular theoretical frame. The paradox is reminiscent of the one the literary philosopher Maurice Blanchot highlights with regard to 'the everyday', that is, mundane, insignificant existence (Blanchot 1993). The everyday exists, but only *outside* theory and conceptual categories like 'true' and 'false' or 'beginning' and 'end'. To try to represent it through art or theory is to make it *significant* in a way that dissolves its very particularity.

Philosophical anguish: *The Philosopher's Pupil*

Derrida haunts *Metaphysics as a Guide to Morals*, then, because he figures as a kind of intellectual double of Murdoch, bringing out the inherent contradictions in her thought. Where she wants to preserve a boundary between philosophy and literature, he wants to break it down. He is a philosopher who brings the literary into philosophy, she is a novelist who wishes to keep it out. Derrida is a thinker who is engaged on project – the attempt to deal with the contingent without recourse to system – which dovetails uncomfortably with Murdoch's own, for it is much less systematic. Reading Murdoch in terms of Derrida helps us see that the contingent in her work is essentially an *idea* about contingency. Although she refers continuously to the value of the particular, a *representation* of it is in fact very difficult to find in her writing (though of course this is not exactly a failure on her part, given the nature of fiction). What we have instead is a simulacrum of the contingent, made possible by Murdoch's philosophical supplement. Her fascination with the contingent is a fantasy of, rather than a nostalgia for, the particular.

This brings us back to *The Philosopher's Pupil*, which we can read in the light of the above discussion, for it is the novel which explores the relationship between philosophy and literature perhaps more deeply and more contradictorily than any of Murdoch's others. It is like so many of them, though, in that its central energy comes from the relationship between two men, the enchanter-philosopher Rozanov and his erstwhile pupil George McCaffrey.

Rozanov, after a life of academic and public success, has reached crisis-point, severely disillusioned with philosophy and the rest of existence as a result. What chiefly depresses and frustrates him is his inability to think and write with absolute clarity: 'If only he could get down deep enough, grasp the difficulties deep deep down and learn to think in an *entirely new way*. [...] He longed to live with ordinariness and see it simply with clear calm eyes. A *simple* lucidity seemed always close at hand, never achieved' (*PP* 135). Murdoch said shortly after publication of the novel that Rozanov's story reflects the 'anguish of the philosopher' which 'comes about because philosophy touches impossibility... It's impossible for the human mind to dominate the things which haunt it' (Haffenden 1985: 199). The urge to dominate what haunts him is beginning to make itself felt in Rozanov's everyday life, too, most troublingly when he decides, unsolicited, to arrange the marriage of his granddaughter to Tom McCaffrey.

Like Rozanov, George McCaffrey is also deeply troubled, chiefly as a result of what he feels to be a brutal rejection by Rozanov, who much earlier abruptly stopped his tuition and subsequently sought to avoid any contact with him. George has consequently chosen to embrace mystification, his every statement and action seemingly an attempt to move away from rationality, stubbornly frustrating the attempts of

others to understand his motives. The novel begins with him impulsively trying to kill his wife Stella by driving their car into a canal. After
Rozanov's most recent snub George 'had been suddenly possessed by
wild destructive hatred; only it was not really hatred, he *could not* hate
John Robert, it was madness' (*PP* 138).

The contrasting desires of both men – the former to achieve order and
clarity, the latter to create chaos – relate to a deeper opposition between
two philosophical positions. On one side there is Murdoch's own philosophy, represented by Rozanov (who is described as a neo-Platonist
[*PP* 83], and is obsessed by the 'the uncategorized manifold, the ultimate
jumble of the world, before which the metaphysician covers his eyes'
[*PP* 133]), and on the other we have an embodiment of a quasi-Nietzschean
ideal of 'beyond good and evil', a man who has decided that if there is
no moral structure against which to measure our actions, then everything
is permissible, even murder (*PP* 223).

In an important sense, behind this opposition is a more wide-ranging
opposition between philosophy and literature. Where Rozanov is clearly
interested in similar philosophical problems to his author, and also
shares her puritanical desire to write down *nothing but the truth* in
philosophy (*PP* 134), George can be – and has been – regarded as the
prime representative of the carnivalesque literary spirit that can be seen
at work in the novel (Heusel 1995: 120–5). George is the novel's 'dangerous
supplement', wandering through the text disrupting stable relationships
and crossing boundaries. He plays a similar role, in other words, to that
of Derrida in *Metaphysics as a Guide to Morals*, and, true to the logic
of deconstruction, the mystifying, disruptive supplement comes to
contaminate the prioritized conception of clarity and purity. George
doggedly draws Rozanov down from his lofty perch and forces him to
engage in the chaotic jumbled world beneath, provoking him until the
philosopher feels that 'George had won. John Robert was now as
obsessed with George as George was with John Robert' (*PP* 416). A major
factor in his descent is his encounter with the muddle of existence in a
more traumatic personal sense, in the form of his growing awareness
that he has incestuous feelings towards his 17-year-old granddaughter,
Hattie Meynell. After he painfully confesses his feelings to her, Hattie is
disgusted at the transformation, barely able to look at him, 'at the cool
dignified remote philosopher, the guardian of her childhood, suddenly
transformed into this pathetic spitting moaning maniac' (*PP* 456).

This outcome appears to validate the views of those critics who have
argued that the literary wins out over the philosophical in the novel
(Bradbury 2000; Heusel 1995). At the very least, it seems that the two

forces come to co-exist, just as Rozanov and George become mutually dependable in a master–slave dialectic. In a Bakhtinian reading of the novel Barbara Stevens Heusel has explored the dialogical nature of *The Philosopher's Pupil*, showing how philosophy in the shape of Rozanov is 'discrowned' thereby causing philosophical discourse to become stripped of its privileged status and made to take its place only as one of the many competing discourses in a supremely carnivalesque text (Heusel 1995: 119–25).

The problem with this reading, however, is that it does not take sufficient account of the other major embodiment of a philosophical position in the novel, the mysterious narrator 'N'. More so than George, it is he who represents 'literature' in this text – literature, that is, in its special guise as the 'realist novel', the conventions of which N exposes, and a genre, as I suggested earlier, inevitably informed by a philosophy. Though there is a sense in which N's shadowy role amounts to a dialogical intermingling of previously separate identities in the structure of fiction – author, narrator, character – (as Heusel's Bakhtinian reading posits [Heusel 1995: 122]) in fact he occupies a position superior to all the characters, and is equal to no less than Murdoch's voice itself: the reference to 'a certain lady' at the end of the novel yokes author and N firmly together.

Like the philosophical aspects of her fiction, the metafictional or postmodern aspects have been played down by Murdoch as nothing more than a supplement, just 'play', 'a little game to amuse a small number of kindly readers' (Amsterdam 1988). But the self-reflexive elements in *The Philosopher's Pupil* suggest that they are supplementary in the destabilizing deconstructive sense, too. N's presence in the novel, particularly when he descends into the action at strategic points, is a constant reminder that the apparently 'natural' unfolding of the story, the realistic world of Ennistone and the independent-seeming characters are all the product of a detailed process of construction on the part of the novelist. Realism is in fact made possible by the theoretical process that postmodern fiction chooses to lay bare; the difference between realism and postmodernism is, in this respect, no more than a question of visibility. The game has been loaded from the start, the interpenetration of ideas has been organized by N/M all along. In this sense *The Philosopher's Pupil* never escapes the author's grasp. So while there is undoubtedly a degree of carnivalesque polyphony, the author's voice retains the final authoritative word. Rozanov's philosophy might be deconstructed by the events of the novel, but the philosophy that gave rise to the creation of the novel and determines its very disposition – namely Murdoch's philosophy of fiction, expressed through her spokesperson, N – remains intact.

The currency of ideas

In a sense the philosophy precedes the fiction in Iris Murdoch simply because of the co-existence of her two kinds of text, philosophical and literary. Reading Murdoch's non-fiction, in other words (which many people interested in her novels will do, certainly those who write about them), helps to produce a particular reading of her fiction. This is clear from the way critical readings of her novels frequently concentrate on the philosophical markers they contain which point to the philosophy outside: for example, the passage from fantasy to reality, the interplay of the necessary and the contingent, the relevance of Plato's allegory of the cave. Her characters wrestle with dilemmas we recognize from the philosophy and speak a language informed by its reference-points. Consider George's conviction that 'he could not sin' (*PP* 96), for example, or his protestation to Rozanov: 'You flayed me, you took away my life-illusions, you killed my self-love' (*PP* 222). But *The Philosopher's Pupil* shows that the philosophy precedes the fiction in an even more deep-rooted sense, in that the organization characterization and plot of Murdoch's novels are governed by her philosophy and literary theory.

This is something the novelist Joyce Carol Oates discerned in her essay, 'Sacred and Profane Iris Murdoch'. Oates argues that in contrast to Murdoch's definition of the highest art, 'her own ambitious, disturbing and eerily eccentric novels are stichomythic structures in which ideas, not things, and certainly not human beings, flourish' (Oates 1999: 1). This, she suggests, is because of Murdoch's Platonism. For Plato, the conventional relation between reality and unreality is reversed (i.e. the everyday world is unreal and illusory, while the real world is the transcendent metaphysical world of the forms), and it follows that the ideas in Murdoch's novels are more real than the everyday world she seeks to depict (Oates 1999: 3–4). Her novels resemble philosophical 'debates' or structures 'in which near-symmetrical, balanced forces war with one another', with Murdoch operating at the level of 'the gods' (Oates 1999: 2), visibly shaping and ordering the debate within. Rather than the machinations of her plots, which are absorbing but 'inconsequential' and threaten 'to dissipate all seriousness', it is the proliferation of 'off-hand, gnomic, always provocative remarks – essays in miniature, really' offered by her characters that give Murdoch's novels 'their intelligence, their gravity' (Oates 1999: 6). This means that Murdoch's aim to create independent-seeming characters is inevitably compromised, too, as Murdoch comes increasingly in her fiction to rely on 'a certain category of personage [...] to make her primary ideas explicit' (e.g. Brendan in *Henry and Cato*, Edgar in *The Sacred and Profane Love Machine*, Arthur in *A Word Child*), characters who enter the novel as 'self-conscious gods-from-the-machine who confront the protagonist with certain gnomic observations that might be applicable to any human dilemma' (Oates 1999: 7).

Oates's insights here are certainly relevant to *The Philosopher's Pupil*. At the heart of the novel is a series of scenes in which two men engage in philosophical debate – Rozanov and George, of course, but even more centrally, Rozanov and the doubting priest (a familiar Murdoch type) Father Bernard Jacoby. The structural importance of such homosocial couplings in this novel and others suggests that the libidinal energy of Murdoch's fiction comes from the currency of ideas circulating within. But the chief merit of Oates's reading is that she treats Murdoch as a contradictory writer from the outset. Not that this in itself amounts to an especially unusual response to Murdoch's work, for the contradictions between her theory and practice have fuelled many criticisms of her work since the beginning. But it has proved difficult for those who admire Murdoch's writing to resist the temptation to try to iron out the contradictions or to demonstrate that they are inconsequential. Oates's reading suggests we do not have to try: to understand Murdoch we must appreciate that, more than just supplementary, the contradictions, paradoxes, *aporias* in Murdoch's thought are what drive the work.

Postscript: Reading Iris Murdoch

> I think we might helpfully distinguish between permissiveness –
> meaning sexual promiscuity – and tolerance. It is good to be
> tolerant, bad to be promiscuous. This is a rough general guide!
>
> Iris Murdoch, interview with S. B. Sagare (1987)

In *Picturing the Human*, her 2000 study of Murdoch's philosophy, Maria
Antonaccio comments that '[i]t is difficult to write about Murdoch
without being drawn into her life and personality, rather than concentrating on the substance of her thought' (Antonaccio 2000: v). This
statement is a measure of the radical change that has recently taken
place in 'Murdoch studies'. Had Antonaccio been writing before the
author's well-documented illness and death instead of after, one might
have expected her to say the exact opposite. For years Murdoch's work
had a curious, almost magical ability to ward off biographical readings.
Little in the way of substantial biographical detail was readily available,
due to Murdoch's reluctance to speak about her life outside her work.
The lack of information was complemented by her insistence in her
literary theory that the serious author had a duty to 'expel' herself from
her work. Why look for her if she was not likely to be there?

The succession of biographical portraits that followed Murdoch's
death changed all this. John Bayley's trilogy of memoirs (1999–2002),
Richard Eyre's biopic *Iris* (2001), Conradi's exhaustive 'official' biography
(2001) and A. N. Wilson's mischievous portrait *Iris Murdoch: As I Knew
Her* (2003)[1] together provide a wealth of information about all aspects
of her life and work: her extraordinary promiscuity, the contents of her
private journals, even her personal hygiene. Where before her death one
could complain of knowing too little, afterwards many argued that we
knew too much. The outcome is that we now have another figure to

place alongside the caricature of a private, puritanical, near 'saint' that prevailed before. Enter 'IM' (to use the shorthand version favoured in Conradi's and Wilson's biographies), a complex, sexualized being, capable of cruelty and deception as much as kindness and wit. Ironically, it seems that the author herself has been posthumously subjected to the kind of 'flaying', the forcible stripping away of the illusions about the self, which her characters undergo in countless examples of her fiction. In a review of the film version of Bayley's book Martin Amis wrote of Murdoch's 'fall'.[2]

Of course, reading the life through the work – and *vice versa* – in this way is perhaps a temptation that should be resisted. After all the influence of theories such as Wimsatt and Beardsley's 'intentional fallacy' and Barthes 'death of the author' are still, quite rightly, strong in literary criticism. Yet all the attention on Murdoch's personality has had a curious effect on the work: it has returned her to her own fiction, where previously she seemed strangely absent from it. Where once it seemed that she was hard to find in her novels apart from the traces of her recognisable intellectual interests, now it seems she is everywhere in it.

Consider, for example, what is perhaps the striking centrepiece of Peter Conradi's biography of Murdoch: its revelations about her sado-masochistic affair with the author and thinker Elias Canetti. Conradi is careful to add that Murdoch 'did not judge a proclivity for masochism harshly', and that masochism 'was only one part of her highly complex nature' (Conradi 2001: 358). But a psychoanalyst would remain unpersuaded by this statement. In Lacanian terms, a subject's psychic 'structure' (neurotic, psychotic or perverse) determines their entire experience of their self and their world. We could surmise that although masochism in its erotogenic form was something that manifested itself only sporadically in Murdoch's life, the structure of masochism might have determined many of the patterns in her dealings with others, just as it seems to have governed the organization of power in her fictional world.

For what is the hysterical and eccentric world of her novels if not a sustained and keenly understood presentation of the masochistic universe? In his famous essay on masochism, 'Coldness and Cruelty' (Deleuze 1989), the philosopher Gilles Deleuze argues that what distinguishes masochism from sadism is not material or moral qualities but *formal* ones. It is not the content of masochistic activities that is important (neither the particular means of visiting pain, beatings or piercings, whatever, nor the guilt-feelings Freud was preoccupied with in his consideration of masochism) but the particular context that the subject sets up and the role s/he plays in the narrative. A sadist might appear in the masochistic universe, but he is only a sadist from the perspective of the masochist.[3] A 'proper' sadist is not what a masochist requires, for integral to the masochistic structure is the need to mould a torturer through persuasion, something often achieved formally via an agreed contract.

This suggests a way of understanding the particular distribution of power amongst Murdoch's characters. Her fictional world is dominated by a succession of enchanter-figures who rule over others like cruel tyrants, punishing them emotionally, often enjoying them sexually. But it would be a mistake to characterize these characters as *sadistic*, even though they embody something of the characteristic sadistic coldness in their disregard for the feelings of others. What makes them powerful is the way that others enable them to *remain* powerful. Murdoch's masochistic characters – the women who imagine they are in love with a powerful enchanter and surrender themselves to him abjectly and the men who are willing to become their slaves (e.g. Tommy/Arthur in *A Word Child* or Harriet Gavender/Edgar Demarnay in *The Sacred and Profane Love Machine*) – often offer themselves completely and explicitly to their imagined tormentor: 'Julius, I could be your slave'; 'I don't want a slave', 'I would do anything you wanted, perform any penance' (*FHD* 142–3). Murdoch's stories, in other words, present the enchanter figures from the overall perspective of the masochist rather than the sadist.

My point here is not to try and prove through reference to her novels that Murdoch was indeed masochistic to the core, nor that we should now comb through her novels in search of autobiographical scenes of masochistic enjoyment. Rather, the correspondence between masochism in Murdoch's life and work shows how a greater knowledge of the author can open up new ways of reading her fiction. I have chosen to focus on masochism not simply because of its presence in the biography, but because, intriguingly, it is something that also happens to be central to Murdoch's theory of literary production.

Now we can assess Murdoch's work as 'complete' (though of course it was by no means conceived as a project) we could contend that what amounts to her most valuable contribution to literary theory is her theory of *authorship*. As a conclusion to this book, then, which has dealt with the peculiar way that Murdoch 'hides behind' a series of surrogate authors in her first-person retrospective novels, I want to use the remainder of this postscript to examine this theory in more depth, by concentrating on the significance it attributes to masochism. To do so means, inevitably, considering how Murdoch's fiction itself relates to her theory of authorship. After recasting her theory of literary production in the light of masochism in her biography I will look in turn at the only two novels in her body of work which present us with deliberate, lengthy portraits of novelists 'proper' (i.e. characters who are *practising* novelists for the duration of the story, presented 'from the inside'): *The Black Prince* and *The Sacred and Profane Love Machine*.[4] It seems significant that these two characters, Bradley Pearson and Monty Small, should appear in novels written one after the other, and from what is surely her key period as a writer, the 1970s. It is reasonable to assume that both are the result of Murdoch exploring her art seriously *in* her art for perhaps the first time.

Authorship as masochism

Murdoch's theory of artistic production is founded upon what we might call an 'ethics of impersonality'. Like the good person, she maintained, a novelist should engage in the literary equivalent of *ascesis*, peeling away the egotistical layers of self which cling to her work to leave the representation of pure 'reality' in all its contingent glory. She argues in *The Sovereignty of Good* that '[t]he chief enemy of excellence in morality (and also in art) is personal fantasy: the tissue of self-aggrandizing and consoling wishes and dreams which prevents one from seeing what is there outside one' (*SG* 59). In practice this means the writer must resist the temptation to give in to this fantasy by featuring in her work herself or imposing pre-existing schema or judgement upon it. Characters should develop 'independently' of the author and each other and not be subservient to the demands of the plot. '[T]he greatest art', Murdoch says, 'is "impersonal" because it shows us the world, our world and not another one, with a clarity which startles and delights us simply because we are not used to looking at the real world at all' (*SG* 65). Or, as she put more clearly still in 1978:

> The bad writer gives way to personal obsession and exalts some characters and demeans others without any concern for truth or justice, that is without any suitable aesthetic "explanation". [. . .] The good writer is the just, intelligent judge. He justifies his placing of his characters by some sort of *work* which he does in the book. (Magee 1978)

This 'work', in other words, ensures that the author's own preferences, his/her own morality, if you like, should be *demonstrated* or *implied* rather than stated or represented directly: an author's touch should be felt rather than seen. What she values in Shakespeare, the great exemplar of her ethics of impersonality, is that, stylistically, his work has his signature right through, yet if we look for *him* as author in his text, he is nowhere to be found.

Advocating impersonality is not an unusual impulse in a twentieth-century author. Rather, it has been perhaps the most dominant feature of modern theories of authorship from romanticism (e.g. Schiller, Coleridge, Keats) to modernism (Eliot and Joyce) and poststructuralism (Barthes, perhaps even Bakhtin). Most of all, though, the body of thought Murdoch most resembles in her approach to authorship is psychoanalysis. Despite her misgivings about psychoanalysis this should not be a surprise, as its language is frequently invoked in her discussions of literature. In early polemical pieces like 'The Sublime and the Good', 'The Sublime and the Beautiful Revisited' and 'Against Dryness', for example, she charges currents within contemporary fiction with indulging in fantasy or being 'neurotic'. Her counter theory, the emphasis on preventing personal fantasy from dominating art, can be understood as a variation of the Freudian notion of sublimation, by which, in Murdoch's own words in *The Fire and the Sun*, '[t]he destructive power of the neurosis is foiled by art; the art object expresses the neurotic conflict and defuses it' (*FS* 42).

Murdoch's theory of artistic production rests on a principle not unlike that which underpins much of Freud's writings on aesthetics, such as his 1907 essay 'Creative Writers and Daydreaming': art arises out of the effort to defuse our natural desires. Freud's paper is regarded, for good reason, as unsatisfactory because in arguing that creative writing is simply a matter of the writer using aesthetic form to present a disguised version of his or her own day-dreams, Freud falls into the trap literature tutors tirelessly point out to their students, of the dangers of regarding fiction as disguised autobiography. On another level, of course, Murdoch and Freud part company, because art for Freud remains a disguised expression of selfish impulses no matter its *quality*, while for Murdoch, the better the art the further away it is from personal desire. Fundamentally, however, Murdoch would seem to share Freud's view that the seductions of the unconscious – the artist's compulsions and fantasies – are never far away from artistic endeavour.

This idea is developed most clearly in *The Sovereignty of Good*, Murdoch's most sustained engagement with Freudian theory. Here she expands on the rather general references to the dangers of 'personal obsession' and 'fantasy' in previous works and focuses on one particular kind of fantasy structure which endangers artistic creation, masochism:

A chief enemy to [...] clarity of vision, whether in art or in morals, is the system to which the technical name of sado-masochism has been given. It is the peculiar subtlety of this system that, while constantly leading attention and energy back into the self, it can produce, almost all the way as it were to the summit, plausible imitations of what is good. Refined sado-masochism can ruin art which is too good to be ruined by the cruder vulgarities of self-indulgence. One's self is interesting, so one's motives are interesting, and the unworthiness of one's motives is interesting. (*SG* 68)

This passage is not far from depicting authorship as an inherently perverse activity: whenever an author aims at achieving clarity of vision, masochistic impulses are ready to derail the process. Artistic creation is presented here as nothing other than a struggle against masochism, the implication being that, if left to its own devices – without careful attention – art will naturally become an outlet for masochistic desire.

Murdoch bases her argument here upon a fundamental characteristic masochism, the element of *masquerade*. If masochism is removed from a purely sexual context and refined (sublimated) into artistic production, she argues, it can present itself as something virtuous – that is, telling the truth about the reality of the world around us – when in fact it is driven by a secret egotism which invests personal emotional energy in what it depicts. Depicting suffering is really a way of feeding a dangerous interest in one's own self: of gaining pleasure from enduring apparent unpleasure.[5] Support for this account of masochism can be found in Deleuze's exemplary reading of masochism, which shows how masochism presents itself as passive suffering when in fact it has engineered its own passivity through busy preparatory activity. The masochistic contract persuades the torturer to act in a certain way. Thus the secret pleasure of the masochist derives not from being severely punished by an external agency, but by fashioning one's *own* punishment by moulding this agency oneself. Masochism is not a matter of laying oneself open to the will of another, but willing that other into being.

Murdoch's theory of the novel, then, is founded upon a kind of aesthetic equivalent of Freud's 'primary masochism'. Primary masochism, as Freud argues in his 1924 essay 'The Economic Problem of Masochism' (Freud 1984c) is the result of the ego's efforts to commandeer unruly libidinal impulses to ensure the resolution of the Oedipus complex. But this means that the energy from the id asserts itself elsewhere, in the formation of an overbearing superego. Masochism can thus be regarded as a 'norm of behaviour' rather than a sexual perversion. This was an important moment of reconceptualization for Freud, as it overturned his longheld view that sadism was the primary impulse in the psyche.

He was led to introduce a new category of masochism, 'moral masochism', which was the result of a continued tension between masochistic ego and sadistic superego.

The theory of 'moral masochism' can further clarify Murdoch's theory of authorship. Her conception of the author, constantly subject to masochistic impulses, is the equivalent of the ego in Freud's structure, while the ethical ideal of impersonality, a safeguard against this process, figures as a version of the superego. It is doubtful how useful this analogy would prove in examining the work of many other writers, but it certainly seems an accurate way of figuring Murdoch's *own* strategy for avoiding falling into the masochistic trap in her fiction. Her two characteristic writing 'selves', novelist and philosopher, function in her work like the ego and the superego in the psyche. That is, her philosophical self advances an 'official' theory of authorship (in her non-fiction writings – interviews, philosophy and literary criticism) which involves laying down injunctions, prohibitions and codes of behaviour. With all the characteristic rhetoric of the superego, this persona reminds Murdoch that the *good* author keeps herself out of her work, strives to create characters who are not indulgent versions of herself, and avoids imposing consoling pattern. The authorial self which actually writes the fiction is analogous to the ego, trying to steer a course between the demands of the superego and the desires of the unconscious.

The tension which results can be explored in the Murdoch novel which deals head on with the complexities of authoring fiction, *The Black Prince*. A. S. Byatt and Richard Todd have already considered this novel in terms of Murdoch's understanding of masochism, pointing out that Bradley derives pleasure from the humiliation and punishment he suffers in his story (Byatt 1976; Todd 1979). As such, he serves as a perfect exemplification of the kind of ingenious artist who presents his story as a tale of purification when in fact it is driven by the *jouissance* he derives from the idea of suffering. We might add that this is intensified by the first-person retrospective form, bearing in mind as we read that, according to the logic of the novel, it is *Bradley* who has chosen to present himself in this way, wallowing in his own humiliation. Important, too, is the presence of Loxias, the shadowy editor, who functions as a kind of superegoic entity in Bradley's mind, policing his artistic desires in the way the 'sadistic' superego operates in Freud's theory of 'moral masochism'.

In this way *The Black Prince* serves to illustrate Murdoch's argument in *The Sovereignty of Good* that '[m]asochism is the artist's greatest and most subtle enemy' (*SG* 87). At the same time, though, it is important to recognise that *The Black Prince* is a novel which is deeply concerned with the question of masquerade. Combined with its treatment of authorship and masochism this leads us, in fact, to question its compatibility with Murdoch's argument in *The Sovereignty of Good*. More specifically it problematizes her conviction about the potential of masochism as an arbiter of literary *value*.

The Black Prince is well known as the novel in which Murdoch flirts continuously with appearing in her own fiction, dividing herself into (at least) two authors, Bradley Pearson and Arnold Baffin. As the prolific writer of best-selling intellectual romances Arnold represents the 'public' version of her authorial *persona*, while Bradley figures as her more puritanical serious side (the one closest – in tandem of course with Loxias – to her superego). The layers of masquerade are set out most tantalizingly in the scene which figures as the thematic core of the novel, the *Hamlet* tutorial. Here Bradley argues that in daring to make his own identity crisis into the central issue in the play, Shakespeare reveals himself to be the 'king of masochists', putting on display his own suffering, such as the trauma of his Oedipal conflict, other 'obsessions' like his melancholia and misogyny, and, most of all, the torments of being a writer. It is a daring piece of literary exhibitionism, Bradley argues, because Shakespeare advertises his own obsessions in a language deliberately so powerful as to be accessible to anyone, a kind of literary exhibitionism (*BP* 199–200).

If we follow the logic established by the embedded diegetic layers of this text, it means of course that whatever Bradley says of Shakespeare does not just apply to himself but to Iris Murdoch too. Shakespeare 'is at his most cryptic when he is talking about himself' (*BP* 198), says Bradley. The artist 'appears, however much he may imagine that he hides, in the revealed extension of his work' (*BP* 12). The implication is that in *The Black Prince* Murdoch is performing an act just as daring, just as exhibitionist as Shakespeare's in *Hamlet*. Furthermore it implies that it is just as *masochistic*, too, because at all points it directs its energies back into the self of its author.

The paradox of *The Black Prince* is that it works beautifully in spite of – indeed because of – contravening most of the injunctions laid down by Murdoch's 'superego': it is exquisitely patterned, deeply self-reflexive, and mysteriously autobiographical. But because of its paradoxical status in Murdoch's body of work it compromises the rhetoric of her ethics of impersonality. For another way of conceiving of the significance of masquerade in masochism is to say that masochism problematizes the act of *interpretation*, for it complicates notions of intention and the will.

Over the last couple of decades this has been debated in legal studies, as in the infamous 'Spanner' case in 1993.[6] Can someone be guilty of perpetrating violence on a person, if prior consent has been given via a contract?

It is a similar kind of undecideability that we find in highly metafictional texts like *The Black Prince*. Though we identify with Bradley Pearson – just as we do with Hamlet – we cannot be absolutely sure in the end if his version of events is correct. We cannot be certain which of the interpretations of his narrative offered by the other characters in the postscripts, if any, is the correct one. In this sense, Murdoch has managed to keep her distance from her characters, in Bakhtinian terms: we are not sure which view she endorses. Yet, crucially, this sense of indeterminacy prevails when it comes to the question of masochism and the novel. For at the end it is unclear whether the narrative Bradley produces is the outcome of having been led from his ordeal to some greater apprehension of reality, or whether it is merely an example of the 'refined' sadomasochism which can masquerade as good art. In this novel, you never can tell: all the acts of criticism it contains – from Bradley's partial reviews of Arnold's novels to the postscripts analysing his own narrative – contain insights, 'truths', but which are skewed by desire. This aspect of the novel, Murdoch's most sustained practical enquiry into the theory and practice of authorship, complicates her literary theory. How can we tell whether any good work of art is *really* a good work of art or one that is only *pretending* to be one?

Monsters and mothers: *The Sacred and Profane Love Machine*

In the light of the deconstructive nature of *The Black Prince* it is interesting to consider how Murdoch deals with the question of authorship in the novel which followed it, *The Sacred and Profane Love Machine*. This text seems to be fuelled by some of the excess energy from its predecessor as far as this theme is concerned. Where Murdoch divides herself between Arnold and Bradley in *The Black Prince*, *The Sacred and Profane Love Machine* shifts the hypodiegetic levels down one degree: instead of a real writer splitting herself into two fictional characters we have a fictional writer dividing himself into two fictional characters. Monty Small has split off part of himself to form a fictional detective, Milo Fane. Milo is a fantasy version of Monty, the 'ideal ego' in psychoanalytic terms, a creation who magnifies his strengths and eliminates his weaknesses. But Monty has come to despise him precisely because of this strength. Instead of his hero salving his sense of inadequacy his existence constantly reminds him of it. Moreover, he is unable to 'kill him off'. As the novel begins Monty is haunted by Milo, feeling that his own creation is stalking him inside his own house (*SPLM* 33).

As a thriller writer Monty is a practitioner of the kind of fiction which exemplifies Murdoch's (and many others) category of 'bad art'. In her 1978 interview with Magee she says, '[o]ne can see how the thriller or the sentimental picture may be simply a stimulus to the private fantasies of the reader or viewer' (Magee 1978). Monty himself subscribes to this definition, calling himself a 'failed novelist'. The detective and thriller genres are bywords for wish-fulfilment in art, and for the disappointment that artists feel in themselves,[7] and this is how they tend to signify within Murdoch's fiction, despite the similarity between her own handling of narrative suspense and that of the thriller writer.[8] Emma Sands is also an author of detective novels. Her writing is never discussed in *An Unofficial Rose*, except for a comic scene where we listen to a reading of a couple of sentences from one of her books. Instead her profession serves to emphasize her role as enchanter in the lives of the characters of the novel, who are treated by her (a classic Murdochian 'artist-figure') as characters to be manipulated into a plot of her making. Her role in the novel is really a small one, but it embodies a warning about the responsibility a novelist should feel, not just to her characters, but to those who engage with her characters as if they are real. The function of Emma Sands is to underline the value of fiction-making, but also its dangers.

The dangers are also suggested, more powerfully, by the experiences of Monty Small. As well as Milo Fane Monty has created another character who does not appear in the pages of any novel, but is used by his psychoanalyst friend Blaise Gavender as an alibi: a fictitious patient who provides cover for his visits to his mistress. In contrast to the ascetic Milo, 'Magnus Bowles' is an exaggeration of Monty's 'other' side, his neurotic, hypersensitive persona. Magnus is a 'failed artist' (*SPLM* 113), and as such menaces Monty just as doggedly as Milo: 'Was he destined to begin his manhood as Milo Fane and to complete it as Magnus Bowles?' (*SPLM* 113). Black comedy is eventually derived from the fact that Harriet, Blaise's wife – who is the victim of the pretence – comes to care deeply for Magnus Bowles. His 'death' is experienced by her as the final straw, the last of a series of losses of people she depended upon, and hastens her nervous breakdown.

Monty's fictional characters contribute to an overall focus in *The Sacred and Profane Love Machine* on the way that dead or non-existent people affect the living. Besides being stalked by Milo Fane Monty is haunted by the voice of his dead wife Sophie. Suspense is increased in the plot as

Murdoch cleverly defers, for much of the novel, an explanation as to why Monty grieves so excessively for Sophie. The reason, we eventually realize, is that it is because he killed her in order to relieve her suffering from cancer. He is so tormented that he is unable, somewhat masochistically, to prevent himself repeatedly playing a tape-recording of Sophie's voice made just before she died. The sheer uncanniness of her voice is felt by Harriet, who overhears it when Monty is playing it back (*SPLM* 242), and worries that either Sophie's ghost inhabits his house or that she is not really dead but hidden inside. In a symbolic sense, of course, this is accurate. In keeping with the way the uncanny operates in Murdoch's retrospective fiction, Sophie's tape-recorded voice (as something familiar which manifests itself in a disturbingly unfamiliar context) shows how we cannot elude the grasp of the traumatic past.

Sophie's voice, like the power wielded by Milo and Magnus, is therefore part of a particular concern in *The Sacred and Profane Love Machine* with the question of 'offspring', with the bits that we remove from or bracket off from ourselves, hoping to achieve a cleansing effect, but which return to haunt us. The idea of creation is evoked most obviously by the novel's concern with motherhood. Three of the male characters, Monty, David Gavender and Edgar Demarnay, attempt to keep the potentially suffocating attentions of their mothers at bay, while the plot turns on the mothering of Blaise's son Luca by his mistress Emily McHugh. This theme, Peter Conradi has suggested, explains the original title of the novel, *A Monster and its Monster* (Conradi 1989: 211). Yet the only part of the text to which this title would seem to relate directly is a nightmare Monty has about a hideous decapitated monster whose baby clings to its side weeping. While this symbolizes the novel's dark take on the destructive mother–son bond, it also underlines the *Frankenstein*-like relationship Monty endures with his own creations.[9]

When we consider this in terms of Murdoch's theory of authorship it seems that the capacity of Monty's characters to somehow exist beyond the parameters their creator has set for them is the uncanny obverse of one of the central tenets of her theory, that authors should create characters who transcend their function in the story. Here an author does just this, but unintentionally, not because of his 'love' for them but out of selfish – not to say masochistic (certainly in the case of Milo Fane, a character designed to make him suffer) – impulses. As a result he is persecuted by them. Like *The Black Prince*, then, *The Sacred and Profane Love Machine* is on one level a cautionary tale which springs from the same moral source as Murdoch's ethics of impersonality. Unlike *The Black Prince*, however, in which Murdoch's metafictional experimentation takes on a life of its own and escapes her control, she has written its follow-up without directly inhabiting the figure of the author to any obvious degree. *The Sacred and Profane Love Machine* presents us with a portrait of a masochistic author without being the obvious product of a masochistic author.

Notes

1 Revisiting the sublime and the beautiful: Iris Murdoch's realism

1. The connection between romanticism and modernism is not by any means unprecedented, of course. See, for example, Waugh (1992) and Jameson (1981).
2. The influence is most clearly apparent in Murdoch's book on Sartre (82–3), and she refers to Lukács in the interview with Magee (1978). See Lukács (1950, 1963).
3. Two useful discussions of Murdoch's construction of an underlying myth in her earlier novels can be found in Souvage (1962) and Byatt (1965).
4. Murdoch's attitude towards myth is examined in relation to modernism in Wasson (1969) and Byatt (1991).
5. See, for example, Philippe Lacoue-Labarthe and Jean-Luc Nancy, *The Literary Absolute: The Theory of Literature in German Romanticism* (New York: State University of New York Press 1988) and Paul Hamilton, *Wordsworth* (Brighton: Harvester 1986).
6. For a thorough, informative discussion of Murdoch's engagement with Western philosophy, see Heusel (1995).
7. A detailed assessment of the significance of Weil on Murdoch's philosophy can be found in Byatt (1965).
8. See, for example, Bersani (1992), Belsey (1980) and Eagleton (1986a).
9. See Goode (1966), the chapter 'Character and Liberalism' in Bergonzi (1970) and Bayley (1974).
10. This quotation comes from an interview in *The Listener*, 4 April 1968, cited in Bergonzi (1970).
11. Gordon (1995: 89).
12. The term psychoanalysis, as Bruno Bettelheim has explained, resulted from Freud's deep humanist aspiration to be 'midwife of the soul' – a phrase used by the American poet and former patient of Freud, Hilda Doolittle (Bettelheim 1982).
13. I am arguing here that Murdoch's attitude to Freud is ambivalent. She is by no means a 'Freudian' – as she takes pains to insist (in the interview with Rose [1968], for example) – yet it is going too far to say that she is involved in a 'feud' with Freud, as Jack Turner does in *Murdoch v. Freud: A Freudian Look at an Anti-Freudian* (1993).
14. BBC interview 1971, quoted in Todd (1979).

2 The insistence of the past

1. See the chapters 'Looking Backwards' and 'Between Nostalgia and Nightmare' in Bergonzi (1970: 104–48, 149–87).

2. See Hutcheon (1988) and Lee (1990). Its sensitivity towards the question of accessing the real in my view dissociates historiographic metafiction from much of the ironic playfulness many see as representative of postmodern culture. And if its attitude to the past is nostalgic, it is certainly not the empty dehistoricized nostalgia Fredric Jameson associates with postmodernism (Jameson 1991).

3. In an interview with S. B. Sagare Murdoch claims that '[t]he idea about abolishing the central characters was really a kind of joke in a way. I didn't mean that literally I would do this but that very often a novelist may find that the minor characters have more individuality than the central characters' (Sagare 2001).

4. Murdoch repeated similar views in a conversation with me on 28 July 1994.

5. In a letter to his friend Pfister, quoted by Bettelheim, Freud speaks of his aim to entrust psychoanalysis 'to a profession that doesn't yet exist, a profession of secular ministers of souls, who don't have to be physicians and must not be priests' (Bettelheim 1982: 35).

3   Narrative as redemption: *The Bell*

1. Iris Murdoch, 'A House of Theory' in Conradi 1999, 171–86 (172).

2. Howard German, 'Allusion in the Early Novels of Iris Murdoch', *Modern Fiction Studies* XV: 2, Autumn 1969: 361–77.

3. A. S. Byatt speculates that Imber evokes connotations of 'umber' or 'umbra' (shades or shadows) (Byatt 1999: xii). A more prosaic explanation for Murdoch's choice of name is the fact that there is a real Imber in Wiltshire – or rather *was*, until the village was requisitioned by the Army in 1943. It now stands as a ghost village, the only original buildings left being the Manor House, which is called Imber Court, the nearby church of St Giles, and the old pub called The Bell.

4. John Milton (1644) *Areopagitica: A Speech for the Liberty of Unlicensed Printing to the Parliament of England.* In John Milton, *Complete English Poems, of Education, Areopagitica* (London: Phoenix 1993).

5. Iris Murdoch, 'Vision and Choice in Morality' in Conradi (1999), 76–98.

4   Author and hero: Murdoch's first-person retrospective novels

1. Barthes (1977: 111). 'External focalization' is used by Gérard Genette in *Narrative Discourse* (1980) while 'psychonarration' is Dorrit Cohn's term (1978). For a detailed exploration of this form of narration, see Rimmon-Kenan (1983).

2. Other valid comparisons with modernist authors can be made. Virginia Woolf is similarly concerned with how the flux of reality is divided up artificially by various forms, and her novels also regard love as the supreme binding force. As I have already suggested, a comparison with Lawrence is worthwhile too. Despite their obvious differences (most clear, in fact, when it comes to narrative voice) both conceive of the psyche in similarly Platonic-Freudian terms and present this via dramatic 'set-pieces' (compare, for example, Gerard on the horse at the level-crossing in *Women in Love*, and Rain Carter's car in *The*

Sandcastle). Malcolm Bradbury compares Woolf and Murdoch in his essay '"A House Fit for Free Characters": The Novels of Iris Murdoch' (1973), while Gordon (1995) discusses Murdoch and Lawrence.

3. There are only a couple of exceptions: see the chapter 'The Role of the Narrator' in Johnson (1987: 20–54) or McCall (1991).

4. In my conversation with Murdoch, Oxford, 28 July 1994.

5. Peter Conradi has discussed the similarities between Murdoch's heroes and Dostoevsky's (see Conradi 1988, 1989).

6. See Conradi (1989: 297, n2). His book also makes some valid comparisons between her work and romance.

7. The extra power which results from witnessing the narrator actually reliving his past can be suggested if we imagine third-person versions of Murdoch's first-person texts. This is not in fact as hypothetical as it may seem, in fact, for the stage adaptations of three of Murdoch's first-person novels also involve the application of an alternative text to the same basic story: *A Severed Head* (1963, with J. B. Priestley), *The Italian Girl* (1968, with James Saunders), and her own adaptation of *The Black Prince* (1989). As conversion into a different medium, these adaptations illustrate the importance of the retrospective dimension.

The suitability of these particular works for conversion is easily apparent. Each has a small cast, a compact range of settings and a concise plot, without the reader requiring to be filled in on a great deal of background information. All three depict a favourite Murdochian situation, 'a poor, rather gullible, confused man stumbling on from one awful blow to another' (Rose 1968). Yet these advantages must be weighed against the large amount of abridgement required to adapt a work made up largely of narratorial introspection, which must necessarily be a major obstacle when converting a first-person novel into a play.

Without this dimension, *A Severed Head* and *The Italian Girl*, although just as entertaining as the originals, are ultimately no more than uncanny likenesses. Deprived of the tortured workings of Martin's mind, *A Severed Head* is reduced to a witty 'Restoration' comedy of manners – much the same, in fact, as Harold Hobson's reductive interpretation, expressed in a *Sunday Times* review, of the novel as a meditation on 'the ineptitude of the English in illicit love, upon their quaint staggerings when they stray from the straight and narrow path'. Martin's love for Honor Klein, which in the novel is made to seem far more intense than any other of the many love affairs, is, in the play, in danger of appearing like just one more meaningless sexual liaison, a product of the permissive era in which the novel is set. *The Times* drama critic, reviewing the play in 1963, commended the play for its comedy and its crisp presentation of Murdoch's 'scrupulously articulate and emotionally entangled world', but detected something missing. He or she recognized that Honor Klein 'holds a position of deeper significance in the play. But it is hard to decide precisely what this is. [. . .] At this symbolic level the adaptation does not manage to carry the novel's content into the theatre, and the result is more arbitrary than illuminating' ('Every Laugh Well Placed', *The Times*, 8 May 1963).

Similarly, though the play version of *The Italian Girl* does manage to echo the Gothic atmosphere of the original (chiefly as a result of the melodramatic manner which the stage directions encourage the actors to adopt) it results in a diminishing of Edmund's character. Where he is portrayed sympathetically in the novel, as a man beset by a damaging other-fixation and a deeply nostalgic

longing to return to childhood, in the play he becomes, as *The Times*'s
reviewer saw him, a prudish moralist whose only role is to go around 'telling
everyone unconvincingly that sex is bad' ('Surprise and a Little Fun', *The
Times*, 7 February 1968).

   The play version of *The Black Prince* is Murdoch's most accomplished adaptation, and the only one of the three to retain the retrospective aspect of the
novel, the sense of the narrator reliving previous events. Its metafictional
debate about the nature of art is paralleled, naturally, by the use of the play
within a play. Bradley tells the audience, 'I have changed my beloved into
art. I have preserved her inside this frame. [Gestures to indicate the prison,
the theatre.] This is her immortality – from this embrace she cannot escape.
So speaks the artist' (*BP*, play version, 299–300). Yet still we miss Bradley's written
meditations. As he says of Hamlet, Bradley himself is words; but unlike Hamlet,
he is not just the words he speaks but the words he writes. Bradley's final
soliloquy suggests that Murdoch is aware of this fact, when he reveals that
the play the audience has just seen is his own artistic re-creation of what
happened: 'I lost my Julian. But I wrote my book. [Takes book out of table
drawer and stands]' (*BP* 299). Yet Bradley has written a novel, not a play.
Thus the strong sense of the surrogate author's independence, which drives
the first-person novels, inevitably cannot be reproduced on stage. To use
Hamburger's terminology, a play is not a feigned reality statement, like the
first-person novel. The autonomy of his text is finally lost, as is a little of the
revisionary force of the postscripts (still present, as the Epilogue), because
the audience has of course seen the events with its own eyes.

8. It is worth pointing out here that not all the artists in Murdoch's fiction fit
   the definition of 'artist-figures' (those who manipulate others around them
   like novelists). For example, the painter Bledyard in *The Sandcastle* and the
   thriller-writer Monty Small in *The Sacred and Profane Love Machine* have aspirations towards the Good which cannot simply be dismissed as falsely
   consolatory, though they do not approximate the saintly.

9. In describing the self-begetting novel as metafictional, it is necessary to consider
   Waugh's view that it is not necessarily 'postmodernist': 'The emphasis is on the
   development of the narrator, on the modernist concern of consciousness rather
   than the post-modernist one of fictionality (as in, for example, André Gide's
   Les Faux-Monnayeurs)' (Waugh 1984: 14). Yet we can say, I think, that the self-
   begetting novel is postmodernist in the sense that it exhibits a self-consciousness
   about its own process of construction, which often – as in the case of Murdoch's
   artist-novels – involves an exploration of fictionality.

10. See Waugh (1984: 19, 99), Alexander (1990: 168), Stevenson (1991: 29) and
    Hutcheon (1984: 102), who remarks on the foregrounding of reading in
    A Word Child.

11. In Genette's terminology, these time-spheres correspond to the 'extradiegetic'
    and 'diegetic' levels of narration.

5   Reading past truth: *Under the Net* and *The Black Prince*

1. Murdoch herself says something very similar in the interview with Magee,
   a statement which serves to underline the view that *The Black Prince* is her

most personally reflexive work: 'Of course philosophers have unconscious minds too, and philosophy can relieve our fears; it is often revealing to ask a philosopher, "what is he afraid of?"' (Magee 1978).

2. Those (e.g. the present author) who like to psychoanalyse fictional characters may be interested in the light Bradley's epistemophilia sheds on two of his psychological problems, his sexual impotence and his 'writer's block'. Freud says that, for the epistemophiliac, the satisfaction which results from thinking his way to the heart of a problem 'is experienced as a *sexual* satisfaction' (Freud 1984a: 124). Given Bradley's inability to penetrate the heart of a mystery, it is perhaps not surprising that he is impotent. Furthermore, according to Freud, the result of the sexualization of the thought-process means that the subject prefers to dwell on thoughts rather than act. This prompts another of the novel's many links with literature's most celebrated procrastinator. Terry Eagleton has in fact linked the concept of epistemophilia to *Hamlet* (Eagleton 1986b: 65). Whereas Othello is manifestly an epistemophiliac, he suggests, Hamlet himself represents the heart of everyone else's mystery. He is certainly the heart of Bradley's.

3. Murdoch's contemporary Philip Larkin once described his meeting with her: 'she is very nice, but given to asking questions: "Where do you live? How many rooms? What kind of carpet? What kind of pictures? What do you eat? How do you cook?" etc. A real novelist's interest...' (Letter to Barbara Pym, 26 June 1971, *Selected Letters of Philip Larkin 1940–1985*, ed. Anthony Thwaite [London: Faber 1992], 439).

4. Peter Brooks comments that the English translation of Barthes' phrase '*la passion du sens*' does not do justice to its ambivalence in French, where it means 'both the passion *for* meaning and the passion *of* meaning: the active quest of the reader for those shaping ends that, terminating the dynamic process of reading, promise to bestow meaning and significance on the beginning and the middle' (Brooks 1992: 19).

5. See, for example, Byatt (1976), and the section on *The Black Prince* in the reissue of her *Degrees of Freedom* (1965).

6. Most of Murdoch's own fiction – certainly this novel – conforms to neither approach, but instead amounts to a combination of the two. Her art is both 'fun' and 'an aspect of the good life' (*BP* 187) – a dialogue between both viewpoints.

7. See the interview with Ziegler and Bigsby (1982).

8. *The Black Prince*'s rhetoric about the power of the word is plentiful. Bradley uses words as a 'barrier' to protect himself from Arnold (*BP* 82), admires *Hamlet* for showing that words can be a powerful redemptive force 'in the lives of those without identity, that is human beings' (*BP* 199), and realizes he can become a murderer in the eyes of the law simply by confessing (*BP* 388). He places special value on the written word, for it has special ability to effect change. He invests letters with 'magical power', for 'to desiderate something in a letter is, I often irrationally feel, tantamount to bringing it about' (*BP* 62–3). His faith is shown to be perfectly rational after all later in the novel when Arnold's letter declaring his love for Christian is found by Rachel who then kills him in a jealous rage. Above all, words are the vehicle for his ultimate artistic desire, to 'travel that path, through truth, absurdity, simplicity, to silence' (*BP* 392) by writing a great work of art.

9. Such injustice is quite at home, however, in a genre of postmodernist fiction to which *The Black Prince* could loosely be linked, the antidetective story. Put simply, examples of this kind of fiction (like Paul Auster's *City of Glass* and Peter Ackroyd's *Hawksmoor*, to name but two) create a sense of disorder where the classic, modernist detective story emphasizes order. See McHale (1992: 291).

10. See the readings of the novel given in Conradi (1989) and Dipple (1984) for a fuller account of this interpretation.

11. The extent of Murdoch's insistence at Amsterdam that *The Black Prince* is relatively simple to decipher, despite the mystification, is in fact quite striking. She denies that the postscripts destabilize the narrative, because of their brevity compared with Bradley's story and because of the unreliability of each writer. She agrees that Julian's admission 'I think the child I was loved the man Pearson was' (*BP* 411), is a casual way of saying 'actually it's all true ... all this did happen, you may take what you've just been reading about as true; but the implication is that *she* could have told it better'. She acknowledges some readers will remain puzzled by the ambiguity of the novel, but hopes it is only a 'small number', for she did not deliberately include 'contradictory constructions'. In the end, she trusts Bradley and Loxias' rhetoric is convincing.

6   The writing cure: *A Severed Head* and *A Word Child*

1. Conradi (1989) offers an illuminating examination of the opposition between the Murdochian 'open' and 'closed' novel – or an essentially crystalline version versus the kind of realism which approximates Murdoch's aesthetic of the sublime.

2. Her critics have tended to divide Murdoch's work into three main phases, the middle one – commonly seen as her most successful – beginning with *The Nice and the Good* (1968) and ending with *The Sea, the Sea* (1978).

3. The novel itself seems to have exerted an uncanny fascination over Murdoch, who regarded it as one of her favourites. It is bodied forth in her later fiction: Honor Klein, its most uncanny character, is mentioned in *The Sea, the Sea* as an example of a difficult part for an actress to play; in *An Unofficial Rose*, a bottle of Lynch-Gibbon wine is opened. Despite her confessed affection for the novel, it is conspicuous by its absence as Murdoch forgets its title when trying to recall her first-person novels at the conference at Caen. A further example of its habit of returning comes in 1964, when Murdoch adapted it – replayed it – for the stage.

4. Freud's essay on the uncanny is one of his most important contributions to literary theory, and has been particularly useful in the study of the fantastic. The essay itself has also been comprehensively analysed and deconstructed: for some examples, see Wright (1984: 142–50).

5. Where in the novel Honor cuts in half a napkin thrown in the air, she uses in the play a far more significant object: she decapitates a small figurine of Bishamon.

6. Freud notes that '*heimlich* is a word the meaning of which develops in the direction of ambivalence, until it finally coincides with its opposite,

unheimlich' (Freud 1990: 347) arguing that this is because the uncanny 'is nothing new or alien, but something which is familiar and old-established in the mind and which has become alienated from it only through the process of repression' (Freud 1990: 363–4).

7. See Brooks' chapter in the same volume, 'Repetition, Repression, and Return: The Plotting of *Great Expectations*' (1992: 113–42) for an example of such a text. In my readings of Murdoch's novels in this chapter I am indebted to Brooks' work on repetition in psychoanalysis and literature.

8. An illuminating discussion about the importance of Frazer's work in understanding *A Severed Head* can be found in Byatt (1991).

9. While these allusions suggest that Martin sees his story as one of mythic proportions, they also show how Murdoch tantalizes the reader with the illusion that there is a 'crystalline' myth underlying the novel. Besides the Orpheus and Medusa connections, which I have referred to, there are many other allusions to mythology. Palmer and Antonia are likened to Ares and Hephaistos. In finally capturing Honor, Martin resembles Perseus, the decapitator of Medusa, the capturer of the severed head. Palmer is compared to Dionysus, his philosophy that a person must act as his heart compels him ('Only let your imagination encompass what your heart privately desires. Tell yourself: nothing is impossible' [*SH* 168]) fitting for the god of mystic ecstasy. To make the allusions still more entangled, Dionysus is connected with Orpheus (some see both as founding the Eleusinian mysteries) and, most significantly in the light of Martin's defeat of Palmer, Perseus, who in resisting the cult of Dionysus fought and drowned him. In order to coerce her into keeping quiet about their affair Martin tells Georgie of how Psyche was promised her child would become a god if she remained silent about her pregnancy. Psyche was the most beautiful of three sisters just as Georgie is the most beautiful of Martin's three partners.

The myth of Psyche is also particularly relevant to the novel as a whole. Despite its obvious connection with the soul, her story also involves a descent to the underworld, and suggests the choice Freud examines in his essay 'The Theme of the Three Caskets' (Penguin Freud Library, vol. 14 [Harmondsworth: Penguin 1990], 233–48), between the symbolic roles of mother, beloved and Mother Earth (the inorganic state) – which we might see as the roles played by Antonia, Georgie and Honor in Martin's story. Furthermore, the tale of Amor and Psyche concerns the extreme love of a mother for her son. Amor's mother is Venus – to whom Honor is compared – and one of her lovers is Mars (Palmer).

10. It would be possible, of course, to consider her sublime aesthetic from a psychoanalytic perspective. The repetition at the heart of the plot serves as an eruption of the real in the symbolic, a version of what we might call the 'Lacanian sublime'.

11. We could return at this point to *A Word Child*'s meditation on *King Lear*. Hilary's decision to pay back the universe resembles Edmund's, and his belief in the 'gods' echoes a similar theme in the play (at one point Clifford Larr quotes Gloucester's 'As flies to wanton boys are we to the gods...'). Other shared themes (besides the central concern with redemptive suffering, which I discussed previously) include the difficulty of finding an appropriate discourse for suffering, Hilary's frequently expressed fears of going mad, and

the way that descriptions of stormy weather, particularly incessant rain and strong winds, become more common as the story gathers pace.

12. For examples of these texts, and Brooks' development of his theory, see the chapters 'Narrative Transaction and Transference' and 'An Unreadable Report: Conrad's *Heart of Darkness*' in Brooks (1992), and also the essay 'Changes in the Margins: Construction, Transference, and Narrative' in Brooks (1994).

13. This notion is central to Brooks' *Reading for the Plot*, which contends that 'plot is the internal logic of the discourse of mortality' (Brooks 1992: 22).

14. In *A Word Child*, to give an example, a comment like 'As I may sometimes seem in what follows...' (*WC* 7) implicitly foregrounds the narrative act. But besides this kind of remark, there is only one direct address to the reader ('which I must leave the reader to determine' [*WC* 60]) and one explicit acknowledgement that he is writing: 'Then I put a hand on her arm. I felt the rough cold snow-dusted surface of the coat sleeve and can feel its texture this moment as I write' (*WC* 312).

15. Brooks reiterates Genette's belief that 'one can tell a story without any reference to the place of its telling, the location from which it is proffered, but that one cannot tell a story without indications of the time of telling in relation to the told' (Brooks 1992: 21). Contained in this statement is an implicit recognition of the importance of the epic situation, but consonant first-person novels like *A Severed Head* and *A Word Child* suggest that when interpreting a first-person novel we do require a more precise idea of the length of time which has elapsed between story and narration, as well as the place where narration occurs, that Brooks and Genette acknowledge.

16. Byatt's reading of *A Severed Head* (in *Degrees of Freedom* 1965) explains how the novel sets up a dialogue between the Freudian and Sartrean interpretations of the Medusa image, which links to its central themes of 'enslavement' and 'liberation', and the breaking of taboo (something she explores further in her 1991 essay '"The Omnipotence of Thought"...'). She takes her cue from a footnote in *Sartre: Romantic Rationalist* where Murdoch compares Freud's and Sartre's reading of Medusa as, respectively, 'a castration fear' and 'our general fear of being observed', and wonders aloud 'how one would set about determining which was "correct"' (*S* 125). Yet these interpretations are not oppositions so much as two sides of the same coin, for the psychoanalytic understanding of castration could be said to incorporate the Sartrean notion of symbolic imprisonment.

7   The ambivalence of coming home: *The Italian Girl* and *The Sea, the Sea*

1. Nostalgia is evident not just in Murdoch's fiction and her literary theory, but also appeared fleetingly – surprisingly perhaps – on those rare occasions when she spoke autobiographically. She was an only child who was born in Dublin and moved to London at the age of one: 'I lived in a perfect trinity of love. It made me expect that, in a way, everything is going to be like that, since it was a very deep harmony' (Haffenden 1985). The sense of loss in these words is also apparent when she linked her fascination with brothers

and sisters and twins to her experience as an only child, seeking to recreate in fiction 'the lost, other person whom one is looking for' (Caen 1978). Similarly Murdoch's personal experience of exile contributes to the nostalgic strain in her work. Her departure from Ireland and subsequent detachment from her Irish relatives made her realize 'as I grow older that we were wanderers, and I've only recently realized that I'm a kind of exile, a displaced person. I identify with exiles' (Haffenden 1985). Being an exile, needless to say, is as much about time as it is about space, as it involves the longing to return to a home which is no longer accessible, perhaps because it never existed in the way we imagine it.

2. 'In the literary artistic chronotope, spatial and temporal indicators are fused into one carefully thought-out, concrete whole. Time, as it were, thickens, takes on flesh, becomes artistically visible; likewise space becomes charged and responsive to the movements of time, plot and history. This intersection of axes and fusion of indicators characterizes the artistic chronotope' (Bakhtin 1996: 184). The space–time juxtaposition is frequently visible in the 'post-Proustian' nostalgic tradition of late modernism, in Hartley's *The Go-Between* ('The past is a foreign country: they do things differently there' [Harmondsworth: Penguin 1986], 7), or the elaborate form of Durrell's *Alexandria Quartet* which explicitly sets out to weld together space and time.

3. From my conversation with Murdoch (Oxford, 28 July 1994).

4. This, and all subsequent quotations from Murdoch on Proust, are taken from her short yet extremely incisive reading of *A la Recherche du temps perdu* in *Metaphysics as a Guide to Morals* (262–4).

5. Genette's discussion of this kind of narration contains other insights which are relevant to *The Sea, the Sea*. He regards it as the most complex type of narration 'since the story and the narrating can become entangled in such a way that the latter has an effect on the former', a development, as we have seen, which occurs in Murdoch's novel. *The Sea, the Sea* also bears out his claim that 'the journal form loosens up to result in a sort of monologue after the event' (Genette 1980: 217).

6. Johnson's theory of the deconstructive subtext, discussed in Chapter 4, is most convincing when applied to present-tense narrative, as we can see in Lorna Martens' similar argument about the diary-novel (Martens 1985).

7. The importance of preserving a particular understanding of the past is illustrated in a similar way in *A Severed Head* and *A Word Child*. Upon discovering his wife's long-standing deception with his brother, Martin experiences it as an injury to his past rather than to himself (*SH* 195–6). Similarly, Crystal's revelation about her brief affair with Gunnar has a dramatic effect on Hilary: 'I wonder if you know what this is doing to me?', he asks her. 'You've changed the past' (*WC* 253).

8 Philosophy's dangerous pupil: *Metaphysics as a Guide to Morals*, Derrida and *The Philosopher's Pupil*

1. Skhlovsky says that '[i]t is common practice to assert that Tristram Shandy is not a novel. Those who speak in this way regard opera alone as true music, while a symphony for them is mere chaos. *Tristram Shandy* is the most typical novel in world literature' (Shklovsky 1991).

2. See Derek Attridge's *Jacques Derrida: Acts of Literature* (London and New York: Routledge 1992) for a collection of Derrida's explorations of the relation between literature and philosophy.
3. As Derek Attridge points out, Derrida's notion of writing as a phenomenon which eludes conventional notions of identity, temporality, origin, activity/passivity depends 'on the opposition between the sensible and the intelligible [which] is a longstanding metaphysical one' (Attridge 1992: 9). Derrida himself is well aware of the impossibility of ever completely escaping the conceptual motivations of metaphysics.

Postscript: reading Iris Murdoch

1. John Bayley, *Iris: A Memoir of Iris Murdoch* (1998), *Iris and the Friends: A Year of Memories* (1999), *The Widower's House* (2002); Peter J. Conradi, *Iris Murdoch: A Life* (London: Harper Collins 2001); A. N. Wilson, *Iris Murdoch: As I Knew Her* (London: Hutchison 2003).
2. Martin Amis, 'Age Will Win', *The Guardian*, 21 December 2001.
3. Deleuze's essay insists that we should be wary of the automatic pairing together of sadism and masochism, as 'their processes and formations are entirely different' (Deleuze 1989: 46).
4. If we leave to one side the novelists-by-proxy who narrate Murdoch's first-person retrospective novels, the fact is that there are only five novelists 'proper' in all her fiction. Besides Bradley and Monty we have: Emma Sands (*The Unofficial Rose*), Garth Gibson Grey (*An Accidental Man*) and Arnold Baffin (*The Black Prince*). Unlike Bradley and Monty the first two are peripheral characters, and Arnold is only seen through the framework of Bradley's prejudiced narrative. An exceptional case is Jake Donahue, for it is only at the end of *Under the Net* that he is really – consciously, that is – a novelist. As a self-begetting novel, however, this decision means that the logic of *Under the Net* is that he has therefore 'written' the whole thing from the start.
5. It is worth pointing out that Murdoch here is surely referring only to masochism rather than sadism, even though she uses the term 'sadomasochism'. Her insights do not seem to apply to sadism which is purely, overtly egotistical in her terms, compared to masochism, which has the capacity to give the *illusion* of being something other than it is.
6. Operation Spanner was a police investigation, begun in 1987, in which a group of men were charged with the murder of a teenage rent-boy. The men successfully argued in court that the death was the result of a sadomasochistic practice which had gone tragically wrong.
7. 'Hard-boiled' detective writer Dashiell Hammett always wanted to write a 'real' novel, but never could. Ian Fleming, much like Monty Small, created a fictional character, James Bond, who compensated for his own inadequacies.
8. Murdoch does explicitly draw on, or parody, the conventions of the detective novel on two occasions. *The Nice and the Good* begins with an apparent suicide, and a detective is swiftly called, while *The Black Prince*, which begins with an attempted murder and ends with a real one, could, as I argued in Chapter 5, be read as a metaphysical 'whodunnit' in which the role of detective is played by the reader.

9. Monty is, therefore, like Victor Frankenstein, a kind of father. It is interesting, however, that in a novel so full of mothers, Blaise is the only real father. As a variation on the Murdochian enchanter-figure, though much weaker and less charismatic than Julius King or Hilary Burde, it is tempting to regard him as a combination of both the father-figures which Lacan classified in relation to Freud's discussion of Oedipal conflict in *Totem and Taboo*. In one sense he represents the 'symbolic father' in that he sets down the law which the other characters must adhere to. Paradoxically, though, he is representative of another, archaic, primordial, law too: as the 'obscene father' he also wants the boundaries he has erected to come down so that he can exploit the chaos. In one of his hypocritical self-indulgent letters to his wife Harriet, he tells her 'I am acting with my eyes open. I *see* how awful all this is, what an outrage, what a crime. But I am placed between crime and crime and I have to move' (*SPLM* 247).

Select Bibliography and References

Major Works by Iris Murdoch

Novels

Under the Net (London, 1954).
The Bell (London, 1958).
A Severed Head (London, 1961).
An Unofficial Rose (London, 1962).
The Unicorn (London, 1963).
The Italian Girl (London, 1964).
The Time of the Angels (London, 1966).
The Nice and the Good (London, 1968).
A Fairly Honourable Defeat (London, 1970).
An Accidental Man (London, 1971).
The Black Prince (London, 1973).
The Sacred and Profane Love Machine (London, 1974).
A Word Child (London, 1975).
The Sea, the Sea (London, 1978).
The Philosopher's Pupil (London, 1983).
The Good Apprentice (London, 1985).
The Message to the Planet (London, 1989).
The Green Knight (London, 1993).
Jackson's Dilemma (London, 1995).

Plays

A Severed Head, with J. B. Priestley (London: Chatto and Windus, 1964).
The Italian Girl, with James Saunders (London: Samuel French, 1968).
The Black Prince (London: Chatto and Windus, 1989).

Philosophy and criticism (a selection)

Sartre: Romantic Rationalist (London, 1953). Reissued with new introduction, (Harmondsworth: Penguin, 1989).
'Knowing the Void', *Spectator*, 197 (1956), 613–14.
'T. S. Eliot as a Moralist', in *T. S. Eliot: A Symposium for his 70th Birthday*, ed. Neville Braybrooke (London, 1958), 52–60.
'A House of Theory', *Partisan Review*, 27 (1959), 17–31.
'The Sublime and the Good', *Chicago Review*, 13 (1959), 42–55.
'The Sublime and the Beautiful Revisited', *Yale Review*, 49 (1959), 247–71.
'Against Dryness', *Encounter*, 16 January 1961, 16–20.
Existentialists and Mystics, 1970 (Birmingham: Delos Press, 1993).
The Sovereignty of Good, 1970 (London: Routledge, 1985).
'Salvation by Words', *New York Review of Books*, 15 June 1972, 4.

The Fire and the Sun: Why Plato Banished the Artists, 1977 (Oxford: Oxford University Press, 1978).
Acastos: Two Platonic Dialogues, 1986 (Harmondsworth: Penguin, 1987).
Metaphysics as a Guide to Morals (London: Chatto and Windus, 1992).

Interviews (a selection)

Kermode, Frank (1963) 'House of Fiction: Interviews with Seven English Novelists', in *The Novel Today*, revised edition, ed. Malcolm Bradbury (London: Fontana, 1990), 119–22.
Rose, W. K. (1968) 'Iris Murdoch, Informally', *London Magazine*, 59–73.
Bradbury, Malcolm (1976) 'Iris Murdoch in Conversation, 17 February 1976', British Council Tape no. RS 2001.
Caen (1978) 'Rencontres avec Iris Murdoch', ed. Jean-Louis Chevalier, Centre de Recherches de Littérature et Linguistique des Pays de Langue Anglaise, Université de Caen, France.
Magee, Brian (1978) 'Philosophy and Literature: A Dialogue with Iris Murdoch', *Men of Ideas: Some Creators of Contemporary Philosophy* (Oxford: Oxford University Press), 244–66.
Haffenden, John (1985) *Novelists in Interview* (London: Methuen).
Ziegler, H. and C. W. E. Bigsby (1982) 'Iris Murdoch', in *The Radical Imagination and the Liberal Tradition: Interviews with English and American Novelists* (London: Junction Books), 209–30.
Amsterdam (1988) *Encounters with Iris Murdoch*, ed. Richard Todd (Amsterdam: Free University Press).

Other references

Alexander, Marguerite (1990) *Flights from Realism: Strategies in Postmodernist British and American Fiction* (London: Edward Arnold).
Amis, Martin (1980) Review of *Nuns and Soldiers*, *The Observer*, 7 September.
Antonaccio, Maria (2000) *Picturing the Human: The Moral Thought of Iris Murdoch* (Oxford: Oxford University Press).
Appleyard, Brian (1990) *The Pleasures of Peace: Art and Imagination in Post-War Britain* (London: Faber and Faber).
Attridge, Derek (1992) *Jacques Derrida: Acts of Literature* (London and New York: Routledge).
Bakhtin, Mikhail (1973) *Problems of Dostoevsky's Poetics*, trans. R. W. Rotsel (Ann Arbor: Ardis).
—— (1995) *Bakhtinian Thought: An Introductory Reader*, ed. Simon Dentith (London: Routledge).
—— (1996) *The Bakhtin Reader*, ed. Pam Morris (London: Edward Arnold).
Barnes, Julian (1984) *Flaubert's Parrot* (London: Picador).
Barthes, Roland (1976) *The Pleasure of the Text*, trans. Richard Miller (London: Jonathan Cape).
—— (1977) 'Introduction to the Structural Analysis of Fiction', *Image–Music–Text*, trans. Stephen Heath (Glasgow: Fontana).
Bayley, John (1960) *The Characters of Love* (London: Constable).
—— (1974) 'Character and Consciousness', *New Literary History*, 5 (Winter), 225–35.

Beebe, Maurice (1964) *Ivory Towers and Sacred Founts: The Artist as Hero in Fiction from Goethe to Joyce* (New York: New York University Press).

Belsey, Catherine (1980) *Critical Practice* (London: Methuen).

Bergonzi, Bernard (1970) *The Situation of the Novel* (London: Macmillan).

—— (1993) *Wartime and Aftermath: English Literature and its Background 1939–60* (Oxford: Oxford University Press).

Bersani, Leo (1992) 'Realism and the Fear of Desire', in *Realism*, ed. Lilian R. Furst (London: Longman), 240–60.

Bettelheim, Bruno (1982) *Freud and Man's Soul* (Harmondsworth: Penguin).

Blanchot, Maurice (1993) 'Everyday Speech', *The Infinite Conversation*, trans. Susan Hanson (Minneapolis and London: University of Minnesota Press, 1993), 238–45.

Bloom, Harold (1975) *A Map of Misreading* (Oxford: Oxford University Press)

—— ed. (1986) *Iris Murdoch: Modern Critical Views* (New York: Chelsea House).

Booth, Wayne (1961) *The Rhetoric of Fiction* (Chicago: The University of Chicago Press).

Bradbury, Malcolm (1962) 'Iris Murdoch's under the Net', *Critical Quarterly*, Spring, 47–54.

—— (1973) '"A House Fit for Free Characters": The Novels of Iris Murdoch', in *No, Not Bloomsbury* (London: Arena, 1987).

—— (1993) *The Modern British Novel* (London: Secker and Warburg).

—— (2000) Introduction to *The Philosopher's Pupil* (London: Vintage).

Brooks, Peter (1992) *Reading for the Plot: Design and Intention in Narrative* (Cambridge, Mass.: Harvard University Press).

—— (1994) *Psychoanalysis and Storytelling* (Oxford: Blackwell).

Brooks-Davies, Douglas (1989) *Fielding, Dickens, Gosse, Iris Murdoch and Oedipal Hamlet* (Basingstoke: Macmillan).

Byatt, A. S. (1965) *Degrees of Freedom* (London: Chatto and Windus). Reissued 1984 (London: Vintage).

—— (1976) *Iris Murdoch* (London: Longman).

—— (1979) 'People in Paper Houses: Attitudes to "Realism" and "Experiment" in English Postwar Fiction', in *The Contemporary English Novel*, eds M. Bradbury and D. Palmer (London: Edward Arnold).

—— (1991) '"The Omnipotence of Thought": Frazer, Freud and Post-Modernist Fiction', in *Passions of the Mind: Selected Writings* (London: Chatto and Windus).

Chatman, Seymour (1978) *Story and Discourse: Narrative Structure in Fiction and Film* (Ithaca: New York: Cornell University Press).

Cohn, Dorrit (1978) *Transparent Minds: Narrative Modes for Presenting Consciousness in Fiction* (Princeton, New Jersey: Princeton University Press).

Conradi, Peter J. (1988) 'Iris Murdoch and Dostoevksy', in *Encounters with Iris Murdoch*, ed. Richard Todd (Amsterdam: Free University Press).

—— (1989) *Iris Murdoch: The Saint and the Artist*, 2nd edition (London: Macmillan).

—— (2001) *Iris Murdoch: A Life* (London: Harper Collins).

Danto, Arthur C. (1991) *Sartre*, 2nd edition (London: Fontana Press).

Davis, Lennard, J. (1983) *Factual Fictions: The Origins of the English Novel* (New York: New York University Press).

Deleuze, Gilles (1989) *Masochism: Coldness and Cruelty* (New York: Urzone, Inc.).

Derrida, Jacques (1967) *Of Grammatology*, trans. Gayatri Chakravorty Spivak (Baltimore: Johns Hopkins University Press).

—— (1978) *Writing and Difference*, trans. Alan Bass (London: Routledge).

Dipple, Elizabeth (1984) *Iris Murdoch: Work for the Spirit* (London: Methuen).
—— (1988) *The Unresolvable Plot: Reading Contemporary Fiction* (London: Routledge).
Docherty, Thomas (1991) 'Postmodern Characterization: The Ethics of Alterity', in *Postmodernism and Contemporary Fiction*, ed. Edmund J. Smyth (London: Batsford), 169–88.
Dudek, Louis (1976) *The First Person in Literature* (Toronto: Canadian Broadcasting Corporation).
Eagleton, Terry (1986a) 'Liberality and Order: The Criticism of John Bayley', in *Against the Grain* (London: Verso), 33–47.
—— (1986b) *William Shakespeare* (Oxford: Basil Blackwell).
—— (1992) 'The Good, the True and the Beautiful', *The Guardian*, 20 October.
Fletcher, John and Malcolm Bradbury (1976) 'The Introverted Novel', in *Modernism 1890–1930*, eds Malcolm Bradbury and James McFarlane (Harmondsworth: Penguin), 394–415.
Foucault, Michel, ed. (1978) *I, Pierre Rivière, having slaughtered my mother, my sister and my brother . . . A case of Patricide in the 19th Century*, trans. Frank Jellinek (Harmondsworth: Peregrine).
Freud, Sigmund (1924) 'Recollection, Repetition and Working Through', in *Collected Papers*, vol. 2, trans. Joan Rivière (London: Hogarth Press).
—— (1973) *New Introductory Lectures*, Pelican Freud Library, vol. 2 (Harmondsworth: Pelican).
—— (1974) 'Medusa's Head', in *The Standard Edition of the Complete Psychological Works of Sigmund Freud*, trans. James Strachey, vol. 18 (London: The Hogarth Press, 1953–74), 273–6.
—— (1984a) 'Notes Upon a Case of Obsessional Neurosis ["The Rat Man"]', *Case Histories II*, Pelican Freud Library, vol. 9 (Harmondsworth: Pelican), 36–128.
—— (1984b) 'Psychoanalytic Notes Upon an Autobiographical Account of a Case of Paranoia (Dementia Paranoides) [Schreber]', in *Case Histories II*, Pelican Freud Library, vol. 9 (Harmondsworth: Pelican), 138–223.
—— (1984c) 'The Economic Problem of Masochism', in *On Metapsychology: The Theory of Psychoanalysis*, Pelican Freud Library, vol. 11 (Harmondsworth: Penguin, 1984).
—— (1986) 'Beyond the Pleasure Principle', in *The Essentials of Psychoanalysis* (Harmondsworth: Pelican), 218–68.
—— (1987) 'Totem and Taboo', in *The Origins of Religion*, Pelican Freud Library, vol. 13 (Harmondsworth: Pelican, 1987), 143–4.
—— (1990) 'The "Uncanny"', in *Art and Literature*, Penguin Freud Library, vol. 14 (Harmondsworth: Penguin), 335–76.
Frye, Northrop (1957) *Anatomy of Criticism: Four Essays* (Princeton, New Jersey: Princeton University Press).
Garber, Marjorie (1987) *Shakespeare's Ghostwriters: Literature as Uncanny Causality* (London: Methuen).
Gasiorek, Andrejz (1995) *Post-War British Fiction: Realism and After* (London: Edward Arnold).
Genette, Gérard (1980) *Narrative Discourse*, trans. Jane E. Lewin (Oxford: Basil Blackwell).
Goode, John (1966) 'Character and Henry James', *New Left Review*, 40 (November/December), 55–75.

Gordon, David J. (1995) *Iris Murdoch's Fables of Unselfing* (University of Missouri Press).

Hamburger, Käte (1957, 1973) *The Logic of Literature*, trans. Marilynn J. Rose, 2nd revised edition (London: Indiana University Press).

Hartill, Rosemary (1989) *Writers Revealed* (London: BBC Books).

Hertz, Neil (1985) 'Freud and the Sandman', *The End of the Line: Essays on Psychoanalysis and the Sublime* (New York: Columbia University Press), 97–121.

Heusel, Barbara Stevens (1995) *Patterned Aimlessness: Iris Murdoch's Novels of the 1970s and 1980s* (Athens: University of Georgia Press).

Higdon, David Leon (1984) *Shadows of the Past in Contemporary British Fiction* (London: Macmillan).

Hutcheon, Linda (1984) *Narcissistic Narrative: The Metafictional Paradox* (London: Methuen).

—— (1988) *A Poetics of Postmodernism: History, Theory, Fiction* (London: Routledge).

Jameson, Fredric (1981) *The Political Unconscious: Narrative as a Socially Symbolic Act* (London: Methuen).

—— (1991) *Postmodernism, or the Cultural Logic of Late Capitalism* (London: Verso).

Johnson, Deborah (1987) *Iris Murdoch* (Brighton: Harvester).

Kane, Richard (1988) *Iris Murdoch, Muriel Spark and John Fowles: Didactic Demons in Modern Fiction* (London and Toronto: Associated University Press).

Kellman, Steven G. (1976) 'The Fiction of Self-Begetting', *Modern Language Notes*, 91 (December), 1243–56.

—— (1980) *The Self-Begetting Novel* (London: Macmillan).

Kemp, Peter (1969) 'The Fight against Fantasy', *Modern Fiction Studies*, 15 (1969), 403–15.

Kennedy, Alan (1974) *The Protean Self: Dramatic Action in Contemporary Fiction* (London: Macmillan).

Kermode, Frank (1971) 'Iris Murdoch', in *Modern Essays* (London: Fontana).

Kristeva, Julia (1989) *Black Sun: Depression and Melancholia* (New York: Columbia University Press).

Lacan, Jacques (1986) *The Four Fundamental Concepts of Psycho-analysis* (Harmondsworth: Peregrine).

Lanser, Susan S. (1981) *The Narrative Act: Point of View in Prose Fiction* (Princeton, New Jersey: Princeton University Press).

Laplanche, Jean and Pontalis, Jean-Bertrand (1981) *The Language of Psychoanalysis* (London: The Hogarth Press Ltd).

Lee, Alison (1990) *Realism and Power: Postmodern British Fiction* (London: Routledge).

Lemaire, Anika (1977) *Jacques Lacan*, trans. David Macey (London: Routledge).

Levenson, Michael (2001) 'Iris Murdoch: The Philosophic Fifties and *The Bell*', *Modern Fiction Studies* 47:3, 558–79.

Lodge, David (1986) *Working with Structuralism: Essays and Reviews on Nineteenth- and Twentieth-Century Literature* (London: Ark).

Loveday, Simon (1985) *The Romances of John Fowles* (London: Macmillan).

Lukács, Georg (1950) *Studies in European Realism: A Sociological Survey of the Writings of Balzac* (London: Hillway Publishing Co.).

—— (1963) *The Meaning of Contemporary Realism* (London: Merlin Press).

Lyotard, Jean-François (1985) 'Answering the Question: What is Postmodernism?' in *The Postmodern Condition: A Report on Knowledge* (Manchester: Manchester University Press).

MacCabe, Colin (1974) 'Realism and the Cinema: Notes on some Brechtian Theses', in *Literary Theory: A Reader*, eds Philip Rice and Patricia Waugh, 2nd revised edition (London: Edward Arnold, 1992), 134–42.

McCall, Lenora (1991) 'The Solipsistic Narrator in Iris Murdoch' (unpubl. PhD dissertation, University of South Carolina).

McHale, Brian (1987) *Postmodernist Fiction* (London: Methuen).

—— (1992) *Constructing Postmodernism* (London: Routledge).

Martens, Lorna (1985) *The Diary Novel* (Cambridge: Cambridge University Press).

Moretti, Franco (1983) 'Clues', *Signs Taken as Wonders* (London: Verso).

O'Connor, William Van (1963) *The New University Wits and the End of Modernism* (Carbondale: Southern Illinois University Press).

Oates, Joyce Carol (1999) 'Sacred and Profane Iris Murdoch', *The Profane Art: Essays and Reviews* (New York: Dutton). Accessed online, 11 April 1999: http://www.usfca.edu/fac-staff/sourtherr/murdoch.html.

Ramanathan, Suguna (1990) *Iris Murdoch: Figures of Good* (London: Macmillan).

Ricoeur, Paul (1984) 'Time Traversed: Remembrance of Things Past', in *A Ricoeur Reader: Reflection and Imagination*, ed. Mario J. Valdés (London: Harvester).

Rimmon-Kenan, Shlomith (1983) *Narrative Fiction: Contemporary Poetics* (London: Routledge).

Romberg, Bertil (1962) *Studies in the Narrative Technique of the First-Person Novel* (Lund: Almqvist and Wiksell).

Rorty, Richard (1989) *Contingency, Irony and Solidarity* (Cambridge: Cambridge University Press).

Roth, Philip (1961) 'Writing American Fiction', in *The Novel Today: Contemporary Writers on Modern Fiction*, ed. Malcolm Bradbury (London: Fontana Press, 1990).

Sacher-Masoch, Leopold von (1989) *Masochism: Venus in Furs* (New York: Urzone, Inc.).

Sagare, S. B. (2001) 'An Interview with Iris Murdoch', *Modern Fiction Studies* 47:3, 696–714.

Sage, Lorna (1977) 'The Savage Sideshow', *New Review*, 4, 39–40.

Scanlan, Margaret (1992) 'The Problem of the Past in Iris Murdoch's *Nuns and Soldiers*', in *Critical Essays on Iris Murdoch*, ed. Lindsey Tucker (New York: G. K. Hall and Co.), 176–87.

Scholes, Robert (1974) *Structuralism in Literature* (London: Yale University Press).

Shklovsky, Victor (1991) *The Theory of Prose* (Dalkey Archive Press).

Souvage, Jacques (1962) 'Symbol as Narrative Device: an Interpretation of Iris Murdoch's *The Bell*', *English Studies*, 43:2 (April), 81–96.

Stanzel, Franz (1984) *A Theory of Narrative*, trans. Charlotte Goedsche, 2nd edition (Cambridge: Cambridge University Press).

Stevenson, Randall (1991) 'Postmodernism and Contemporary Fiction in Britain', in *Postmodernism and Contemporary Fiction*, ed. Edmund J. Smyth (London: Batsford), 19–35.

Sussman, Henry (1990) 'Psychoanalysis Modern and Post-Modern', in *Psychoanalysis and...*, eds Richard Feldstein and Henry Sussman (London: Routledge), 129–50.

Swinden, Patrick (1973) *Unofficial Selves: Character in the Novel from Dickens to the Present Day* (London: Macmillan).

Todd, Richard (1979) *The Shakespearian Interest* (London: Vision).

—— (1984) *Iris Murdoch* (London: Methuen).

Todorov, Tzvetan (1973) *The Fantastic: A Structural Approach to a Literary Genre*, trans. Richard Howard (Cleveland, Ohio).
—— (1980) 'Reading as Construction', trans. Marilyn A. August, in *The Reader in the Text*, eds Susan R. Suleiman and Inge Crosman (Princeton, New Jersey: Princeton University Press), 67–82.
Turner, Jack (1993) *Murdoch v. Freud: A Freudian Look at an Anti-Freudian* (New York: Peter Lang Publishing Inc.).
Wasson, Richard (1969) 'Notes on a New Sensibility', *Partisan Review*, 36, 460–77.
Waugh, Patricia (1984) *Metafiction: The Theory and Practice of Self-Conscious Fiction* (London: Routledge).
—— (1992) *Practising Postmodernism/Reading Modernism* (London: Edward Arnold).
Wright, Elizabeth (1984) *Psychoanalytic Criticism: Theory in Practice* (London: Methuen).
Ziegler, H. and C. W. E. Bigsby (1982) 'Iris Murdoch', in *The Radical Imagination and the Liberal Tradition: Interviews with English and American Novelists* (London: Junction Books), 209–30.
Žižek, Slavoj (1990) 'The Limits of the Semiotic Approach to Psychoanalysis', trans. Sylvie Newman, in *Psychoanalysis and...*, eds Richard Feldstein and Henry Sussman (London: Routledge), 89–110.
—— (1991) *Looking Awry: An Introduction to Lacan through Popular Culture* (Cambridge, MA: MIT Press).
—— ed. (1992) *Everything You Always Wanted to Know about Lacan (But Were Afraid to Ask Hitchcock)* (London: Verso).

Index